The Master of
Puppets

Also by Molly J. Bragg

Mail Order Bride

Hearts of Heroes
Scatter

Transistor

The Master of Puppets

Puppets

The War of Souls 1

Molly J. Bragg

Desert Palm Press

The Master of Puppets
(The War of Souls - Book 1)

By Molly J. Bragg

©2022 Molly J. Bragg

ISBN (book) 9781954213494
ISBN (epub) 9781954213500

Desert Palm Press
1961 Main Street, Suite 220
Watsonville, California 95076
www.desertpalmpress.com

Editor: Kaycee Hawn
Cover Design: Jeanette Eileen Widjaja

Printed in the United States of America
First Edition November 2022

Acknowledgements:

I would like to acknowledge Beck Use, Kelly Fitzsimons and Isca Irangwe. Without them, this book might never have gotten finished. I'd also like to thank my wonderful editor Kaycee Hawn for not only editing with a light hand but having a turnaround time that boggles the mind, and Lee Fitzsimmons for giving me a chance to share my work with the world.

Dedication:

For Tabby and Wendi, who helped me realize it's time to move on with my life instead of wallowing in the past. I love you both, and I can't thank you enough for the well timed kicks in the backside you've both given me over the years.

Chapter One

"WHAT ARE THOSE?" JAKARI asked, staring at the hologram floating in the middle of the medical bay.

"Those are humans," Dubari said. "Dominant intelligent species of Sol 3, AKA Terra, AKA Earth."

"They named their planet after dirt?" Jakari asked.

"According to the report from Napati's unit," Dubari said.

"That's…"

"Primitive? Barbaric? Dumb?" Dubari asked. "Honestly, what do you expect from a species that's still debating whether they are the only intelligent life in the universe?"

"I was going to say weird," Jakari said.

Dubari shrugged. "That too."

Jakari sat down near the hologram and dropped her hand on the control interface point on the arm of the chair, bringing up the vital statistics on 'humans.' The report from Napati included about ten million genetic profiles and a reproductive algorithm that would allow them to 'breed' unique profiles for her and Dubari to use. That was fairly standard for an infiltration package. What wasn't standard was the humans themselves.

In the ten thousand or so years she'd been alive, Jakari had seen a lot of aliens. Big ones, small ones, flora and fauna evolved. Predators, scavengers, and grazers. Carnivores, omnivores, herbivores, chemivores, and photovores. Oxygen breathers and methane breathers and water breathers. Even a handful of species like her own that had long since left their purely organic origins behind in favor of techno-organic or even fully robotic bodies. There was a lot of variety, but she hadn't seen anything quite like humans before.

The lower segment of their legs didn't end in a proper paw or hoof. Instead, it was shortened into a kind of elongated hand with vestigial fingers at the forward end. The whole thing was pressed against the ground as some weird sort of ped. There was a joint where it connected to the rest of the leg, that had a bit more mobility than a joint in that place normally would, but the main joints of the leg were the knee between the upper and middle segments and the hip joint.

There was no tail, which must have made balancing even harder with the oddly shaped peds. The sex organs on the male just sort of dangled loosely between the legs instead of withdrawing into the body or into some sort of protective sheath. The lower spine had an odd bend in it. The female had enlarged mammary glands, even when they weren't actively nursing their young. The arms were normal enough, she supposed.

They actually had a better range of motion in the shoulder than most species. A short neck, which was common enough, but then the head. The face was oddly flat, the fangs were undersized to the point of uselessness, and there was a huge, flat plate of bone above the eyelids. The strangest thing was the hair. They only had hair in significant quantities under the shoulder joints, around their sex organs, and on the top and back of the head. The males did grow hair on their lower face after they reached maturity, but Jakari could hardly see the point. They were mostly just big, pink, naked things.

"Was there anything in our orders about why we're going to this planet?" Jakari asked.

"Just that it was a high priority mission, and that Napati would brief us when we arrived," Dubari said.

"Wonderful," Jakari said. "I hate going in blind."

"You hate going in."

Jakari looked over at Dubari, who had a grin on their face. She shrugged because what they said was true. She hated their job. It was necessary, and they were both good at it, and what they did probably had more impact on the course of the war than any number of battles and sieges, but it didn't mean she had to like it.

"I just want to know who we're supposed to kill," she said.

"Does it really matter?" Dubari asked.

Jakari had to bite her tongue, because of course it mattered. Assassinating some dumb, young lieutenant leading a resource scouting mission wasn't going to have any sort of lasting effect on the war, and would be a waste of their time. Not that she seriously believed that was their mission. Napati was second-in-command of the entire Suil Agam. She wouldn't be out here on some godforsaken mudball if there wasn't a reason. The problem was, Jakari no longer trusted Arthan to have a good reason. Not since Cruthanna. What had happened there had broken her faith in Arthan, and the more she watched him, the more apparent it became that most of what he did these days was about holding on to power, and not enough of it was about actually ending the war.

"Arthan assigned us this mission personally," Dubari said. "It's got to be important."

"I hope so," Jakari said. She looked back at the hologram of the humans. "And if we have to wear that, I hope it's quick."

"Are you going to pick a male form this time?"

"Do I ever pick a male form?" Jakari asked.

Dubari laughed. "No."

"Then what makes you think I'd do it this time?"

"I thought you finally might be getting bored of the whole woman thing."

Jakari shook her head and told the computer to 'breed' a set of genetic profiles for her.

"You could try it," Dubari said.

Jakari didn't answer, but then she didn't have to. It was an old argument between them. Dubari had been born centuries after the Migration. They'd never really known what it was like to have a body that couldn't be reshaped at will, or how much that body could become a part of your identity. Jakari had been born a woman decades before the Migration, and she had liked being a woman. Dubari, like most of the Gadan born after the Migration, viewed gender as a relic of the past. They didn't understand why shifting into a male form made Jakari want to crawl out of her skin.

She'd done it plenty of times when it was necessary to see a mission through, but it always made her uncomfortable in a way that shape shifting in general didn't. Dubari thought it was a weakness, something that would help the enemy spot her, but she figured if it wasn't something she could shake after ten thousand years, no amount of nagging or teasing was going to change her mind. So, when the computer finished breeding the profiles she requested, she loaded them into her Phylactery's memory core, along with the movement and combat algorithms, language pack, and sample clothing packs that had been sent along with the report. While all of that was loading, she displayed the first genetic profile in the holoprojector and started scrolling through them, trying to find one she liked.

"They're very pink, aren't they?" Dubari asked.

"Apparently they come in different colors," Jakari said. "The pink ones are just the most common in the area we'll be operating in." Jakari stopped scrolling as a new image filled the projection.

"That one, you think?" Dubari asked.

"I like the brown better than the pink," Jakari said. "This one is listed as 'Afro-Latino,' whatever that means."

"How do they survive without fur or scales?" Dubari asked.

"I don't know," Jakari said. "Maybe the hide is tougher than it looks."

"It would have to be," Dubari said. "Go on, give it a try."

Jakari nodded and pulled up the clothing packs. She frowned as she realized they all included some form of ped covering. She'd always hated wearing anything on her paws, but apparently these human 'feet' were delicate enough to need protection, so she didn't have a choice. She scrolled through the outfits until she found something she liked. Heavy black leg coverings, a blue underlayer that covered the torso and upper arms, and a hide outer layer that covered the torso and arms. There were also undergarments that covered the genitals and some sort of elastic contraption that restricted the movement of the enlarged mammary glands. She tweaked the settings until the hair on the head was trimmed short in something called a 'pixie cut.' At that point, she figured it was about as good as she was going to get, so she stood up and shifted, reorganizing the Techno-Organic Polymorphic matter that made up her body until it settled down into the correct form. An exact duplicate, down to the genetic level, of the human woman in the hologram.

"Not bad," Dubari said. Jakari detected a bit of envy in their tone, but that was nothing new. She had always been a better shapeshifter than them. It came with having centuries more practice, though she also suspected that part of it was that shape shifting was a skill she'd had to work hard to learn as an adult, rather than an inborn ability she'd had her whole life. She worked at it, and even now, she spent a few hours a week practicing.

She took a couple of steps, using the movement algorithms Napati's unit had sent along. They were surprisingly well-optimized, considering how long Napati had been on the planet. Jakari was also a little surprised by how stable the form felt. She had expected to have to lean forward to keep from falling over backwards, but instead she found that she could stand up straight. Walking was a little scary. It was less walking and more falling forward and catching yourself over and over, but it worked well enough. She even managed to run a couple of laps around the medical compartment before she sat back down.

"Well?" Dubari asked. "What do you think?"

4

"I think it will do," she said. "Pick a form and we'll give the combat algorithms a try."

* * * *

Mamachi watched the transport ship light up the night sky as it came in for a landing. It had the flat disk shape of all warp-capable spacecraft, but some of the craft's TOP matter hull had been reconfigured to create control surfaces to aid with maneuverability and to give the craft a long nose, which helped it cut through the atmosphere at supersonic speeds. Those features melted back into the main disk as the craft came to a stop over the designated landing pad. It hovered briefly as it extended six landing legs, then gently set down on them. Once it had settled onto the ground, the boarding ramp lowered, and two human forms came down the ramp.

Mamachi couldn't keep a smile off their face. There was no question as to which one was Jakari. She always chose a female form. Which meant that the male human had to be her partner Dubari. Mamachi wanted to run forward and pull Jakari into a hug. It had been far, far too long since they'd seen her. Almost three decades. Unfortunately, however much Mamachi wished they could just spend time with one of their oldest friends, threats to the Suil Agam had to come first, and they hadn't faced a threat like this in thousands of years.

Mamachi watched as Napati and Special Agent Gomez stepped forward to greet Jakari and Dubari.

"I am Napati," she said with a bow. "This is special agent in charge, Silvia Gomez. A human. She is our liaison with the local government."

"I am Jakari."

"I am Dubari."

The formal introductions were a necessary ritual in a culture made up of shapeshifters, especially when meeting in new forms, but once they were done, the tension and formality of it fell away, and Jakari stepped forward and hugged Napati.

"It's good to see you again," Jakari said.

"It's good to see you, too," Napati said. "How have you been?"

Jakari sighed and stepped back. "You know how it is," she said. "The old man keeps us busy."

"So I've heard," Napati said. Mamachi could hear the disapproval in her voice. They knew it came from Napati's disapproval of the types of missions Jakari was assigned, rather than disapproval of her, but it didn't stop Mamachi from frowning. They respected Napati a great deal, but they suspected they would never see eye to eye with them about this. If Jakari could pull off the mission she was here for, it might very well help end the war, and Mamachi had more reason than most to want an end to the fighting.

Jakari turned to Gomez. "Special Agent Silvia Gomez, I am Colonel Jakari of the Suil Agam Army. This is my partner, Major Dubari. Thank you for welcoming us to your world."

"Thank you for coming," Gomez said. "If you're as effective as General Napati says, I'm hopeful that you might be able to end the threat to my world and my people."

"We'll do our best," Jakari said. She looked over at where Mamachi stood.

"Is that Mamachi?" Jakari asked.

"It is," Napati said.

Jakari smiled and walked over to Mamachi, looking them up and down.

"Don't you dare," Mamachi said.

Jakari smiled, and before Mamachi could react, she bent down and drove a shoulder into their waist. She wrapped her arms around them and stood up, lifting Mamachi over her shoulder and spinning around as they both laughed. After a few spins, Jakari bent down, planting Mamachi back on their feet and letting them go.

"How have you been?" Jakari asked as she stood up, a smile on her face and laughter in her voice.

"Good," Mamachi said. "I got deployed here over a year before the Char Oram arrived."

"Time away from the fighting," Jakari said, her smile getting even bigger. "Did you enjoy it?"

"Very much," Mamachi said.

Jakari reached out and squeezed Mamachi's shoulder. "I'm glad for you, old friend."

"Thank you," Mamachi said. "I wish we had time to talk, but things are bad, and time is of the essence."

"Then I guess we should start the briefing."

* * * *

Jakari followed Napati and her team into a large building while one of Napati's troops moved her ship into a hangar. Apparently, they were trying to keep the presence of aliens on the planet from the locals. She didn't really see the point, but it was a trivial thing. She was a lot more interested in why Napati, of all people, had called in the Suil's top assassins. Napati hated assassination as a tactic and as a strategy. She thought it was beneath them.

There was probably a time Jakari would have agreed, but the occupation had taught her a few very hard lessons in just how low she was willing to sink in order to end a war, and the facts were, assassination was really effective as both a weapon of terror and a weapon of war, and Jakari was really, really good at it.

Dubari was arguably better, but that's because they were still a true believer. They still believed every word out of Arthan's mouth was divine truth. Jakari didn't give a shit about Arthan and his vision. She just wanted to end the war, and she was more than willing to shatter any Phylactery it took to make that happen. Even Arthan's. Hell, especially Arthan's.

Napati led them to a briefing room. It couldn't be anything else. Briefing rooms and conference rooms were surprisingly consistent across alien cultures, as was an almost bone-deep aversion to them. Napati took the head of the table and the human Gomez sat to Napati's right. Mamachi sat to Napati's left. Jakari took the one on Gomez's right, and Dubari took the seat on Mamachi's left.

"So, why are we here?" Jakari asked.

"I'll allow Mamachi to explain," Napati said.

Jakari looked over at Mamachi and smiled. Their human form looked young, with bright golden hair, light brown skin, and dark brown eyes, but they had the same confidence Jakari had seen when they'd met on Cruthanna all those years ago.

"Six standard cycles ago, I received a report from a source that Cikara was planning an expedition that would take them off Cruthanna. I was hesitant to believe it, since none of the Triumvirate have left Cruthanna in almost a millennium, but the report came from a reliable source, so I thought it bore further investigation. I approached Napati and asked if I could be dispatched to the world Cikara had supposedly chosen as their intended destination to see if the report was true. Napati agreed, and I came to Earth.

"When I arrived, I used local resources to build a monitoring station that would allow me to detect incoming warp signatures, and then I waited. About a year after I arrived, I detected a dreadnought dropping out of warp. I only got a brief look before it cloaked, but it was enough to confirm it was a Char ship. At that point I contacted the local government, in the person of Special Agent Gomez, and I opened diplomatic relations and received permission for a Suil expeditionary force to come to Earth to counter the Char forces. Once I had permission, I sent a message to General Napati, and she arrived with her forces two local months later.

"For the last five local years, we have only had brief skirmishes with Char forces, but about two years ago, the same source that warned us of Cikara's expedition contacted us again. They told us that Cikara was on Earth, and that they were here to develop a new weapon. We had no idea of the nature of the weapon, or how big a threat it would pose, but given that Cikara was overseeing its development personally, we have been doing everything we can to gather additional intel. Two months ago, we got lucky."

Mamachi placed their hand on one of the interface points on the table and a hologram appeared, showing a human form in a containment cell.

"This is a Helot," Mamachi said. "It's Cikara's new weapon. We captured two of them when Cikara's forces attempted to rob a military base."

The hologram shifted from a live feed to a rendered model of the human form. Then the human form peeled away, leaving something that looked like a Phylactery, but was bigger.

"What is that?" Jakari asked.

"It's a device called a Shroud. It's designed to encase a Phylactery, and once it does, it suppresses all memories stored in the Phylactery prior to being linked to the Shroud. It then loads a number of preset forms into the Phylactery, along with combat and movement algorithms associated with those forms, and it writes in a limited personality that is absolutely loyal to the Char Oram."

Jakari suddenly understood exactly why she was on Earth. What she was looking at was a monstrosity. Gadan were techno-organic beings. They didn't have a set form and could reshape their body at will, but the Phylactery was where their mind was stored. A small spherical computer that held all their memory and knowledge. This new device basically erased the person inside the Phylactery it was attached to and replaced them with computer code.

"So if they capture one of us, they can attach one of these Shrouds to our Phylactery and turn us into some sort of mindless drone soldier?" Dubari asked.

"It's worse than that," Mamachi said. "The two Helots we captured were not Gadans. They were humans. Cikara's transferring human minds into Phylacteries and then attaching Shrouds to them."

"They're turning humans into mindless cannon fodder," Jakari said.

"Exactly," Mamachi said. "Right now, they're grabbing humans in small numbers and working on perfecting the technology, but there are nearly seven point seven billion humans on this planet. If this goes into mass production, the war will be over, and the Char will win."

Mamachi looked over to Napati, who gave them a small nod.

"I reported our findings to Arthan, and he sent the two of you here. Your mission is to kill Cikara and destroy both the weapon system and all research related to it," Napati said.

"How the hell are we supposed to do that?" Dubari asked.

"I don't know," Napati said. "As it stands, we don't even know the location of Cikara's dreadnought, much less how we could get someone onboard."

"I might have an idea," Jakari said.

Dubari turned to look at her. "Is it a good one?"

"No. It's a crazy, stupid, dangerous idea that's more likely to get us killed than the target."

"Well, that's never stopped us before," Dubari said.

"That's because we're both idiots," Jakari said. She turned back to Mamachi. "You said that Cikara's grabbing humans in small numbers."

"Yes," Mamachi said.

"Where from?" Jakari asked.

"A city called Dallas," Mamachi said.

Chapter Two

PEOPLE WERE IDIOTS. THIS was not new information. Hayami had been on the job for twelve years, first as a beat cop, then as a detective, and the amount of sheer stupidity she had seen occasionally made her wonder if mother nature should just wipe out humanity and start over with a smarter species. Like cats, or crows.

The most recent example of human stupidity was the pack of glammed-up girls walking down the sidewalk right in front of her. Despite numerous public safety advisories; despite the fact that there were black and whites patrolling the streets downtown constantly; despite the fact that twenty-three people had been grabbed off the streets of downtown Dallas in the last six months; five girls in their early to mid-twenties were just walking down the street in the middle of downtown, headed to one of the nightclubs.

They might as well have been wearing signs saying, 'Kidnap us, we're easy targets!'

She was watching them file into one of the clubs when her phone rang. She reached down and hit the accept button without looking at the caller ID, and immediately regretted it.

"Takahashi," she said.

"You're downtown again, aren't you?" Michelle asked.

"What? No," Hayami said.

"Oh, really? Then where are you?"

"I'm at home, trying to decide what I want to watch on Netflix."

"Oh, really? So, if I knocked on your front door right now, you'd get up and let me in?"

Hayami sighed. "You're standing on my porch, aren't you?"

"I'm standing on your porch with pizza and a six pack, and you're downtown again."

"I'm downtown again," Hayami said.

"Damn it, Yami, what the fuck?"

"I'm trying to solve the damn case," Hayami said. A bit of motion caught her eye, and she watched as a woman riding a big, red touring motorcycle pulled into the parking lot across the street from her.

"By sitting downtown and watching idiots take stupid risks?" Michelle asked. "That's what we have black and whites for. You should be at home, resting. You're never going to solve anything if you're exhausted all the time."

"I can't just sit at home and do nothing. Whatever's going on is escalating." She watched the woman on the motorcycle take off her helmet.

"I know," Michelle said, "but you're not working this case alone. There's a reason we've got a whole task force on this."

"Well, the task force isn't doing any better than I am, are they?" Hayami asked as she watched the woman lock her helmet in the storage box mounted above the rear wheel of the bike.

"We're all working our asses off," Michelle said. "Why are you taking this one so personally? You're usually pretty good about separating work from your life."

"I don't know," Hayami said as she watched the woman start walking. "This feels different, somehow. Bigger."

"What the hell does that mean?"

"I don't know, but my gut is telling me that we need to shut down whatever is going on fast. I..." Hayami stopped as she saw the woman turn down a side street.

"Yami?"

"I've got to go," Hayami said.

"What? Why?"

She didn't answer. She just grabbed her phone out of the docking cradle, climbed out of the car, and slammed the door.

"Stupid fucking people," she muttered to herself as she ran across the street. The woman was doing everything she wasn't supposed to be doing. Moving alone at night on a side street. It was almost like she wanted to get grabbed. Hayami shoved her phone in her pocket and did a quick check to make sure her gun was where it should be as she started down the same side street as the woman.

"Hey, wait up!" she called. The woman ignored her, so she picked up her pace again. She'd almost reached her when she heard a heavy vehicle behind her. She glanced back to see a brown delivery van coming down the street towards them, and felt a chill run down her spine.

"Fuck," she said as she turned back around. She ran the last few feet to catch up with the woman and grabbed her by the shoulder. The woman spun around.

"Let go," she snapped.

"We've got to get out of here," Hayami said.

The woman looked over her shoulder, and instead of the fear Hayami expected, there was a look of pure annoyance. Before either of them could say anything, the van rolled to a stop, and four men jumped out. Hayami grabbed her gun.

"Dallas PD!" she yelled. "Down on the ground, now!"

The men from the van didn't even slow down. Hayami took a step back as she picked a target and fired. The distance between them was so short there was no way she could have missed. The man she'd targeted rocked back from the impact, but he didn't slow down or stop. She fired again, putting three more rounds into the same guy before he grabbed her gun and ripped it out of her hands. She watched, stunned, as he crushed it like it was made of playdough, then tossed it aside. She turned and tried to run, but she didn't get more than two steps before she was lifted off the ground and tossed over a shoulder.

The same man she had shot in the chest four times carried her to the back of the van and tossed her in. Another man was waiting for her there. He grabbed her wrists, slipped a pair of zip cuffs on, and cinched them tight. The van pulled away from the curb and started accelerating while the man who had tied her up searched her. He found her phone, badge, cuffs, knife, spare magazines, and backup gun, tossing each out of the back of the already moving van. The other woman didn't seem to have anything on her worth tossing other than a phone.

While he was searching her, Hayami did a quick headcount. Her, the woman, the four men who had grabbed them, and a driver. Hayami looked over at the woman. She was tall, with skin just a little darker than Hayami's own, and had short, close-cut hair. She was still looking at Hayami with nothing but annoyance on her face.

"You couldn't have just minded your own business?" the woman asked in a tone that made it sound like Hayami had spoiled a surprise party or something.

"Shut up," one of the men said. He drove the command home by punching the woman in the face hard enough that her head bounced off the side of the van. Hayami was a little shocked, because rather than a broken nose and unconsciousness, which was what she'd expected, the blow didn't seem to do anything except make the woman look even more annoyed. At least at first. The woman glared at the man who hit her for a few seconds, then leaned her head back and closed her eyes, leaving Hayami to face their kidnappers by herself.

* * * *

Jakari leaned her head back against the side of the van and closed her eyes, because she always found it easier to remote pilot a Talus without visual distractions. She reached out through one of her Phylactery's control links to one of her Shims and felt it respond, almost eagerly asking for commands. She sent them, and fifteen blocks away, the motorcycle she'd left behind roared to life. The three saddlebags and the front fairing flowed together, morphing to form a rider for the bike that looked a lot like Jakari's current human form. The bike righted itself and backed out of the parking spot as the kickstand folded away, then it rushed forward, turning down the same street Jakari had been walking down, then tearing after the van.

She wanted to scream in rage and frustration as she guided the motorcycle along the streets. She'd been roaming downtown Dallas for almost a week playing fat, happy, and stupid while waiting for Cikara's people to grab her, and the night it finally worked, some stupid human had to get in the way. Why couldn't the woman have just minded her own damn business?

She had to admit, there was a part of her that had admired the woman. After all, few people would risk their life to try and save a total stranger. And when the danger appeared, the woman had kept her head and reacted like a warrior, producing a weapon and trying to put down her enemies. It would have worked if her enemies had been human, but trying to get a kill with a projectile weapon while you were fighting a Gadan was next to impossible. There was a reason both the Suil and the Char used directed energy weapons. The only way to get a kill was to destroy the Phylactery, and Phylacteries were tiny. Hitting one with a bullet was next to impossible.

Jakari shifted her attention back to her Talus as the rear of the van came into view through the sensors on the motorcycle. It wouldn't take long for the Char soldiers to spot the motorcycle and figure out what it was, so she would have to do this quickly. She gunned the motorcycle's engine and brought it up along the passenger's side of the van, the side she was leaning against. She pulled her legs up and planted them on the floor of the van, which got the Char soldiers' attention, but before they could do anything, the rider on her motorcycle reached out and drove its hand through the paneling, tearing a hole in the side of the van. Jakari used her feet to kick off, shoving herself out of the hole in the side of the van with inhuman strength at the same time the motorcycle launched itself into the air.

She heard the human woman scream, and she understood. For a human, the move would have been suicide, but Jakari wasn't human. Far from it. As she flew out of the van, her body gave up the human form it had been holding, even as her Talus began to morph. She hit the rider in the chest, but instead of knocking it off the motorcycle, or tipping over the motorcycle, the mass of the rider, the motorcycle, and Jakari's body all merged and flowed together. TOP matter, the substance which made up Gadan bodies as well as their technology, reorganized itself as Jakari and her motorcycle took on a new, single form.

The new form stood three meters tall and looked like a giant, metal Gadan. Purple armored skin, proper digitigrade legs ending in paws with razor sharp alloy claws. A tail for balance, a round torso, strong arms, sharp talons at the end of the fingers and a head with a proper snout instead of the smushed face of a human.

Jakari hit the ground running, her massive strides easily keeping up with the van, but she didn't have a lot of time. The van had already started to morph as well. She swiped at it with both arms, tearing a gap. She reached in and snatched the human through the gap before it could close and then jumped again, morphing as she sailed through the air. She split her own mass from the Talus, resuming her human form as the Talus morphed back into a motorcycle.

"Hold on to me," Jakari yelled. The human wrapped her arms tightly around Jakari's waist, and a moment later, the motorcycle hit the ground with tooth-jarring force. There wasn't a lot she could do to cushion the landing for her passenger, but she hoped it wasn't too much for the woman. She managed to hold on, so Jakari took that as a good sign. She gunned the throttle, accelerating the bike far faster than any human-built engine could manage.

"Jakari to Mamachi," she said as she started swerving back and forth across the road, trying to make them harder to hit. "I've been made. Five Char in pursuit with one Class Three construct. Assistance required."

"Support inbound," Mamachi said. "ETA ten minutes."

"Fuck," Jakari said as the first plasma blast dug a hole in the road off to her left. There was no way she was going to last ten minutes while babysitting a human. If she were alone, there wouldn't be a problem. She'd put her and her Talus up against five Char goons and a Class Three any day—but humans were squishy, and given that she'd blown a shot at Cikara's ship to rescue this one, she wanted to keep her alive.

She swung onto a cross street, morphing the bike through the turn, shifting the center of mass so it held to the road instead of turning into an uncontrolled skid. The human screamed, but Jakari ignored it. She had to if she wanted to keep them alive.

"I need a battlefield," Jakari said. "Guide me."

"There's an airport four miles from you," Mamachi said.

"Too many people," Jakari said. "I need something empty."

"Got it!" Mamachi said. "I'm sending you the guide path now."

A red line superimposed itself over the middle of the road, telling her she was headed in the right direction for now, just as another plasma bolt dug a hole in the pavement. She risked a glance in the mirror and saw a Char hover sled following. Not a particularly formidable enemy, and if she was alone, she would turn and fight, but her human passenger complicated things. Still, no reason she couldn't fight back a bit.

She morphed the bike's saddle bags into rear-facing plasma cannons. She'd have to time her shots carefully since she actually gave a shit about collateral damage and innocent bystanders, but as she swerved back across the centerline of the hover sled, her targeting system locked on and she fired. The shot hit the center of the sloping glacis plate on the front of the sled and gouged a huge trench in the armor, but didn't manage to cut through and hit any of the Char soldiers, and before she could get off a follow up shot, TOP matter flowed into the trench and solidified, repairing the damage.

"What is that thing?" the human yelled.

"Bad news," Jakari said. The red line turned yellow and an arrow pointing left popped up, indicating an upcoming left turn. She braced for it, and when she reached the right cross street, she slung them through another impossible turn and gunned the engine again, hoping to gain ground.

The human didn't scream this time. She just held on tight and leaned into the turn, but Jakari could smell the fear hormones coming off the human. She was terrified, and Jakari wished there was something she could do about that.

"Help is on the way," she said, hoping it would calm her. She didn't tell her there was no way in the galaxy that the help in question would arrive in time to do any good.

She saw the hover sled reappear in the rear-view mirror and said to hell with it. An alien tank was chasing her down the street. She wasn't going to die to maintain cover that was already blown. She kicked the motorcycle into the air and morphed it, converting it into a grav sled. As vehicles went, it wasn't that far removed from the motorcycle, only instead of wheels, it rode on columns of antigravity, which made it a hell of a lot faster. She shoved the throttle forward, running from the hover sled faster than they could follow.

They flew under some sort of elevated roadway and then through an intersection that led them into some sort of shopping area, when Mamachi spoke up.

"You're coming up on a bridge over an empty riverbed. The riverbed is your battleground. Best I can do."

"It will work," Jakari said as the bridge came into view. She drove out onto it and throttled up the anti-grav, lifting the grav sled high enough to jump the guard rail. She hit the ground below and stopped.

"What are you doing?" the human asked.

"Get off," Jakari said. "I can't fight them and protect you at the same time. Get up under the bridge and hide. Wait until they're distracted and run back to that shopping area. There were people there."

The human had the sense not to argue. She climbed off the grav sled and ran back under the bridge. Jakari didn't waste any more time. She put a good bit of space between her and the bridge, then shifted back into her mech form and turned around. She deployed the plasma cannon on her right arm and waited until she saw the hover sled approaching the bridge. She fired once; a single, tight beam shot. Not enough to do any damage, but just enough to get their attention.

The sled turned towards her and came down into the riverbed. As it approached, four of the five Char soldiers jumped out and the hover sled began to morph.

"Oh, this day just gets better and better," Jakari said as she braced for the fight to come.

* * * *

Hayami had never questioned her own bravery. She'd stared down hardened criminals, raided drug labs, arrested men twice her size, and even gone back to the job after taking a bullet on her vest. She knew she wasn't a coward, but she couldn't help but feel like one as she ran away from a fight. She crawled up the embankment that supported one end of the Inwood Road bridge, tucking herself into the darkness where the bottom of the bridge met the top of the embankment. Then she turned and watched.

She watched as the woman from the van—Jakari, she'd called herself when she was calling for help —stopped the...whatever it was she was riding and turned it around. It began to change shape, moving and flowing like liquid as it surrounded her, slowly growing to maybe ten feet tall, and taking the form of some sort of purple anthropomorphic cat.

It was enough to make Hayami wonder if she'd finally lost it. If the stress from work had finally made her crack. She'd grown up on her dad's rather extensive anime collection. She knew a mech when she saw it. She also knew they didn't exist. Not really. But there one was, raising some kind of weapon.

There was a bright blue flash, and Hayami blinked, trying to clear the spots out of her eyes. A moment later, the strange tank-like vehicle that had been chasing them sailed over the side of the bridge, stopping just before it hit the ground. The four men who had grabbed her and Jakari jumped out of the vehicle before it started to morph the same way Jakari's vehicle did, flowing like a liquid from one form to the next. Only this form was twenty feet tall.

The fight started before the larger mech had finished taking on its new shape. Jakari fired five shots into the larger machine, then broke into a run. The men lifted their arms, and Hayami wasn't sure if they had weapons, or if their arms morphed the way the vehicles had, but they started shooting plasma at Jakari's mech.

Jakari dodged, flipped, rolled, jumped, and maybe even danced her way around the plasma fire coming at her. The whole time she kept up a steady stream of return fire. She used her left arm to pump shot after shot into the larger mech, which couldn't seem to finish its transformation while getting hit. Her right arm targeted the men on foot, but they were every bit as fast and nimble as she was. They used their numbers to their advantage, spreading out so she couldn't hit more than one of them with a single shot.

Hayami knew she should use the distraction of the battle to run and get help, but she couldn't move, couldn't take her eyes off what was happening. She was terrified for Jakari. She didn't know the woman at all, but she knew that Jakari had saved her life. She also knew that she had unintentionally blown a mission that could have stopped the kidnappings cold. She'd been right about something bigger going on, even though she had no idea what she had walked into, and she couldn't bring herself to leave the woman who had saved her behind. Even if she couldn't help.

The first death was as sudden as it was unexpected. Jakari was still keeping up a stream of fire into the larger mech, staging it and blowing pieces off, but one of the men tried to come at her from the side, and she suddenly jerked her left arm around and fired, leaving nothing of him but a burn mark on the grass.

The kill cost her, though. The break in fire was enough to allow the larger mech the chance to change a piece of itself into a shield, and when Jakari turned her attention back to the larger mech, she could no longer hit the main body, and it was able to finish taking on its new form.

After three shots splashed against the shield, Jakari seemed to give up on the larger mech and turned both guns on the men. The second kill came almost immediately. The men weren't ready for the change in tactics, and Jakari caught one of them with a shot from her left arm.

The third kill came just a moment later when Jakari charged one of the two remaining men. She kicked him into the air and shot him as he fell. She had just turned toward the last of the men when a blast from the larger mech hit her, knocking her back and blowing the right arm off her mech.

The larger mech swung its shield in front of it as Jakari started to raise her left arm to fire at it, but at the last second her arm dropped, and she fired into the larger mech's foot, blowing it off at the ankle. The larger mech toppled over, flailing the whole way down. As the larger mech fell, Jakari's mech morphed again, shrinking even as it grew a replacement for its right arm.

The last man tried to get a shot in while Jakari was morphing, but he missed. Jakari turned and fired, hitting him with both of her plasma cannons before her mech had even settled completely into its new form. With the last man gone, Jakari turned her attention back to the larger mech. It had grown a new foot and was getting back up, but Jakari charged it. It started firing at her, but Jakari dodged this way and that, avoiding the shots until she was so close Hayami didn't know how the larger mech could miss, but Jakari sprang into the air, jumping over the next plasma bolt and coming down on top of the larger mech.

Jakari's mech's legs morphed, turning into giant spikes. She drove both of them into the larger mech's torso as she wrapped her arms around its neck. It reached up, clawing at her, but something big launched out of the back of Jakari's mech, and as Hayami watched, it turned into something that looked like a dog with bat wings, flying away from the two mechs as fast as it could. Hayami looked back at the two mechs just in time to see them both explode.

Chapter Three

JAKARI CIRCLED THE BATTLEFIELD in her pterocanis form, trying to burn off some of her rage. She hated losing a Talus. It wasn't that they were hard to replace. Connect a Shim to your Phylactery, then stick it in a mass of TOP matter, and you had a new Talus. The problem was, no two Shims ever felt quite the same, and it took time to get used to a new one. That was time she wasn't fighting at her best.

She could have taken down the Char without using the self-destruct on her Talus, but a Class One against a Class Three in an open battlefield wasn't a fight she wanted to have when there was a time constraint. Keeping the locals from knowing there were aliens among them was still listed as a mission priority, which meant she'd needed to end the fight and end it fast.

There was nothing for it, though. The battle was over, and her Talus and the Char Talus were both expanding vapor. The difference was the Char soldier hadn't had the good sense to bail out. She wondered who they were. Were they a recent recruit, someone just a few decades old who didn't know when to cut and run? Or were they someone who had fought in the rebellion and just made a mistake? Did they even know what they were fighting for? And what about the foot soldiers she'd killed? How many centuries or millennia of lived experience had she erased from the universe that night?

God, she was so tired of all of this. It was all such a waste.

She circled lower and lower until she came in for a landing, touching down near the bridge, then shifted back into her human form.

"You're alive!"

Jakari spun around, morphing her right hand into a plasma cannon and pointing it at the person who'd spoken, only to relax a moment later as she realized it was the human who she'd rescued. She morphed the plasma cannon back into a hand.

"You were supposed to go and find help," Jakari said. "Someone to get you away from here."

"I didn't want to leave you," she said. "You saved my life."

"And you...forget it. Get out of here."

"You're kidding, right?"

"No. Just, get out of here. Forget you saw any of this."

"I can't do that," the woman said.

"Why not?"

"I'm a cop," she said.

"Fuck." Local law enforcement. Just what she needed. "Jakari to Mamachi. Where's my backup?"

"Close. Two minutes."

"We've got a security breach," Jakari said. "Local law enforcement."

"That's not good," Mamachi said. "Gomez is not going to be happy."

"Yeah. She can get in line. My Talus is gone. I'm going to need transport for two."

Jakari turned and looked at the human. "You have a name?" she asked.

"Detective Hayami Takahashi. Dallas Police Department. And who are you?"

"You can call me Jakari," she said.

"That a first name or a last name?" Hayami asked.

"That's an only name," she said.

"Okay," Hayami said. Jakari got the feeling she didn't believe her, but there wasn't a lot she could do about that. "You want to tell me what just happened?"

"You stuck your nose into something that's way above your head," Jakari said.

"Except it's not," Hayami said. "I'm one of the detectives working the kidnappings downtown. You know, like what happened to us."

"Well, I suppose that would explain why you walked into the middle of a perfectly good trap," Jakari said.

"So you *were* looking to get kidnapped," Hayami said.

Jakari shook her head. "I can't talk to you about this. You're going to have to wait and talk to my boss."

"Your boss?"

"You'll see soon enough," Jakari said as she spotted her backup. "Our ride is here."

* * * *

Cikara looked up from the display as the door to their office opened. Bayadani stepped inside and came to attention. Cikara felt a small wave of disquiet at the sight of them. Even after five local years wearing one, the sight of the human forms still disturbed Cikara. They missed their true form and longed to return to Cruthanna, however impossible the current situation made that.

"Yes?" Cikara asked.

"Forgive the interruption, General, but there's a situation you should be aware of."

"Go on," Cikara said.

"The Collection team is dead."

"What?" Cikara asked. "How?"

"They grabbed two specimens for conversion, but shortly after the grab, a Class One Talus attacked them. One of the specimens turned out to be a Suil operative. They attempted to escape with the other specimen, but the Collection team gave chase. The Suil operative led them into a dry riverbed where they turned to fight. After that, we don't know exactly what happened, but we lost the Collection team's comm beacons one by one."

"They had a Class Three Talus!" Cikara said. "How could they lose to a Class One?"

"I believe the Class One was piloted by Jakari, General."

Cikara slumped back in their chair, shocked by what they had just heard. Jakari was here?

"What makes you believe that?" Cikara asked.

Bayadani stepped forward and placed their hand on an interface point on Cikara's desk. The holoprojector in the center of the desk came to life, projecting an image of a Class One Talus in a mech configuration, and Cikara felt a chill run down their spine. One of the quirks of the way Gadan technology worked was that no two Talus users would ever create forms that were completely identical. They might start from the same templates, but a Talus was a living extension of the user, and the more experienced a user was, the more their Talus tended to reflect the user's personality and experience. The more experienced a Talus user was, the easier it was to identify them by the quirks of their mech forms.

"You know them better than I do, General," Bayadani said.

"Her," Cikara said.

"Ah, yes," Bayadani said. "I forgot that she's a Migrant."

"That's definitely her," Cikara said. "That means her little partner is here too."

"Dubari," Bayadani said.

"Have you informed Nira of this?" Cikara asked.

"No, but the chances that she doesn't know are slim."

Cikara wished they could argue, but that was one of the unfortunate side effects of having the Char's chief spy master looking over their shoulder. She always knew everything. In this case, that might actually be a good thing, though. Jakari had been a thorn in the Char's side since the civil war began. Jaya had issued dozens of bounties on her, but no one had ever been able to collect. Nira would love the chance to remove Jakari from the board. Anything to appease her master.

"Do we have an ident scan of Jakari's human form?" Cikara asked.

"We have scans for both her and the human who was with her," Bayadani said. The hologram switched from Jakari's Talus to an image of two women. Cikara had spent enough time studying the humans to learn their phenotypes. One of the women looked Japanese, though she had darker than normal skin for that ethnic group, and hair that was a closer fit to various African groups. Possibly mixed race, then. The other woman had slightly darker skin and short-cropped hair. Light-skinned African or mixed race. Both were attractive, as humans considered such things. Cikara had learned to read the signs even if they didn't see the appeal of the creatures.

"Which one is which?"

Bayadani pointed at the one that wasn't Japanese. "That's Jakari."

"And who is the other one?"

"We're unsure. Possibly an agent of the human government."

Cikara thought about it. That would make sense. The Suil had been working with the local government and had been assisted by humans in some of their previous encounters with them on this world.

"Do you think you could take Jakari?" Cikara asked. They knew there was no way Bayadani could, but they were curious to see if Bayadani realized their own limitations.

"No," Bayadani said. "Not alone. I'm good, but..."

Cikara nodded, reassured that Bayadani had a realistic understanding of their own skills. That would be important when it came time to be rid of Nira. Cikara took a moment, turning it over in their head. Up until now, the Suil presence on Earth had been little more than a minor nuisance, but if Jakari was here, it was very likely they had worked out what Cikara was doing. That wasn't unexpected after they had captured a couple of Cikara's Helots, but it also meant that Jakari was here for them. It was hardly the first time an assassin had targeted them, but it was the first time they were actually afraid. Jakari wasn't just any assassin, and Jakari knew them. They'd fought side by side often enough during the rebellion. And then there had been the incident with Mamachi.

"Send Birat and Ghuma out. Give them the ident scan of this human and tell them I want a location on the Suil base of operations. It's time we dealt with them."

"Birat and Ghuma?" Bayadani asked. "Are you sure you want to send them?"

"Yes," Cikara said. "Them and only them."

"Nira would not be happy about that."

"Nira is not in command," Cikara said. "Send them."

"Of course, General," Bayadani said. They turned and left without further comment.

Cikara closed their eyes, turning everything over in their head. They thought they'd have more time before they had to deal with the Suil, but what was done was done, and this could be an opportunity. If Cikara could just redirect Jakari's attention onto Nira, the plan might still work. Perhaps kill her human associate and make it look like Nira was to blame.

They wondered for a moment if they could actually recruit Jakari. It had been a long time since the two of them spoke, not since the incident with Mamachi on Cruthanna, but if Jakari was still anything like the person Cikara remembered, she might be willing to work with Cikara if it meant an end to the war. It was likely wishful thinking, but Cikara didn't want to kill any more friends. They didn't even want to kill Nira, Jaya, Saka, and Arthan, but they had realized a long time ago that the war would never end as long as the four of them were alive. Killing Nira, Jaya, and Saka would be relatively easy, but Cikara wasn't sure how to get to Arthan, and if they could convince Jakari to help, she might be the key to that.

They looked back down at the display they'd been working on before they'd been interrupted, dismissing the idea. It was wishful thinking, and Cikara had done too much of that of late, but they were tired of war and short on hope.

* * * *

Hayami wasn't sure what on Earth was going on. She'd been shuffled into the back of a Humvee and driven to a military base northeast of Dallas, which she supposed made some sense. The machines she'd seen that night would have had to be military, but that still didn't explain why people were being kidnapped. It didn't explain the kind of technology

24

she'd seen. She'd read enough sci-fi to know what she'd seen had to have been some kind of nanotechnology, but that didn't make sense. None of it made sense. Not what she'd seen, not a military base she'd never heard of, not the way she'd been shoved into an interrogation room as soon as she'd arrived. Someone had checked on her every fifteen minutes, bringing her water, food, and escorting her to a restroom when she needed it, but she'd been sitting there for almost six hours, and she was exhausted.

She needed to call in what had happened, but how the hell could she explain it? No one was going to believe she'd seen giant robots fighting in the Trinity riverbed. No one was going to believe she'd seen a woman who could apparently turn into a giant bat dog or turn her hands into energy weapons. No one was going to believe she'd shot someone four times and they hadn't even flinched. She wasn't sure she believed it, and she'd seen it with her own eyes. She finally had a break in the case after six months and no one was going to believe any of it, assuming the military didn't throw her in some black site so she could never tell anyone anything.

She turned at the sound of the door opening. Jakari and two people she hadn't seen before came into the room. One was a dark-haired woman wearing a black suit and carrying a handful of evidence bags. The other was a blonde man with a deep tan and brown eyes. He was wearing black pants and a white t-shirt, but looked like he would be more at home riding a surfboard out in California. Jakari and the woman sat down across from Hayami while the man grabbed a chair out of the corner and pulled it up to the end of the table. The woman laid out the evidence bags in front of Hayami, and she immediately recognized her badge, her phone, her cuffs, her knife, her spare magazines, and her backup gun.

"Where did you get these?" Hayami said.

"You were apparently on the phone with your partner when you got grabbed. She heard the shots and called it in. The Dallas PD traced your phone and found your things scattered in the road where the kidnappers had dumped them."

"Where's my other gun?" Hayami asked.

"In our evidence lock up. You won't be getting it back," the woman said. "Now, I do apologize for keeping you waiting so long, but you've left us with a huge mess to clean up."

"I've left you with a mess?" Hayami asked.

"Yes," the woman said. "I'm Special Agent in Charge, Silvia Gomez, DHS. Tonight, you walked right into the middle of a matter of national security. Our agent had to blow her cover to keep you from being kidnapped, which meant blowing an entire op. One we may not be able to repeat. Now, would you like to tell me what the hell you were doing?"

"My job," Hayami said. "People have been disappearing in that part of town for months. I'm part of a joint DPD/FBI task force looking into the disappearances."

"Your lieutenant at the DPD said you are part of their Human Trafficking task force," Gomez said.

"That's right. We caught the case because the first victims were girls in their early twenties. We thought it was a human trafficking grab until victims who didn't fit that profile started to disappear."

"That still doesn't explain what you were doing downtown tonight, or why you approached my agent."

"I was downtown because we've gone six months without a break in the case. I was watching for any potential suspect vehicles, or anyone suspicious. People casing the area. People disabling traffic cams. I was trying to find some clue to tell me where twenty-three missing people have gone."

"And why did you approach my agent?"

"Because I saw her walking down an unlit side street on her own. I was worried she was going to get grabbed and I wanted to protect her."

Gomez looked over at Jakari, who nodded.

"I can't fault your instincts, but Jesus, you picked the wrong person to help," Gomez said.

"So you did want her to get grabbed."

"Yes," Gomez said. "We'd been parading her around in the danger zone for six days, hoping they would grab her."

"And you didn't think to let the Dallas PD or the FBI in on your plans?" Hayami asked.

"No, we didn't," Gomez said. "You might have noticed that all of this is way above your pay grade."

"Well, that's stupid," Hayami said. "We've been working the case for six months. You could have brought us in on this. We've got hundreds of hours of surveillance. We've got videos of four of the grabs. We could have helped you."

"The only thing you could help us do, Detective, is exactly what you did. Help us blow an op. We have no idea if the people we are trying to catch have eyes and ears inside the Dallas PD. We don't know if they have selected Dallas as a grab site simply because it's convenient, or because they have a way of avoiding law enforcement or both. In short, informing you would have put my agent at risk."

"Okay, enough," Jakari said.

Gomez turned towards her. "What?"

"The woman was doing her job," Jakari said. "I don't know anything about how you people handle your law enforcement, but from what I can see, she seems to have been doing it well. Yeah, she got in the way. Yeah, I'm pissed the op is blown. But she didn't do anything wrong, and busting her ass is counterproductive."

"Well, what do you suggest?"

"I don't know," Jakari said. "I have no idea if the Char transmitted ident scans back to their ship, but if they did, she'll be a target. I'd say stick her in a safehouse somewhere and be done with it."

"Safehouse?" Hayami said. "You can't be serious. And who are the Char? What's an ident scan? What kind of ship?"

Gomez glared at Jakari, but the man spoke for the first time.

"Jakari, opsec," he said.

"Seriously?" Jakari asked. "She saw me using my Talus. She saw me fighting another Talus. She saw me morph into a pterocanis when I bailed out, and she saw me turn my hand into a plasma cannon. I really don't think there's much point in worrying about it now."

"That's not the point," the man said. "The less she knows, the better."

"The lieutenant has a point," Gomez said to Jakari. "Detective Hayami is Dallas PD. We can't just stick her in a safehouse without explaining what's going on to her superiors, and even if we did explain, they're going to raise hell. I don't think we can hold her."

"No one is holding me," Hayami said.

"It would be for your own safety," the man said. "You don't have any idea how dangerous these people are."

Hayami looked over at him. "Do you have a name, lieutenant?"

"Mamachi," he said.

"Well, Lieutenant Mamachi, I'm a cop. I'm not used to hiding from the bad guys," Hayami said. "Whoever these people are, they have kidnapped almost two dozen people off the streets in my town. I want a piece of them."

"That's not your call," Gomez said.

"Maybe it should be," Mamachi said.

"What?" Gomez asked.

"She has a point," Mamachi said. "Her task force has been watching the disappearances for six months. If they stay on the investigation, something like this is going to happen again. And there's also the fact that we've had a lot of luck with cooperation between..." He trailed off without finishing the sentence, which left Hayami a little confused.

Gomez looked at her, then back at Mamachi. "You sure the general would go for it?"

"The general isn't the one who insisted on keeping what's going on out of the public eye. She would actually prefer more open cooperation between us because it would make things easier."

Gomez shrugged. "Fine," she said. "It's your call. I'm just here to keep it out of the papers."

"What are you talking about?" Hayami asked.

Mamachi turned towards her. "After this incident, Homeland Security is going to have to take over the investigation into the kidnappings. We can't risk Dallas PD or the FBI getting further involved. The risk of exposure, and the risk to the lives of your people is too great. However, as Colonel Jakari points out, you've already seen a great deal of what's going on. Since the people we're fighting most likely have your picture, at the very least, you are already on their radar. What I'm proposing is that, instead of putting you into protective custody, we bring you into our operation and pair you with one of our people."

"I like that option," Hayami said.

"It will be dangerous," Mamachi said. "If they know who you are, you will be a target."

"I can live with that."

"Good," Mamachi said. "Then it's settled. You'll work with Jakari."

"What?" Jakari asked. "No! Absolutely not!"

"Okay," Hayami said. "I'm not feeling the love."

Jakari looked at her. "I already have a partner," she said. "And I can't protect a squishy in a fight."

"Did you just call me a squishy?" Hayami asked.

"Yes," Jakari said, before turning back to Mamachi. "I'm not here to make nice with the locals. I'm here to kill Cikara."

"I know why you're here," Mamachi said.

"Who's Cikara?" Hayami asked.

"Then you know I can't spend my time babysitting some defenseless local," Jakari said.

"She won't be defenseless," Mamachi said. "We can equip her with gear that will make her considerably less squishy. As for your mission, you can't kill Cikara until you can find them, and right now, the detective may be your best bet for actually finding them."

Jakari stopped and stared at Mamachi for a moment, then looked over at Hayami.

"If they have her ident scan, you know they'll come for her," Mamachi said.

"I don't want to use her as bait," Jakari said, turning back to Mamachi.

"I don't either," Mamachi said. "Part of the reason we're here is to protect humans. But if we don't find a way to stop Cikara, there won't be any humans left, and not long after that, there won't be any Suil left either, which means there won't be anything standing in the way of Jaya."

"Fuck," Jakari said. She turned back to Hayami. "Are you sure you're okay with this?"

"Being dangled as bait for people who ride around in twenty-foot-tall battle mechs kidnaping random people and doing God knows what to them? No. I'm definitely not okay with that. But people are disappearing, and it sounds like whatever is going on is really fucking bad, so...sign me up."

Chapter Four

"I THOUGHT YOU SAID you were taking me somewhere so you could fill me in on what's going on," Hayami said as she looked around the building Jakari had led her to. It was a massive hangar with a smooth, glossy white floor and an arched roof supported by exposed steel beams. That wasn't out of the ordinary, but what was strange were the huge tanks that filled the back half of the building. They looked like something out of a brewery and were all connected with a series of overhead pipes that led to what looked like some kind of spigot. The spigot was on a pivot, and under the area where it could reach, there were a series of molds, like the kind you would use to pour prefab concrete shapes. Each of the molds was a simple rectangle, and the only real difference between them seemed to be size. They ran from a small one about the size of a laundry basket up to one the size of a large shipping container. A single woman sat at a desk near the molds, watching TV on her computer screen.

"I am," Jakari said as she led them towards the woman at the desk. "I'm taking you home so you can get some sleep, and I'll give you the full briefing when you wake up, but we need a way to get there."

"So you're getting another one of those robot things?" Hayami asked.

"It's called a Talus, and yes," Jakari said.

The woman glanced up as they approached and frowned. She paused and minimized her show and turned slightly in her chair so she was facing them as they reached her desk.

"I am Jakari."

"I am Iksha," the woman said. "How can I help?"

"My Talus was destroyed. I need a new one," Jakari said.

"What class?" the woman asked.

"Class One," Jakari said.

The woman turned back to her desk and pulled up a different application on her computer, clicked on something, then typed in a password. The spigot swung around so it was over one of the smaller molds, this one a little bigger than a coffin, and a dark gray liquid the color of pencil lead started pouring out. It kept pouring until the mold was filled, then the liquid stopped, and what was still between the spigot and the top of the mold flowed back up into the spigot, leaving the mold filled exactly to capacity.

Jakari walked over to the mold and Hayami followed. She put her left hand on the surface of the liquid, which solidified the moment she touched it. Hayami watched as a small cylinder maybe half an inch long and an eighth inch in diameter rose out of the hard surface. Jakari picked the cylinder up with her right hand and lifted her left hand off the surface. As soon as she lifted her hand, the contents of the mold became liquid again. She held the cylinder up in the palm of her right hand, and Hayami watched as the cylinder melted and soaked into Jakari's skin, disappearing.

"This will take a minute," Jakari said. Before Hayami could say anything, Jakari turned the same gray color as the liquid in the mold and stood there, frozen like a statue. Hayami stepped back in shock and looked over at Iksha, who was watching with a bored expression on her face as if people turning into graphite statues was a routine and particularly boring part of her day.

"First time you've seen it, huh?" Iksha asked.

"What the fuck is happening?" Hayami asked.

"They are making a Shim," Iksha said. "It's what lets them control a Talus and lets it hold a form without a Gadan being in direct physical contact."

Hayami turned back to Jakari, not having any better an idea of what was going on than she had before, but she didn't have to wait long. The graphite color faded away a moment later as Jakari returned to her normal flesh and blood self except for a patch in the middle of the palm of her right hand. The cylinder from before rose out of the patch before it returned to its normal color. Jakari turned and dropped the cylinder into the liquid in the mold. It sank quickly below the surface, and as soon as it disappeared, the liquid started flowing over the side of the mold. Hayami stepped back and watched in stunned disbelief as the liquid took on the form of the motorcycle she'd seen earlier in the evening, with two helmets resting on the seat.

Jakari stepped forward and picked up one of the helmets, holding it out for Hayami. "I understand these are legally mandated," she said.

"Yeah," Hayami said, taking the helmet cautiously. Jakari took the other one and pulled it on, then climbed onto the bike. Hayami pulled her helmet on a bit reluctantly, but it felt solid and normal enough. She clipped the chip strap closed, then climbed on the bike behind Jakari.

"You know where we're going?" Hayami asked.

"Yeah," Jakari said. "Your address was in your police file, and I'm tapped into GPS."

Hayami wrapped her arms around Jakari as she started the motorcycle, wondering what the hell she'd gotten herself into.

* * * *

Mamachi walked back to their quarters, disappointed in the late hour. They had hoped to be done early enough to spend some of the evening with Skylar. It had never been a realistic hope, but they'd missed her terribly the last week. They'd gotten so used to her constant company during the year they'd lived on Earth before the Char arrived that being separated from her left them with a physical ache. After five years, it was something they'd learned to manage. It helped that they usually got to spend at least some time with her during the evenings, but the last week had been night after night of sitting on comms, waiting for any word from Jakari that she'd been grabbed.

They reached their quarters and punched in the security code in the keypad. The light on the lock changed from red to green, and Mamachi opened the door and stepped inside. They froze, the sound of breathing instantly alerting them to the presence of someone in their quarters. They morphed their eyes from human form to their Gadan form so they could see better and smiled when they spotted the huge lump in their bed. They eased the door closed and morphed their clothes into a pair of pajamas as they crossed the room and sat down on the edge of the bed, a huge smile on their face.

Skylar was curled up in a ball in the middle of their bed, snoring gently. Her curly brown hair was spread out over the pillow she was sleeping on and she had her arms wrapped around the other pillow, clutching it tightly. Mamachi reached down, gently brushing a few strands of hair out of her face.

Skylar let out a small hum and slowly opened her eyes.

"Hey," she said in a sleepy voice.

"Hey yourself," Mamachi said. "What are you doing here?"

"Missed you," she said. She took the pillow she'd been holding and laid it up near the head of the bed. "Lay down."

They smiled and stood up, then pulled back the covers and climbed beneath them as Skylar straightened out on the bed. They slipped an arm around her, and she rested her head on their shoulder.

"Better," she said. "How'd it go?"

"It was a mess," Mamachi said, but they didn't continue. A soft snore coming from Skylar let them know she was already asleep again. Mamachi couldn't stop themself from smiling. It was funny, really. They'd been fighting the Char for almost seventeen hundred years, but it wasn't until they'd met Skylar that they felt like they had something to fight for, and now all they wanted was for the war to be over, to have the freedom to choose their own life so they could choose to stay here on Earth with her.

It was probably a fantasy. They didn't even know if Skylar would want them to stay. They hoped. Some days it felt like the hope was all that kept them going, but they weren't sure, and they were afraid to ask because it felt like a dream. The war had started four thousand years before they were even born. Hoping that it would end so they could stay here and enjoy the few decades of life a human had was madness, but it was the first time in their entire life Mamachi could remember truly wanting something just for themselves.

They pulled Skylar closer against their side and shut their eyes, dropping into a rest cycle, hoping that Skylar would still be there in the morning. Maybe they could get breakfast together before work pulled them apart for the day.

* * * *

It was close to 5:00 AM by the time they pulled into the driveway of Hayami's house. Since her cruiser wasn't there, she went ahead and opened the garage so Jakari could park her Talus inside. The last thing she needed was one of her neighbors getting nosy about why there was a motorcycle in her driveway. Once the Talus was parked, she led Jakari into the house.

"You own this place?" Jakari asked.

"The bank owns most of it," Hayami said. "I'm five years into a twenty-year mortgage."

"I don't know what that means," Jakari said.

"Oh," Hayami said. "Um...it's not important. For practical purposes, yes, I own this place."

Jakari nodded. "You should get some rest," she said. "I'll stand guard."

"I'd rather you tell me what the hell is going on," Hayami said.

Jakari frowned. "I was under the impression that humans needed at least eight hours of sleep every twenty-four," she said.

"You keep talking about humans like you're not one," Hayami said.

"I'm not. I thought that was clear by now," Jakari said.

"So what are you, exactly?"

"I'm a Gadan," Jakari said. "Don't you need sleep?"

"I do, but I'm not going to be able to sleep until you tell me what's going on," Hayami said.

"The files I have on humans say that lack of sleep can be dangerous. Even deadly."

"It takes about three days without sleep before there's any serious issues," Hayami said. "I'll be fine."

"Okay," Jakari said. "Is there somewhere we can sit down?"

Hayami led the way to the living room, sat down in the easy chair, and gestured to the couch. Jakari sat down on the couch and held out her right hand. The center turned the same graphite color as before and a small disk with a lens in the center rose out of it. Jakari leaned forward and set the disk on the coffee table. The lens on the disk lit up and a hologram appeared above it, showing an image of a bar spiral galaxy. Most of the galaxy appeared bright white, but there was a single, bright red point of light about two thirds of the way to the edge.

"This is what your people call the Milky Way Galaxy. The red dot is our current location." The image expanded and another dot appeared, this time bright green. "This is my homeworld. Cruthanna. It's about six thousand lightyears from here in the general direction of galactic spin.

"My people, the Gadan, were like you once. Purely organic beings." The image of the galaxy vanished, replaced by an animated image of a creature that looked like a combination of an anthropomorphic hairless cat and a lizard. It had the general look of a cat. Digitigrade hind legs, a torso that was thicker front to back than side to side, a long tail, a triangular head with a pronounced snout and tall ears that turned this way and that. The arms were built more like human arms than cat arms and ended with hands tipped with curved claws. The claws retracted and extended as a muscle in the forearm tensed and relaxed. Unlike hairless cats on earth, there wasn't any loose, wrinkled skin. Instead, the skin was taut, and the body was covered with scales. The creature in the image was mostly red with a pale, tan belly and blue diamond patterns in the scales.

"We were a peaceful people then. Largely content to stay in our own star system. We had FTL technology and used it to trade with a few of our neighbors, but we hadn't established any colonies other than some asteroid mining facilities and a few resource extraction facilities on various moons in our own system. We hadn't fought a war in hundreds of your years."

"Then the Seichu came." The image of the catlike Gadan was replaced by a different creature, and Hayami honestly had no real basis for comparison. The closest she could think of was some sort of combination between a frog and an octopus. It had four-toed webbed feet at the end of digitigrade legs, a flat body, long, four-fingered webbed hands, and a flat, triangular head with eyes on top. It was all stoutly built, like it was meant to carry a lot of weight, but then there were the tentacles. Thick, massive things attached to the back of the head, with suction cups and spiked tips. Each one was long enough to hang down the back to the creature's lower knees, but as Hayami watched, the tentacles lifted and swayed and moved in ways that made her want to run away from what she was seeing.

"They were from a resource-poor star system not far from ours. They'd exhausted their world, mined it bare, burned through all their fossil fuels, tapped out the world's small supply of extractable ores. Every resource they had was nearly spent, and they were looking for more. They chose our world thinking we would be a soft target, but they were wrong. Just because we hadn't fought a war in a long time didn't mean we couldn't.

"We were predators once. We'd worked hard to overcome our nature, but when they started killing us, the veneer of civilization slipped, and we fought back like the killers we were. The war was vicious and brutal. We answered every atrocity they committed with a reprisal, and in the end we were winning, but we underestimated how far they were willing to go.

"They sued for peace and sent a ship carrying an ambassador to negotiate terms. As soon as the ship entered our atmosphere, it exploded, spraying a bioweapon across the face of our world. A full third the population died the first day, but the rest of us lingered."

Hayami looked up from the hologram, her detective instinct kicking in. There was something about how cold, how mechanical the recitation was, combined with the haunted look in Jakari's eyes, that told a horrible story. It was hard to believe if all of this happened ten thousand years ago, but she'd seen a lot of things that were hard to believe that night.

"You lived through this?" she asked.

"I did," Jakari said.

"How old are you?"

"I was forty-six of your years old when the bioweapon was dropped."

"How is that possible?" Hayami asked.

"One of our scientists had been researching a way to transfer minds into computers as a way to extend life. His technology became our salvation. He created a device called a Phylactery." The image of the Seichu was replaced with an image of a graphite-colored sphere about the size of a golf ball. "It's a techno-organic computer. A mix of carbon-based nanotechnology and genetically-engineered biology. Each Phylactery can hold a single mind, and they were easy enough to make because they could be grown from the techno-organic materials we already used to make up a large amount of our technology. Techno-organic materials which were immune to the bioweapon."

"So you're a cyborg?" Hayami asked.

"You could call us that," Jakari said. "It's not entirely accurate though. A cyborg is usually an organic being with technology grafted onto them. We're a blend of the technological and organic from the genetic level up. The difference is important, because the new technology gave us remarkable abilities. Things a cyborg could never do. We could reshape ourselves at will. Form our bodies into tools or weapons. What we couldn't do was match the Seichu for sheer numbers. Barely a quarter of our pre-bioweapon population survived long enough to undergo the Migration.

"When they came again, they outnumbered us. We were still recovering from the bioweapon, and we hadn't realized the true potential of our new forms yet. They conquered us easily, but by the time they did, barely ten percent of our pre-bioweapon population remained. Less than a billion of us."

"Were you a soldier?" Hayami asked.

"Me?" Jakari asked. "No. I was a gardener. Before the bioweapon, I'd never done anything more violent than pull a few weeds. When they were recruiting soldiers, they gave me an aptitude test. It said I lacked the capacity for violence necessary to be a soldier."

"I think they got that wrong," Hayami said.

"I don't know," Jakari said. "Before the bioweapon, they might have been right, but watching as your wife dies a slow, painful death does things to you. It changes you in ways that aren't for the better. After the bioweapon, after she died, I hated the Seichu.

"I didn't know it was possible to hate like that. Before the Seichu, my idea of hate was limited to scale mites and torsha soup, but then I watched Aashi die, and I learned what real hatred was. When they came, when they took our planet, I fought back. I killed every one of them I could lay hands on. In alleyways, in their homes. I used guns and knives, but bombs were my favorite. I'd attach them to public transports, wait until they were full, and blow-up dozens of them. I brought down buildings on their heads. One time, I even blew up an entire cruise ship. Dropped it right out of orbit."

"You were a terrorist," Hayami said, more than a little horrified.

"Yes," Jakari said, something like pride in her voice. "I was a spectacular terrorist. I didn't care who I killed, as long as they were Seichu. Not until Napati found me. She taught me to direct my efforts. Brought me into the rebellion. That's where I met Jaya, Cikara, Saka, and Arthan. Arthan was the leader of the rebellion. Napati, Jaya, Cikara, and Saka were his generals, and I became his chief assassin.

"I had a gift for it. I could get into places no one else could. Reach targets that were unreachable. Napati found me 200 years into the occupation, and for another 800 years, I killed anyone Arthan told me to until the rebellion was over, and we'd wiped out the Seichu."

"You killed them all?" Hayami asked.

"A few escaped," Jakari said, sounding disappointed. "Two or three transports' worth. However, many escaped their old homeworld before our warships arrived. When open war broke out near the end, we didn't take prisoners. A thousand years is a long time to hate someone, and the Seichu treated us worse than animals. We were nothing but toys to them, to be broken and tossed aside. The things they did...you can't even begin to imagine. We killed them all because they deserved it. Everyone we could find, and if we ever found any more, we would cheerfully finish the job because they still deserve it for what they did to us. Not that we deserve much better.

"They call those of us who were alive before the bioweapon Migrants because we migrated from purely organic to techno-organic bodies. Of the two point five billion or so of us who originally underwent Migration, there are maybe a hundred thousand left today. The Seichu killed a billion and a half during the conquest, and maybe another two hundred thousand of us during the occupation. The other seven hundred thousand was our own doing.

"After the rebellion, after we drove the Seichu off our homeworld Cruthanna, the Migrants formed a political party called the Suil Agam with Arthan as our leader. The Suil wanted peace. We wanted to return to the life we had before the Seichu, and we had huge popular support, even among those born during the occupation. The Seichu were gone, and for a lot of us, they'd taken our taste for war with them. We wanted to go back to the way it was before. A simple, peaceful life, without the day-to-day horrors of the occupation. That's the platform our candidates ran on, and we won almost every election.

"Once we had control of the government, we started restoring our world, we established off-world colonies, we made alliances with the aliens around us. We used our technology to ensure everyone was fed and provided for. We thought it would be a new golden age, but we were wrong.

"Char Oram, the opposing political party founded by Jara, Cikara, and Saka, believed that the only way our people would ever be safe, the only way to protect ourselves against anyone else who would conquer us, was to build an empire and conquer them first. When the Char couldn't win at the ballot box, they turned to the same tactics they'd used against the Seichu. They assassinated the Senate and started a war.

"It was easy for them to take Cruthanna. Most of the Suil supporters had moved out to the colonies, looking for a home that didn't remind them of the horrors of the occupation. They drove the Suil off Cruthanna completely, and we've been fighting a bloody civil war ever since. Nearly three quarters of the colonies fell to Char control, and the only way we've been able to hold on is the support of our alien allies. There have been lulls in the fighting sometimes. A few years here, a few decades there. Once we went two centuries without a single battle, but sooner or later, one side or the other will think they have an advantage and attack.

"Which is how we got to where we are. Cikara, the second-in-command of the Char Oram, is here on your planet. They're working on a way to turn your people into soldiers for their cause. They're putting them into techno-organic bodies like ours, but they're attaching a mind control device to their Phylactery that makes them loyal to the Char. That's what the disappearances have been about. Earth is offering them more than seven billion potential soldiers. Enough to overwhelm the Suil and end the war. Enough to start building their galactic empire."

"Why Earth?" Hayami said. "If we're six thousand lightyears from your world, why come here?"

"Because you can't fight back," Jakari said. "I don't know how they found your world, but compared to the other alien species we've encountered, your people are technologically primitive. You barely have space flight; your weapons are useless against us unless you want to start dropping nukes. Cikara picked you because you can't resist.

"The people you're looking for, the people who have been kidnapped. They've been converted already. We've captured two of them, and they have bodies like mine, but their minds are locked inside their Phylacteries and we don't know how to get them out."

"Why were you trying to get captured last night?" Hayami asked.

"Because I was sent here to kill Cikara and to destroy their research, to end the threat this weapon poses, but we don't know where their ship is. Their stealth technology is just as good as ours, if not better. Getting captured was the fastest way to find their ship. They would take me there, thinking I was nothing more than a human, and once I was onboard, I would escape, kill Cikara, destroy their research, and let Napati know where the ship was so she could destroy it."

"And I blew it," Hayami said.

"You didn't know," Jakari said. "You were trying to help me. I was angry at the time, but it's not your fault. You did the right thing."

"But how many people will die because of me?" Hayami asked.

"None," Jakari said. "I made the decision to break cover. Anyone who dies, that's on me. I could have traded your life for passage onto Cikara's ship. I chose to save you instead."

"Why?" Hayami asked. "If this Cikara is really as dangerous as you say, why did you break cover? Why save me?"

Jakari looked at Hayami as if the question itself made her uncomfortable, and instead of answering, she reached out and picked up the holoprojector. The device merged back into her hand and she stood up.

"You should go to bed," Jakari said. "I'll keep watch."

"But—"

"Go to bed," Jakari said. "I'll keep watch."

Hayami nodded. "Okay. If you want to get some sleep, the couch is comfortable. Honestly, I end up falling asleep there a couple of times a week. There are blankets and pillows in the cabinet over there if you want them."

Jakari didn't answer. She just walked over to the window and pushed the curtain aside to look out. Hayami sighed and headed for her bedroom, wondering why such a simple question had provoked such a reaction.

Chapter Five

ONE OF THE FIRST things Hayami noticed when she laid down that morning was that it was hard to sleep with a self-confessed terrorist and assassin wandering around your house. She usually didn't have any trouble getting to sleep, especially when she'd been up all night, but that morning, she lay in bed tossing and turning, going over what she'd been told in her head. She was a little surprised the alien part didn't bother her. Not nearly as much as the way Jakari had talked about blowing up public transit vehicles and buildings and spaceships.

It conjured up horrible images. The twin towers collapsing, airplane wreckage spread out in a field, the Oklahoma Federal building in ruins. Burned-out school buses and still burning car bombs. Images that had haunted her when she'd taken anti-terrorist training courses. She tried to tell herself it was different. Jakari's world was occupied by people who had killed ninety percent of her race. That it would be more like a Jewish woman fighting back against the Nazis, or the French resistance during World War II, but she wasn't sure she believed that.

Jakari's people had fought back, but they hadn't just driven their enemies off their world. They'd committed a far more thorough genocide than their oppressors had. Jakari hadn't said anything about the Seichu having anything like the technological immortality that her people had. After a thousand years, were any of the people who had conquered her world still alive? Were the Seichu really such cruel rulers that they deserved what had happened to them? Was Hayami a better judge of that than a woman who had lived through the horrors of the war and the occupation?

She had so many questions, but the one that bothered her more than any other was why Jakari had saved her. If Jakari was the monster she claimed to be, a terrorist who spent centuries slaughtering her enemy without restraint, an assassin who had been killing professionally for thousands of years without remorse, why would she hesitate to let the enemy kill one person if it meant a chance to get close to her target?

It didn't make any sense to her at all, and Hayami hated things that didn't make sense. They offended her detective's brain, and Jakari did not make sense. Not even a little bit.

* * * *

"Why? If this Cikara is really as dangerous as you say, why did you break cover? Why save me?"

The question echoed through her head and Jakari had to fight down the anger that it brought with it. Why save her? How could Jakari explain? How could she make someone who hadn't seen the things she'd seen, done the things she'd done, understand?

Jakari had killed so many people in just the first year of the occupation that she'd lost count. It hadn't mattered to her how many she'd killed. The answer was always the same. Not enough. Never enough. Not as long as a single Seichu drew breath. She'd hated and she'd killed and she'd hated some more. She'd practically drowned herself in the foul-smelling blue ichor of Seichu blood, wanting to erase who she'd been before the war. A gardener. What use was a gardener in a universe filled with monsters?

She'd been powerless to protect Aashi. What good was a fucking gardener against a bioweapon? She'd failed Aashi. She'd failed the woman she loved. She was useless and worthless, so she stopped being a gardener. She remade herself into an avenging personification of death. She started with pruning knives and trowels and other tools of her former trade. Moved into fertilizer bombs, and then into better tools. With her new techno-organic mind, her natural gift for chemistry became positive genius. She designed her own explosives. She learned how to design circuits and build detonators from electronic junk fished out of the Seichu's trash, and she killed them.

She killed them with their own waste, with their own excess, with the very evidence of their crimes against a peaceful people who had never done them harm before they first attacked. She made their blood flow like a river. It never brought her any satisfaction, never brought her any joy. It was simply her purpose. Her reason to go on existing. She would make them pay. Every last one.

Then she'd met Napati, and she'd found a better way. She still killed Seichu, but she didn't do it at random anymore. She picked her targets more carefully. A bomb in the right place, a bit of poison gas at the right moment, a knife in the right neck could save lives at the same time as it eased her thirst for retribution.

It took time. It took centuries, but they did it. They ended the Seichu. Billions had come to Cruthanna after the bioweapon. When the rebellion ended, the transport ships that had escaped couldn't have carried more than a few dozen. Then they had gone to the Seichu's world and turned every square millimeter into radioactive glass. She'd looked at the world she'd helped liberate and thought of all the blood she'd spilled to do it, and she'd felt nothing. She looked at the world she'd helped turn into a cinder and she felt nothing. There was no sense of triumph. No sense of joy or satisfaction. All that had been left was grief for everything she'd lost.

When it was all over, she'd gone back to being a gardener. She'd done it because aside from killing people, it was the only skill she had. It was then, kneeling in a newly planted sabuja berry patch, that she'd felt joy for the first time since Aashi died. She'd made things grow. She'd nurtured life, cultivated it, shaped it, and made it beautiful. She'd began to feel like a person again. Then the Char killed the Senate, and the war had started all over again.

She'd expected Arthan's call. She'd agreed to go back, not because she wanted to kill anymore, but because she'd wanted to protect life the way Napati had taught her. The right knife in the right neck and the right time to save lives.

How do you explain that to someone who had never seen the things she'd had seen? How do you explain that after you'd spent ten thousand years doing nothing but ending life, that life was the most precious thing in the universe?

Why did she save Hayami? Because she had to. Because there was no way she couldn't save her. Because if she'd let Hayami die, then it was all a lie. If she let Hayami die, then her mission wasn't about saving lives, it was about killing someone.

If she let Hayami die, she was still that wounded, enraged animal who cared more about screaming her grief into the void and lashing out at the architects of her pain than about protecting the people who were still living.

Why save Hayami?

How could she not? How could she trade an innocent life for a mission and still live with herself? Hayami was innocent. Her whole world was innocent. They'd done nothing to bring this on themselves, any more than the Gadan had done something to bring on the Seichu, and Jakari would not have any part in their destruction.

* * * *

Hayami woke up to the sound of knocking. Well, no, not knocking. Banging. Someone was banging on the front door. Loudly. She looked over at the clock and groaned. It was 8:15 AM, which meant she might have gotten an hour's worth of sleep. She considered ignoring the banging and going back to sleep until she heard the front door open.

"Who the hell are—" Michelle started to ask, only to get cut off with a shout. There was the sound of something being slammed against a wall and the door slamming shut.

"What the fuck!"

"Who are you?" Jakari demanded as Hayami scrambled out of bed and ran for the living room.

"Let go of her!" Hayami yelled as she ran into the living room. Jakari had Michelle up against the wall with a weird-looking pistol pointed at her face.

Jakari looked at her. "You know this person?"

"She's my partner!"

"They were trying to break down the front door," Jakari said.

"She wasn't," Hayami said. "Now let her go."

Jakari lowered the pistol and stepped back, taking her hand off Michelle's chest.

"What the fuck?" Michelle asked.

"What are you doing here, Michelle?" Hayami asked.

"What am I doing here?" Michelle asked. "I'm checking on my fucking partner. The one I heard get kidnapped last night. The one who apparently spent the night in DHS custody. The one who isn't answering her fucking phone."

"My phone?" Hayami asked.

"Yeah. The one I've called a dozen fucking times this morning, since DHS said you were released around 4:00 AM."

"Right," Hayami said. "Wait here. And don't shoot each other!"

She turned and marched back into her bedroom and found her phone where it was laying on her bedside table. It was turned off. She groaned and turned it back on as she headed back out into the living room, where Michelle was glaring at Jakari and Jakari sat with a disinterested look on her face.

"DHS turned it off," Hayami said. "I forgot to turn it back on when they cut me loose."

"You forgot?" Michelle asked.

"It was a long night," Hayami said.

"For a lot of us," Michelle said. "You scared the fucking piss out of me. And who the fuck is she?"

Hayami looked over at Jakari, not sure how to answer that question, but Jakari apparently had an answer. She reached into her pocket and pulled out an ID folio.

"Special Agent Jack Arias, Department of Homeland Security."

"You're Homeland Security?" Michelle asked.

"That's what I just said." Jakari turned to Hayami. "Does she have a hearing defect?"

"No," Hayami said. "You know what, I'm not awake enough for this shit. Michelle, make some coffee. Jack, try not to kill anyone. I'm going to go take a shower and put some clothes on."

"But you haven't had enough sleep," Jakari said.

"That's what the coffee is for," Hayami said. She looked at Michelle. "Make it strong. None of that lightweight bullshit you drink."

"Yes ma'am," Michelle said, snapping off a salute before marching into the kitchen.

Jakari gave Hayami a confused look, but she ignored it and went to get a shower.

* * * *

Jakari sat back down on the couch and opened a connection to the planetary information network. What Mamachi had called the internet. It wasn't an ideal way to communicate, but Mamachi had told her that it was more secure for them because even if the Char wanted to try, there was no way they could sort through all the data flowing across the net to zero in on and eavesdrop on their communications. Especially if they used encryption.

Jakari opened a link to Mamachi, using the data path they had given her before she left the base to send a text-only message.

Jakari: I require non-emergency assistance.

Mamachi: What with?

Jakari: Another human arrived at Hayami's residence and attempted to break down the door. I reacted by drawing a weapon on the attacking human, but this upset Hayami. She said the human in question was her partner.

Mamachi: Send me a record of the interaction.

Jakari pulled up the memory file and encoded it as an audio-visual log, then transmitted it to Mamachi and waited. It took a couple of minutes before Mamachi responded.

Mamachi: I understand the source of the error. I made the same mistake once as well. Michelle was not trying to break the door down.

Humans often engage in hyperbolic speech and behavior as a way to communicate emotion. Especially distress or frustration. Michelle was concerned for the wellbeing of Hayami and upset that Hayami had not responded to their attempt at communication through the cell phone. Hayami was upset with you because of a perceived overreaction to what she considers normal behavior.

Jakari: That's considered normal behavior?

Mamachi: Normal might be an exaggeration, but it's not considered behavior that warrants an armed response. Skylar, the human who I first made contact with, still sometimes reminds me that I pulled a plasma pistol on her mother.

Jakari: How am I supposed to distinguish between actual attacks and hyperbolic behavior?

Mamachi: If the attack is directed towards a living individual and not property, you may intervene. Also, if the attacker is using a weapon and not simply their hands, you may assume that you can respond in kind. Provided the weapon does not have the word 'Nerf' emblazoned on the side.

Jakari: What is 'Nerf'?

Mamachi: 'Nerf' is the name of a local manufacturer that makes weapons which are used for recreational combat simulation. The ammo is composed of a soft plastic foam which cannot harm the target. Humans become quite agitated if you respond to 'Nerf' weapons with plasma cannons.

Jakari: I will keep that in mind.

Mamachi: Do you require any further assistance?

Jakari: Not at this time. Thank you.

Mamachi: You're welcome.

Jakari closed the connection to Mamachi and wondered what other bizarre behavior she would encounter while dealing with these humans.

No sooner had the thought passed through her head then she jumped to her feet, morphing her hand into a plasma cannon at the sound of a horrible grinding noise coming from the kitchen. Her first instinct was to run in, weapon ready, but after what had just happened, and the lack of calls for help or sounds of distress, Jakari morphed her hand back to human form and went to investigate, hoping this was some other bizarre human custom she had yet to encounter.

* * * *

Hayami did her best to shower and get dressed quickly, worried about how much of a disaster things between Jakari and Michelle could become while she wasn't there to referee. When she came out of the bedroom, she was a little relieved that there were no plasma burns or bullet holes in the walls, but disturbed by the fact that neither Michelle nor Jakari were anywhere to be found. If it wasn't for the smell of coffee coming from the kitchen, she'd have checked to see if they'd gone outside to duel to the death or something. Instead, she followed the siren song of caffeine into the kitchen and found Michelle and Jakari staring at each other over the kitchen table, each with a steaming mug sitting in front of them. Michelle had already committed sacrilege and contaminated her coffee with half and half, while Jakari's cup looked untouched. Hayami picked up her favorite mug—a ceramic one custom printed with a piece of Eliza and Goliath fan art from the old Disney Gargoyles TV Show —and poured herself a cup of coffee, then walked over and sat down at the table.

Jakari watched her with a look of horror as she took a sip of her coffee.

"You don't like it?" Hayami asked.

"It smells wonderful, but it tastes like burnt plastic."

"Hold that thought," Hayami said. She got up and grabbed a spoon from the drawer and came back over to the table. She scooped two teaspoons worth of sugar into Jakari's coffee and stirred it for a minute.

"Try it now."

Jakari gave her a dubious look but lifted it up and took a sip. The look on her face changed from reluctance to shock.

"That is good!" she said.

"How have you never had coffee before?" Michelle asked.

"Michelle," Hayami said. "Drop it."

"What?" Michelle asked. "Why? Homeland here starts the day by sticking some kind of gun in my face 'cause I knocked a little loud, and doesn't know what coffee is. I'm not allowed to ask questions?"

"Jack is here to protect me," Hayami said. "Because the kidnappers have a picture of my face, and there's a chance that they'll come after me again."

"Dallas PD can protect you," Michelle said.

"No, you can't," Jakari said.

Michelle started to bristle, and Hayami reached out and put a hand on her shoulder.

"She's right," Hayami said. "I hate to admit it, but DPD is seriously outgunned here."

"So DPD can't protect you, but Homeland here can?"

"It's not personal. There's just more going on here than we realized."

"Then tell me," Michelle said. "What the hell happened last night?"

"DHS has been working the kidnappings from a different angle than we have. Jack was undercover as bait. The idea was for her to get grabbed and then for her team to track the kidnappers back to their base. When I saw her go down a deserted side street by herself, I went after her to try and protect her, and ended up getting grabbed along with her. When she wasn't the only person grabbed, she made the decision to abort the op. The kidnappers did not come quietly. They're all dead, and they torched the van. DHS is trying to pull anything they can from the wreck, but there wasn't a lot left by the time they put it out. Whoever is running the kidnappings has pictures of mine and Jack's faces. So, a facial recognition algorithm or two and they'll know who I am, at the very least, and come after me. That's why Jack is here."

"So, what? She's going to be riding along on all of our cases?" Michelle asked.

"No," Hayami said. "I'm being temporarily reassigned. DHS is taking over the kidnapping investigations."

"You're kidding me," Michelle said. "They can't do that. It's our case!"

"They can," Hayami said. "The special agent in charge is going to meet with the lieutenant and the FBI lead on the case at around 11:00 AM, and after that, I'll be attached to the DHS team until this is done."

"What the hell, Yami?"

"I'm sorry, Michelle, but you do not want any part of this. Trust me. I wish to God I'd stayed home last night, because I know shit I do not want to know. And because maybe if I had, all of this would be over, but it's done. And please, just this once, I'm begging you to leave it alone."

"You're serious?" Michelle asked. "We've been partners since the day you made detective."

"I know, and I'm not trying to shut you out. I'm trying to protect you."

"I don't need protection," Michelle said.

"Yeah, you do," Hayami said. "This isn't some group of Eurotrash running teenage girls. DHS is involved for a reason."

"Then tell me what the hell is going on!"

"She can't," Jack said. "It's classified.

"That's bullshit."

"No, it's not," Hayami said. "Go in to work. I'll be by a little later to get some things and talk to the lieutenant."

"Fine," Michelle said as she stood up.

"Do you know what happened to my cruiser?" Hayami asked.

"It's in impound. Tagged as evidence."

"Okay," Hayami said. "Saves me a trip downtown."

"Whatever," Michelle said. "See you around, partner."

Michelle left without another word, slamming the door on her way out. Hayami didn't really blame her. Michelle was normally a pretty good person, but she could be an absolute bitch when she was pissed, and she was obviously pissed.

"I'm sorry," Jakari said.

"About what?"

"I didn't mean to cause you problems with your partner," Jakari said.

"She'll come around once the mad wears off," Hayami said. "She always does. It will just take a little longer this time."

"How long?"

"How long do you think it will take to wrap up this mess with Cikara?"

"I have no idea," Jakari said.

"Same answer, plus about two weeks," Hayami said. "Finish your coffee. I need to go buy a new gun."

Chapter Six

A BLUE ASTON MARTIN Vantage and a red Chevy Suburban pulled into the driveway of Hayami's house. A person stepped out of each in perfect unison, though the people couldn't have been more different if they tried.

The person who stepped out of the Aston Martin was small. By human standards, roughly five foot, three inches tall. They wore a shiny blue three-piece suit with a matching tie. Their face was clean shaven and their hair was all combed over to the left side, ending at their chin. Their face had an androgenous look, making it hard to tell if they were male or female. Something further complicated by the hints of makeup.

The person who stepped out of the Suburban was six foot, four inches and made of bulging muscles. They looked like a bodybuilder and wore their hair in a crew cut. Anyone who looked at them would immediately assume they were male. The sculpted pecs, the lack of breasts, the broad shoulders, and narrow hips lending to that assumption. They were dressed in black combat boots, black fatigue pants, a white t-shirt, and a brown leather jacket with dark tinted aviator sunglasses.

Both of them looked around, taking in the area, searching for enemies. Once they were sure there was no attack coming, they headed up onto the porch. The smaller one tested the door and found it locked, so he pressed a fingertip against the keyhole. The tip of the finger turned a dark graphite color and flowed into the keyhole. A moment later, there was a click as the lock opened. They pulled their finger away and repeated the process on the deadbolt, then opened the door.

Both of them filed inside, their hands morphing into plasma cannons as they did. They moved through the house quickly, searching for their targets. One they expected to be fairly easy. Nothing more than a human. The other they expected to be much harder. Jakari was a legend, after all.

The initial search came up empty, no human, no Jakari, no vehicle they could pull GPS information from, so they started a more thorough search, taking care not to leave any evidence of their presence. They didn't find much. A few bills, a stack of takeout menus. A drawer in the nightstand full of items whose use neither of them particularly cared to think about.

In the end, they didn't find anything that would point them at the Suil base, so they left the way they came, careful to lock both locks behind them.

"Where to now?" the larger one asked.

"This human works for the Dallas Police Department," the smaller one said.

"Are you sure that's wise?" the larger one asked. "It will attract a lot of attention."

"That's what we want," the smaller one said. "Attract attention. Draw the Suil out. Follow them back to their base and then call in a strike."

The larger one shrugged. "If you say so."

"I do," the smaller one said. "I just need to make a quick call along the way."

* * * *

Aside from a few bar fights broken up by MPs, Jakari had never really dealt with law enforcement before. She'd never had so much as a traffic citation before the bioweapon, and during the occupation, the Seichu's idea of law enforcement amounted to throwing any Gadan even suspected of a crime into the gladiator pits. A place Jakari escaped from at least five times. During the civil war, she'd been under military authority, so civilian law enforcement left her alone on Suil worlds, and on Char worlds it was nothing more than an obstacle between her and her target, which made walking into the police station where Hayami worked a novel experience.

Hayami escorted her past a desk manned by an officer in uniform and led her into a large room filled with various people who didn't wear uniforms, but had badges clipped to their belts, or wore them on lanyards around their neck. They all sat at desks, drinking coffee and typing away on computers or reading files. A few had people sitting beside their desks that they were talking to. It was all very loud and busy and more than a little confusing.

Hayami pointed Jakari to a chair next to her desk, and she sat down while Hayami began filling out paperwork to let the department know she had purchased a new gun and would be carrying it on duty from now on. Jakari wasn't sure why that was important, and given how much grumbling Hayami was doing, neither was she, but apparently it was a task that had to be completed.

Michelle showed up after a few minutes and took a seat at the desk directly across from Hayami's, and proceeded to glare at Jakari for some reason. She was tempted to ask what the problem was, but the look Hayami was giving her told her that would be a bad idea.

Hayami finished her paperwork after about a half an hour and took out a stack of files from one of the drawers in her desk.

"Are those the kidnapping files?" Michelle asked.

"Yes," Hayami said. "I—"

"Takahashi, Anderson, get your asses in here," someone called out.

"And there's us," Hayami said. "Come on."

Jakari followed Hayami and Michelle across the room to a closed off office where Special Agent Gomez was waiting with a man she didn't recognize.

"Lieutenant," Hayami said. "Special Agent Gomez."

There weren't enough chairs in the office, so Jakari took a spot against the back wall, figuring the humans probably needed them more than she did. Gomez already had one, and the lieutenant had another. Jakari was a little annoyed when Michelle took the third and final chair, since Hayami hadn't had a full sleep cycle, but Hayami didn't say anything, so Jakari let it pass.

"Lieutenant, this is Special Agent Jack Arias. DHS. Jack, this is Lieutenant Isaac Hall. Dallas PD," Gomez said.

"Nice to meet you," Jakari said.

"Can't say the same," Hall said. "I hear you're stealing one of my best detectives."

Jakari didn't respond because she didn't know what the appropriate human response was, and because there was nothing she could do about his unhappiness. The decision had been made without her approval either, and she wasn't exactly happy about it herself. The lack of response seemed to make Lieutenant Hall agitated, but fortunately, Gomez cut in, saving Jakari from having to figure out how to solve the issue.

"Special Agent Arias isn't the one who made the decision, lieutenant. That was me, and you can direct any ire you have in my direction. She's just doing her job."

"And what is her job, exactly?" he asked.

"To track down the terrorists who are grabbing people off the streets of Dallas," Gomez said.

"And what makes you think this is the work of terrorists?" Hall asked.

"We have intel you don't. Intel that, unfortunately, we can't share."

"Right," Hall said. "Am I allowed to ask my detective what the hell happened last night?"

"By all means," Gomez said.

Hall turned to Hayami. "Well?"

"I was downtown trying to catch a break in the case," Hayami said.

"Off the clock?" Hall asked.

Hayami sighed. "Yes sir," she said.

"I'll yell at you for that later. Finish your report."

Jakari turned and looked out the window, tuning out Hayami's recitation of the previous night. She let her internal system record the conversation in case she needed to reference it later, but she'd already heard the fake version of the story several times, and she'd lived the real version, so there wasn't a lot she could get from it.

She watched the detectives moving around the large room, trying to figure out all the things they were doing, but something over by the door attracted her attention, and if she still had a heart, it would have skipped a beat.

"Gomez," Jakari said without looking away from the sight of a small human in a shiny blue suit, "what would be the fastest way to signal a general evacuation of the building?"

"Fire alarm," Gomez said. "Why?"

Jakari turned towards her. "How do I signal one of those?"

Gomez nodded towards a red box on the wall. Jakari stepped over and pulled the lever marked, 'Pull Down.' The building filled with the sound of a shrieking alarm.

"What the hell are you doing?" Hall asked.

"We have hostiles in the building," Jakari said, looking out at the person in the blue suit.

"How many?" Gomez asked as she grabbed a heavy black backpack off the floor.

"At least two," Jakari said.

"They're here?" Hayami asked.

"Yes," Jakari said. "The person in the blue suit. That's Ghuma. The big one beside them is Birat. Ghuma's one of their intel specialists. Birat is a heavy weapons specialist."

Gomez stood up and slipped her arms through the straps on her backpack. "Lieutenant, get as many of your people out of here as possible. This is about to get ugly."

"There are two terrorists in my bullpen, and you want me to evacuate the building?" Hall asked. "Are you crazy or just stupid?"

"Sir, listen to them," Hayami said. "We can't fight these people."

Jakari was watching Ghuma and Birat. They weren't trying to stop any of the humans from leaving the building, which was good, but they were looking around for people who weren't trying to evacuate, which was bad. She saw the moment Ghuma spotted her, the way a thin, gloating smile spread across their face.

"They've spotted us," Jakari said. "Hall, take Michelle and get out. I'll try to stall for time."

"Will that work?" Gomez asked.

"It might," Jakari said.

She stepped out of the office and walked towards Ghuma with her hands up. Birat kept a close eye on her, but she kept her gaze fixed on Ghuma. When the two of them were together, Ghuma was always the one in charge.

"Hey, Ghuma," she said. "Been a long time."

"But you still recognized me," Ghuma said. "I'm flattered."

"It's the color," Jakari said. "Still suits you, even in this form."

"Thank you," Ghuma said. "You always did have more of a sense of style than most of your comrades."

Jakari glanced around, noting that the 'bullpen,' as Hall had called it, was largely clear, before turning back to Ghuma.

"Cikara send you after me?" she asked.

"You and your human pet," Ghuma said.

"I don't suppose it would do any good to tell you the human was just a cop who was trying to keep me from getting grabbed. Wrong place, wrong time. She's not one of our allies."

"Don't care," Ghuma said. "Orders are orders, and you know how Cikara gets when theirs aren't carried out."

"I do," Jakari said. "Any chance we could do this somewhere less public?"

"Sure," Ghuma said. "You tell me where the Suil base is and we can finish this in one big blaze of fire and death."

"Well, you know I can't do that," Jakari said. "How about you tell me where the Char base is, and we'll come to your place for the party?"

"Cikara doesn't like uninvited guests," Ghuma said.

"So Cikara is here," Jakari said. "Good to know."

"She's stalling for time," Birat said.

"I know that, love," Ghuma said. "Doesn't mean we can't mind our manners."

Jakari glanced over at the office and saw that the only one left there was Gomez, who gave a small nod. She turned back to Ghuma.

"Building's empty," Jakari said. "No more reason to stall."

"You sure you don't want to just surrender?" Ghuma said. "It could save us a lot of messy fighting."

"Hmmm..." Jakari said. "I'm going to have to go with..." She jerked her hand up, morphing it into a plasma cannon, and fired. "...no!"

Ghuma and Birat both managed to dodge, though Ghuma caught the edge of the blast, which scorched them on the left side. They hit the ground and shed the burned TOP matter, reforming their suit without the jacket as both their hands turned into cannons. Birat raised their arm, their hand already replaced with a tri-barrel rotary cannon. Jakari dodged out of the way before Birat could line up a shot. They turned to follow her, but caught a blast from the office that burned their arm away at the elbow.

Gomez burst through the wall, wrapped in power armor and carrying a pair of plasma pistols. She kept firing at Birat, driving them and Ghuma further away as Jakari started firing at Ghuma. Ghuma shifted into their Gadan form, using the extra mobility to their advantage. They leapt into the air, firing at Jakari. Jakari responded by rolling out of the line of fire and firing into the patch of floor where Ghuma was going to land. Ghuma slammed into the compromised floor and went right through.

Jakari turned and opened fire at Birat, taking some of the pressure off Gomez, who was dodging as fast as she could in the power armor. Birat turned towards what they no doubt perceived as the greater threat and started pouring fire in Jakari's direction. Jakari dove towards the floor and rolled while Gomez picked up a heavy metal desk and chucked it at Birat.

The desk slammed into him, giving Jakari the opening she needed. She scrambled to her feet and charged across the room, scooping

Gomez up in the process, and dove out the window, landing on her feet three stories below. She set Gomez down as she sent a command to her Talus.

"This is about to get real public," Jakari said.

"Can't be helped," Gomez said. "Do what you need to do."

Jakari nodded as her bike rolled up beside her. She climbed onto it and revved the engine as Ghuma and Birat came running out of the building. They made for a blue car and a red truck that were racing to meet them.

"Take care of Hayami," Jakari said, and gunned the throttle, accelerating away from Gomez. She glanced back in her rear view, watching as Ghuma and Birat both gave chase.

"Gomez, do you read?" she called.

"Loud and clear."

"They're following me. Get Hayami and get back to base."

"Understood."

Jakari switched comm channels. "Mamachi, do you read?"

"Loud and clear. What's up?"

"Ghuma and Birat are on my tail. Ghuma is in a Class Two Light, and Birat is in a Class Two Heavy. I'm leading them away from Gomez and Hayami, but I'm not sure I can hold both of them by myself. I need support, and not ten minutes from now."

"Roger that," Mamachi said. "I'm scrambling a pair of Class Four flyers, and a Class Five Heavy flyer."

"Where the fuck were they last night?" Jakari asked.

"We didn't have the templates last night," Mamachi said. "Gomez only authorized us to scan the template vehicles this morning."

"Fine," Jakari said. "Just get them here."

"They're in the air and enroute."

She glanced back, relieved to see that Ghuma and Birat were both still following. She just needed to keep it that way until backup arrived.

* * * *

Vrusti watched as Ghuma and Birat pulled away from the human law enforcement outpost. They didn't pay the fight or Ghuma and Birat's departure much thought. They had their own mission. They had spotted the human woman target as soon as she had rushed out and stayed close. Vrusti's current form was small, and humans tended not to notice it unless it called attention to itself, so staying close to the human was easy, and when Jakari had jumped out of the building carrying a human in TOP matter armor, Vrusti knew their time was coming.

They watched as the armored human hurried over to the target human and pulled her towards a vehicle. Vrusti followed, and once they were sure which vehicle they were taking, they rushed under it. The humans were all too busy to see a small black cat rush under a car. They were also too busy to see that cat's body reshape itself and attach itself to the undercarriage as a simple black box.

When the car pulled out of the parking lot and headed north, Vrusti settled into their new perch and waited as the humans took them to their target, completely unaware of the fact that they were giving the location of their base away.

* * * *

Jakari cut between two cars as she wove through traffic, doing her best to put as much distance between her, Ghuma, and Birat as she could without actually losing them. Ghuma was closer because the small blue sports car was better able to maneuver around other vehicles than the big red SUV, but something felt off. The Suil were trying their best to keep the alien presence on Earth under wraps at the request of the various Earth governments, but the night before, the Char had shown no hesitation about exposing themselves and their weapons. So why weren't Ghuma and Birat firing at her? They couldn't think they'd spooked her badly enough that she'd run straight back to the Suil base.

She heard a rhythmic thumping sound coming from up ahead and spotted a pair of odd-looking aircraft headed her way. They had a spinning blade over top of the main body of the craft. It had a sort of rounded front that turned into a long, boxy middle, then tapered back to a narrow tail that had a vertical stabilizer with two horizontal control surfaces coming off it, and another one of those spinning blades, this time pointed horizontally, coming off the tail.

"Mamachi, I see two flyers incoming," Jakari said.

"That's your backup. Third one is a bit slower but is on the way."

The flyers swung wide and circled around to get behind Ghuma and Birat. They seemed to realize backup had arrived, and rather than fight, they took the next exit off the highway. The flyers went in pursuit, but the feeling Jakari had that something was wrong just got worse. Ghuma and Birat might not be the most loyal troops the Char had ever seen, but they were both fighters. For them to just run away didn't make sense.

"Jakari to Gomez, do you read?"

"Gomez here, I read you."

"Hostiles have broken pursuit on my end. Is everything okay with you?"

"We're fine. Enroute to base with no signs of pursuit."

"Acknowledged," Jakari said. "Keep your eyes open. Something feels off about all of this."

"Understood."

* * * *

"Stop the car," Hayami said.

"What?" Gomez asked.

"Stop the car!" Hayami said, a bit more forcefully this time.

Gomez didn't ask any more questions. She just pulled over onto the shoulder. The moment the car was stopped, Hayami got out of the car and dropped down on the ground. She pulled out her flashlight and clicked it on, shining it under the car, looking for anything that didn't belong. Gomez came around the car and knelt beside her.

"What are you doing?" Gomez asked.

"Looking for a tracker," Hayami said.

"Why?" Gomez asked.

"You heard Jakari. She said something feels off, and she's right. They had to know who I am. How else would they have known to look for us at the station? And there were two of them. When Jakari made her breakout, why not send the heavy after her, and the lighter one after me?"

"Maybe they lost you in the crowd?" Gomez said.

"Maybe, but all the more reason for one of them to stay and try to find me again," she said.

"Do you see anything down there?" Gomez asked.

"No," she said. "But that doesn't mean there isn't anything."

"Move," Gomez said.

Hayami got up and moved out of the way. Gomez, still wearing the armor she'd come out of the station in, laid down on the ground. The helmet of the armor snapped closed again, and she looked under the car for a minute.

"Son of a bitch," she said. She reached under the car and pulled out a black box. She stood up as the helmet of her armor retracted. "You were right."

"Yeah," Hayami said. "I wonder what—"

The black box started shifting in front of them, quickly morphing from a simple box into a small black cat. Before either of them could do anything to stop it, the cat kicked free of Gomez's grip, and shot off into the bushes.

"What the fuck?" Hayami asked.

"I don't know," Gomez said. She reached up and hit a button to activate her comm. "Gomez to base. We're going to need a pickup and a containment team."

Chapter Seven

IT WAS JUST AFTER 3:00 PM when the blue Ford Mustang Shelby GT 500 pulled over to the side of the road. The passenger's side door swung open, and a black cat ran out of the bushes and jumped into the passenger's seat. As soon as the cat was in the car, the door swung closed, and the Mustang pulled back into traffic.

Inside the car, the cat jumped into the back seat where a large plastic trunk was sitting. The trunk and the cat both turned a dark graphite and flowed together, then the resultant mass extended a tentacle into the front seat, and slowly, the entire mass flowed along the length of the tentacle, taking the form of a young human woman. Once the transformation was complete, they reached up and pulled on their seatbelt.

"What happened?" Ghuma asked.

"The human target, Hayami, guessed that we had to be tracking them. The other human, Gomez, the one with the TOP matter armor, used the sensors in the armor to spot me. I managed to escape, but they found and destroyed the additional trackers I left on the vehicle," Vrusti said. "I did manage to get an ident scan of Gomez."

"Excellent," Ghuma said.

"Do you think Cikara will be angry that we didn't find their base?" Vrusti asked.

"I think that's for me to worry about," Ghuma said. "You weren't officially assigned to this mission, so you won't get caught in any fallout."

"You'll cover for me that way?" Vrusti asked.

"Of course," Ghuma said. "Contrary to what you may have heard, I'm not a complete bastard. Besides, you're useful. You can't be useful to me if Cikara assigns you to waste management or something else ridiculous."

"That's not as reassuring as I thought it would be," Vrusti said.

"Sorry, kid. This is war. I like you, but if it's a choice between you or me, or you or Birat, I'm going to pick me and Birat every time."

"Well, at least I know where I stand," Vrusti said.

"That's better than you'll get with most of the Char," Ghuma said.

"Yeah," Vrusti said. "I've noticed that."

* * * *

Jakari felt a wave of relief wash over her as Hayami stepped off the 'Blackhawk.' Jakari had been brought back to base on the third flyer, a larger one that had two of the blades on top. The humans had called it a Chinook. The names didn't make any sense to Jakari, but both types of vehicles apparently fell under the 'helicopter' label.

Jakari waited impatiently as Hayami and Gomez got clear of the helicopter and then ran over to them. Once she reached them, she looked Hayami over carefully.

"Are you okay? Do we need to take you to the medical bay?" Jakari asked.

"I'm fine," Hayami said. "What about the people back at the station?"

"No humans were injured," Jakari said. "The building is still structurally sound, though depending on how quickly your construction teams work, it may take some time before it's usable again."

"Great," Hayami said, voice dripping with sarcasm.

"How did you know you were being tracked?" Jakari asked.

"It made sense," Hayami said. "You're the stronger fighter. If they chased you off, it would make sense for us to retreat to somewhere safe. If they wanted the location of the base, then it would make sense to have a tracker or a tail on us. I had been watching for a tail, but when you said something felt off, I knew it had to be a tracker."

"I never would have thought of it," Jakari said.

"Why not?" Hayami asked.

"Taluses are living extensions of us. We could feel any sort of device attached to our Talus as if it were attached directly to our body. What they did would only have worked on a human vehicle."

"So you're saying we make you vulnerable?" Hayami asked, her tone cutting, and Jakari immediately realized what she'd done wrong.

"No," Jakari said with a shake of her head. "Not at all. I'm saying that we're lucky you were aware of your own weaknesses. You saved a lot of lives today. We're in your debt."

Hayami smiled at that. "Just doing my job," she said.

"Doing it very well," Jakari said. "Come on. We need to get you fitted with your control implants. If you're going to work with us, you need to be able to use the equipment we've designed for humans."

"Implants?" Hayami asked.

"It's okay," Gomez said. "I've had them for years. They're perfectly safe, and you can remove them at any time."

"Right," Hayami said. "Maybe a little more detail first?"

"We can do that," Gomez said.

* * * *

Cikara smiled as they felt a call come in on their internal comm. They opened a channel and smiled as Ghuma appeared in their heads-up display.

"Ghuma," Cikara said. "Do you have good news for me?"

"Not yet, General," Ghuma said. "The human target is more clever than we gave them credit for. They spotted the tracking device we planted on their human-built vehicle. It wasn't a complete loss, however. We know for sure that their base is located to the northeast of the city and we have a general area. It's only a matter of time before we have an exact location."

"Good work," Cikara said. "When you have that location, be sure to contact me on my private band. Do not go through ships' comms."

"Of course, General," Ghuma said.

"And Ghuma, move quickly," Cikara said. "It's imperative that we find their base before Jakari finds ours. Otherwise, you and Birat might find yourselves at Nira's tender mercies."

Ghuma shuddered. "Understood."

Cikara cut the connection and leaned back in their chair. Whatever Bayadani thought about Ghuma and Birat, they produced results. They weren't always the quietest about it, but that hardly mattered as long as they got a location for the Suil base.

Nira would know, of course, that Ghuma and Birat were working for Cikara, but that didn't worry them. They knew who Nira's agents onboard were, and had people of their own carefully positioned to remove them. When the time came, Nira would be on her own. Still phenomenally dangerous, but she was just one woman, and quantity had a quality all its own.

The biggest danger would be Nira sabotaging the ship in some way, and Cikara had contingencies against that. Modifications to the normal ship Scripts, as well as replacing the Scripts on a regular basis. They hoped that Nira wouldn't act against them without direct orders from Jaya, but Nira's presence meant that she more than likely already had contingency orders to remove Cikara.

Which made the real question whether to move against Nira now, or after they had the base location. Moving now would likely tip their hand with Jaya, but waiting meant Nira might move against them first.

Cikara hated this. They weren't built for plotting and scheming. They were a scientist and a weapons designer, and yes, over the millennia they'd become a highly-skilled field commander by simple necessity, but plotting the downfall of two governments was not within their skillset. There was just no one else to do it. Jaya and Arthan would never end the war without a genocide. Saka's insanity was growing by the day, and Nira was too loyal to Jaya to even realize how blind Jaya had become to the reality of their situation. Napati was, ironically, the only one of them who Cikara trusted, and Napati was just as likely to kill them on sight as she was to listen to them if they tried to sue for peace.

It was enough to make Cikara long for the gladiator pits. Things had been so much easier back then. Just kill the next opponent put in front of you. That was something Cikara had gotten very, very good at.

* * * *

Hayami followed Jakari and Gomez into the medical bay at the base, still feeling more than a little nervous. They'd both insisted that it would be best to let the medic explain how the implants would work. Hayami still wasn't sure she wanted to even get in the same room with anything called an 'implant.' Being able to use Gadan weapons did have a certain appeal. She hated the fact that the most useful thing she'd been able to do in both of her encounters with the Char was run away, but the idea of putting alien tech in her body was only slightly less appealing than the idea of putting Earth tech in her body.

"Rayak," Jakari said as an older man stepped into view. Hayami was surprised to find out that he was a Gadan. All the Gadan she'd met so far looked young, in their prime, but the man in front of her had gray hair and age lines on his hands and face. He looked more like someone's grandfather than a shapeshifting alien soldier.

"Jakari," Rayak said in an annoyed tone. "You don't look like you're hurt, so why are you bothering me?"

"I'm not," Jakari said. "This is Hayami Takahashi. She's a human law enforcement officer. She's going to be working with us for a while. She needs implants so she can use the equipment we've adapted for the humans, but she's a little nervous about it and has some questions."

"Another human?" Rayak said, shaking his head. "You'd think we couldn't fight our own damn war."

Rayak looked at Hayami. "I suppose if you're nervous about this, that's a sign that you're smarter than the other humans who've wandered through my medical bay. Not that your primitive human brain could understand half of what our technology does."

"Rayak," Jakari said in a warning tone. "Be nice."

"Hmph! Have you met me?" Rayak said. He pointed at one of the beds. "You, human. Sit there and ask your questions."

Hayami looked at Jakari and Gomez, who both gave her a small nod. She walked over and sat down on the bed.

"So, how exactly do these implants work?" Hayami said.

"Magic," Rayak said. "Are you done?"

"Rayak, explain it to her," Jakari said.

"Fine," Rayak said. "Stupid waste of time if you ask me, but no one ever does." He looked at Hayami. "The first step is the injection of a techno organic computer called a 'Script.' Scripts are what we use to create pieces of our technology that are not permanently linked to a Gadan mind stored in a Phylactery. Do you know what all of those words mean?"

"So, a Script is like a Shim, except that it's not connected to a Phylactery the way a Shim is."

Rayak's face lit up with surprise. "Maybe you're not as dumb as the other humans after all," he said. "That's exactly right. The main difference between a Shim and a Script is that a Shim is connected to the mind of a Gadan and can be controlled without physical contact. In order to control a Script, you have to be in direct physical contact with the device that contains a Script. We call those devices Fixtures."

"Okay," Hayami said. "A Shim is a computer that controls a Talus, and a Script is a computer that controls a Fixture."

"That's right," Rayak said.

"So why are you going to put a Script inside me?" Hayami asked.

"Because you don't have a Phylactery, so you can't control a Shim," Rayak said. "And since you can't control a Shim, you can't control a Talus. So what we're going to do is put a Script in you, and then we're going to inject TOP matter into you."

"TOP matter is what Gadan bodies are made out of?"

"Yes," Rayak said. "Gadan bodies are called Vessels, though that term doesn't get used a lot. Vessels, Taluses, and Fixtures are all made of TOP matter. TOP matter stands for—"

"Techno-Organic Polymorphic matter. I've got that part," Hayami said. "And the Script inside me will control the TOP matter you inject me with."

"Very good," Rayak said. "The Script will instruct the TOP matter to form a neural interface. The TOP matter will then connect itself to all the nerve trunks in your body, as well as burrowing its way into your spine and sending runners up into your brain."

"That sounds painful," Hayami said.

"It is. Incredibly."

"He's lying," Gomez said. "He sedates you. You don't feel a thing."

Rayak glared at Gomez for a minute. "Anyway, as I was saying, the Script creates a neural interface which replicates the control links in a Phylactery. It will allow you to control a limited number of Shims. You won't have anywhere near the bandwidth a true Phylactery will have, but it's enough to control a Class Point-Five Talus and a couple of weapons."

Hayami looked over at Gomez. "That's what you were wearing? A Talus?"

"Yeah," Gomez said. "It's kind of limited in function, but it's enough to protect you against the edge of a plasma blast. Not a direct hit, though."

"It will also increase your strength, stamina, speed, and endurance," Rayak said. "It has a built-in comms system, a full sensor suite, and a medical support package, but you can't reshape it on the fly the way a Gadan does with a true Talus. You won't have the bandwidth, and honestly, your brain doesn't work fast enough."

"And what happens when all of this is over? I just walk around with these implants in my body my whole life?"

"No," Rayak said. "You can actually purge the implants from your body any time you want, but if you do it without outside assistance, it will be incredibly painful. Like ripping nerves out of your body with your bare hands. If you come back here, we can sedate you, and the process will be painless."

"And this is safe?" Hayami asked.

"Oh, no," Rayak said. "Not even a little bit. I mean, the procedure itself is perfectly safe, but you'll be out there fighting Char soldiers who have thousands of years of combat experience. You try fighting one of them alone, and you won't stand a chance. You'll die screaming."

"Right," Hayami said. She looked over at Jakari.

"He's not wrong about that," Jakari said. "The reason I want you to have the implants is to make you less squishy. Not because I expect you to go toe-to-toe with Char troopers."

"So you still expect me to run away?" Hayami asked.

"I don't want you to die," Jakari said. "If I had my way, you never would have gotten involved in this. No human would. But you did, so I want to maximize your chances of survival. And I've seen enough of you to know you're not going to keep running away, even if it is the smart thing to do. So if you want to keep working with me, you take the implants. Otherwise, Gomez is going to confine you to base."

"Fine," Hayami said. She looked at Rayak. "Do it."

Rayak shook his head. "Well, there goes my hopes for a smart human," he said as he headed over towards a supply locker.

Hayami couldn't help but agree with him.

* * * *

Jakari watched as Rayak swabbed the back of Hayami's neck with some sort of pink gel. The anesthetic had taken hold a few minutes ago and she was lying face down on the bed with her face positioned over a hole so it wouldn't impede her breathing, but Jakari didn't like it. Seeing Hayami so still didn't feel right at all. Jakari hadn't known her long, but as long as she had known her, she'd been constantly in motion. Talking, asking questions, going through paperwork. Even when she was just sitting and thinking, she never really sat still. Now she was quiet and motionless, and it felt wrong to Jakari.

"What is that you're doing?" Jakari asked, not able to stand still herself.

Rayak sighed. "I'm applying a healing accelerant," he said. "I have to use a large-bore needle to get the Script in place, and this will help close up the hole by the time she wakes up."

Jakari frowned. He hadn't said anything about that when he was explaining how the implants worked, and it seemed like the sort of thing Hayami would have wanted to know.

He set the gel aside and picked up a large syringe. He uncapped it, pinched up an area of skin just above her spine, and slipped the needle in, then pressed the plunger down. Once it was all the way down, he pulled the needle out of the end of the syringe and attached it to a hose that was filled with the dark graphite color of TOP matter.

"You don't have to stay for this," he said. "The process takes about twelve hours."

"Why so long?"

"Because human tissue is delicate. If I feed in the TOP matter too fast, it will damage her, and after it's in place, I have to inject more of the healing accelerant or it will take her weeks to recover."

"Where did you get the healing accelerant?"

"It's an old nanotech medicine from before the Migration. I had the recipe stored in my Phylactery. It wasn't hard to adapt it to humans," Rayak said. His tone was surprisingly gentle. "You don't need to worry about her. I promise I'll take good care of her."

"I know you will," Jakari said. "I'm not worried, but she's my responsibility."

"I see," he said.

"She's a fighter," Jakari said.

"I had noticed that," Rayak said. "A lot of these humans are. Gomez, and that one that Mamachi is fond of."

"Skylar," Jakari said.

"Is that their name?" Rayak asked.

Jakari had to fight not to smile at that, because she knew damn well that Rayak knew Skylar's name. No one could spend much time with Mamachi and not hear Skylar's name.

"Well, if you're going to stay here, you might as well make yourself useful. Come over here, I'll show you how to monitor the infusion so I can do some real work."

Jakari walked over and looked at the monitor, listening carefully as Rayak began to explain what she was seeing.

Chapter Eight

"IT'S NOW BEEN FOUR days since the alleged terror attack at Police Headquarters in Dallas, with no news as to which terrorist organization is behind the attack or what their motivation and demands might be. Sources inside the Dallas PD speaking on condition of anonymity say that the attack is somehow connected to the recent string of mass kidnappings in downtown that have left at least twenty-three people missing, with unconfirmed reports that the number may be even higher. In related news, the manhunt continues for these two men who are suspected of carrying out the terror attack at Police Headquarters. No word yet on whether or not they are also involved in the kidnappings."

Hayami sighed and shook her head as she looked back down at her breakfast. She cut herself another bite from her pancakes and chewed it slowly, more than a little amazed at just how good pancakes from an army cafeteria were.

"I see the carb cravings have kicked in," someone said.

Hayami looked up and saw a young woman with long, curly brown hair standing next to her table. She was attractive, in a girl next door kind of way. Deep brown eyes, a cute nose. A little heavy on the smokey eyeshadow look. She was wearing a Cure band T-shirt over a pair of those God-awful tan camouflage pants most of the soldiers wore. Hayami recognized her instantly as the girl she'd seen talking to Mamachi on multiple occasions, but she'd never gotten her name.

"I'm sorry?" she said.

"Carb cravings," the girl said. "You just got your implants, right?"

"How did you know?"

"You've got three stacks of pancakes," the girl said. "Can I sit?"

"Sure," Hayami said.

The girl sat down and put her tray on the table. It shocked Hayami a little. It had two stacks of pancakes, two chocolate croissants, and what looked like two eclairs with bacon on them, along with a few strips of bacon, a couple of sausage links, and a mound of scrambled eggs covered in ketchup.

"I'm Skylar," the girl said. "Skylar Peyton."

"Hayami Takahashi," Hayami said. "Nice to meet you."

"Likewise," the girl said as she speared one of the sausage links with her fork. She dipped it in the ketchup on top of her eggs and then bit it in half, chewing cheerfully. She waved her fork at Hayami's plate. She covered her mouth with her other hand. "Eat," she said around a mouth full of sausage.

Hayami cut another bite of her pancakes and started chewing.

"The carb cravings are going to overpower everything else," Skylar said after she swallowed her food. "It's the TOP matter. The nanotech is carbon-based, so you need more carbohydrates than before to maintain it, but you have to keep up your protein and fat intake as well. Otherwise, you'll develop deficiencies."

"Really?" Hayami asked.

"Yeah," Skylar said as she held up a bottle of orange juice. "And watch your vitamin intake too. One idiot actually managed to give himself scurvy."

"Scurvy? You're kidding."

Skylar nodded. "You'll see. The carb cravings are nuts. I've had the implants longer than anyone else here, and sometimes I wake up in the middle of the night halfway through a pint of Americone Dream."

"They're that bad?"

"Our bodies aren't really made to handle the TOP matter. It's not toxic or anything. It's all the same fatty acids and aminos in Earth food, but the Gadan's bodies do a lot of recycling that ours can't, so we have to eat to make up the difference."

"They didn't tell me any of that when I got the implants," Hayami said.

"Don't hold it against them," Skylar said. "Rayak hasn't lived in a fully organic body in ten thousand years. You tend to forget little details. Mamachi and a lot of the others were born into the TOP matter bodies, so they've never had to deal with food the way we have."

"I've seen them eat," Hayami said.

"Yeah, but how much and how often," Skylar said. She lifted her hand and waved at someone. Hayami turned and saw Mamachi headed their way.

"Hey," Mamachi said. "You mind if I join the two of you?"

Skylar gave Hayami a look.

"Not at all," Hayami said.

"Thanks," Mamachi said as they sat down. Skylar immediately pushed the two bacon topped eclairs towards them.

"Two bacon maple glazed," she said.

"Oh!" Mamachi said, practically bouncing in their seat. "Thank you!" They took a bite of one of them and let out a moan that was vaguely pornographic. Skylar just looked at them with a big dopey grin on her face.

"Those donuts will last them for days," Skylar said.

"Really?" Hayami asked.

Mamachi nodded as they chewed slowly, obviously savoring their meal. "It's true," they said, once they swallowed. "Most of our energy comes from collecting ambient environmental energy, which allows our body to reprocess a lot of what you would use up as chemical energy. Mostly, we just need to replace small amounts of mass lost due to environmental factors. If anything, Skylar's understating how long I could survive on these. I could probably go a couple of weeks without anything else. It wouldn't be comfortable after about the tenth day, though."

Hayami made note of that, since it could be useful information later. She turned to Skylar. "You said you were the first one to get the implants."

"Yeah," Skylar said. "I was actually the one to make first contact with the Gadan. I was out in the desert and I saw what I thought was a plane go down. I went to help, and instead of a downed plane, I found a flying saucer, complete with an alien."

"A flying saucer?" Hayami asked.

"You haven't seen one of their ships yet?" Skylar asked.

"No," Hayami said.

"You should ask Jakari to show you," Skylar said. "They really are flying saucers."

"Really?"

"It makes the warp drive more efficient," Mamachi said. "Warp drive requires a circular engine, so we put that around the edge of the ship, but length in the direction of travel affects power consumption, so we make the ship as flat as possible and just fill in all the space inside the ring. I didn't get why Skylar found it so funny until she showed me a bunch of old movies."

"Wait, you showed an actual alien a bunch of alien invasion movies?" Hayami asked.

Skylar shrugged. "It seemed like a good idea at the time?"

Hayami burst out laughing.

"Klaatu barada nikto," Mamachi said, making Hayami laugh even harder.

"ET phone home," Skylar said.

"Do or do not. There is no try," Mamachi said.

"Stop," Hayami begged, gasping for breath.

"Think we should let her off easy?" Skylar asked.

"Sure," Mamachi said. "Just this once."

Hayami glared at both of them as she caught her breath. "You two are trouble."

Skylar smiled. "We do try," she said. "So, what are you doing today?"

"I'm supposed to meet Jakari after breakfast," she said. "We're going to look at the data we have from the kidnappings and all of your previous skirmishes with the Char and see if we can use any of it to help us narrow down where they are."

"Oh, can we come with you?" Mamachi asked. "I haven't had a chance to annoy Jakari in forever."

"Sure," Hayami said. "Why not?"

* * * *

Jakari looked up from the hologram she and Dubari were studying at the sound of the door to the conference room opening, and smiled as Hayami, Mamachi, and Skylar entered the room.

"I come bearing gifts," Hayami said. She set a plate down on the table with four oblong items on it. The items smelled of cooked meat and sugar.

"What are they?" Dubari asked.

"Food," Hayami said as she, Skylar, and Mamachi took a seat.

"They're bacon maple glazed donuts," Mamachi said, bouncing in their seat a little with each word. "Try them. They're delicious."

Jakari took one of the donuts and bit into it cautiously. Mamachi's idea of what constituted food didn't always match up with hers, but in this case, she was pleasantly surprised.

"That is good," she said after she swallowed the first bite.

Dubari reached out and picked up one of the donuts, giving it a dubious look before biting into it. A moment later, there was a moan of satisfaction.

"Told you," Mamachi said. Dubari rolled their eyes, but kept eating.

"Made any progress?" Hayami asked.

"Nothing so far," Jakari said. "We've run every predictive algorithm we have, and nothing."

"Maybe that's the issue," Hayami said.

"What do you mean?" Jakari asked.

"Well, you're using predictive algorithms to figure out where Cikara is, right?"

"Yes," Jakari said.

"But wouldn't they have access to those same algorithms, or at least ones very similar?"

"Yes."

"So maybe they are using the algorithm to choose where not to operate in order to throw off your search."

"That doesn't make any sense," Dubari said.

"Actually, it does," Mamachi said. "The way our predictive algorithms work is they use the locations of the various encounters we've had to predict the location of the base, operating on the assumption that Cikara is choosing targets based on convenience. Basically, any time they grab something, they do it from the nearest location to minimize resources expended on the acquisition."

"We use a similar technique to calculate the locations of criminal's homes based on the location of their crimes," Hayami said.

Mamachi nodded. "But if I wanted to avoid detection, I could select an alternate location as a center of activity, then let a computer algorithm choose my targets based on optimizing from that alternate location."

"So basically, you tell the computer to pretend that your base is, say, fifty miles west of where it actually is, and to choose targets based on the fake location?" Jakari asked.

"Exactly," Mamachi said.

"Well, that would explain why the algorithms aren't working," Dubari said. "But it doesn't do much to help us find Cikara."

"No, it doesn't," Jakari said.

"I still say we should just go with my plan," Dubari said.

"No," Jakari said.

"It would be the fastest way to finish the mission," Dubari said.

"What's your plan?" Mamachi asked.

"We leak the location of our base, and when Cikara moves in to attack, Jakari and I board their ship and kill them."

"Are you insane?" Mamachi asked.

"It's a good plan," Dubari said. "It brings Cikara out in the open so Jakari and I can get at them, and it offers Napati a chance to destroy their ship."

"Do you know the kind of damage destroying a Char Dreadnought would do to the surrounding area?" Mamachi asked.

"So evacuate it," Dubari said.

"You're talking about more than ten million people," Mamachi said. "The Dallas-Fort Worth Metroplex is one of the largest urban areas in this hemisphere."

"Yeah, so what?" Dubari asked. "We're talking about a shot at Cikara. One of the Triumvirate. Cikara is the second-in-command of the entire Char Oram. It would be the biggest victory we've had since we retook Santipurna."

"No," Jakari said.

"But—"

"No," Jakari repeated. "We're not going to invite an attack that would damage a human city. Cikara is our primary objective, but mission parameters call for us to keep our presence a secret from the general human population if at all possible. Right now, we're not to the point where it's necessary to discard that objective."

"Fine," Dubari said. They stood up. "I'm going to go for a walk. See if I can come up with any other ideas."

Jakari watched as they stormed out of the room and did her best to keep her temper in check.

"How bad would it be if we destroyed Cikara's ship?" Skylar asked.

"Bad," Mamachi said. "The standard fuel load for a Char Dreadnought is about 100 kilograms of antimatter."

"That sounds bad," Skylar said.

"Destruction out to at least 250 kilometers in every direction. Everyone in the Dallas Fort-Worth area would be dead, and the area would be soaked in lethal levels of radiation," Mamachi said. "The radiation would dissipate fairly quickly, but all that would be left behind would be a giant, lifeless burn mark where the cities used to be."

Skylar looked out the door after Dubari. "They can't seriously want to risk that, can they?"

"For a shot at the Triumvirate?" Jakari asked. "They wouldn't even hesitate if the city was still full."

"Jesus fuck," Skylar said.

"Don't judge them too harshly," Jakari said. "They were born into the middle of a brutal war, and as soon as it ended, another one started. They don't have any idea what peace is like."

"Neither do I," Mamachi said. "But I still know better than to kill ten million people just to get at one target."

Jakari reached out and took Mamachi's hand, squeezing it. "That's because you're better than the rest of us," she said. "You always have been."

Mamachi shook their head. "I'm not. You—"

"You are," Jakari said. "Don't let what happened on Cruthanna cloud your judgment. You were my mission."

"That's a load of crap," Mamachi said. "If I were your mission, you would have taken off and left me when I didn't make the pickup window."

"You were just a kid," Jakari said. "You had no business being on that mission in the first place, and I sure as hell wasn't going to leave you to die."

"See?" Mamachi said. "Not just your mission."

"You guys want to tell us what happened on Cruthanna?" Hayami asked.

"No," both of them said in perfect unison.

"Don't feel too bad," Skylar said. "I've known Mamachi for six years and they won't tell me either."

* * * *

Cikara stood in their lab, staring at the latest iteration of the Shroud. They'd already sent the updates to the twenty-one test subjects and received acknowledgement that the Shrouds inside them had rebuilt themselves to the new specifications, but they needed new test subjects. These new Shrouds were close to the final design. Cikara had finally added the heuristic subroutines to the core programming, meaning the Helots would be capable of learning and improving from their starting point. They would still begin life as little more than automatons, but the longer they survived, the more effective soldiers they would become.

The next step—the *final* step in perfecting the technology—would be the mesh network. Linking all the Helots together so they could share their learning, and when any Helot learned something, they would all learn it.

Just a little more time and everything would come together. Cikara would have the ultimate weapon. Removing Jaya and Saka would be easy, and once Arthan was gone, Cikara could force a peace treaty with the Helots as leverage. The Suil could have their way. A return to peace. While the Char would have the Helots to protect the Gadan from any enemies. An immortal army whose ranks could be refilled from the ranks of the criminals and even the enemies of the Gadan. An army who would be loyal to Cikara, and to the Char cause. The preservation and safety of the Gadan for all time. Jaya's failed dream of an empire could be cast aside and the rifts in Gadan society could finally be repaired. All it would cost would be this one world of primitives. A small price to pay.

The only obstacle in Cikara's way now was Nira. She would have to go before Cikara prepared the last update to the Shroud technology. The update that would also imbed loyalty to Cikara, rather than Jaya.

Cikara turned at the sound of the lab door opening and watched as Nira walked into the room. Her human form was every bit as intimidating as her Gadan form, the scar across her face ever present. It was an affectation, of course. Many of the Migrants carried such things over. Scars, tattoos, signs of age, gender. But for some reason, on Nira, it was particularly disturbing. Perhaps it was the ugliness of the scar. The way it ran from the upper right side of her face, down through the right eye, across the nose and down to the left jaw. Maybe it was the clearly artificial right eye. Silver with a gold iris and a black pupil.

Whatever the reason, even after knowing her for thousands of years, Cikara was frightened of her. Only a fool wouldn't be. Of the four of them who had come out of the Gladiator pits together, Cikara, Saka, Nira, and Jaya, only Jaya was deadlier. If it came to it, Cikara didn't doubt their abilities against Saka, but there was no way they could take Nira or Jaya in a fair fight.

Nira crossed the lab, and Cikara wondered if the moment had come. If Nira had finally received the order from Jaya to remove them. If so, they should have picked a venue other than Cikara's lab. Cikara readied themself, waiting for the first move, the first blow, but Nira simply held out a tablet. Cikara took it and looked down to see two humans. Nyala King and Hikaru Takahashi.

Cikara looked up at Nira. "The human woman's parents?" they asked.

Nira didn't answer, but that wasn't unusual. She was known for going decades without uttering a word. Instead, she simply turned and left the lab. Cikara touched the interface point on the edge of the tablet, loading the contents into their Phylactery, then pulled up their comm link.

"Ghuma," Cikara said.

"Yes?" Ghuma asked.

"I have some information you might find useful..."

* * * *

Hayami leaned back and rubbed her eyes. They'd been working for hours, and she needed a break or she was going to get a headache. Mamachi had been kind enough to run and fetch lunch for her and Skylar. Hayami suspected it was more for Skylar's benefit than hers, but she didn't really mind. What did bother her was that after nearly six hours staring at maps and charts and going over incident reports and police reports and Mamachi's original recordings of the Char ship's first arrival, they still couldn't pin down a location for where it could be.

Hayami couldn't figure out how the hell you could hide a ten-kilometer-wide flying saucer in North Texas, but somehow, this Cikara had found a way to do it.

"I think we need a break," Hayami said.

"Agreed," Skylar said. "If I look at one more map, my eyes are going to start bleeding."

Mamachi looked at Skylar with concern, but she waved them off.

"Figure of speech," she said.

Mamachi just nodded their head.

"A break might be a good idea," Jakari said. "Honestly, I'm at a loss for where to look next."

Hayami leaned back in her seat and looked at Jakari. "Can I ask a question?"

"Of course," Jakari said.

"How does gender work among your people?" Hayami asked. "I honestly haven't been able to pin that down. You and Napati use female pronouns. Rayak uses male pronouns. Mamachi uses neutral pronouns, and apparently so does Cikara."

"It's related to age," Jakari said. "Most of our people who use a fixed gender are Migrants. People who were alive before the bioweapon. We grew up with a fixed gender. It was part of our identity and self-image. Some Migrants have lost that over the millennia and switched to a genderless identity. Usually, you see that in the younger Migrants, the ones who were just children when the bioweapon was deployed. The vast majority of us who had reached adulthood before the bioweapon still have a preference with regard to our gender. Most of those born after the Migration don't have a lot of use for the concept of gender. The words kind of fell out of use in our language, except for the rare case when you're addressing a Migrant."

"How does reproduction work? If you're not fully organic..."

"It's the same process we use to generate unique forms when we have to disguise ourselves as a different species. Each of us had our genes sequenced as part of the Migration, so our full genetic profile is recorded in our Phylactery. When we choose to have children, the Phylacteries of the parents link and run through a simulated breeding process to create a genetic profile for the child, which is then embedded in a new Phylactery. The Phylactery is placed into a TOP matter body, along with a device called a Form Lock. The Form Lock holds the body in the shape of a Gadan child until the child's mind has developed enough to be able to use the various abilities that come with having a TOP matter body. The Form Lock will typically break down between the child's twelfth and sixteenth year."

"So, the new mind isn't fully formed?" Hayami asked.

"No," Jakari said. "If it was, we wouldn't be here. If you could create a fully-formed mind using regular reproduction, there wouldn't be a need for the Helot tech. The mind in a new Phylactery is a newborn mind. It has to be trained just like a regular mind."

"And you can't copy minds either?" Hayami asked.

"No," Jakari said. "Rayak would know more about why it doesn't work. He's probably the most conversant with the Phylactery technology of anyone in the Suil. All I know is, trying to copy a mind usually ends up killing the test subject."

"Yikes," Hayami said.

"Yeah," Jakari said. "The Seichu did some really fucked up things during the occupation."

"So, how about changing that subject?" Skylar asked, which made Hayami and Mamachi laugh, and Jakari raise an eyebrow.

"That was not subtle," Jakari said.

"Yeah. My idea of subtle is hitting things with a wrench," Skylar said. She looked over at Hayami. "Before all of this, I restored classic cars for a living."

"What do you actually do now?" Hayami asked.

"Well, I don't fix cars, because most of the ones around here are made of goop. I mostly work as one of Mamachi's analysts. I know the Gadan better than any of the other humans on the base, and I've been helping them analyze data since before they linked up with the government. I've gotten pretty good at it. I've also spent a lot of time analyzing Gadan tech. We're still a century or two away from anything close to the level of nanotech engineering that goes into TOP matter, but if my work is ever declassified, you're going to see some serious shit."

"That sounds interesting," Hayami said.

"Most days," Skylar said. "Some days I miss my wrenches and my angle grinders. The worst thing I ever had to worry about when I was rebuilding a car was accidently stripping a bolt or having to patch the sheet metal because it had rusted through. Here, if I screw up, people die."

"So, how about changing that subject?" Hayami asked.

"Zero points for subtlety, but ten out of ten for humor," Skylar said.

"It was getting morbid," Hayami said. "Which might make my next question a bit ironic." She turned to Jakari. "You mentioned having a wife."

"I did," Jakari said.

"What was she like?" Hayami asked. "You mentioned getting passed over for the draft when the Seichu invaded. Did she go fight?"

Jakari smiled and shook her head. "No," she said. "Aashi was declared an essential worker. Too important to be sent to war."

"What did she do?" Hayami asked.

"She was a teacher of young children. Ones too young for formal education. We had day camps for our children from the time they were two until they were five years old. They would go and learn to socialize and be watched to identify those who had issues with socialization so they could be helped. There were games to develop cognitive and motor functions. Story periods so they could learn attentive listening skills."

"Preschool," Hayami said. "We have something similar."

"Preschool," Jakari said. "That's a good name for it. Aashi loved it. She was wonderful with children. Kind and attentive. The reading period was her favorite part of the day. We have these creatures in our mythology. I'm not really sure how to describe them. We called them Takatiki. They were long creatures with four legs and massive wings. They were covered in fur, and they could control the weather. They breathed ice and snow and hail and lightning, and they gathered treasure and built great nests out of it inside caves."

"They sound like dragons. Only, dragons breathe fire and have scales."

"Maybe," Jakari said. "I'd have to see one of your dragons, but Aashi loved the Takatiki. She had a toy one that was the size of a child that she slept with every night. When reading period came for her students, she would always read them books about the Takatiki. She even wrote a series of books about a Takatiki named Bandhu. She was a great lonely beast who found a lost Gadan girl named Shrivali and adopted her as her own daughter. There were dozens of books about Bandhu and Shrivali going on adventures. Her students loved them. I loved them. On rest days, I used to lay on our basking stone and ask her to read them to me just so I could hear her voice."

"She sounds amazing," Hayami said.

"She was," Jakari said. "I was always amazed by how soft and gentle and kind she was. Before we met, she'd had a hard life. Her parents weren't good people. The first time I laid eyes on her, she was laughing, and I just fell in love with her right there. I watched her until she stopped laughing, then I turned to my friend who was with me and I said, 'I'm going to marry her.' He looked at me like I was a mad woman, but I walked up to her and I introduced myself, and I practically begged her to let me take her on a date."

"I'm guessing it went well?" Hayami asked.

"Oh, no," Jakari said. "It was without a doubt the worst date in the history of Gadan. I arrived late. We'd barely left the house when it began to rain, and by the time we reached the restaurant, we were soaking wet and they'd given our table away. We ended up having dinner in a horrible little diner, and instead of a walk by the lake like I'd planned, we ended the evening by riding home in a taxi so we wouldn't get rained on again, but it was one of the best nights of my life. I walked her to her door in the pouring down rain, holding my coat over her head to keep her dry, and when we got to the door, she kissed me and told me she'd had a wonderful night, and asked when we could do it again."

"What did you say?" Hayami asked.

"I asked her to marry me," Jakari said. "She said to take her on another date first. She kept saying that for six months, and I kept asking at the end of every date, until one night, she said yes."

"It sounds beautiful," Hayami said.

"It was. She was. It wasn't perfect. We fought—all couples do—but we always made up, and there was never a single moment I was with her that I wanted to be anywhere else." Jakari looked at Hayami. "Have you ever been in love?"

"Not like that," Hayami said. "Maybe not at all. I thought I was a few times, but honestly, I'm horrible at relationships. I've never found a woman that understands my job and the commitment it takes."

"Maybe your focus is on the wrong thing," Jakari said.

"What do you mean?"

"You're still young. You still have time to find a life, love, happiness. If that's what you want, maybe you should give up the job."

"Give up being a cop?" Hayami asked.

"Maybe," Jakari said. "I do what I do because I don't have very much left. A few friends here and there. All people who are part of the war. Most days, what gets me out of bed is the anger and the pain and the grief. Ten thousand years and it's still as fresh as the day she died, and I get up wanting more than anything to make sure no one else has to feel that. But some days, more the older I get, what gets me on my feet is the hope that this is the day that someone like Ghuma, or Birat, or Cikara will get lucky, and it will finally be over.

"I've told Mamachi more times than I can count that they should get out. Leave the Suil. Build a life. Be happy. They never listen, but maybe you will. When this is over, remember that being a cop or a soldier is just a job. Walk away from it. Find what makes you happy. You're not like us. You don't have eternity ahead of you. Enjoy the years you have."

"I...um..." Hayami stammered, not sure what to say to what she'd just heard. Jakari seemed to understand. She smiled, though it didn't quite reach her eyes.

"How about changing that subject?" Jakari asked.

* * * *

Ghuma stepped out of the blue Corvette as Birat stepped out of the red GMC Yukon. Ghuma waited while Birat trotted up the driveway to stand next to them, and then, with a small nod, the two of them walked up to the porch of the house they'd been watching for hours.

Ghuma knocked and waited for a couple of minutes until a black woman with a large head of curly black hair opened the door.

"Can I help you?" she asked.

"Yes, ma'am," Ghuma said as he pulled up a small ID folio and held it up for her to see. "I'm Special Agent Ghuma Char of the Department of Homeland Security. This is my partner, Birat Oram. Ma'am, I'm not sure if you're aware of this, but your daughter is currently working with us to help solve the disappearances in downtown Dallas."

"Yes," the woman said. "She told me."

"Well, ma'am. We've been assigned as your security detail because there's a chance your daughter has been targeted. Up until now, we've just been keeping discreet surveillance. We didn't want to disrupt you and your husband's lives. However, ma'am, we have information that leads us to believe that you and your husband may have been targeted in an attempt to draw your daughter out. For your own safety, ma'am, we need you and your husband to come with us to a safehouse."

"Oh," the woman said. "Do we have time to pack?"

"No, ma'am," Ghuma said. "I'm afraid the hostile forces are very close by. We need to leave now."

"All right," the woman said. "Just one moment." She turned away from the door. "Hikaru, two DHS agents are here. They want to take us into protective custody."

Ghuma smiled, thinking this was going to be easier than they expected. A thought which was quickly erased when the woman suddenly dove out of the way, and people in black suits carrying heavy plasma rifles came around the corner firing.

Chapter Nine

"DO WE HAVE ANY topographical maps that were made after the Char ship arrived?" Hayami said. "Maybe we could do a comparison against any topo maps from before and see if there's been any significant changes to the topography that might be related to burying a huge flying saucer."

"That's...a really good idea," Mamachi said.

"You don't have to sound so surprised," Hayami said.

Mamachi looked over at her. "Sorry. I'm just annoyed that I never thought of it."

"I'm guessing you've never spent any time out in the woods looking for unmarked graves," Hayami said. "Freshly turned earth is a big clue. This is the same thing, just on a bigger scale."

"I don't know about topo maps, but we night have some satellite images we could—"

Before Mamachi could finish whatever they were saying, a small woman with bright pink hair opened the door and stepped inside.

"There's been an attack," she said.

"Where?" Jakari asked.

"Two Char agents just tried to kidnap the detective's parents at their home," the pink-haired woman said.

"What?" Hayami asked, her heart slamming against her chest in a panic as she got to her feet. "Are my parents okay?"

"They're fine," Jakari said. "They were moved to a safehouse the night you and I were grabbed."

Hayami stared at Jakari for a moment, wanting to scream at her, to demand to know how she could not have told her something like that, but she didn't. She would save that conversation for later, when they were alone. Instead, she turned back to the pink-haired woman. "Did we catch the attackers?"

"No," the woman said. "Prack has people in pursuit right now, but the Char agents managed to slip the trap."

Jakari stood up. "Come on," she said. "Let's go and see what's happening."

Hayami nodded as Skylar and Mamachi stood up as well. The pink-haired woman turned and led them out of the conference room and down the hall to an elevator. All of them piled in and the elevator started down, but then something odd happened. After it descended for a few seconds, it stopped and started moving sideways. That continued for a couple of minutes, then the doors opened into a part of the base Hayami hadn't seen before.

The corridors were just a little taller than they should be, and the floor had an odd give to it, like they were walking on some kind of rubber mat. The lighting was lower than was comfortable and the walls seemed to radiate warmth. The colors didn't seem quite right, either. There were a lot of reds, but in places where you would expect lettering that would stand out, it was done entirely in black, which made no sense.

They turned the corner and headed through a large door with more of that strange black lettering and walked into something that looked like it came right out of a science fiction movie. A room filled with workstations, holograms floating above each one as giant, scaled, cat-like creatures in varying colors sat at those stations, twisting and manipulating those holograms with their hands. There were a few humans, or at least human-looking people, mixed in among the lizard-cat people. The other end of the room ended in a balcony, as they approached, Hayami could see another level down below, filled with more of the lizard-cat people, but the far wall had a three-story tall, floor to ceiling display showing what looked like a live feed from a helicopter flying over traffic in downtown Dallas.

"Prack," the pink-haired girl said.

A truly massive human turned around. He was about six foot, six inches, and weighed maybe 300 pounds, all of it pure muscle. His bicep had to be at least as thick as Hayami's waist.

"Hey, Kida," Prack said.

"They wanted to see what was going on," the pink-haired woman, Kida, said.

Prack looked at the group, and Hayami thought she saw a touch of disappointment on his face, but he nodded and turned back to the massive display.

"It's Ghuma and Birat," Prack said. "They turned up at the Takahashi residence about twenty minutes ago. The soldier we had impersonating Ms. King answered the door, and Ghuma identified themself and Birat as DHS agents sent to take Ms. King and Mr. Takahashi into custody. Our person gave the signal and a couple of our troops engaged with plasma rifles. Ghuma and Birat both took hits but managed to reach their Taluses. We have a pair of Blackhawk Taluses in pursuit, but we can't affect capture because they are still in the city limits, and we'd have to reveal ourselves in order to bring crippling weapons to bear."

"What about Ms. King and Mr. Takahashi?" Jakari asked.

"They're safe and secure. No indication that our safehouse has been compromised," Prack said.

Jakari turned to Hayami. "Would you like them brought here?" she asked.

"You'd do that?" Hayami said.

"Of course," Jakari said.

"Let me think about it," Hayami said.

Jakari nodded and turned back to Prack. "Can you get a tight beam signal on Ghuma on an open channel?"

"Sure," Prack said. "What for?"

"I want to talk to them."

"Gangesh, I need you to lay a tight beam comm signal on the target. Open channel," Prack said as he reached down and entered a command on his console. "I'm sending you a relay signal now."

Prack waited a minute until an alert popped up on his screen, then he turned to Jakari and nodded.

"Ghuma, can you hear me?" Jakari asked.

"Jakari," Ghuma said, dragging out her name a bit. "Twice in one week. People will talk."

"In your dreams," Jakari said. "Besides, I'd never do that to Birat. I actually respect them."

"Oh, you wound me," Ghuma said.

"Not yet," Jakari said. "But give me time."

"Now you're the one dreaming," Ghuma said. "So, as much as I'm enjoying our little back and forth, I'm assuming this call has a purpose?"

"It does," Jakari said. "I'm going to send you a comm packet encrypted with Cikara's public key. I'd like you to pass it on for me."

"Sending the boss love letters? That doesn't seem like you, Jakari. What are you up to?"

"I'm just looking to chat with an old friend," Jakari said. "Will you pass on the comm packet?"

"What's in it for me?" Ghuma asked.

"I'll call off the pursuit," Jakari said.

"Really?" Ghuma asked.

"Tell you what," Jakari said. "I'll transmit the packet. If the flyers pull back, you can pass on the comm packet. Otherwise, you can delete it."

"Now that does sound good," Ghuma said. "You have a deal."

Jakari stepped forward and put her hand on one of the silver interface points on the console.

"I have the packet," Ghuma said. "Now, call off your friends."

Jakari turned to Prack. "Call off the pursuit," she said.

Prack looked like he wanted to argue, but instead he just nodded. "Gangesh, Swati, fall back and discontinue pursuit."

The image on the display shifted as the helicopter swung in a circle and headed back the way they came. Prack reached down and entered a command on the console.

"Comm channel closed," Prack said. "You sure letting them go was a good idea? Those two have caused a lot of damage."

"I know," Jakari said. "But Cikara is the target, and I want to talk to them."

Prack nodded. "I'll set up a comm relay for you. Two satellite bounces and three ground side relays."

"Good," Jakari said. "The comm packet I sent told him to call in forty-eight local hours. I'm hoping we'll have found their ship by then."

"Good luck with that," Prack said. "Um...is there any reason Dubari isn't with you?"

"They weren't with us when Kida came and found us," Jakari said. "Have they not been to see you yet?"

"No," Prack said. "I sent them a message, letting them know I was assigned here, but I never got a response."

Jakari reached up and rested a hand on their shoulder. "Want me to knock some sense into them?"

"No," Prack said. "It's fine. If they don't want to see me, I understand."

"It's not fine," Jakari said. "I'll talk to them."

"Thanks," Prack said.

"No problem," Jakari said. "I still owe you for pulling me out of that building during the bombing of Comdar."

Prack laughed. "Didn't you save my life three separate times during the fifth battle of Crodain?"

"I have no clue what happened at fifth Crodain," Jakari said. "I got hit with one of those lightning shells the first day of the fight and spent most of the battle out of my mind on repair and pain suppression algorithms. You could tell me I danced naked in front of the Seichu Governing Council and I wouldn't be able to deny it."

Prack smiled. "That actually explains a lot about what happened at the victory party."

Jakari smiled. "Never tell me," she said before turning back to Hayami and the rest of the group. "Come on. We still have a base to find."

* * * *

Cikara tapped the comm request flashing in their HUD. "Go ahead."

"No joy on the human's parents," Ghuma said. "Suil commandos were waiting for us."

"Interesting," Cikara said. "I wonder if Nira's intel was bad, or if she was deliberately trying to get you and Birat killed."

"Hard to say, though if I were a betting person, I would bet my money on the latter. Nira's Intel is rarely bad."

"Yes," Cikara said. "I'd had that thought myself. I take it you and Birat escaped with your Vessels intact?"

"Nothing that can't be patched with a TOP matter infusion," Ghuma said. "Something interesting did happen though."

"Oh?"

"Jakari contacted us while the commandos were chasing us. She offered to call them off in exchange for me passing on a comm packet to you."

"I see," Cikara said. "Go ahead and send it."

"Transmitting now," Ghuma said.

"I have it," Cikara said. "Have you isolated the location of the Suil base yet?"

"Not yet," Ghuma said. "We have three candidate sites. We just need another forty-eight hours to narrow it down."

"Excellent work," Cikara said.

"Do you want us to come back to the ship when we have the location?"

"No," Cikara said. "Send me the information on a secure channel, then proceed to the Beta site. I have a feeling our current location will be compromised shortly."

"Understood," Ghuma said. "And Cikara..."

"Yes?"

"Take care of yourself."

"I will."

Cikara cut the connection and opened the comm packet. It included a time, a comm frequency, and an encryption key, plus a short message consisting of only three words.

'Let's talk—Jakari.'

Interesting.

Definitely very interesting.

* * * *

"Could we have a few minutes alone?" Hayami asked as the four of them got back to the conference room. Mamachi gave Jakari a questioning look, but she just nodded, already having a bit of an idea what this might be about.

"Grab some drinks," Jakari said. "I'm sure we could all use them."

"Of course," Mamachi said. They turned and headed towards the cafeteria, and Skylar followed them. Jakari led Hayami inside the conference room and shut the door, then sat down in the same spot she'd sat for most of the day.

"How could you not tell me that my parents had been taken into protective custody?" Hayami asked.

"It didn't occur to me," Jakari said. "I heard Gomez give the order after your initial debrief, but I didn't think anything else about it until Kida mentioned that Ghuma and Birat had tried to grab your parents."

"You didn't think anything else about it?" Hayami said, her voice thick with anger and frustration.

"No," Jakari said. "It never would have occurred to me to secure your parents, but when I heard Gomez give the order, I just filed it away as something that had been taken care of. I'm sorry. All I can say is that it's been a very long time since I've given any thought to something like that."

Hayami stared at her for a moment, and Jakari could see the anger draining out of her. "Yeah," she said. "I suppose it has been a while since you had parents to think about."

Jakari could have let it go at that, and she probably should have, but she felt a strange reluctance to let Hayami's misinterpretation of what she'd said stand.

"That's not what I meant," Jakari said. "You're here, working with me, and you see me acting like a soldier, or maybe like one of your police officers. Reviewing documents, investigating, trying to locate the people who have committed crimes on your world, and I think it gives you the wrong impression. I'm not a soldier. I'm not a police officer. I'm not here to get justice for the dead, or to protect the innocent. Those are just happy byproducts if my mission is successful.

"I'm an assassin. I came to your world to kill someone. That's what I do. I take life. My superiors point me at a target, and they tell me that person needs to die for the good of the people on Suil-controlled worlds. I go, and I kill them, and I hope that what I've done makes things better. So when I say it's been a long time since I've given any thought to something like that, what I mean is, it's been a long time since I've had to think about how to protect someone at all. Most of my attention is given over to finding my targets, figuring out how to reach them, how to kill them, and how to escape afterwards."

Hayami stared at Jakari for a couple of minutes in total silence before she shook her head. "How can you live like that?"

"I don't know," Jakari said. "Sometimes, I think the only reason I'm still alive is because I've gotten in the habit of not dying, and I don't know how to break it."

"Your life sucks," Hayami said.

Jakari shrugged. "Do you want to see your parents?"

"Yes," Hayami said. "Please. I need to know they're okay."

"I'll make sure it happens," Jakari said.

"Thank you."

"You're welcome," Jakari said. "And I am sorry. You deserve better. I wish I was still capable of it."

She turned back to the maps they had been studying and began to search for Cikara's base again. She could feel Hayami looking at her, but neither of them said anything until Mamachi and Skylar got back with their drinks.

* * * *

"What do you think they're talking about?" Skylar asked as they headed for the cafeteria.

"I would guess that Hayami is angry that Jakari didn't mention that Hayami's parents had been moved to a safehouse."

"That is kind of a big thing to not mention," Skylar said.

"I know," Mamachi said.

"You and Jakari seem close," Skylar said. "How come you've never mentioned her before?"

"Because of the way we met," Mamachi said.

"On Cruthanna?" Skylar asked.

"Yes," Mamachi said.

"And you won't tell me what happened there?" Skylar asked.

Mamachi looked over at her. "It's a long story," they said. "Cruthanna wasn't just one mission. It's our homeworld, and the Char have controlled it for millennia. I was assigned there as a spy for centuries, but most of the time, when I think of it, I think of the way it ended, and that's not a happy memory."

"I'm sorry," Skylar said. "I shouldn't have asked."

"No, it's okay. I just...I don't like to talk about it because everyone thinks that what happened makes me this big hero, but I don't feel that way. I just feel scared. It's been fifteen hundred years and I'm still afraid when I think about it."

Skylar reached over and took their hand. "Whatever happened, you made it through. You're here now. You're safe."

They nodded. "I know," they said. "I just...Jakari was there, and Napati sort of understands. Everyone else who has heard the story looks at me differently, and I don't...I don't want you to look at me that way."

"What way?" Skylar asked.

"Like I'm something I'm not. Like I'm a hero instead of someone who just got lucky."

"I already think you're a hero," Skylar said.

"Don't," Mamachi said. "It's not a joke."

Skylar stopped and turned to face them. "I'm not joking," she said. "You came to this world alone, on a hunch. On the off chance that a tip you got from the enemy might be true. You lived in an alien world for a year. You learned our language, our culture, you learned how to live in one of our bodies, how to fight in it, and you watched the sky the whole time. And when Cikara arrived, you were the one who negotiated a treaty with the US Government and the United Nations to allow your people to come here to help us. All of that takes courage and commitment and bravery. So when I look at you, I already see a hero."

Mamachi looked away from her, not quite able to take the intensity they saw in her eyes. "When we finish today, come with me back to my quarters. I'll tell you the story."

"You don't have to," Skylar said.

They turned to look at her again. "I want to. I want you to understand."

"Okay," Skylar said. "I'd like that."

Chapter Ten

"MAMACHI, COULD I HAVE a word?" Jakari asked.

Mamachi stopped and looked at Jakari for a second, then turned to Skylar. "Why don't you go and grab dinner? I'll catch up."

"Sure," Skylar said. She turned to Hayami. "Want to hit the cafeteria with me?"

"Lead the way," Hayami said.

The two of them disappeared out of the doorway and Mamachi closed it behind them, then turned back to Jakari.

"What is it?"

"I'm worried about you," Jakari said. "You seem nervous about something."

"Skylar asked me about Cruthanna again. I agreed to tell her what happened."

"Are you sure you want to do that?" Jakari asked. "Those aren't exactly the fondest memories for either of us."

"She's my friend," Mamachi said. "And what happened on Cruthanna…"

"I know," Jakari said. "I could go with you, if you want. Be there when you tell her."

"You'd do that?" Mamachi asked.

"For you."

"But what happened…what you had to do…"

"I remember," Jakari said. "What I did, and what you did."

"I didn't do anything other than get lucky," Mamachi said.

"I think we both know it was a little bit more than that," Jakari said. "Would you mind if I brought Hayami?"

"You want to tell her?"

"No," Jakari said. "But I think I need to. I don't think she understands who I am, and if we're going to work together, she needs to."

"Cruthanna is not who you are," Mamachi said.

"Cruthanna is exactly who I am," Jakari said.

Mamachi stared at her for a long time, then finally shook their head. "Bring her if you want, but I'll tell her the truth."

"That's exactly what I want."

* * * *

Mamachi could tell that Skylar was a little surprised when they told her that Jakari and Hayami would be coming back to their quarters, but like always, she just rolled with it and gave them one of those brilliant smiles that made Mamachi long for the end of the war. They knew that it wouldn't really change anything. Skylar was human, her life was short and fleeting, and she would want to spend it with someone like herself. Someone she could raise a family with, grow old with, someone who wasn't saddled with all the baggage that came with being a Suil soldier. But in those moments when she looked at them, smiled at them, Mamachi could pretend they could be together, that they could be something more than just friends. In those moments, for the first time in their life, Mamachi truly understood why the war was worth fighting and winning.

They wondered if Skylar was right. If she would still look at them the same way after they heard the truth about Cruthanna. They wanted to believe she would, that what happened wouldn't come between them, but Mamachi hated Cruthanna and everything about it. People called them a hero, but Jakari was the real hero, and she would never believe that. Not after the things she had to do. Mamachi understood. They carried the same guilt, even if they hadn't been the one to pull the trigger.

The four of them walked into Mamachi's quarters, the ones on the human part of the base, not the ones they had been assigned on Napati's ship, and when they got there, Skylar punched in the security code and they stepped inside. The quarters were better appointed than most on base. A lot of that had to do with the fact that, despite their young age, Mamachi was the equivalent of a human colonel, and Napati's intelligence officer. Instead of just a twin XL bed, a desk, a chair, a wardrobe and a footlocker, the quarters had a sofa, a TV, a pair of easy chairs, a full-sized bed, and its own en suite, plus a small refrigerator.

Mamachi headed for the sofa and Skylar followed, taking a seat next to them, leaving the easy chairs for Hayami and Jakari. They closed their eyes and took a deep breath, feeling the dread spread through them. Skylar took their hand, threading their fingers together and giving their hand a squeeze. They opened their eyes and smiled at her.

"Take your time," she said. Mamachi squeezed her hand back and looked over at Jakari.

"I'm here," Jakari said. "You're safe."

Mamachi nodded and took another deep breath, letting it out slowly.

"I'm a little over two thousand Earth years old," Mamachi said. "I was born on the Suil-controlled colony world of Bailenua, and from the time I was born, I had a friend. Their name was Karusa, and they were the child of Jitrinda and Subhash. They were just a few months older than me, and my parents, Dipen and Alok, had been friends with their parents since Bailenua had been settled, nearly seven thousand years earlier. We were young, and we were stupid, and at barely three hundred years of age, we got the brilliant idea to sign up with the Suil. We were going to go off and fight and win the war.

"I wouldn't find out for a long time why Arthan himself took an interest in us, but he did. The moment we graduated from the academy, he approached us about a special mission. He wanted us to go to Cruthanna, to the homeworld, as spies. We were young, and we were stupid, and we accepted, and went off to win the war.

"We were on Cruthanna for two hundred years. We started at the bottom, pretending to be from the Char-controlled colonies, pretending we were friends whose families had been killed in the fighting, pretending we hated the Suil and wanted to help the Char win the war. We went to the academy and we stood out. It's easy to excel when you've already taken all the classes before. We got postings and we worked hard. We climbed our way up, eventually making our way into the Triumvirate's direct service. I worked for Cikara for almost fifty years, while Karusa worked for Jaya, but then we were both transferred to Nira's intelligence team.

"We were young, and we were stupid, and we thought it was the perfect place for spies to be, but we were both wrong, just for very different reasons."

* * * *

Crodain, Cruthanna. Year of Freedom 7538 (Gadan Reckoning) 485 AD (Earth Reckoning)

Mamachi smiled at Karusa as they sat down across the table and passed over a cup of tea.

"Good morning," Mamachi said.

"Morning," Karusa grumbled.

"You seem grouchier than usual," Mamachi said. "Something wrong?"

"Gadha kept me up all night," Karusa said.

"You do know we can go several days without sleep, right?"

"Yeah, which would be fine if she hadn't done the same thing all week."

"You know you could put her in her tank for the night, right?" Mamachi asked.

Karusa glared, and Mamachi had to fight not to laugh. Karusa made a big deal of being tough and all business, but a tiny little agacha had them wrapped around her foreclaw. It was actually kind of adorable.

"She likes to sleep on my chest," Karusa said. "It's a body heat thing."

"So you've told me," Mamachi said. "What does she do when you aren't at home?"

"I leave her under a heat lamp most days," Karusa said. "But she just shed her skin and she's always clingy after."

"So what do you do on days after she sheds her skin?" Mamachi asked.

"The same," Karusa said.

"Uh-huh," Mamachi said. "What do you really do on days after..." They stopped talking and looked at the neckline of Karusa's shirt, where a small, pink nose was sticking out.

"What?" Karusa asked.

"Nothing," Mamachi said.

Karusa frowned and took another sip of their coffee as the nose inched its way a little further out of their shirt.

"Are you going back by your apartment before you head into the office?"

"No, why would I?"

"No reason," Mamachi said before taking a long drink of their tea.

* * * *

Cikara called.

Mamachi stopped and turned around to see Cikara jogging down the hall to catch up with them. They gave them a smile and a wave as Cikara came to a stop.

"What can I do for you, boss?" Mamachi asked.

Cikara smiled. "Not your boss anymore," they said.

"You're the second-in-command of the entire Char Oram," Mamachi said. "I'm pretty sure I can still call you boss, even if I report to Nira these days."

Cikara laughed. "I guess so," Cikara said. "Somedays, I forget I'm anything more than a scientist."

"That sounds like a good problem to have," Mamachi said. "It means your staff are doing their jobs."

"Yeah. I guess it does. I wanted to ask if you got a chance to look over those new Suil weapon designs?"

"New Suil weapon designs?" Mamachi asked.

"Yeah," Cikara said. "One of my people got a set of schematics for a new Suil design, and it looked really familiar. I thought it might be an attempt to reverse engineer one of ours, but then I realized it's a design pattern we never actually released to our troops. I sent it to Nira's office for analysis and logged a request that you be on the evaluation team to see if we have a leak, or if they just hit on a similar design."

Mamachi felt a small knot forming in their stomach. "It hasn't come across my desk, but if you have the designs with you, I'd be happy to take a look."

"Sure," Cikara said.

Mamachi held out their tablet, and Cikara touched one of the access points, downloading the design schematics. "I'll look at them as soon as I have a spare moment," Mamachi said.

"Thanks," Cikara said. "And if you ever get tired of playing spook, I'd love to have you back on my team."

"I'll think about it," Mamachi said. "I only left because Jaya convinced me I could do more for the war effort in intel, but I miss you guys."

"That's because you were a good fit," Cikara said. "And because Jaya poaches all the best talent." They reached out and slapped Mamachi's shoulder. "Thanks again. I'll look forward to your report."

"It's good to see you, General."

"It's good to see you too, Major."

Mamachi watched as Cikara turned and headed off to their office, then turned and headed for their own. If Cikara had specifically asked for Mamachi to review an intel report and it hadn't reached their desk, something was wrong. Very, very wrong.

* * * *

Mamachi leaned back in their chair, watching Karusa slip Babama nuts to the small pink snout sticking out of the neckline of their shirt. Karusa loved Gadha, and if Mamachi was honest, they did too. The agacha was cute and friendly, and Karusa had spoiled her rotten ever since they had found her under a bush in the parking lot outside their apartment, still sitting in her just-hatched shell. Sneaking her into work was a new one, but Mamachi shouldn't be surprised given how clingy Gadha got after shedding.

They would have to make plans for Gadha. It shouldn't be that hard. A carry sling and a couple of cans of food pellets. Agacha built up fat reserves along the sides of their bodies to last them if they had to go a prolonged period without food, so it wouldn't be a big deal if she had to miss a feeding or two. Just make sure Gadha's water sacks were full before they left.

Mamachi would go by one of their blind drops on the way home and drop the request for emergency extraction. It was possible, in theory, that Karusa wasn't blown, but Mamachi wouldn't chance it. The two of them had gone in together, so they would go home together.

Mamachi just wished they knew how they'd gotten blown. They'd done everything right. They'd rotated their dead drops, they never talked to anyone about their work. They never even talked to Karusa about it. But the evidence didn't lie. Mamachi had looked through the reports they'd been assigned over the last couple of months and compared it to the intel sources they'd developed on their own that didn't come through official channels. The ones that Nira didn't know about. The differences told a story. Mamachi had been blown about six days earlier, and Nira was trying to use them to feed false intel to the Suil.

"Karusa," Mamachi said, making them jump a little and try to hide the nut they were about to feed Gadha.

"Yes?"

"I'm going to cut out a couple of minutes early. Cikara asked me to look at something for them, and I want to drop off the report before end of day. Let Nira know where I am if she comes by?"

"Sure," Karusa said.

Mamachi stood up and started pulling on their coat. "You want to come by tonight? A new set of Comdar Sunrise episodes dropped a few days ago, and I was thinking of starting them."

"I don't know," Karusa said. "You know how Gadha is when she's just shed."

"Bring her along," Mamachi said. "I'll pick up some sabuja berries for them."

"Okay," Karusa said, and Mamachi felt a bit of relief when Karusa didn't show any visible reaction to the use of one of their code words.

"See you later," Mamachi said as they picked up their tablet and headed for the door.

* * * *

Mamachi had always questioned the wisdom of sending them and Karusa in together. Over the decades, they had been happy to know that there was someone they could trust, someone who would always have their back if things went sideways, but it also meant that if one of them got made, it dramatically increased the risk the other was in. Mamachi would much rather have not known if there were any other spies in the Triumvirate's Palace, because they couldn't give up what they didn't know.

But, knowing Karusa was there, Mamachi had always gone out of their way to not ever let Karusa know where their dead drops were, and taken care to never figure out where Karusa's drops were. Mamachi had gone out of their way to avoid even speculating. They regretted that just a bit as they walked home that night. They'd been able to hit three of their drops without deviating from their normal path home, other than to pick up some sabuja berries, and at each of those drops, they'd sent a single word. 'Cream.'

The word has been chosen at random. It had no meaning related to the mission, but it was the predesignated code word that meant 'Our cover has been blown, and we need extraction.' They wished, more than anything, that they could have dropped it at every one of their own dead drops and at all of Karusa's, just to be sure.

When they arrived at their apartment, they went ahead and started getting ready for the evening. They made a pot of tea, washed the sabuja berries, and got down a pot of Babama nuts for Gadha, then pulled up Comdar Sunrise on the holoprojector. Everything was ready by the time Karusa knocked on the door. Mamachi walked over and let them in, smiling at the sight of Gadha riding inside Karusa's shift. Her entire head was poking out, fresh pink skin showing. In a few days, the pink would be gone, and Gadha would be back to her color-changing, nearly-invisible self, but for now, Mamachi could appreciate just how insanely cute she was. They reached up and ran a finger along the top of Gadha's head, earning an appreciative croak.

"Come in," Mamachi said.

Karusa stepped inside and dropped down on the couch. "God, what a day," they said.

"What happened?" Mamachi asked.

"Intel report came in late. We had to do a lot of reshuffling to deal with it."

"Has that been happening to you a lot of late?" Mamachi asked.

"No" Karusa said. "Why do you ask?"

"Something similar happened to me. Cikara flagged an intel report for me to look at, but it never got delivered to my desk. They gave me a copy personally, and I reviewed it and took it back to them."

"That's why you left early," Karusa said. "I was wondering."

"Yeah," Mamachi said as they sat down next to Karusa on the couch. They reached over and took Karusa's hand, their palm morphing into an access point. Karusa linked to the access point, opening a direct, and more importantly, undetectable and untappable commlink between them.

"Can we just sit a minute?" Mamachi said. "I know I promised you horrible romantic melodrama, but…"

"It's fine," Karusa said out loud.

<What's going on?> Karusa sent over the commlink.

<My cover is blown,> Mamachi sent.

<You're sure?> Karusa asked.

<Positive. I've already requested extraction.>

<When?>

<I made the drops tonight. Our ride home should be here within five days.>

<A lot can happen in five days,> Karusa sent.

<I know.>

"How was Nira with everything?" Mamachi asked.

"Fine, I would guess. I didn't see her today."

Mamachi let out a yawn and leaned in against Karusa. "Did Gadha enjoy her trip to the office?"

"What?" Karusa said. "I didn't take Gadha to the office!"

"So, you were just dropping Babama nuts down your shirt for no reason?" Mamachi asked.

"I wasn't…" Karusa sighed. "Fine. I didn't want to leave her. She was really frantic any time I tried to put her in the tank, and I figured it wouldn't do any harm."

"It's okay," Mamachi said as they dropped their head on Karusa's shoulder. "I won't tell Nira if you don't."

Karusa let go of Mamachi's hand and wrapped their arm around Mamachi's shoulders. "Thanks," they said. "Now, I was promised trashy melodrama."

"Fine," Mamachi said, and started the first episode of the new batch of Comdar Sunrise.

* * * *

It might seem like a bad idea to get up and go to work for an enemy that knew you were a spy, and Mamachi would never have pretended there wasn't a bit of risk involved, but their evac was five days away. If Nira didn't realize Mamachi knew they had been made, then the best thing to do was to go on as if nothing had changed. To keep showing up to work and be the good little funnel of bad intel right into the Suil Intelligence Agency's office. Let Nira think that she was still in control of the situation and just mark all the reports with a special key in the cipher to let the home office know they were so much bullshit.

That's why they got up the next morning, met Karusa for tea like they always did, and then marched right into the Triumvirate's Palace the same way they had every day for the last 160 years. They stopped by Cikara's office on the way in and asked if they'd had a chance to read the report. Cikara had said yes with a smile and thanked them for getting to it so quickly. Then Mamachi had headed up to Nira's office, saying hi to friends and acquaintances along the way. They made a few jokes, laughed at a few stories, and arrived at their desk five minutes early, just like every other day. They took off their coat and hung it on the back of their chair, then they sat down, getting ready to start the day.

Nira walked into the office, accompanied by a pair of security officers. That, in and of itself, wasn't at all unusual, but Mamachi knew as soon as they saw her that they'd guessed wrong. That they should have taken Karusa and run for it the night before. Mamachi knew they had no hope against Nira. They might have had some of the best training you could get, both in the Suil before they were sent to Cruthanna and in the Char after, but Nira had thousands of years more experience, and if she were smart, she would have picked security officers almost as old as she was.

Still, Mamachi had worked in Nira's office for 110 years. That was a long time to think, a long time to plan, and a long time to prepare, so as Nira and the security officers approached, they rested their hands on one of their workstation's access points.

"Major Mamachi," one of the security officers said. "By order of Nira, and on the Authority of the Char Oram, you are under arrest for—"

Mamachi never did find out what the specific charges against them were. Four of the security turrets built into the ceiling dropped down and opened fire. The security officers vanished in a blast of plasma as the first two turrets hit them square in the chest. The third turret blew a hole in the wall, creating an escape route for Mamachi, while the fourth one targeted and tried its best to kill Nira, who somehow simply wasn't there.

Mamachi didn't wait to sort it out. They leapt over their desk and ran through the hole in the wall as the alarms started blaring. As they ran, they threw open a special frequency they'd set up two centuries before in their comm system and transmitted a single word. 'Run.' The message was so heavily encrypted that it would take centuries to break the security without the appropriate key, but with any luck, by then it would be too late. Karusa would have gotten the message and disappeared into one of the bolt holes they had prepared over the last two centuries.

At least, Mamachi hoped. Right now, they had other problems. Ones they had thankfully prepared for. As they rounded a corner heading towards the stairwell, one of the massive decorative planters that lined the hallway began to move. It dumped soil and plants on the floor as it took a vaguely Gadan form. Mamachi ran right to it, the TOP matter of their body merging with the Talus they had created almost a century earlier. Despite being a century old, the Talus was far from out of date. Mamachi, as one of the analysts specifically tasked with evaluating the threat posed by new Suil weapons, had access to all the Char's latest patterns. Instead of stepping into a set of power armor that was a century out of date, Mamachi stepped into a set of power armor that wouldn't be rolled out to Char troopers for months.

Talus in place, Mamachi ran right past the door to the stairwell and raised both of their arms, deploying a pair of resonance cannons and firing into the clear armored polymer sheet that filled the windows. The sonic weapons shattered the polymer like glass, and Mamachi jumped out of the hole.

For one brief moment, Mamachi looked down at the nearly five kilometer drop and wondered if maybe there had been a better exit strategy. Then the power armor's counter grav generator kicked on, the wings snapped into place, the thrusters fired, and Mamachi flew out over the city. They didn't try to stay at altitude though. Up in the air they would stick out like a sore thumb. Instead, they went into a controlled dive, heading down below the roofline of the arcologies and the skyscrapers, running for the lower levels of the city where it was easy to disappear.

They just had to stay hidden for five days and hope like hell that Karusa had gotten their message and would make the rendezvous.

* * * *

Mamachi moved through the streets quickly, doing their best to keep from getting caught on any of the security feeds. They'd already shifted their appearance five times since they'd escaped from the Palace that morning, and they had very carefully hidden the Talus close to one of their safehouses. They were terrified that Karusa had been caught, but they couldn't do anything about that right now.

They hurried across the street, slipping through a break in traffic and ducking into an apartment building. The place was cheap, but well-maintained and near the spaceport. As far as the landlord knew, Mamachi was a spacer who spent most of their time off world but didn't want to live out of a hotel when they were on Cruthanna. It was a good cover story that explained why the rent was paid a year at a time, and today, it would save Mamachi's life. Hopefully.

They opened the door to the apartment and flipped on the lights, sighing with relief. They closed the door and did a quick check, making sure no one was in the room, then lay down on the bed and let out a breath.

The last sound they heard was a dull whump as an immobilizer spike erupted out of the bed and impaled them through the stomach. They never even felt the electric discharge that forced their Phylactery into defensive lockdown, but they did feel the terror and helplessness as the darkness took them.

Chapter Eleven

Crodain, Cruthanna. Year of Freedom 7538 (Gadan Reckoning) 485 AD (Earth Reckoning)

JAKARI TOOK A SIP of her tea and tried not to curse. The tea was delicious. Something she got every time she was on Cruthanna, which was more often than people would expect given how many death warrants the Char had issued for her. She'd actually stopped counting somewhere around a thousand, but that was almost two millennia ago. What made her angry, and unable to enjoy the tea, was the fact that Karusa and Mamachi had definitely been captured.

She wondered which one of them had fucked up and gotten their cover blown, but the truth was, it hardly mattered. That was the problem with sending in agents in pairs. If one got blown, the other almost always followed. She'd known that going in, just like she'd known that there wasn't much of a chance of a successful extraction when she'd received the request from Arthan.

She also knew the fucker had only asked her to extract them because it was Karusa. Jakari had never gotten on particularly well with Aashi's family. They were all horrible people, with the noted exceptions of Aashi herself, and her younger brother Subhash. Jakari and Subhash had actually been pretty good friends before the bioweapon, and while they could hardly be called close these days, Jakari had tried to keep up with him. She'd been happy for him when he had gotten married, and when Karusa had been born, she'd visited and cried happy tears for the first time in a very, very long time.

The idea that some small part of Aashi had been reborn in a new life had been overwhelming, and Jakari had felt something for the first time in longer than she really wanted to think about. It hadn't been enough to convince her to walk away from her job. In fact, it had made her more dedicated, more determined than before. She wanted to end the war for someone, instead of just because she was sick of the fighting.

Then she'd found out that Karusa had decided to join the Suil, and she'd tried everything to stop it, but Karusa was determined. When Jakari had found out that Karusa had been recruited for intelligence work, at first she'd been relieved. Most intel officers spent their lives behind nice, safe desks. Then she'd found out that Karusa had been chosen to be a field asset. She'd almost killed Arthan on the spot.

When she'd arrived on Cruthanna five days ago, she'd hoped that Karusa or Mamachi had realized they were blown early enough to call for help before they were arrested. There hadn't been much hope, but this was Karusa. Jakari would have walked into Jaya's arms if it meant saving them.

Five days on the planet, five of the scheduled rendezvous, and each one had been crawling with Nira's Security Officers. They'd been undercover, trying their best to hide who and what they were, but there were always tells. Little details that were wrong. Sometimes Jakari didn't even know exactly what it was that gave them away, but once she spotted them, she could always pick out all the details that just weren't right.

The fact that all the meets had been ambushes meant that Karusa or Mamachi had given them up. Jakari didn't want to think about what that would mean, and if it had been anyone else, she would have gone back to the ship after the first meet and gotten as far from Cruthanna as possible. But it was Karusa. She couldn't leave Karusa. She'd never be able to live with herself. So instead she drank her tea, and when she was finished, she paid her bill and headed into the city.

* * * *

Mamachi opened their eyes slowly, bracing for the pain of the blinding lights in their eyes, but it never came. Instead, they were left with the other agonies their body was inflicting on them. They looked over at their right arm. A massive bolt was driven through the center of the hand, the bolt's head turned down crushingly tight. Four fingers were missing, and a cuff around the wrist drove sharp teeth into the flesh. Strips of skin had been peeled off the arm, leaving the muscle exposed, nails had been driven through the bones at intervals, and the shoulder was visibly dislocated.

They turned to look at their left arm, which was when they realized their left eye had been plucked out. They had to turn their head a lot further than they normally would have to see their left arm. It was in roughly the same shape, though it looked like they had passed out before Saka had finished, because they still had two fingers left on that hand.

They turned their head back to face forward and spit out the blood that had been collecting in their mouth. As soon as it was out of their body, it turned a graphite color as it fell into the pool of TOP matter below them. The same pool that held the TOP matter that used to be their eye, their fingers, their teeth, their left leg below the second knee, the toes of their right paw, and the blood that was leaking out of all the places spikes had been driven through their torso.

They wanted to heal, to repair the wounds, but the first thing Saka had done before Mamachi had even woken up after being captured, was implant a Form Lock. The Form Lock prevented Mamachi from controlling the TOP matter that made up their body. No healing, no shape shifting, no escaping. This one, unlike a normal Form Lock, also prevented Mamachi from running any of the pain suppression algorithms they had stored in their Phylactery.

Saka had taken a device designed to help children learn to control their bodies as they grew up and turned it into something to make torture more effective. Mamachi shouldn't be surprised. They'd known Saka was insane before they'd even agreed to take the assignment on Cruthanna. They'd had nightmares about getting caught and turned over to them for interrogation. Of course, now they weren't nightmares. They were memories and they were far, far worse than anything Mamachi had ever imagined.

The door opened, and Mamachi looked over to see Saka, Jaya, Nira, and Cikara all walk into the room. They let their head drop and closed their eye quickly, hoping none of them would realize they were awake.

"Are you serious?" Jaya asked. "They're a traitor. They worked in your office for fifty years, lied to your face every day, and you're objecting to us interrogating them?"

"This isn't interrogation," Cikara said. "This is torture."

"This is effective," Saka said.

"Really?" Cikara asked. "Because it was my understanding that you hadn't gotten a single bit of information out of them."

"True," Saka admitted. "This subject is unusually resilient in the face of my normal methods."

"You see?" Cikara said. "You're allowing this to go on when it's not even getting any results."

"What does it matter?" Jaya asked. "It's just a Suil spy."

"It matters because I fought a war to stop things like this!" Cikara shouted. "Look around you. Doesn't this room remind you of any place?"

"What are you getting at, Cikara?" Jaya asked.

"You want me to say it?" Cikara asked. "Fine. This room looks more like a Seichu torture chamber than an interrogation room."

"Watch yourself, Cikara," Jaya said.

"Or what?" Cikara asked.

"Don't think I've forgotten that our friend here came up through your office."

"And then they worked for your little pet over there for more than a century. Maybe you should string her up next. Let Saka see if they can get her to talk."

"Enough!" Jaya shouted. "I will not go easy on a traitor just because you've lost your stomach for making hard decisions."

"This isn't a hard decision," Cikara said. "This is cruelty for cruelty's sake. This is what we wiped the Seichu out for, and now you're condoning it. I don't care if they are a spy, or a traitor. No one deserves this. If they aren't talking, kill them and be done with it, but this is beneath us."

"You don't get to decide that!" Jaya said. "Arthan sent this traitor here to make fools of us, and I mean to send Arthan a recording of every moment of agony we put their little pet through."

"So that's what this is about?" Cikara asked. "You and your fucking pride?"

"Get out!" Jaya shouted.

"Fine," Cikara said. "Just be sure to release the recording to the public so they all know what the Char Oram has become."

Mamachi heard the door open and then close again.

"You can stop pretending to be asleep now," Saka said.

Mamachi opened their eye and lifted their head. "I didn't want to interrupt your little chat," they said.

"Ah," Jaya said. "Did you think Cikara's pleas for mercy would help?"

"Not really," Mamachi said. "I already knew you were insane."

"I'm not the one who tried to spy on the rulers of the Char Oram," Jaya said.

"Yeah," Mamachi said. "I admit that was a mistake. I mean, it only took you two hundred years to catch me."

A look of rage spread over Jaya's face, and they slammed their hand down on a button that Mamachi knew all too well by now. The frame they were strapped to fell forward into the pool of TOP matter, and Mamachi felt the Form Lock reset. All the pain went away as their body absorbed TOP matter out of the pool, regrowing skin and fingers as nails and spikes and bolts fell free. When it was over, the frame lifted out of the pool, and Mamachi was in perfect health. Two arms and two legs, ten fingers and eight toes, two eyes, two ears, all their teeth and scales. A tube even swung around, offering them water, and they latched on and drank greedily, quenching their thirst. Once they'd drunk their fill, the tube swung away, and Mamachi looked down at Jaya, Saka, and Nira, knowing very well what came next. Or at least, they thought they did.

"Start by cutting out their tongue," Jaya said.

Mamachi looked over at Saka.

"That is not logical," Saka said. "They will be unable to communicate any useful information."

"I don't care," Jaya said. "Cut out their tongue."

"Very well," Saka said as they picked up a knife and a pair of forceps.

* * * *

"You know they're probably dead by now," Dubari said.

"I know," Jakari said.

"Even if they aren't dead, we have no way of knowing where they're being held."

"I know."

"Even if we could find out where they are being held, the chances that we could get in, get them, get back out, and get off-planet are pretty much zero."

"I know."

"Our cover has also started to wear a little thin. A tramp freighter sitting idle for five days is going to raise some flags."

"I know."

"Just making sure," Dubari said.

"You can leave if you want," Jakari said. "I can find another way off world."

"You're my partner," Dubari said. "You stay, I stay."

"Even if it gets you killed?" Jakari asked.

"Even if it gets me killed," Dubari said. "So, what are we going to do?"

"Today was the last of the pre-scheduled meets," Jakari said. "Which means we activate the contingency plan."

"You know that if they've given up the meets, they've probably also given up the dead drops," Dubari said.

"I know," Jakari said. "But right now, I'm more interested in figuring out which one of them gave up the meets."

"Why?" Dubari asked.

"Because every bit of data is something we didn't know before," Jakari said. "Also, if one of them hasn't given up their drops yet, it makes it more likely they are alive."

"Good point. You want me to make the drops?"

"No," Jakari said. "I've got it."

* * * *

Dead drops were an old part of spy craft. No one was really sure when they were invented, but they'd been in use for thousands of years. They'd also evolved in that time. A dead drop had long since stopped being about the physical transfer of paper, microfilm, or other objects, and long since become about data. Most dead drops consisted of a small wireless transceiver, a data storage device, and a power supply.

The transceiver would sit and listen until it got a specific wake signal, then it would open an encrypted data channel for burst transmission. It would then either receive and store an encrypted data packet, or it would transmit and dump its stored data, depending on which command it received. Most of them also contained a small self-destruct device that would destroy the device beyond any chance of data retrieval if it was removed from its secure location.

Because of the nature of the dead drop, the person using it never had to physically visit the drop. Most of the burst transmitters had a decent range. The ones currently used by the Suil were good up to a half a kilometer. That meant that the person using it could visit the tea shop that had the drop embedded inside the wall, they could buy fruit at the produce stand next door, they could spend a pleasant afternoon at the massage parlor across the street, or they could just walk down the street without doing any of that.

Jakari visited the massage parlor, and somewhere between having her toe pads rubbed with lotion and having her ears brushed, she sent a burst transmission to one of Mamachi's dead drops with a location for a new meet.

Two hours later, wearing a different face and feeling more relaxed than she had in days, Jakari walked into a small toy shop on the other side of the city, picked up a souvenir for a child she didn't have, and sent a burst transmission arranging a different meet to one of Karusa's dead drops.

That done, Jakari went back to the spaceport and boarded her and Dubari's ship, which had been loaded with a cargo they were supposed to drop on one of the Char colony worlds in five days. They lifted out of the spaceport, and once they cleared the planet, they set a least-time course for said colony, shooting off at high warp. Then, about half a light year out from Cruthanna, they dropped out of warp, ejected their cargo, swapped out their faces and bodies, reconfigured their ship, and after a little bouncing around in deep space, warped back into Cruthanna space and requested a docking berth using a different ship registry and credit account.

They touched back down at just after midnight, and then they waited.

* * * *

"I want to talk to the prisoner," Cikara said.

Mamachi opened their eyes and looked over to see Cikara and Saka facing off against each other.

"Why?" Saka asked.

"Because I do," Cikara said.

"There is no reason for you to talk to the prisoner," Saka said.

"Wanting to is all the reason I need," Cikara said.

"I am in charge of the prisoner's interrogation," Saka said.

"I know," Cikara said. "Look, Saka, Mamachi worked in my office for fifty years. I considered them a friend, and they betrayed me. Is it really that hard to believe that I might want to ask them why they did it?"

"No," Saka said. "You have always been...emotional."

"Fine," Cikara said. "I'm emotional. But please, just give me a few minutes."

"Very well," Saka said. "You will need to reset the Form Lock. They currently do not have a tongue."

"Fine," Cikara said. "Leave us."

Saka didn't move.

"That's an order!" Cikara snapped.

Saka turned and marched out of the room. Once they were gone, Cikara turned and began working at the console. Mamachi couldn't see what they were doing, but when they were finished, they pulled a small device out of their pocket and activated it, then slipped it back into their pocket before hitting the button to lower Mamachi into the pool of TOP matter and reset the Form Lock.

When the cycle was complete, Mamachi was lifted out of the pool of TOP matter. The water tube dropped down to where Mamachi could reach it, but they didn't latch on. They didn't want the brief moment of comfort drinking would bring. Not if the torture was just going to start again.

"Drink," Cikara said.

"What's the point?" Mamachi said. "You're just going to torture me some more."

"No," Cikara said. "I won't. I hate this."

Mamachi looked down at them for a moment, thinking about it. They'd heard Cikara arguing against the torture earlier. It might be a ploy. Give Mamachi someone they could trust, someone to open up to, and then once Mamachi had spilled everything, Cikara would betray them. Mamachi nodded and latched onto the water tube, drinking deeply. If that was the game, Mamachi needed a clear head to take advantage, and dehydration wouldn't help.

"I'm sorry this is happening to you," Cikara said.

"Your friends don't seem sorry," Mamachi said.

"I know, but this isn't what the Char Oram is supposed to be," Cikara said. "This is the kind of thing we're supposed to protect Gadan from."

"Great job," Mamachi said.

"I want to help you," Cikara said.

"Kill me," Mamachi said. "Just, rip out my Phylactery and crush it."

"No," Cikara said, shaking their head.

"That's the only way you can help me," Mamachi said. "Kill me or let me go."

"Do you have a way off world?"

"No," Mamachi said.

"Is there someone I can contact? Someone who can help you if you get free?"

"I wouldn't tell you if there was," Mamachi said.

"Please," Cikara said. "Let me help you."

Mamachi stared at them for a minute. This was the moment where they had to decide if they believed Cikara or not. If they did, there was a chance they could escape. If they didn't, then at least they could warn off the extraction team. Assuming they were still out there.

They thought about what they knew of Cikara, of the years they'd spent working for them, of the casual talks and encounters, of Cikara's reaction to war news and to various political situations. Cikara was the weak link in the Triumvirate. That much was easy to see. They believed in the Char wholeheartedly, but they had never been onboard with some of Jaya and Saka's methods. Was that enough to get Mamachi to trust them with fellow agent's lives?

Not even close.

"Okay," Mamachi said. "If you want to help, here's what you need to do."

* * * *

Jakari's stomach sank as they walked into the small tea shop. They were half an hour early for the meet, but it didn't really matter. They had spotted three Security Officers sitting out on the patio. The meet was blown. She walked up to the counter and ordered a cup of tea to go, and once it was ready, she turned and headed out of the shop.

Karusa had given up their dead drops and their encryption codes, which meant, more than likely, they were either dead or being tortured to try to break Mamachi. Jakari wasn't sure which one to hope for at this point, but either way, it was possible Mamachi was still alive, so that had to come first.

Jakari sipped her tea as she walked deeper into the city, heading for the second meet.

* * * *

"Jakari, do you read?" Dubari asked over comms.

"Loud and clear," Jakari sent back without actually saying the words out loud.

"We got a posting on the info net requesting a meet."

"Mamachi or Karusa?" Jakari asked.

"Mamachi," Dubari asked. "But there are several keywords."

"Go on."

"The message indicates that Mamachi is captured, the meet is with an intermediary, and the intermediary is likely a hostile agent."

"Fuck," Jakari muttered. They were sitting at the meet site they had set up for Mamachi, and it was clean, but Mamachi hadn't shown.

That was a good sign for Mamachi being alive, but the message Dubari was reporting was a bad sign. The message was basically Mamachi sending them a warning, 'I'm captured, and they have someone playing ally to try and get me to lure you into a trap.'

Mamachi was essentially telling them to run. That the situation was hopeless. Every instinct Jakari had told her to listen, to get the fuck off Cruthanna for the next century. To write Mamachi and Karusa off as lost assets.

"Where's the meet?"

"You're going?" Dubari asked.

"It's Karusa," Jakari said.

"Yeah," Dubari said with a heavy sigh. "It's Karusa. The meet is at a tea shop near the Palace. I'm sending the address now."

"Thanks, Dubari," she said.

"You're my partner," Dubari said.

"Still," Jakari said. "Thanks."

* * * *

Jakari walked into Freedom Square outside the Triumvirate Palace just a few minutes before the scheduled meet. She knew coming here was insane. The square was always full of Security Officers, so there was no way to be sure it wasn't an ambush. If anyone other than Karusa had been on the line, Jakari would never have come, but they were, so here she was.

She nearly froze when she spotted her contact. They were sitting outside the tea shop, a data pad propped up with a picture of a pretty Gadan standing on the beach displayed, just the way it was supposed to be. What shocked her was the person sitting at the table. Cikara. Second-in-command of the Triumvirate.

This was insane. She should leave. She should get off the planet right now. This had to be a trap.

She walked into the tea shop and bought a cup, then came back out and sat down directly across from Cikara.

"I have to admit, I never thought I'd see you again," Jakari said.

Cikara looked at her. "I'm sorry," they said. "But I'm waiting for someone."

"Yes," Jakari said. "I understand you're looking to sell a hover sled."

Cikara stiffened slightly at the code words. "If the price is right," they responded.

"Well, as long as it's not an arm and a leg, I'm sure we can work something out."

Cikara leaned back in their chair and took a sip of their tea. "Do I know you?"

"I am Jakari."

Cikara's eyes went wide. "I..."

"Not who you were expecting?" Jakari asked.

"No," Cikara said. "Are you going to kill me?"

"That depends on what you have to say."

Cikara nodded. "I suppose that's fair," they said. "After what I've seen the last few days, I'm not sure I wouldn't deserve it."

"Well, then, you'd better give me a reason not to turn you into a ball of expanding plasma."

"Mamachi is being held in the Palace," Cikara said. "I've arranged for there to be a small security breach tonight, an hour after midnight. They will have everything they need to make it out of the building. If you're in place to meet them, you could get them off world."

"Why?"

"What?"

"Why are you doing this?"

"Does it matter?"

"If you expect me to trust you, it matters very much."

"Because this is not who we are supposed to be," Cikara said. "The Char is supposed to protect our people. Not torture them. They've done things to that child that would make even a Seichu torturer flinch."

"And I'm supposed to believe you care?"

"If you want to save them," Cikara said. "Look, I'm not saying I would have lifted a finger if Jaya had ordered Mamachi executed. They're a spy. Espionage carries a death sentence, but that's justice. What's happening in Saka's lab is an abomination."

"Is Mamachi the only prisoner?"

"As far as I know," Cikara said. "Why do you ask?"

"We don't leave our people behind. If you've arranged for Mamachi to escape, they'll bring any other prisoners with them. I need to know how many people I need to get off world."

"As far as I've seen, Mamachi is the only prisoner in Saka's lab. If there are any more in the building, I don't know about them. I'm sorry."

"Okay," Jakari said. She picked up her tea and took a sip. "So, tell me, what have you been up to for the last seven and a half thousand years?"

"You want to talk?" Cikara asked.

"Well, the square is full of Security Officers, and it would look awfully suspicious if we only talked for two minutes. So let's finish our tea and have a nice conversation, and then we'll go our separate ways. And if tonight turns out to be a trap, I'll come back tomorrow and kill you."

Cikara's eyes went wide, but Jakari just smiled and took another sip of her tea.

.

Chapter Twelve

Crodain, Cruthanna. Year of Freedom 7538 (Gadan Reckoning) 485 AD (Earth Reckoning)

MAMACHI DIDN'T BOTHER WITH a catalog of their injuries. It would have been hard to do anyway, since both of their eyes were gone this time. At first, they weren't even sure what had woken them up until they realized they were being lowered into the TOP matter pool again. The thought of starting the torture again was enough to make them cry, if they had still been able. They'd managed to hold out however long they'd been in custody, but they weren't sure how much longer they could last. The cycle of torture and healing and torture and healing was wearing them down. They wanted it to stop or they wanted to die. They didn't care which anymore.

They screamed as the Form Lock reset. Somehow, the lack of pain was worse than the pain now. Maybe it was the anticipation of what was to come that hurt. They didn't know. All they knew was that they had to fight, had to hold out. So when the frame they were locked to lifted them upright again, they jerked against their restraints, and to their surprise, the restraints gave way, dropping them back into the pool again. There was a terrible ripping pain in their back as they fell, like a piece of them was being torn out, but the pain faded almost instantly, and they felt their control of their body snap back.

They lifted themselves out of the pool, turned to look at the frame, and saw the Form Lock dangling from the end of a cable, and it hit them. They were free. They were free and standing in a pool of TOP matter.

A million questions ran through Mamachi's mind, but the only ones that really mattered were: 'how much time did they have?', 'where was Karusa?', 'would escaping be easier with or without a Talus?', 'did they dare take the time to look for Karusa?'

They knew the answer to that last one was a resounding 'no' even as they climbed out of the TOP matter pool and made their way over to the computer. A few quick commands and they were in. Mamachi had more than a century with the system. If Nira thought she was going to remove all the back doors they'd installed in the space of a couple of weeks, she wasn't as smart as Mamachi gave her credit for.

A quick query told them that Karusa wasn't being held in the building, but they couldn't find any information on where Karusa was being held. They checked the clock. Ten minutes after one in the morning. Without a clue where to start, there was no way to find Karusa now. They would have to escape, find some place to hide, and make another run at it later. Maybe Karusa had gotten lucky and escaped, but if Mamachi didn't move now, they would be back up on that torture rack.

They walked over to the pool and stuck their hand in, siphoning a bit of TOP matter into their form, increasing their size as they took on a new look, complete with a Security Officer uniform and fake badge. Once they were settled into their new form, they headed for the door, moving as fast as they could while initiating a stored subroutine to build a Shim. It wouldn't be nearly as fast as doing it manually, but if they needed one later, they'd rather not have to build one on the fly.

* * * *

Freedom Square at 1:15 in the morning wasn't a lot different than Freedom Square in the middle of the afternoon. It was well lit, crowded, and most of the businesses were open. It was the perfect place to grab an escaped prisoner without anyone being the wiser. Or it would be, if she had any idea what the escaped prisoner looked like. She watched the front door with her own eyes, while she watched all the other entrances and exits through the various cameras that she'd spent the day putting in place. If Cikara was telling the truth, Mamachi should be exiting the Palace any minute. Jakari just had to be sure they picked the right person to approach.

A massive Security Officer stepped out of the front door of the Palace and started down the steps. Jakari hesitated for just a moment, because it was just a little too ridiculous. Sneaking out disguised as a guard? There was no way the kid could be that crazy. Except a second after that thought ran through Jakari's head, the Palace alarms went off full blast, and every Security Officer in the square except one turned and started running towards the Palace.

Jakari stood up and moved as quickly as she could without attracting attention, which was a lot quicker than it usually would be. No one wanted to be anywhere near Freedom Square during a security alert. Too much chance of getting arrested just in case, or getting caught in a crossfire. The mad scramble for safety let Jakari get right next to the oversized security guard before they noticed her approach, and by the time they did notice, Jakari already had a plasma cannon pressed against their side.

"Keep walking," Jakari said.

"Who are you?" the security guard asked.

"That depends on who you tell me you are," Jakari said. "If you give me the right answer, I'm the person saving your life. If you give me the wrong answer, I'm the person turning you into an expanding cloud of vapor. So, 'meadow.'"

"Golden-haired pollen fly," the Security Officer said.

"I am Jakari," she said as she morphed the plasma cannon back into her hand.

"I am Mamachi."

"Are you alone?" Jakari asked.

"Yes," Mamachi said.

Jakari felt a pain like a knife sink into her heart. Karusa wasn't with them. They'd expected that, but the confirmation hurt.

"Where to?" Mamachi asked.

"Just keep walking," she said.

They were just exiting Freedom Square when the first of the flyers arrived. Heavily armored grav vans opened to drop squads of Security Officers in Class One Taluses. She led them down a block from the square to a public lot, and then pointed at one of the air cars.

"That one," she said.

Mamachi ducked around to the passenger's side while Jakari climbed into the driver's seat. Once they were in, she tinted the windows so they were solid black from the outside, then lifted the car out of its parking spot.

"Lose the big guy and the uniform."

Mamachi shrugged off the excess TOP matter, which Jakari absorbed into the seat, then shunted into a tank in the trunk. Once they were a more normal size, Mamachi shifted into a new face. Satisfied with their new disguise, Jakari put the car into a climb, shifting its color and design as they moved through the middle altitudes where Security and traffic didn't have any cameras. She also shifted her own face and body, then shifted the windows to transparent before they reached the traffic lanes.

"Go ahead and ask," Jakari said.

"I can't and you know it," Mamachi said.

"Yeah, and if the question had the answer you wanted, you wouldn't need to ask in the first place."

Mamachi dropped their head, because it was true. Neither of them could use Karusa's name, in case the other wasn't who they claimed to be and Karusa hadn't been blown, but the fact that they couldn't share information without putting Karusa in danger meant they couldn't compare notes and maybe figure out where Karusa was.

"Do you know how you got blown?" Jakari asked.

"No idea," Mamachi said. "The Char were good and careful. I was compromised six days before I realized it. When I did, I did my best not to give any clues, but I put an extraction call in three of my dead drops. It's possible one of them was compromised because they came to arrest me the next morning when I reported to work."

"Is that where they took you?"

"No. I had contingencies."

"What contingencies?"

"I'd stashed a Class One Talus on my floor. When they tried to arrest me, I put it on and jumped out the window."

"Bet they weren't expecting that," Jakari said.

"Wish I could say the same about my safehouse," Mamachi said.

"They caught you at your safehouse?"

"Yeah. No idea how they found it, but I walked in, did a quick inspection. Place was empty, but they'd put an immobilizer spike inside the mattress."

"Damn," Jakari said. "Chest?"

"Stomach."

"Ouch," Jakari said. "Can you handle a Class Two?"

"I've run a Class Four," Mamachi said.

Jakari looked over at them. "I thought you were five hundred years old."

"I am," Mamachi said.

"Never met anyone under a thousand who could handle a Class Three, much less a Four."

"Now you have," Mamachi said.

Jakari shrugged.

"We're headed away from the spaceport," Mamachi said.

"Took you this long to notice?"

"Thought you might be circling around."

"I'm not," Jakari said.

"Want to tell me where we're headed then?"

"Someplace safe," Jakari said.

"Only place safe is off world."

"Yeah, but the spaceport is locked down and they'll be doing a search of all ships."

"You have a way around that?"

"I do," Jakari said.

Mamachi leaned back in their seat. Jakari could tell they weren't happy with the answer, but she didn't really care.

* * * *

Mamachi stared at the vat of TOP matter in front of them, then looked over at the cargo containers.

"This is your plan?" they asked.

"You have a better one?" Jakari asked.

"No," Mamachi said. "I don't suppose I do."

"Good," Jakari said. "Then let's get started."

She walked over to the vat and opened the spigot, and the graphite liquid began to spill out into a large mold. At the same time, a tendril extended from the hood of the air car and touched the rapidly forming puddle in the bottom of the mold. As soon as the tendril touched the puddle, the air car started changing shape, growing and twisting quickly until it finally turned into a grav crane. Once it reached its final form, the tendril withdrew, leaving the puddle to begin filling up the mold.

"You have the schematic ready?" Jakari asked.

"Yeah," Mamachi said. They walked up to the mold and raised their hand, extruding the Shim they had created after their escape and dropping it into the rapidly growing pool of TOP matter now filling the mold. Mamachi sent a mental command through the Shim, and the TOP matter flowed out of the mold, leaving behind a tendril connected to the vat so it could continue to draw in more TOP matter until a second grav crane was sitting next to the first. When that was done, Mamachi disconnected the tendril from the vat, and TOP matter began spilling into the mold again. Jakari touched a button on the vat and the TOP matter reversed its flow, drawing everything in the mold back into the vat before the spigot closed itself off.

"Let's go," Jakari said. She walked over to her Talus and climbed up into the cockpit. Mamachi followed suit, climbing into their newly made Talus. They took a second, familiarizing themself with the controls. They hadn't flown a grav crane in centuries. Not since the academy. They were simple vehicles; a pilot's compartment, a massive anti-gravity generator, and a cluster of high output ion engines, all attached to four adjustable arms that attached to the corners of cargo containers.

Jakari lifted her crane off the ground, floated over to one of the two cargo containers Mamachi had been eyeing earlier, and latched on, then lifted into the sky. Mamachi did the same, locking on to the second container and lifting into the air. Once Mamachi was in the air, Jakari started forward, heading towards the spaceport at a leisurely pace. Mamachi followed, doing their best to ignore the sight of security vehicles swarming all over the city.

Mamachi listened nervously as they were challenged by the security forces around the spaceport, but Jakari just calmly gave their flight authorization and delivery code. Relief flooded through them as they were given clearance to land in the appropriate docking bay. They followed Jakari in and set down next to her. They quickly set their cargo container down on the floor of the bay, then parked a couple dozen meters away and exited their crane just as a pair of Security Officers walked into the landing bay.

Mamachi waited next to the cargo container as the Security Officers approached.

"Manifest," one of the officers said.

Before Mamachi could hand over the manifest, there were two thunderous impacts from behind. Mamachi turned to see a pair of Taluses standing there with the Triumvirate Security Insignia emblazoned on the chest of one of them, and the Triumvirate Insignia emblazoned on the other. Both of them had their cannons raised.

"Thank you, Officers," Jaya's voice said from the Talus with the Triumvirate Insignia on it, "but we'll take it from here."

Both of the Security Officers bowed deeply before turning and running for the door. Once they were gone, Jaya's Talus took a couple of steps to the side, getting a better line of fire on Jakari.

"Now, which one of you is Mamachi?" Jaya asked.

Mamachi shifted back into their normal appearance and stared up at the Talus.

"And who's your little friend?" Jaya asked.

Jakari stepped up to stand beside them and shifted into a form Mamachi had never seen before. One they assumed was her true face.

"Hey, Jaya," Jakari said in the same tone one might use to greet an old friend they hadn't seen in a while. "It's been a long time."

"Jakari?" Jaya asked in a gleeful tone. "Well, this is a happy day."

"Aunt Jakari?" a voice asked from the other Talus. A voice Mamachi knew all too well. One that Jakari apparently knew too, from the way she reacted.

"Karusa?' Jakari asked.

Jaya's Talus looked back and forth between Jakari and Karusa's Talus. "You two know each other?" Jaya asked, sounding even more delighted than before.

The chest of Karusa's Talus cracked open and they jumped out, landing on the floor of the docking bay.

"Aunt Jakari, what are you doing here?" Karusa asked.

"Well, I came to take you and your friend home," Jakari said.

"You wasted a trip," Karusa said. "I am home."

Jakari nodded her head. "All right," she said. "I'm going to go out on a limb here and guess that you're the one who told the Char about Mamachi?"

"I had to," Karusa said.

"You gave me up?" Mamachi asked, not able to believe it. All the evidence was in front of them. The fact that Karusa was in a Security Talus, the fact that they'd basically just confessed to it, but it didn't make sense. Karusa was their friend. Karusa had been their friend their entire life.

"I didn't want to," Karusa said. "I tried to make you see reason."

"What are you talking about?"

"They lied to us. Our whole lives, they lied to us. They never showed us what the Seichu did. They never showed us the torture rooms, the gladiator pits, the slave brothels. They never showed us the markets where we were bought and sold like animals. But Jaya and Nira did. They told me the truth, and the more I saw, the more I realized the Char Oram is right. We have to protect ourselves. We have to be strong.

"I tried to get you to see that. All those talks we had about the Seichu and the rebellion. All those nights we sat talking about the Char and their goals. But you never listened. You just talked about how misguided it was to live in fear."

"It is," Mamachi said.

"Not if the fear is legitimate!" Karusa yelled. "How many alien races are there? How many of them would gladly kill us or enslave us to take our resources? How many are like the Seichu?"

"So you gave me up because you're afraid of the Seichu?"

"I gave you up because I knew I could never convince you of the truth," Karusa said. "I cried for weeks when I realized what I had to do. You were my friend my whole life, but you remember what they taught us at the academy. It's our duty to protect the Gadan, at all costs.

"I didn't want to give you up, but you were working for the Suil. They're making us weak. We need to be strong, or the next time a race like the Seichu comes along, they might wipe us out, or worse, they might turn us into slaves, just like the Seichu."

"So you gave me up, let me be tortured? And now what? You're here to kill me?" Mamachi asked.

"No," Karusa said. "No, I begged Jaya for the chance to talk to you. If you tell them everything, if you swear loyalty to the Char, they'll spare you."

"And if I don't?" Mamachi asked.

"Then...then I have to kill you."

Mamachi looked over at Jakari. "I didn't realize they were your family."

"No way you could have," Jakari said. She looked right at Karusa. "What about me, kid?"

"You weren't supposed to be here," Karusa said.

"You didn't think I'd let someone else come if I thought you were in trouble, did you?"

"I wish you had," Karusa said.

"We all make mistakes," Jakari said. "It's not too late to walk away from this one."

"This isn't a mistake," Karusa said. "You never told me the truth either. About what the Seichu did."

"I didn't tell you because I didn't want you to know," Jakari said. "I didn't tell you because I didn't want you to have the nightmares that I have every night. I didn't want you to have to remember the things I remember. The Seichu are gone. That war is over, and this one is nothing but Jaya's fear over an enemy the rest of us have long since put behind us. You made a mistake, kid, but you can still come home."

"You're wrong," Karusa said. "You don't understand the things I've seen."

"Bullshit," Jakari said. "I've lived them. Whatever you've seen, I've lived it. The slave pens, the gladiator pits, the brothels, the torture rooms. I've seen it all. Lived it all. You're scared of stories, but I've lived the reality of it, and I'm telling you, you're wrong. You're listening to a little child who never stopped jumping at shadows."

"Enough!" Jaya said. "Karusa, I gave you your chance. Mamachi will not listen and Jakari is a wanted murderer. It's time to do your duty."

Karusa looked at Jaya's Talus for a moment, then turned around and walked back to their own. They jumped up and landed in the chest cavity, which started to close around them. As it did, Mamachi saw Jakari's Talus start to shift out of its grav crane configuration, and reached out to their own, initiating transformation into a combat mech configuration. Karusa's Talus turned slightly as they raised their arms, pointing their cannons at Mamachi.

"I'm sorry," Karusa said. "I wish you could have seen the truth."

"I'm sorry I didn't see what was happening to you," Mamachi said.

Karusa's plasma cannons started to glow blue, and several things happened at once. Jakari's Talus, which had finished its transformation first, slammed into Karusa's Talus from behind and jerked its arms into the air. Karusa's plasma cannons went off, filling the sky above the docking port with bursts of bright blue plasma. Jaya screamed in shock and surprise. Hidden panels on Jakari's ship opened and plasma cannons dropped down, firing on Jaya's Talus. Mamachi's Talus leapt towards Jaya's, and both Jakari and Mamachi made a run for the ship's boarding ramp.

They might have made it if it had just been Jaya and Karusa. Mamachi was never sure, because the boarding ramp was on the other side of the ship, pointed directly away from them. Maybe if the cargo ramp was open, they could have made it. They would never know, because another Talus dropped out of the air. There was no doubt who it belonged to, not with the bright red slash across the Talus's face. Nira had joined the fight.

Whoever was in the ship switched the ship's cannons from Jaya's Talus to Nira's, but Nira's Talus had a massive shield, and kept it between itself and the cannons as it stalked towards Jakari and Mamachi. Both of them turned and charged back towards where their Taluses were fighting Jaya and Karusa.

They both seemed to have the same thought. Both of their Taluses spun, putting themselves between Mamachi and Jakari and the hostile Taluses. Their backs opened, exposing an inner compartment, and Mamachi and Jakari jumped.

Mamachi lost track of the rest of the battle for a moment as they landed on their Talus and the back swung closed. Their body and the inner walls flowed together as they became one with the Talus, becoming a single, living war machine. They spun again, putting Jaya firmly between themselves and Nira, but Jaya had apparently had enough of being manhandled and fired their jump jets, ripping themselves free of Mamachi's grasp.

Mamachi let them go and brought their arms up, deploying their plasma cannons and firing at Nira, who couldn't bring the shield to bear without exposing themselves to plasma fire from the ship. Nira stumbled back, taking four hits to the chest that left her smoking and staggering. Mamachi glanced up to check Jaya's position and saw Jaya falling directly towards them, a massive sword in hand. Mamachi deployed a small shield and ran a massive electrical current across it as they brought it up, taking the sword strike on the shield at an angle so it would glance off, rather than hit dead on.

When the blade hit Mamachi's shield, the electric current had the desired effect, discharging into Jaya and knocking her back. Mamachi used the momentary reprieve to check the rest of the battlefield. A large hatch on the ship was open, and a Talus Mamachi didn't recognize was fighting Nira, slamming a massive Warhammer down on Nira's shield, and Jakari was still grappling with Karusa. Above them, Security Flyers circled.

Mamachi turned back to Jaya, who now had their own shield out. Mamachi took a moment to deploy a sword and pulled up every sword fighting algorithm they'd ever loaded. They were not ready for this. They were not ready for this. They were facing down Jaya, the most successful gladiator of all time with a sword and a shield. This was the definition of a bad decision.

Jaya moved in, and it was as if the universe had heard Mamachi's very thoughts and decided to prove them right. They weren't even sure what happened, just that every time they tried to block, Jaya's attack was a feint that scored a hit, and every time they tried to attack, Jaya wasn't where they were supposed to be.

They felt a surge of agony as Jaya impaled them and ripped the blade loose. Before they could put the damage right, Jaya attacked again, severing Mamachi's arm. Mamachi staggered back, trying to gain distance. They tried to parry the next sword blow, and unbelievably, they did, turning it aside, only for the edge of Jaya's shield to cave in their face, blinding them for precious seconds as they had to rebuild it. Before they could, they felt their other arm get sliced off. Their sensors came back online just as they saw Jaya raise their blade for another blow and did the only thing they could think of. They deployed a plasma cannon from their stomach and fired it point blank into Jaya's chest.

The explosion blew Mamachi back and they began to stagger, already off balance due to their missing limbs. Jaya screamed in rage, the front of her Talus smoking where Mamachi had blown a hole in it, and deployed four plasma cannons. Mamachi didn't have time to react. They didn't even have time to prepare for the death they were sure was coming. They just reacted with one desperate impulse, reshaping all their weapons and every bit of extra equipment on the Talus into a thick shield covering the center of the mech form.

The four plasma blasts knocked Mamachi back and they slammed into something. Before they could react or move, Jaya hit them again, blowing them through whatever they were pressed up against, and for one brief moment, they thought they were about to die, until they realized what they had been pressed up against.

Every docking bay on every Gadan controlled planet had a large tank of TOP matter in it to use to repair any ships that had taken damage or to provide extra TOP matter to travelers who needed it. TOP matter was the core of Gadan technology. Ships, vehicles, medicine, weapons. All of it required TOP matter, and sometimes lots of it. And Mamachi suddenly found themselves inside a massive tank of it.

They reached out, gathering as much of it as they could to themself as they rifled through their schematic archive. Taluses were not easy things to control. Yes, they were an extension of your body, but most Gadan minds only had so much bandwidth. It was something that expanded as you aged. A young Gadan, someone less than a century, would struggle with anything above a Class One. Even a Class One Heavy might be out of their reach. At two or three centuries, they might be able to handle a Class Two. Most people took a thousand years to be able to handle a Class Three, and about half of the population never moved beyond that. Handling a Class Four or Class Five was considered a gift, even at four or five thousand years old. People who could handle a Class Six were rare in the extreme.

Mamachi loaded a Class Seven schematic, pulling in nearly thirty thousand kilograms of TOP matter. They stood up, the motion tearing apart the tank they had been knocked into. A force shield generator snapped on, as every eye in the docking bay turned towards Mamachi, who was still standing in a veritable lake of TOP matter.

Mamachi reached into their Script archive for a missile design and created hundreds of copies of the Script, spilling them out into the TOP matter. The missiles formed out of the graphite liquid and shot into the sky. Dozens of missiles homed in on every one of the Security vehicles, and the sky filled with blinding flashes and clouds of expanding plasma.

Nira leapt into the air, trying to flee on their jump jets. Mamachi locked on and fired a dozen plasma cannons. At the last second, a small object was shot out of the side of Nira's Talus before the plasma swallowed it and vaporized it. Mamachi tried to lock onto the escaping object, which do doubt held Nira's Phylactery, but it was too small for their targeting sensors, so they turned their attention to Jaya, who was also trying to make a run for it. They locked on, and just as Nira had, Jaya ejected their Phylactery, but unlike Nira, once the Phylactery was clear, Jaya's Talus turned back towards Mamachi, intent on a suicide run. Mamachi vaporized it.

They turned towards Karusa, all their plasma cannons focused on them.

"Get out of the Talus," Mamachi said.

Jakari stepped back away from Karusa, who turned and raised their plasma cannon, pointing them at Mamachi.

"No," they said.

"Karusa, get out of the Talus," Mamachi said.

"Or what?" Karusa said. "You won't kill me."

Mamachi fired four of the cannons, and blew off all four of Karusa's limbs, vaporizing them completely. The head and torso fell to the ground and lay there, unmoving.

"Get out of the Talus," Mamachi said.

The chest of the Talus cracked open, and Karusa climbed out slowly, their hands raised.

"Move away," Mamachi said.

Karusa walked over to where Jakari was standing. Mamachi fired into the Talus, destroying what was left.

Mamachi looked over at the third Talus in their little group.

"Friend of yours?" Mamachi asked.

"Yeah," Jakari said.

"Let's get out of here," Mamachi said.

Jakari's Talus opened and she jumped out. She grabbed Karusa by the arm and started leading them towards the ship. Mamachi opened the chest of their Talus and jumped down, following quickly as the other Talus pilot climbed back into the cargo compartment of the ship.

"Can you handle that thing remotely?" Jakari asked.

"Yeah," Mamachi said. "I should be able to escort us."

"Good," Jakari said. "We'll need it."

Afterwards, Mamachi was never quite sure what the trigger was. They were never sure why Karusa couldn't accept their capture and defeat. It was something that would haunt them for centuries. Karusa jerked free of Jakari's grip and spun around, hands morphing into plasma cannons, both of them pointed at Mamachi. Blue light swelled inside the barrels, and Mamachi knew, beyond a shadow of a doubt, that they were going to die.

The plasma bolt that killed Karusa seemed to come out of nowhere. One second, they were standing there, ready to kill Mamachi, and the next, they were gone, and there was a plasma burn where they had been standing. Mamachi turned towards Jakari, who stood there, staring at the black mark burned into the ground with a look of abject horror in her face. They turned towards Jakari's Talus, which had one arm raised with a plasma cannon aimed at the exact spot where Karusa had been standing, and they understood what had happened.

They turned back towards Jakari.

"We have to go," Mamachi said.

"Yeah," Jakari said, but she didn't move.

"Jakari," Mamachi said, but there was no response, so they did the only thing they could. They picked Jakari up and carried her aboard the ship.

Chapter Thirteen

"YOU KILLED KARUSA?" HAYAMI asked.

"Yes," Jakari said.

"She did it to save my life," Mamachi cut in before Hayami could reply. They didn't like where this was going. "Karusa would have killed me if Jakari hadn't taken that shot."

"I know," Hayami said. "I'm not questioning why she did it. I just…" Hayami turned back to Jakari. "That had to be hard on you. Killing a member of your own family…"

Jakari looked down at the floor, and Mamachi felt a small knot of dread settle into their stomach. They'd had this conversation with Jakari before and knew how it ended.

"It wasn't a conscious decision," Jakari said. "I don't know if that makes it better or worse, but they drew a weapon on Mamachi and I just reacted. I don't even remember firing."

"Did you ever talk to someone about it?" Hayami asked.

"Talk to who?" Jakari asked. "The only people who knew the truth was me, Mamachi, and Dubari. As far as the rest of the Suil was concerned, Karusa died when the Char tried to arrest them."

"You didn't tell their family what happened?" Hayami asked.

"*No!*" Jakari shouted as she looked up, and Mamachi could see the horror on her face. "What was I supposed to do? Go back to Bailenua and tell Subhash that their only child had been a traitor who gave up their best friend to be tortured and murdered by the Char?" She shook her head. "No. No, as far as anyone else is concerned, Karusa died a hero. No one needs to know what they got twisted into."

Hayami looked like she wanted to say something, but Jakari turned away.

"She's right," Mamachi said. "Telling the truth wouldn't have done anyone any good. It took a while to convince Dubari, but they agreed to keep the secret."

"I'm sorry," Skylar said.

Jakari looked over at her. "What?"

"I'm sorry that happened to you. To both of you. That Karusa put you both in a place where you got hurt."

Mamachi squeezed Skylar's hand. She looked over at them and smiled, but the moment was cut short by Jakari standing up.

"We should get some rest," she said. "Meet back in the conference room tomorrow at 9:00 AM and we'll see if we can pin down a location for the Char ship."

Jakari headed for the door. Hayami looked like she was about to follow, but Mamachi waved to get her attention then shook their head. Hayami frowned, but let Jakari go without chasing after her.

"What just happened?" Skylar asked.

"Jakari happened," Mamachi said with a sigh. "She's never really made peace with what happened on Cruthanna. I tried telling her over and over again that it wasn't her fault. That I'm the one who didn't see the signs. That I'm the one who didn't realize Karusa needed to be pulled out before the constant propaganda got to them."

"It's not your fault either," Skylar said.

"I was there," Mamachi said. "Karusa was my friend, my partner, and I didn't see the signs. I let them down and they died because of me."

"That's a crock of shit," Skylar said.

"What?"

"She's right," Hayami said. "Karusa might have been your friend, but they were old enough to make their own choices. You were right there in the middle of everything and you didn't let yourself get brainwashed."

"People make bad decisions," Skylar said. "Karusa made bad decisions. I'm not saying they deserved what happened to them, but you didn't deserve what happened to you either, and you and Jakari don't deserve the pain Karusa caused you."

Mamachi squeezed Skylar's hand again. They knew Skylar and Hayami meant well, but they didn't believe what they were saying. Mamachi had been there, and had apparently missed years, maybe decades of warning signs.

"I'm a little surprised that you and Jakari ended up such good friends," Hayami said.

"So am I, honestly," Mamachi said. "I figured after what happened, she would never want to see me again. Instead, she reached out to Napati and made sure I got assigned to her unit. I think a lot of that was that Jakari knew Napati wouldn't put up with me getting a big head just because I'd survived a fight with Jaya. At first, I figured she was dumping me somewhere I couldn't get into trouble, but she kept coming around, checking on me. It didn't seem to matter where we were stationed.

Every couple of years, she would show up. I think the stretch before she got here was the longest that I'd ever gone without seeing her."

"How long?" Hayami asked.

"Thirty years," Mamachi said. "I talked to her a few times over comms. She said she was busy with missions."

"You think she was avoiding you?" Hayami asked.

"I don't think so," Mamachi asked. "The war has been bad the last few decades. Jaya made another push in the colonies and the fighting has been intense. If it was anyone other than Cikara here on Earth, I doubt Arthan would have sent anyone at all."

"Nice to know how high we rate," Hayami said.

"It's not that," Mamachi said. "Napati would never let an innocent world get swallowed up like that. Neither would most of the other Suil leaders. It's just Arthan."

"Not a nice guy?" Hayami asked.

Mamachi sighed. "I'm not sure Arthan actually cares about anything other than beating Jaya anymore."

"Isn't winning the war what you all want?" Hayami asked.

"Yeah, but...there's a difference between winning the war and beating Jaya," Mamachi said. "When you're fighting a war, sometimes you lose a battle here and there. It just happens. But Arthan obsesses over every defeat. It's all too personal. And he turns on anyone who questions his decisions. He practically accused Napati of treason at one point."

"Sounds like he's unhinged," Hayami said.

"I'm not the best person to judge," Mamachi said. "I hate him."

"Because he sent you to Cruthanna?" Skylar asked.

"No. Because he sent Karusa," Mamachi said. "I pulled their file after I was assigned to Napati's team, and there were tests that indicated that Karusa might be susceptible to propaganda. That they were a bad candidate for deep cover because they could be indoctrinated by Char ideology. Arthan ordered them assigned to the mission over the objections of our training officers."

"Why would he do that?" Skylar asked.

"I have a theory, but if I tell you, both of you have to promise you'll never repeat it."

Skylar nodded, and Mamachi looked over at Hayami. She was a bit more hesitant, but finally, she nodded as well.

"Jakari was Karusa's aunt," Mamachi said. "She's easily the most successful wetwork operative the Suil has. Dubari technically has the same number of successful missions because they're a team, but Jakari is the reason they're so successful. She's pulled off missions that no one else could have."

"I sense a 'but' coming," Hayami said.

"Yeah. She's got a bit of a bad reputation in the intelligence community for going off book. She won't accept a mission without a complete breakdown of the mission's goals. Not just who the target is, but why the Suil wants them eliminated. And if she doesn't think you've picked the right target to accomplish those goals, she'll re-task herself and kill the person she thinks will have the desired impact."

"That can't go over well," Hayami said.

"No," Mamachi said. "Especially not with Arthan. He still uses her, because there is literally no one else who can do some of the things she does, but I think he was looking for a replacement. I think he sent Karusa in to Cruthanna as a way to see if they were good enough to take Jakari's place. If they failed, then Jakari would have every reason to hate the Char, and Jakari's hatred is legendary. The things she did to the Seichu are still whispered about."

"Except the Char didn't kill Karusa," Hayami said.

"Right," Mamachi said.

"So that legendary hatred is pointed squarely at herself," Hayami said.

"Pretty much," Mamachi said. "That's why she ran out of here. You came dangerously close to implying that she's not a horrible person who deserves nothing but misery in their life."

"Do you people just not have therapists?" Hayami asked.

"Oh, we have them," Mamachi said. "But no one uses them. At least, not at our level."

"Why not?" Hayami asked.

"Because the only therapists cleared for the things we deal with are military therapists, and military therapists have a duty to report anything that could be considered a security risk. The moment either of us start talking about what happened at Cruthanna, or at a hundred other places, we would instantly become a security risk."

Hayami stood up. "I'm going to bed, because if I think about this anymore, I'm going to scream."

Mamachi nodded and watched as she left. Once they were alone with Skylar, they let out a sigh.

"I suppose you'll be going too?" they asked.

"I could stay, if you'd like some company," Skylar said.

"I'd like that very much," Mamachi said.

"Give me a minute to get changed," Skylar said. She got up and grabbed a couple of items out of the wardrobe that was full of her things. Mamachi had long since given up on real clothes and just created whatever they needed as part of the shape shifting process.

They got up and locked the door, then shifted into a pair of boxer shorts and climbed into bed. It took about ten minutes before Skylar reappeared wearing a pair of boxer briefs and a tank top. She climbed into bed and wrapped herself around them, and Mamachi held her tight as she drifted off to sleep.

* * * *

Jakari climbed the boarding ramp to her ship and headed for the cockpit. Her mind was all over the place. It always was when she thought about Cruthanna. It was funny. Once, she wouldn't have even thought of it that way. It would just have been home. Even after the occupation, even after the civil war started and she'd been pushed off the planet with the rest of the Suil, it had still been home. Up until that mission. Up until it had become Cruthanna. The world where she'd killed her family.

She dropped down in the pilot's chair and stared straight ahead. There wasn't a lot to see. Just a bright white bulkhead. One of the advantages of a living ship. It cleaned and repaired itself. It always looked like it was sitting in a showroom. One of the disadvantages, too. She'd been flying around in the Sabuja Bramble for almost nine thousand years, but the ship was still top of the line and state of the art because she kept updating the Scripts embedded in the ship with the latest and greatest from Suil Research and Development, from the civilian market, and even, on occasion, from the Char.

It reminded her of herself in a lot of ways. Always fresh, always new, always in peak condition, but at the same time, unimaginably old. She wondered if the ship was as tired as she was. She doubted it. As much as the ship might feel like a reflection of her, it wasn't. It was more like Mamachi, Dubari, and the other, younger Gadan. The ones who were born with the expectation of immortality, of unlimited time and unending second chances. Their minds were formed with that idea as a central part of them. They never had to come to the realization that they would grow old and die. They never learned to look forward to it.

She had. Her life before the bioweapon had been idyllic. She was married to someone she loved so deeply and so passionately that some days, it had been hard to believe that it was real. Aashi was like something out of a dream. A miracle that she treasured and cherished and guarded with everything she was. A miracle the universe had decided she was unworthy of and taken back.

Maybe God, or the universe, or whoever decided such things saw what she really was, or what she would become, and decided that Aashi was too good for her. Maybe they took Aashi away as punishment for all the ways she would fail, or all the horrors she would commit. She didn't know why. All she knew was that it had been the beginning of the end for her. Watching Aashi die had been what started her down the path to becoming the kind of person who could slaughter someone they loved without even thinking about it.

She closed her eyes, trying to tamp down the flood of emotions rolling through her. She was usually better at keeping them from overwhelming her, but too many things were pulling at her. Seeing Mamachi, Cikara being involved, talking about Cruthanna, and worst of all, Hayami. Hayami who was brave and smart and caring and compassionate and who asked dangerous questions that demanded answers Jakari wasn't sure she had.

Why had she blown the op to save one human? At the time, the answer had seemed simple. She couldn't trade an innocent life for the success of her mission. She was an assassin, but she killed for a reason. She killed to protect the innocent. The right knife in the right neck at the right time saved lives. If she let an innocent die, her mission stopped being about saving lives, and became about killing people.

But there was more to it than that. Mamachi and Cikara and Arthan and Karusa and Hayami and Skylar all danced in her head, but more than that, there was Aashi. Aashi who she had failed. Aashi who had died in the first wave of a genocide.

Now humans were facing a genocide. Things had come full circle, only this time, the Gadan weren't the victims, they were the monsters come down from the sky to end all life. And Hayami...Hayami was trying to do what Jakari hadn't been able to do. She was trying to hold back the tide of death.

Hayami was the person Jakari wished she had been. Someone who could stand up and fight back when it still mattered instead of waiting until it was too late, and all that was left was revenge.

Jakari turned her head slightly as she caught the sound of footsteps in the corridor leading to the cockpit. She relaxed a moment later when she realized who it was.

"Hey," Dubari said as they stepped into the cockpit. "You okay?"

"I just want this mission to be over," Jakari said. "I don't like this world."

"That's not the impression I got," Dubari said.

"What?"

"You seem to like your new partner well enough."

"Are you jealous?" Jakari asked.

Dubari scoffed. "Of a human?" they asked. "Don't be ridiculous."

"I just don't want to see any humans get killed," Jakari said. "They're innocent."

"Hardly," Dubari said. "Have you read any of their history?"

"It doesn't matter," Jakari said. "They have no part in our war. They never hurt us, never threatened us, didn't even know we existed before Mamachi arrived. They don't deserve to die just because the Gadan can't get our shit together."

"Agreed," Dubari said as they dropped down into the copilot's chair. "I heard you arranged a talk with Cikara."

"Yeah," Jakari said.

"Why?" Dubari asked.

"Because something about this doesn't feel right," Jakari said.

Dubari stared at her for a minute. "Look, Jakari, you know I'm usually willing to follow your lead, but we cannot go off book on this one. We have a shot at a member of the Triumvirate."

"I know," Jakari said. "And I'm not planning to go off book, but you can't tell me that something about this doesn't feel off to you."

"You're right," Dubari said. "I don't know Cikara as well as you. I didn't fight with them during the rebellion, but from what I do know of them, going after someone's parents isn't really their style."

"It's not. Cikara is more direct. Sending Ghuma and Birat after Hayami is absolutely something they would do, but going after Hayami's parents isn't something they would think of."

"You think someone else is pulling the strings?" Dubari asked.

"Maybe," Jakari asked. "That's why I scheduled the talk. I owe Cikara for what they did on Cruthanna. That's worth at least asking them what the hell is going on."

"You don't owe Cikara shit," Dubari said.

"I disagree," Jakari said. "But don't worry. That won't stop me from killing them."

"Good," Dubari said. "Because as much as I trust you, we absolutely cannot go off book on this one. Killing a Triumvirate member could turn the tide of the war."

"I know," Jakari said.

"Do you?" Dubari asked.

"Better than you," Jakari snapped. "I'm not the one forgetting that the Char rule more than a hundred worlds. I'm not the one who thinks killing the Triumvirate will solve all our problems. And I'm definitely not the one who has my nose so far up Arthan's ass that I can see the back of his teeth."

Dubari flinched and held up their hands. "Easy," they said.

"You're the one who pushed," Jakari said.

"Yeah, I am," Dubari said. "But you've been off your game ever since we got here."

"I'm not off my game," Jakari said. "I'm tired. I'm tired of wondering which old friend I'm going to be sent to kill today. I'm tired of living out of this fucking ship. I'm tired of a war neither side seems to want to end. I'm tired of looking in the mirror and seeing someone who would have been better off if they'd died along with their wife."

"Fuck," Dubari said. "That's a lot. Are you sure you're up for this?"

"I'll be fine," Jakari said. "I'm fine right now, and I'll be fine once we finish this mission and get off this world. I'm always fine."

Dubari nodded. "Maybe, once this is over, you should take a break."

"And do what?" Jakari asked. "I'm not going to get any younger. I'm ten thousand years old. People aren't meant to live that long." She leaned back in her chair and closed her eyes. "Sometimes I wonder if that's why the war has lasted so long. The people in charge just won't fucking die."

"Maybe," Dubari said. "But maybes don't matter. We can only live with the world we have."

"Yeah," Jakari said.

"Just promise me you won't try to get yourself killed," Dubari said.

"I won't," Jakari said. "At this point, surviving is a bad habit, and I don't know how to kick it."

Dubari reached out and squeezed her shoulder. "I know you may not want to hear this, but a lot of people care about you."

"They shouldn't," Jakari said.

"You're wrong about that," Dubari said. "Go get some rest. The sooner we get this mission wrapped, the sooner we get off this shit hole planet."

"I think I'll just sleep here," Jakari said.

"You're sure?" Dubari said.

"Yeah," Jakari said.

"Okay," Dubari said. "Just...comm me if you need anything."

"Sure," Jakari said.

She listened as they got up and headed for the corridor that led to the rest of the ship. They hesitated a moment at the door, but left without another word.

Jakari was asleep before they were completely out of earshot.

* * * *

Hayami lay on the bunk in the quarters she'd been assigned and stared up at the ceiling. The only light in the room was what leaked in under the door from the hallway outside. It wasn't really enough to make out any detail, but then, the ceiling was nothing more than white sheetrock, so it wasn't like she was missing much.

She wished she could sleep, but she couldn't. She kept turning the conversation from earlier in the evening over in her head. The more she learned about Jakari, the more she worried. Jakari was the lynchpin in their plan to stop the Char from turning humanity into mindless robot slaves. And how weird had her life become that that was something she legitimately had to worry about?

The problem was, the more she learned about Jakari, the more she realized that Jakari was a deeply broken person. She'd obviously never really recovered from the death of her wife. She'd been thrust into a horrible, brutal war for survival, and when it was over, she'd been tossed into the middle of an unending civil war and driven off her homeworld. She'd spent thousands of years killing on command for a man who sounded like he was losing his grip on sanity, and then she'd had to kill her... niece/nephew/whatever the gender-neutral term for that was. On top of all of that, she couldn't reach out for help because she couldn't trust a therapist not to turn her in for being angry at the person that she blamed for Karusa's death.

It was too much for anyone, and it was clear to Hayami that Jakari blamed herself for all of it. For the death of her wife, for the things she'd done during the occupation and the civil war, for Karusa's death. She wondered if Jakari even blamed herself for what was happening on

Earth since she didn't kill Cikara when she had the chance all those years ago.

She hadn't missed that Mamachi had a lot of the same issues, but at least Mamachi seemed to have found someone to talk to. Someone who cared about them enough to help. Jakari didn't have a Skylar. She had Dubari, but for whatever reason, Dubari seemed distant, and Hayami got the impression that Jakari didn't quite trust them.

Someone needed to do something. Too much was riding on Jakari. The problem was, no one seemed willing to do anything about it, which just left her. The absolute worst choice in the world. She didn't help people. Not like this. She could solve a murder or a robbery or find a missing person or bring down a trafficking ring, but help someone having mental health issues? She was definitely the wrong person for the job.

The problem was, no one else seemed willing to step up, so she had to try. Otherwise, a whole lot of people were going to die. Maybe everyone. She couldn't let that happen.

Chapter Fourteen

HAYAMI GOT TO THE conference room about half an hour early the next morning, carrying a tray filled with coffee and bacon maple glazed donuts. She expected to find Jakari there, hoping they could talk for a bit before Mamachi and Skylar arrived and they had to get to work, but Jakari was nowhere to be found. Instead, Dubari sat in the room, looking over maps with a frustrated expression.

"Hey," she said.

Dubari looked up from the maps and smiled as soon as they saw the tray. "Hey," they said. "Are those more of those bacon donut things?"

"Yeah," Hayami said. "Two for you and two for Jakari. I would have brought coffee for you, but I wasn't sure how you like yours, and I figured it would be cold by the time you got here anyway."

"That's okay," Dubari said. "I appreciate the thought, but I don't care for coffee." They held up a large paper cup. "I prefer tea."

"Noted," Hayami said. She set the tray down on the table and took a seat. "Where's Jakari?"

"Probably still sleeping," Dubari said as they took two of the donuts from the tray. "She was pretty worn out last night."

"You saw her last night?"

"Yeah," Dubari said. "She racked out on the Bramble."

"The what?"

"Oh, um, sorry. Our ship. Well, her ship, really. The Sabuja Bramble. I have an alarm set if anyone boards her. It went off last night and I went to check it out, but it was just Jakari. She said she was going to sleep there."

"Does she do that often?" Hayami said.

"Yeah. Honestly, we live out of the ship a lot. Having quarters assigned is kind of a rarity. But Jakari's been living on the Bramble since we were driven off Cruthanna. I think she sleeps there because after a few thousand years, it feels like home."

Hayami nodded and took a sip from her coffee. "How long have the two of you been partners?"

"Hard to say," Dubari said. "We worked together a few times during the occupation, and on and off through the civil war. More on than off, honestly, but both of us take individual missions sometimes. Arthan likes to keep us together."

"Why's that?" Hayami said. "I'd think if you were both so effective, he'd want to give you new partners to train."

Dubari took a bite of one of the donuts and chewed it slowly. Hayami suspected they were either trying to decide if they wanted to answer or trying to figure out how to phrase the answer, so she just took a sip of her coffee and waited.

"He keeps us together because I'm good at keeping Jakari on task," Dubari said after they swallowed the bite of donut. "Don't get me wrong. Jakari is really good at her work, but sometimes she can get distracted."

"Distracted?"

"Sometimes, she will pick a different target than the one assigned if she thinks taking out someone different will do more to accomplish the mission objective. It pisses off Headquarters."

"Is that why you're on this mission? To make sure she doesn't get distracted?" Hayami asked.

"I'm on this mission because Cikara is the highest value target we've ever been assigned. Taking them out might actually break the stalemate we've been in."

"Cikara's really that important?"

"Cikara's their chief weapon designer," Dubari said. "On top of that, Cikara's got the best head for strategy of all of the Triumvirate. Jaya's more aggressive, but that makes them more prone to mistakes. Cikara's the one who reins Jaya in most of the time. Without them, Jaya would probably run the Char military into the ground."

"And I'm guessing that wouldn't be a good thing."

"Yeah," Dubari said. "I owe you an apology, by the way."

"For what?"

"For yesterday. I know it probably sounded cold, what I said. It's just, between the Gadan colony worlds and the Suil's alien allies, there are more than two hundred worlds directly involved in the war, and another thousand that would be threatened by Char expansion if they won. On that scale, trading a city for a chance to take out a target as important as Cikara is something we'd accept, but humans aren't used to thinking on that scale. Losing a city for you would be more like losing a planet for us. I didn't take that into account, and I'm sorry."

Hayami nodded. "I appreciate the apology," she said. "I just hope you understand that blowing up Dallas isn't an option."

"Yeah," Dubari said. "But we still need to find Cikara."

"We will," Hayami said.

"I hope so," Dubari said. "Because if we can't, the humans and the Suil are both in a hell of a lot of trouble."

* * * *

Hayami stepped into the cockpit of the ship and had to stop for a moment, frowning slightly at the oppressive heat that filled the room. The rest of the ship had been a relatively moderate temperature, but the bridge felt like the early part of a Texas summer. It had to be at least ninety degrees. She was just thankful it lacked the God-awful humidity of Dallas in the summer.

The ship wasn't what she'd expected. Everything was a shiny white and brightly lit. It wasn't like the ship she'd been in the day before at all. She had no idea why the two ships were so different, but she filed the question away for another day and took in the cockpit. It was a bit odd. There was one chair off to one side, but where you would expect a second chair, there was what looked like a large bowl on a pedestal, with some kind of red lamp above it.

She didn't see Jakari at all, but Dubari had insisted she'd be sleeping in the cockpit, so Hayami had followed the indicators in her HUD and been led here. She stepped into the cockpit, and she heard a soft wheezing sound coming from the bowl, and as she got close enough to see inside, she spotted what could only be Jakari in her natural form. An anthropomorphic cat with no hair, covered in purple and silver scales. She was curled up in a ball, the tops of her back paws pressed against her nose, and her tail wrapped around the top of her head. Her hands were hooked behind the backwards-bent lower knees of her legs, and she let out a wheeze every time her chest rose and fell.

The heat in the cockpit was coming from the red light hanging down above her, and Hayami had to laugh as she realized what she was looking at. It was a combination of a cat curled up in a sunbeam, and a lizard sunning itself on a rock. It was adorable, and Hayami hated the idea of waking her up. Especially since Gadan apparently slept naked. But Jakari was already half an hour late for work, and had slept through every comm call they'd made, so Hayami didn't have much choice.

"Jakari," she said.

Jakari twitched an ear and tightened her grip on her legs, curling into a slightly smaller ball.

"Jakari," Hayami said again.

Jakari growled.

"Jakari."

Jakari reached up with her hand and rubbed her ear while letting out a low grumbling sound.

"Jakari," Hayami said a little louder.

Jakari finally opened her eyes. She looked up for a moment and let out a loud, scolding chitter before closing her eyes.

"Jakari, you're late."

Jakari opened one eye and looked at her for a minute, then huffed and closed her eye again. Hayami got ready to try one more time before she broke out the drill sergeant voice, but Jakari rolled onto her back and stretched. Arms above her head, legs all the way out, somehow even stretching her tail. Hayami could see the muscles rippling under the skin, and with the way Jakari leaned this way and that, she couldn't stop herself.

"Ooh. Big stretch!" she said.

Jakari opened her eye and glared for a minute before she let out another chittering sound. The heat lamp quickly melted up into the ceiling while the bowl morphed into a chair. Jakari stood up and gave one more stretch before her whole body shifted into graphite and quickly reshaped itself, assuming the human shape Hayami was familiar with, complete with clothes and boots. The graphite color vanished, leaving Jakari looking like a perfectly normal, if unfairly attractive woman.

"What time is it?" Jakari asked.

"About 9:40 AM," Hayami said.

"Damn," Jakari said. "I'm sorry."

"It's okay. It looks like you needed the sleep." Hayami tipped her head towards the corridor. "Come on. Mamachi, Dubari, and Skylar are waiting."

Jakari nodded and followed as Hayami led the way.

"Do you always revert to your natural form when you sleep?" she asked.

"No," Jakari said. "I just got cold in the night, and I wasn't sure a human form could stand up to a bask lamp."

"Probably not," Hayami said. "Were your people cold blooded before the Migration?"

"No," Jakari said. "We were mesotherms. Sort of in between cold-blooded and warm-blooded. We can produce internal heat if we need to, but Cruthanna is a lot warmer than most worlds, so we normally just relied on ambient heat. Have you guys made any progress?"

"Not really," Hayami said. "We couldn't find the topographical maps, so we're doing a satellite imagery comparison to see if we can find any changes in the landscape, but it's slow going, and we can't be sure one way or the other."

"Well, if worse comes to worse, I'll figure out something when I talk to Cikara tomorrow."

"You think they'll give away the location of their base?"

"No," Jakari said. "Cikara is many things, but stupid isn't one of them. Something is going on here that we don't know about, and I'm hoping that talking to them will give me a clue as to what it is."

"Okay," Hayami said. Her earlier conversation with Dubari came back to her, and she wondered if Dubari was right about Jakari losing sight of the target. She didn't say anything, but she decided she would keep an eye on her and do her best to help keep her on target.

* * * *

"Okay, seriously, there has got to be a better way to do this," Hayami said as she dropped the tablet she'd been staring at on the table.

"We're open to suggestions," Jakari said. "But so far, the computer hasn't been able to locate even a single candidate by comparing the satellite images, and neither have any of us."

Hayami looked down at the tablet again. It was two pictures of the same empty patch of land taken five years apart. The image on the left was taken before the Char ship landed. The image on the right was taken after. There was virtually no difference, just like the hundreds of other images she'd compared that morning.

How the hell do you hide a ship that big? The Suil had apparently done it by building a military base on top of it, but the Char didn't have the same option. It wasn't like they could just bury a ship and build a town on top of it over...

"We're looking in the wrong place!" Hayami said.

"What?" Jakari asked.

Hayami turned to Mamachi. "How long did it take you to bury Napati's ship?"

"A few hours," Mamachi said. "The military had cleared the land in advance. They shipped in a bunch of prefab buildings and put them up around the perimeter so anyone watching would see the construction and not get suspicious. The ship came in under cloak and used tractor beams to dig out the hole. Then it landed, and a handful of shuttles and drop ships did the backfill, tamped it down, and loaded the excess dirt into dump trucks."

"And the buildings on top of the ship? They're all made of TOP matter, aren't they?" Hayami asked.

"Yes," Mamachi said.

"How many abandoned towns are there around Dallas?" Hayami asked.

"Not a lot," Mamachi said.

"No, but there are some," Hayami said. "Skylar, get on Google. Get a list of ghost towns within a five-hour drive of Dallas."

"On it," Skylar said.

"Mamachi, once she has that, we're going to need satellite imagery."

"Okay," Mamachi said.

She looked over at Jakari, who was staring at her with a look on her face she didn't quite understand.

"What is it?" she asked.

"You cracked it," Jakari said.

"Maybe," Hayami said. "We'll see."

* * * *

"There it is," Skylar said. "Thurber. An old coal mining town."

"Makes sense," Mamachi said. "They could collapse the upper levels of the mines to make room for the ship, then recreate the ruins out of TOP matter."

Hayami stared at the image up on the large display on the wall. It was easy to see the outline of the ship. A large, circular ring where the ruins of the town were disrupted. It stood out clear as day, once you knew what you were looking for. An alien flying saucer, ten kilometers across, that could spell the extinction of the human race.

"We've got the bastards," Dubari said.

"Yeah," Jakari said.

"So, what do we do now?" Hayami asked.

"I still want to talk to Cikara," Jakari said. "Something about this whole thing still feels off."

"But we've got them," Dubari said. "We could go in tonight, take Cikara out, destroy the research, and be on the way home by tomorrow morning."

"We could," Jakari began, "but like I said, something feels off. My gut tells me there's more going on here than we know."

"We should probably run this by Napati," Mamachi said.

Jakari looked over at them and nodded. "Agreed."

* * * *

Vrusti watched from the side of the road as the Army truck approached and waited patiently. As soon as it came to a stop, they bolted, rushing across the space between the road and the bushes where they had been hiding as fast as the cat form body would carry them. They jumped and landed on the bumper, then jumped again, scrambling over the tailgate of the truck and into the cargo bed.

There wasn't a lot of room in the back of the truck, but that didn't bother them at all. They were used to getting into and out of tight places. It was their specialty. They wiggled into a spot near the wheel well and waited as the truck turned down the road to the nearby military base.

The truck stopped a couple of minutes later, and Vrusti listened as the driver showed the guards their ID and orders. The guards did a quick inspection of the truck, checking the underside with mirrors, looking for tracking devices and bombs. They even checked in the bed briefly, but the wheel well hid Vrusti from view. Then, the guards waved the truck through. Vrusti waited a couple of minutes, then moved. They poked their head up over the tailgate to make sure the guard post couldn't see them, then waited until they reached the buildings that made up the base. A quick jump and they were on the ground and headed for one of the hangars.

* * * *

"This is good work," Napati said.

"Agreed," Gomez said.

Jakari looked back and forth between them, trying not to roll her eyes. She knew it was good work. In fact, it was amazing work. She didn't think they would have ever found the ship without Hayami's help. Or at least, it would have taken weeks longer. That wasn't really the question.

"What about my timetable?" Jakari asked.

"I would rather attack as soon as possible," Napati said.

"I understand, and all things being equal, I would agree with you," Jakari said. "But my gut is telling me that something is off about Cikara's behavior. I'm not sure I'll be able to figure it out from one conversation, but I don't want to walk our forces into a trap. All I'm asking for is one more day."

Gomez looked at Napati. "It's your call. You know Jakari better than I do, but from what I've seen, her instincts are pretty good. And if we're really talking about going up against the entire Char force, an extra day to prepare couldn't hurt."

"Agreed," Napati said. "For now, we'll plan on assaulting the Char ship tomorrow night, with the understanding that the timetable may change based on the outcome of Jakari's conversation with Cikara tomorrow afternoon."

"Thank you," Jakari said. She looked around the table, taking in everyone's expression. Dubari didn't look happy, but that might have had more to do with being in the room with Prack than Napati's decision. Prack looked more interested in talking to Dubari than planning an assault. Mamachi, Skylar, Gomez, and Hayami all looked satisfied, while Rayak was his usual grumpy self.

"Okay," Jakari said. "I'll decide on my infiltration team and have it ready by tomorrow morning."

"Excellent," Napati said. "Prack, I'll want your assault plan by then as well."

"Understood," Prack said.

"Then we're done here," Napati said. "Dismissed."

"Dubari," Prack said, "could I have a moment?"

"I need to help Jakari plan the infiltration," Dubari said.

"It's fine," Jakari said. "You can have a few minutes."

Dubari turned and glared at her, but Jakari just shrugged.

"Talk to your dad," she said. "It won't kill you."

Dubari huffed and turned to Prack. "Lead the way."

Jakari turned and headed out of the conference room with Hayami, Mamachi, and Skylar in tow.

"What was that about?" Hayami asked.

"Family squabble," Jakari said. "Dubari's Prack's kid, but they've been fighting."

"For how long?" Hayami asked.

"I don't know. Mamachi, do you remember when Dubari caught Prack with Hamadri?"

"Been about a hundred years," Mamachi said.

"Dubari is mad because they caught their dad having sex?" Skylar asked.

"No, Dubari is mad because they caught their dad having sex with someone other than their mother," Jakari said. "Which would have been justified, if their mother hadn't known about it and been sleeping with Hamadri too."

"Oh," Hayami said.

"Yeah," Jakari said. "Dubari's been a real ass about the whole thing. Won't talk to Prack, won't talk to Charvi, sure as hell won't talk to Hamadri, which makes things really awkward now that Prack, Charvi, and Hamadri are all married."

"I could see that making holiday dinners a bit rough," Hayami said. "But isn't Dubari almost ten thousand years old?"

"Yeah," Jakari said. "Which makes the whole thing ridiculous."

"I would imagine monogamy would be a hard thing to maintain when you live that long," Hayami said.

Jakari shrugged. "I wouldn't know," she said. "My last serious relationship was with my wife."

"That's a long time to be alone," Hayami said.

Jakari looked at Hayami. "Yeah, it is," she said.

"Don't you ever get lonely?" Hayami asked.

Jakari shrugged and turned away, not wanting to answer. Fortunately, Hayami didn't press.

* * * *

Vrusti ducked into the hangar on the edge of the airfield and looked up, smiling the best they could in their cat form as they stared at the Suil transport. The round disc of a ship that was definitely not built by human hands. They activated their comm as they ducked behind a few crates, finding a good hiding spot.

"What's the word?" Ghuma asked.

"It's definitely the Suil base," Vrusti replied.

"Excellent," Ghuma said.

"Should I exfiltrate?"

"No. Stay there. The boss might want more intel."

"Understood."

* * * *

Cikara accepted the comm request from Ghuma and leaned back in their chair. "Report."

"We've found it," Ghuma said.

"Excellent," Cikara said. "Who else knows?"

"Just you, me, Birat, and Vrusti."

"Send me the coordinates and keep it that way," Cikara said.

"Understood," Ghuma said.

The coordinates came through and Cikara cut the comm link, then they commed Bayadani.

"Yes, General?" Bayadani asked.

"Begin preparations to move the ship," Cikara said.

"How soon?" Bayadani asked.

"Nothing is certain, but I want to be able to lift with no more than ten minutes notice by noon tomorrow."

"Understood," Bayadani said. "And what should I tell Nira if she asks?"

"Tell her it's a precaution," Cikara said. "Nothing more."

"Yes, General," Bayadani said.

Cikara cut the comm line and closed their eyes. Nira would insist on attacking Napati's forces directly, which would be a foolish move. Dreadnought versus dreadnought combat was always messy under the best of circumstances, and the Suil would have the humans backing them up. Better to cut and run if it came to it. Park somewhere in the atmosphere and let the cloaking device hide them, but Nira wouldn't see it that way. She was almost as much of an attack dog as Jaya.

Cikara stared at the wall in front of them, turning the entire situation over in their head. Their options were narrowing. They were going to have to kill Nira soon, or Nira was going to move against them. They were sure the only thing Nira was waiting for was for Cikara to finish the Helot technology. As soon as they did, Nira would end them, and they couldn't let that happen. The entire future of the Gadan depended on it.

The wild card was Jakari. Cikara wasn't sure why they wanted to talk, but it might just be enough to turn a messy situation into a shot at a clean victory against Nira. They just needed to survive the day.

Chapter Fifteen

"HAYAMI, WAIT," JAKARI SAID as Hayami was on her way out of the conference room where they'd spent most of the day.

"Yes?" Hayami asked.

Jakari reached up and tapped her ear. "I just got a comm notice. Your parents are here. They've been taken to officer's housing. You could go see them now if you like."

"Thank you," Hayami said. "Um, can you show me where officer's housing is?"

"I can show you," Mamachi said. "That's—"

"No, you can't," Skylar said.

Mamachi turned to face her. "What?"

"We have to run into town. Remember?" The 'remember' was asked in a pointed tone that Jakari didn't seem to understand, but Mamachi apparently picked up on whatever the subtext was.

"Right," Mamachi said. "I forgot." They turned to Hayami. "Sorry."

"It's fine," Hayami said.

Before Mamachi could say anything else, Skylar pulled them out of the room.

"What was that about?" Dubari asked. Jakari was about to tell them she didn't know, but Hayami beat her to it.

"Human thing," Hayami said. "Don't worry about it. Jakari?"

"Right," Jakari said. She stood up and grabbed her empty coffee cup, dropping it in the trash on the way to the door.

"Are you going to sleep on the Bramble again tonight?" Dubari asked.

"I don't think so, but if I do, I'll comm you and save you the trip," Jakari said.

Dubari nodded. "See you in the morning."

Jakari gave them a small nod before she led Hayami out of the conference room and towards the officers' quarters.

"You know the officer's quarters is where Mamachi's room is," Jakari said.

"I know," Hayami said, "but this way, I get to drag you to meet my parents."

Jakari looked over at Hayami. "Any particular reason you want me to meet them?" she asked.

"My mom likes to meet all my friends," Hayami said. "Wants to make sure I'm not hanging around the wrong kind of people."

"And you want to introduce her to me?" Jakari asked. "Because I'm pretty sure I'm the definition of 'the wrong kind of people.'"

"I don't know," Hayami said. "So far, you've saved my life twice, kept the fight at the police station from turning into a bloodbath, and you're trying to save the world."

"I'm an assassin," Jakari said.

"Maybe don't lead with that when I introduce you to Mom," Hayami said.

Jakari shrugged. "I still think this is a bad idea."

"But you're still coming with me," Hayami said.

"You asked me to," Jakari said.

"And that's all it takes?"

"Depending on what you're asking," Jakari said. "If you want me to kill someone, I'd want to know why."

"Maybe don't offer to kill anyone while we're talking to my parents either."

"This is a bad idea," Jakari said.

"Maybe," Hayami said, "but when was the last time you did something that wasn't about the war?"

Jakari thought about it for a minute and frowned at the answer she came up with. "Thirty years, give or take."

"Tell me about it," Hayami said.

"It was the last time I saw Mamachi before coming here," Jakari said. "I was between assignments, and Napati's unit was stationed on Bailenua."

"That's Mamachi's home planet, isn't it?"

"Yeah," Jakari said. "It's the oldest of the colonies, and the biggest. It's the Suil capital. Arthan likes to keep Napati there so he can keep an eye on her. I dropped by to visit Mamachi, and they took me to the Santipurna botanical gardens."

"Did you have a good time?" Hayami asked.

Jakari shook her head. "No."

"Why not?" Hayami asked.

"I kept thinking about Aashi," Jakari said. "How much she would have loved it there. How much she would have liked Mamachi. How many wonderful, beautiful things I never got to share with her."

"I'm sorry," Hayami said.

Jakari shrugged and didn't say anything else until they reached the quarters that had been assigned to Hayami's parents.

"This is it," she said as she showed her ID to one of the guards by the door. "You sure you want me to come in?"

"Yeah," Hayami said as she raised her hand and knocked. They waited in silence until the door opened and a tall woman with dark reddish-brown skin and black, short-cut, tightly-curled hair greeted them. She was dressed in a knee-length white dress with green and gold embroidery around the neck and down the middle of the front, and she wore a gold pendant with a smooth white stone set in the middle.

"Hey, Mom," Hayami said.

"Sweetheart!" her mom said, and pulled Hayami into a hug so tight Hayami's feet left the ground. "I've been so worried about you."

Hayami hugged her back. "I've been worried about you too," she said as her mom set her down. "Where's Dad?"

"I'm right here," a man's voice said from inside the quarters. A moment later, a short man with sallow skin, a long, wide face, big eyes and straight, gray hair appeared. Hayami let go of her mother and pulled him into a hug just as fierce as the one her mother had given her.

"Hey, Dad," she said.

"How's my baby girl?" he asked.

"I'm good. I'm just glad you're both okay." She set her dad down and let him go.

"Us?" Hayami's mom asked. "We've been at a safehouse. What about you?"

"Let's go inside and I'll tell you what I can," Hayami said.

"Come on then," her mom said, stepping back to make room. Hayami stepped inside, and Jakari followed. She gave both of Hayami's parents a small nod as she stepped inside, and got curious looks in return, but neither one said anything until the door was closed.

"Can I get you or your friend something to drink?" Hayami's mom asked. "There's not much, just bottled water and some instant coffee, but you're welcome to it."

"A bottle of water would be great," Jakari said.

"Sweetheart?"

"Please," Hayami said.

Hayami's mother disappeared into the small kitchen while her father led them over to the seating area in the living room.

"Please, have a seat," he said.

Jakari took one of the armchairs and Hayami took the other, and by the time they were seated, her mother had reappeared carrying four bottles of water.

"Thank you," Jakari said as she took hers. She opened it and took a sip while Hayami's parents settled themselves on the couch.

"Mom, Dad," Hayami said, "this is Special Agent Jack Arias of the Department of Homeland Security. Jack, this is my mother, Nyala King, and my father, Hikaru Takahashi."

"Pleased to meet you both," Jakari said.

"Homeland Security?" Nyala asked.

"Yes, ma'am," Jakari said.

Nyala turned to Hayami. "Sweetheart, what's going on? Men from DHS showed up the other night and rushed us out of the house without even letting us pack."

"I'm sorry," Hayami said. "That's my fault."

"What happened?"

"You both know I was working the disappearances downtown, right?" Hayami asked. Both of her parents nodded. "The night DHS showed up at your house, I was downtown working the case. I didn't know that the DHS was working it from a different angle, and I walked into the middle of a sting. It's been all over the news that the disappearances are related to the terrorist attack on DPD headquarters. What hasn't been in the news is that they were there looking for me. When I messed up the sting, they managed to get a picture of my face, and from there, they were able to get everything about me. My name, my home address, your information. DHS took you into protective custody to make sure they couldn't get to me through you."

"So what's going to happen?" Hikaru asked. "Are we going to have to go into Witness Protection or something?"

"We hope not," Jakari said. "We're trying to end this as quickly as possible. Your daughter has been a tremendous help in that regard."

"She has?" Nyala asked.

"Gee, Mom. You don't have to sound so surprised."

"It's not that, sweetheart," Nyala said. She looked Jakari over. "I'm just surprised to hear a Federal Agent give a local cop so much credit. Aren't you the one who says they're all glory hounds?"

"*Mom*," Hayami groaned.

Jakari laughed at the pained tone in Hayami's voice. "I can't speak for other federal agents, but I'm really glad to have your daughter on the team. I can't go into details, but I can tell you that she gave us one of the biggest leads we've had in the case in years."

"That's high praise," Nyala said. "How did you and Hayami meet?"

"She walked into the middle of my sting," Jakari said. "I was annoyed at the time, but it's hard to stay that way when someone is trying to save your life."

"It's hard to stay annoyed at Hayami in general," Nyala said. "She always has the best of intentions."

"Mom, stop," Hayami said.

"It's true," Hikaru said. "One time, I came home from work and found her in the garage with three litters of stray puppies. She'd brought them and their mothers home and spent her whole allowance for the month on heating pads and dog food."

"It took us forever to find homes for all of them," Nyala said.

"Almost all of them," Hikaru said. "We ended up keeping her two favorites."

"She named them Eliza and Goliath after some cartoon she liked," Nyala said.

Jakari smiled and looked over at Hayami, whose cheeks had turned bright red. "That reminds me of my wife," she said. "She was always feeding strays that wandered into our garden."

"You're married?" Nyala asked.

"Oh, um...I was," Jakari said. "She died."

"I'm sorry," Nyala said.

"It's okay," Jakari said. "I shouldn't have brought her up."

"Oh, no," Nyala said. "No. Dear, you shouldn't feel that way. You need to remember the people you've lost."

Jakari looked down. "She's been on my mind the last few days."

"How long ago did you lose her?"

"Mom, don't," Hayami said.

"It's okay," Jakari said. She looked up at Nyala. "Somedays, it seems like ten thousand years and I can feel every second of it, and somedays, I wake up wondering why she isn't next to me."

"It sounds like you really loved her," Nyala said.

"I did," Jakari said.

"Was she a cop like you?"

Jakari laughed and shook her head. "No. No, I couldn't imagine anyone who was less like a cop than Aashi. She was a preschool teacher."

"How did you two meet?" Nyala asked.

"We were at a party to celebrate the new year," Jakari said. "It was like fate. I'd wanted to stay home, but my best friend dragged me down to the town square. I'd been there ten minutes when I heard this laugh. It was like music, and I turned towards the sound, and when I saw her, she took my breath away. I spent the whole night talking to her, trying to convince her to let me take her on a date, and she finally agreed. My friend never let me forget it, either. He made a speech at our wedding about how I'd abandoned him the moment I saw her. I couldn't even argue with him, because it was true."

"Love at first sight," Nyala said. She nodded towards Hayami. "This one thinks it's a silly notion."

"I'd probably agree with her most days, but that night was something special," Jakari said. She took a deep breath. "I should go and let you both spend some time with your daughter."

"Oh, no. You don't have to leave."

"It's okay," Jakari said as she stood up. "It's been lovely meeting both of you, and I'm glad you're safe. We'll do our best to make sure you can go home as quickly as possible."

"I'll see you out," Hayami said. Jakari gave her a small nod and headed for the door. When they reached it, Hayami put her hand on the knob before Jakari could open it. "Are you okay?"

"Yeah," Jakari said. "I'm fine. Really. Go spend some time with your parents."

"Okay," Hayami said. "But if you need someone to talk to…"

Jakari nodded. "Thanks."

Hayami opened the door and Jakari slipped out of the room. She glanced back at the sound of the door closing and wondered for a moment if she'd made a mistake. If maybe she should have stayed. It didn't really matter; it was too late to change her mind, so she headed for her own quarters, hoping she could get some rest.

* * * *

"Really, Mom?" Hayami said as she walked back into the living room.

"What?" Nyala asked.

"She's here for five minutes and you have her talking about her dead wife!"

"She brought it up," Nyala said. "What? Am I a mind reader? She mentions a wife, and I'm just supposed to know the wife is dead?"

Hayami huffed as she dropped back into her chair. "No," she grumbled. "I just...God, I don't even know."

"She seems nice," Nyala said.

"Don't start!" Hayami said.

"What? I can't make an observation now?"

"No," Hayami said. "Not when you can't even see me talking to a woman without starting the wedding plans."

"Now you're just being ridiculous," Nyala said.

"Dad, help me out here," Hayami said.

"Leave me out of this," Hikaru said. "I learned my lesson about you and your girlfriends with that one girl...what was her name? Chiffon, Chevron..."

"Siobhan," Hayami said.

"Right," Hikaru said. "The one that smelled like pot."

"That was patchouli," Hayami said.

"It was cheap pot," Hikaru said. "The patchouli was just to cover it up."

Hayami rolled her eyes. It was an old argument, and she hated it because her dad was right. Siobhan had been a stoner, which was why Hayami dumped her.

"Are you okay, sweetheart?" Nyala asked.

"No," Hayami said. "How the hell am I supposed to be okay? Someone walked into the station and tried to kill me, someone tried to kidnap the two of you to get to me, the woman I'm working with is a god-damned basket case, and the case I'm working is absolutely terrifying, so no, I'm not okay!"

"Come here, Musume," her dad said. Hayami got up and stomped over to the couch and dropped down next to him. He reached up and pulled her into a hug, resting her head on his shoulder the way she used to when she was a little girl.

"You know your mom loves you," he said.

"I know," Hayami said.

"You know I love you."

"I know."

"Your friend seems like she knows what she's doing."

"She does," Hayami said. "She's been doing it a long time, and everyone says she's the best at it."

"But you're worried."

"I'm worried about her," Hayami said. "This case is personal for her for a lot of reasons."

"You think she can't handle it?"

"I think she'll solve the case," Hayami said. "But I'm worried about how she'll handle the fallout. She's a good person, but the job is hard on people, and it's been harder on her than most."

"You care about her," Nyala said.

"Yeah," Hayami said. "She saved my life the night we met. She goes out of her way to take care of people, but no one seems to bother taking care of her, and I hate it."

"You never could stand to see anyone hurting," Hikaru said. "That's why I didn't want you to be a cop."

"Not all of us are cut out to be doctors," Hayami said. "And some of us are definitely not cut out to run a clothing store."

"Like I'd ask you," Nyala said. "You'd spend all day hitting on my customers."

"I'm not that bad," Hayami grumbled.

"Yes, you are," her dad said.

She glared up at him.

"Do I have to bring up the one with the spiked hair? Edna, Eta..."

"Electra," Nyala said.

"That's the one."

"No," Hayami said. "Electra was the one with the nose ring. Echo was the one with the spiked hair."

"You're making your dad's point for him, sweetheart."

"You do remember I'm the one who's going to pick out your nursing home, right?"

* * * *

Vrusti sat on the roof of one of the hangars, their cat form abandoned in favor of a large local bird that was just as black as the cat. This particular variety seemed particularly intelligent. They'd even heard it speaking some of the human language to one of the humans who had come out to feed them. Vrusti had watched from a distance, not quite trusting themselves to fool the human on their first outing in this form.

Besides, they were much more interested in keeping an eye on the building where some of the humans slept. The officers' quarters, which held a prize they hoped would earn them a reward. They had been watching since the prize arrived late in the afternoon, not moving or making a sound lest they attract unwanted attention. The sun had set, night had come and gone, and the sun had come up again before the prize reappeared.

Two people. The human female's parents were escorted out of the building around 10:00 AM and put in the back of an SUV. Once Vrusti was sure the SUV was headed away from the base, they leapt into the air, flying in a straight line for the front gate and then circling until they saw the SUV pass through and get out on the main road. They followed until the SUV was out of sight of the base, then dove, their leg flowing and rippling as a small disk formed in their talon. They swept over the top of the SUV and with a feather light touch, they planted the tracking device before beating their wings and lifting away. Once they were clear of the SUV, they activated their comms.

"Vrusti to Ghuma," they said. "I have good news."

Chapter Sixteen

WHEN THE TIME FOR the comm call with Cikara came, they had to move to a larger conference room. In addition to Jakari; Hayami, Dubari, Mamachi, and Skylar; Napati, Prack, Gomez, Rayak, and Napati's tech specialist Dhom were all piled in and sitting around the table. All of them had strict instructions not to speak, and Dhom had set up an AI filter to remove anything any of them might say, just to be on the safe side.

Jakari would have much rather taken the call alone, but Napati had vetoed that idea fairly quickly when she'd suggested it. Gomez, Dubari, and Hayami hadn't looked thrilled with the idea either. It frustrated her, because she worked better alone. She always had. Even when she was working a mission with Dubari, they generally split the mission into individual tasks. Having someone jiggling her elbow while she was trying to conduct a delicate negotiation wasn't ideal, but she'd just have to deal with it.

When the time came, she reached out and put her hand on the access point on the table and opened the comm. A holoimage of a human form appeared in front of her. A young man with a triangular face, black hair, and delicate features. He was clean shaven and well-groomed and dressed in a black suit with a white shirt and a red tie. She knew enough to tell that he was attractive by human standards, though she still found the flatness of their faces a little weird.

"I am Cikara," the human form said.

"I am Jakari," she said.

"It's been a long time," Cikara said.

"Fifteen hundred years, give or take," Jakari said.

"Something like that. I don't think I asked at the time, but did you enjoy your tea?"

"I did. It's hard to get good Beguni tea out in the colonies."

"You should try the human's Raspberry tea," Cikara said. "It's a bit sweeter than Beguni, but I'm rather taken with it."

"I'll keep that in mind," Jakari said. "Though I don't expect to be on Earth very long."

"Just long enough to kill me," Cikara said.

"Just that long, yes," Jakari said.

"I wish I could say I didn't deserve it, but we both know I do. I did the last time we met, though that time I had something to buy my life with. How is Mamachi, by the way?"

"Alive and well," Jakari said. "As happy as any of us can manage."

"That's good to hear. I was glad that they escaped."

"But not happy to hear I escaped."

"If I told you I was, it would be a lie, and I don't want to lie to you. I'd prefer if you didn't lie to me, either."

"I think that's something we can agree on. No lies."

"Good," Cikara said. "That will make things easier."

"It usually does. So, why are you on Earth?"

"You don't know? That seems unlikely, unless Mamachi isn't as good at their job as they once were."

"I know about the Helot weapon system," Jakari said. "But I want to know why Earth? Why not some other planet? Earth isn't a part of our war, and you never had the same taste for slaughtering innocents that Jaya and Saka do."

"You give me more credit than I really deserve. I have just as much blood on my hands as they do on theirs."

"It's not a question of guilt, old friend. God knows, all of us have enough blood on our hands to fill a river, but there's a difference between being guilty of something and relishing it. You never enjoyed killing. Not even in the gladiator pits. Not the way some of us did."

"True enough. I just loved designing the guns and bombs all of you used to slaughter each other."

"I'm not a priest, Cikara. If you want to unburden your conscience, build a temple and light some incense. I just want to know why you picked Earth."

"I picked it because it's not a part of the war. It's a backwater. Jaya and Saka don't give a damn about it. I could blow it out of space and no one would flinch."

"You were looking for a place to work away from their oversight," Jakari said.

"Yes."

"Did you find it?"

"Yes and no," Cikara said. "They sent Nira with me."

All the Gadan at the table sat up a little straighter at that and started exchanging looks. Jakari tried to ignore it, but she could guess what they were all thinking. Nira was the unofficial fourth member of the Triumvirate. She was every bit as much a part of the entrenched power structure in the Char as Cikara. For Jaya to send her out here when Cikara was already going was damn near unbelievable.

"Are we sticking to the no lying agreement, old friend?" Jakari asked.

"Yes," Cikara said. They reached forward and did something outside of the holo-imager's pickup, and a second image appeared. This one static. A human form, a woman with a thick, ugly scar that ran from the upper right side of her face, down through her right eye, across her nose and down to her left jaw. Her right eye was clearly artificial, silver with a gold iris and a black pupil. Anyone who had ever seen it before would have recognized the scar and the artificial eye, and Jakari didn't doubt for one moment that she was seeing a human form of Nira.

"You're trying to buy your life again," Jakari said.

"Of course I am," Cikara said. "In my place, wouldn't you be trying to do the same?"

"As long as we worked together, you should know me better than that," Jakari said.

"I suppose I should," Cikara said. "But I always tend to forget that you don't actually care whether you live or die. It does make me wonder how you've managed to survive this long."

"It's a bad habit. One I never figured out how to kick."

"Well, Nira might be willing to help with that. If you're interested."

Jakari looked over at Napati, who had a torn look on their face, and felt a wave of annoyance. Napati was a good battlefield leader, but when it came to moments like this she always struggled, and Jakari didn't have time to wait.

"What are your terms?" Jakari asked.

"Nira's life in exchange for mine," Cikara said.

"No," Jakari said.

"No?"

"Nira and the weapon," Jakari said. "You want to live, no more Helots. You give us access to Nira, and once she's dead, you give us root access to your ship's computer so we can purge the Helot research. You agree not to redevelop the tech."

"No," Cikara said. "I can't do that."

"Why not?" Jakari asked.

"Because the moment Nira dies, Jaya and Saka are going to come after me."

"Why would they do that?"

There was a long silence. Seconds stretched into a minute, then two.

"There are things you don't know," Cikara said.

"So, tell me," Jakari said. "If you want to buy your life, you need to make it worth my time."

"Something changed after Mamachi escaped. Losing Karusa did something to Jaya. They were never quite the same again. I think Jaya and Saka suspect I helped Mamachi escape, and I think Jaya blames me for Karusa's death. I think Jaya sent Nira along to kill me as soon as the Helot technology is ready."

"Well, that's sad for you, but that doesn't give me a reason to spare you," Jakari said. "There are more than seven billion innocent people on this planet. I'm not going to kill Nira for you, then fuck off while you commit genocide."

"I need the Helots to fight Jaya and Saka," Cikara said.

"The Helots are off the table," Jakari said. "My mission was to come here, kill you, and destroy the technology. The orders come directly from Arthan himself. Now, I might have some wiggle room if I take Nira out, but the Helot tech has to go."

The link fell silent again, and Jakari sat and watched Cikara thinking, turning things over in their head.

"Who's listening on your end?" Cikara said.

"Napati and her staff. Dubari. A couple of humans," Jakari said.

"What if I could lure Saka and Jaya here?" Cikara asked.

"I'm listening," Jakari said.

"If I send back a report that Nira has been killed, and the Helot technology has been destroyed, Jaya will send Saka out here to kill me and to finish the Helot project. And if Saka dies..."

"Jaya will come to deal with you personally," Jakari said.

"Exactly," Cikara said.

"It's an interesting idea," Jakari said.

"Is it enough to buy my life?" Cikara said.

"Your life in exchange for the Helot tech, Nira, Saka, and Jaya? That is what we're talking about, right?" Jakari asked. "I don't want there to be any ambiguity here."

"Yes," Cikara said. "That's the agreement. What do you say?"

"Give me a moment to discuss it with Napati," Jakari said.

"Don't take too long. Keeping Nira from finding out about this conversation isn't easy, and the longer it goes on..."

"Understood. I'll be quick."

Jakari muted the comm channel and looked at Napati.

"What do you think?" Jakari asked.

"You can't be serious," Dubari said. "They're lying."

"We can argue about it later," Jakari said. "Right now, I need Napati to give me a yes or no."

"Do you think you can trust them?" Napati asked.

"You know what Cikara was like," Jakari said. "What they went through. They didn't have the same taste for power that Jaya and Saka did. They went along with the Char because they were afraid. And given what happened on Cruthanna..."

"What did happen on Cruthanna?" Napati said. "Because it's clear the official report only tells part of the story."

"It's a long story, and we're short of time. The relevant part is that Cikara helped Mamachi escape the tower."

"You didn't think that was relevant when you wrote the report?" Napati asked.

"Ma'am, with respect, about ninety-nine percent of every report I write is fiction. I have operated on the assumption that every report I write goes straight to Nira and the Triumvirate's desks for the last nine thousand years, which is a large part of why I, and most of my contacts on Char worlds, are still alive. If I had put the truth in my report, and it found its way back to Jaya, Nira, or Saka, Cikara would be dead, and we wouldn't have a real shot at bringing down Nira, Jaya, and Saka."

"Which would leave the Char entirely under Cikara's control," Napati said. "Is that something we really want?"

"I'd say yes," Jakari said.

"I'd agree with her," Mamachi said. "I admit that I might be a little biased, given that Cikara saved my life once, but even before that, Cikara has always been the most reasonable of the Triumvirate. A Char under Cikara's control is one we might be able to negotiate a lasting peace with."

"Cikara's also their best strategist," Napati said. "If they aren't inclined to negotiate, having them in charge will make the Char a hell of a lot more dangerous."

Jakari let out a frustrated sigh. "It's a risk, but it's also the first real chance we've had at ending the war in a long time. You're in command, but I am telling you that if it were up to me, I would say yes."

"Oh, for fuck's sake," Rayak said, cutting into the conversation and reminding everyone that he was there. "Make the fucking deal, Napati. We're never going to get a better shot than this. And if Cikara starts getting frisky once the rest of them are out of the way, it's a hell of a lot easier to deal with one problem than four."

Napati stared at Rayak for a second, then turned to Jakari. "Make the deal," she said.

Jakari reopened the comm. "Still there?"

"Yes," Cikara said. "That was faster than I expected."

"We're in," Jakari said.

"Excellent," Cikara said.

"We'll need a show of good faith to start with," Jakari said.

"Such as?"

"The location of your ship."

"I see," Cikara said. "Are you sure you won't just come kill me?"

"We agreed that we wouldn't lie to each other, Cikara. Besides, if I was going to kill you, I would tell you. Just like I did on Cruthanna. It's not like you could stop me."

"That's not as comforting as you think it is."

"But it is true."

"Fine. Transmitting coordinates."

Jakari looked down at the console and saw the coordinates displayed on the screen. They matched up perfectly to what she already knew.

"Got it," Jakari said. "One more thing."

"What is it?"

"I need to personally lay eyes on Nira," Jakari said.

"What?" Cikara asked, panic in their voice.

"Tonight, I'm going to come to your ship, I'm going to slip aboard, and I'm going to find Nira. Once I lay eyes on her, then we have a deal."

"You don't trust me?" Cikara asked.

"I trust you exactly as much as I trusted you on Cruthanna, and just like I said in Freedom Square, if tonight turns out to be a trap, I'll come back tomorrow and kill you. Are we clear on where we stand?"

"Very," Cikara said.

"Good. I'll see you tonight."

Jakari cut the channel and leaned back in her chair, carefully ignoring the way everyone in the room was staring at her.

"You don't think you should ask if I would approve a recon mission to the Char ship?" Napati asked.

Jakari shrugged. "I'm going whether you approve it or not, so I didn't see the point."

"You do remember that I outrank you, right?" Napati asked.

"How long have you known me?" Jakari asked.

"Ninety-eight hundred years, give or take," Napati said.

"And in all that time, have you ever once known me to give a damn if someone outranks me?" Jakari asked.

Napati sighed. "No," she said.

"You knew what she was when you recruited her," Rayak said. "Don't blame the agacha for eating all the imdura."

"What's an agacha?" Gomez asked.

"It's a type of lizard," Mamachi said. "We keep them as pets. They're kind of like cats, personality wise."

"And an imdura?" Skylar asked.

"Imdura used to be food animals," Mamachi said. "Before the migration, Gadan would keep them to snack on. They're kind of like mice."

"Tasty," Jakari said. "Aashi liked to dip hers in Cako syrup."

"Did you ever try them with Garama sauce?" Rayak asked.

"I did once," Napati said. "I didn't like how much it made them squirm."

"You ate them alive?" Skylar asked, sounding horrified.

"Usually," Jakari said. "Sometimes you could get roasted skewers from a street vendor, but you had to be careful. You never knew how fresh they were if they weren't served live. Although, there was this one place in Crodain near the Temple of the Brooding Mother that served them roasted with jellied Pudina."

"I remember that place!" Rayak said. "It was on the same side of the temple as the Shrine of the Eggs, between a little tea shop and the scale scrapers, right?"

"Yeah," Jakari said.

"They had a flatbread topped with pickled Gajari. I got it every time—"

"I'm sorry to interrupt the trip down memory lane, but can we talk about the fact that you just decided to toss our orders out the window?" Dubari said.

Jakari sighed and turned to Dubari. "Well, technically, our orders to kill Cikara came from Napati, and now Napati is giving us new orders."

"That's bullshit, and you know it!" Dubari said. "Napati was just passing on orders from Arthan. We can't go off-book on this."

"For a shot at Nira, Jaya, and Saka and a chance to end the war? You bet your ass I can go off-book," Jakari said.

"I agree with Jakari on this," Napati said. "And as second-in-command of the Suil, and the commander on scene, I will take personal responsibility for the change in plans, but as of right now, I am placing everything that happened here under security seal. What we discussed does not leave this room."

"We should at least inform Arthan," Dubari said.

"It's too big a risk," Napati said. "There is no way I'm transmitting that a member of the Triumvirate is working with us to assassinate the other two. So unless you want to get in a shuttle and deliver a report to Arthan in person, the matter is closed. We will work with Cikara for now, and with a little luck, in a few months, we'll have brought down the Triumvirate."

"Napati's right, kid," Rayak said. "This isn't something we can broadcast. Besides, if we told Arthan about it, he'd just send back detailed instructions on how to fuck it up."

Dubari leaned back in their chair. Jakari could see the anger on their face and wasn't even remotely surprised. Not after the speech they'd given about not going off-book a couple of nights earlier. She hoped Napati's orders were enough to keep them quiet about it, but she doubted it. There would probably be a hell of an argument later, but the biggest issue was that she wouldn't be able to take Dubari with her on the recon mission. She probably wouldn't have anyway, so it wasn't that big a loss.

She looked around at the other people present. Prack was giving Dubari a worried look. Mamachi looked like they were already working on how to deal with the new situation. Dhom looked unreasonably excited, and Jakari tried to remember why they were even there. It took a second to recall that they were Napati's tech specialist. She ignored them and turned to the humans. Skylar and Gomez looked vaguely ill, but Hayami was unreadable.

"Who are you taking with you tonight?" Napati asked.

"Mamachi," Jakari said. "Though they won't actually be going into the ship with me. I'll go alone. Easier to get in, easier to get out. Less chance of discovery."

"Less chance of being able to fight your way out if it's a trap," Prack said. "Let me put together a team to go with you."

"No," Jakari said. "The last thing I need when I'm trying to sneak onto a Char ship is a squad of commandos wrapped in explosives getting underfoot. If it's a trap, I can deal with it as long as I've got Mamachi nearby for support."

"You're sure?" Napati asked.

"I want to go, too," Hayami said.

"No," Jakari said. "Absolutely not."

"Why not?"

"Because it's too dangerous," Jakari said. "The only reason I'm taking Mamachi is because they can pilot a Class Four Talus. They are just going to sit outside the base, waiting to get us out of danger if things go badly."

"If things go badly, they can get both of us out of danger."

"You can't shapeshift," Jakari said, trying to come up with reasons Hayami couldn't go without telling anyone the truth of what she had planned. There were some secrets she preferred to keep.

"Jakari has a point," Mamachi said. "If she gets spotted, all she has to do in order to disappear is break visual contact with the enemy, and her shapeshifting will let her effectively disappear. With you there, that becomes much harder."

"I know it's a risk," Hayami said, "but you're bargaining with the safety of our entire planet. A human should be there."

"She has a point," Gomez said. "I understand that this is your war, but you've brought it to our world. We have a huge stake in what's happening."

"I can't guarantee her safety," Jakari said.

"I'm willing to take the risk."

"Well, I'm not," Jakari said.

"Jakari," Napati said.

Jakari turned towards Napati. "What?"

"The humans have a right to be there."

Jakari sighed and turned to Hayami. "How much do you weigh?"

"Why is that important?" Hayami asked.

"Because it will determine if you can go with me or not," Jakari said.

Hayami frowned. "I'm around 140 pounds," she said.

Jakari turned to Rayak. "What's the maximum mass bandwidth for the implanted neural interface?"

"A hundred kilograms," Rayak said. "About two hundred and twenty pounds."

Jakari turned back to Hayami. "Fine. You can go. If you can learn to remote operate a Talus in the next four hours."

* * * *

Cikara carefully guided their Talus into the abandoned building that concealed the hangar entrance for the ship. A simple mental command sent through the Talus' comm system triggered the floor to split and flow out of the way as Cikara's Talus shifted from a Mercedes-Maybach S-Class into a Gadan aircar. It lifted off the ground and floated out over the opening in the floor, then began the short descent into the hangar.

They had just settled onto the hangar floor when they got a comm request from Ghuma.

"General, I have good news," Ghuma said.

"What is it?" Cikara asked.

"We've located the safehouse where the human woman's parents are being held. Do you want me to bring them in?"

"No," Cikara said. "Observe only."

"Understood," Ghuma said.

Cikara was about to get out of the aircar when a thought occurred to them. "Actually, Ghuma, I have a strange order, but it's important. Listen carefully. The future of the Char may depend on it."

Chapter Seventeen

JAKARI CHECKED THE TIE down strap holding the Talus in place. It was a Class Two. Nearly 1000 kilograms configured as a heavy grav sled. It was a triple chassis design. The central chassis was three meters long with two in-line seats, and held two counter-grav engines, while the secondary chassis on each side held a turbofan engine. The ratchet straps holding it in place in the back of the Class Four, currently configured as a delivery truck, seemed secure enough, so Jakari stood up and looked around, seeing if there was anything else that needed her attention.

"You sure you don't want me to go with you?" Dubari asked.

Jakari turned to see them standing at the back of the truck. "I'm sure," she said.

"You don't trust me not to kill Cikara on sight, do you?" Dubari asked.

"No," Jakari said. "I don't."

Dubari frowned. "Would it kill you to lie about something like that once in a while?"

"I don't see the point," Jakari said.

"You don't think that after all the time we've worked together, I've got your back?"

"It's not my back I'm worried about," Jakari said. "I know I can trust you to watch it, right up to the day Arthan orders you to kill me."

"He wouldn't do that," Dubari said.

"He would, and sooner or later, he will," Jakari said. "Me, Napati, Rayak, and Sonu. The four of us are all that's left of the original resistance. He'll want us gone eventually. The only question is whether he gives the order before or after the Char falls."

"Why do you think he would do that?" Dubari asked.

"Because he's as crazy as Jaya is," Jakari said. "But that's not really the point. The point is, you have orders from Arthan to kill Cikara. You'll carry those orders out. I don't blame you, Dubari. I trust you to do what you think is right. The problem is, your idea of what is right and my idea of what is right don't agree. You think the right thing to do is follow orders. I think the right thing to do is to take the chance to end the war. So until I'm convinced that you're on board with my way of doing things, you're benched."

Dubari sighed and shook their head. "I would have done the recon."

"Maybe," Jakari said. "But I've got it covered."

"Okay," Dubari said.

"How did things go with your dad?" Jakari asked.

"We talked," Dubari said.

"Did you patch things up?"

"Not really," Dubari said.

Jakari sighed. "You need to get over it."

"It's not your business," Dubari said.

"You and Prack are my friends. That makes it my business."

"Jakari..."

"Look, you're lucky. Your parents are still alive. You can walk across the room and talk to your dad. But that could change any time. We could get attacked, or he could die in an attack on the Char ship. The base your mom is serving at could get bombed out of existence tomorrow. And you're letting something stupid keep you from talking to them."

"It's not stupid," Dubari said.

"Yeah, it is," Jakari said. "Look, I get it. You grew up before we really had time to get used to the fact that we're going to live forever. You still want to believe all of those things that we used to believe when we only had a century or so to live our lives. That two people are enough for each other forever. That love is eternal. All those things. But those things were never true. Not when we lived a century. Not now that we live however long we live. I loved Aashi with all my heart and soul, but I still had friends, I still had other people in my life, and so did she. No one can meet all of a person's emotional needs, and it's profoundly unfair of you to expect Prack and Charvi to give up someone they love because it offends your sensibilities. Hamadri is a good person. They love your parents, and your parents love them."

"They're younger than I am!" Dubari said.

"So is ninety-nine percent of the fucking Gadan species! Hamadri is six thousand years old. The fact that your parents are Migrants and you were one of the first generation of native-born means almost anyone they might meet and fall in love with is going to be younger than you. Your parents are people, Dubari. People live, they grow, they change, they fall in and out of love."

"You don't," Dubari said.

"Your parents fell in love, and they have sex with their spouse. That's a hell of a lot healthier than lying in bed and replaying memories of making love to a woman who's been dead for ten thousand years. I'm not someone you should hold up as an example. I'm broken, and I've been that way so long I missed any chance I ever had of getting better.

"Please, I'm saying this as your friend. Go talk to your dad, because if you don't and something happens to him, you might end up like me. And neither of us wants that." Dubari opened their mouth to say something else, but Jakari just pointed out the back of the truck. "*Go!*" she snapped. Dubari turned around and hopped down. She watched for a minute as they headed in Prack's direction, then shook her head and went to check on her second Talus.

* * * *

"You can still wait in the truck," Jakari said as the truck rolled down the highway towards the small Texas ghost town where the Char ship was buried.

Hayami looked over at her, and the expression on Jakari's face made her bite off the snarky reply that was on the tip of her tongue. Jakari looked worried. It was the first time she could recall seeing that expression on her face, and it made her hesitate for a moment and glance over at her Talus.

It had been surprisingly easy to learn the basic controls. Run, jump, stand, sit. It was less a matter of learning how to pilot a machine and more how to redirect muscle impulses to the Talus instead of her own body. It took a lot of concentration at first, but after about thirty minutes, it had been as natural as breathing. Moving through the various shape shifts pre-programmed into the Talus had been a lot harder. Turning hands into guns, making the jump jets pop out of her back and her legs, adjusting what spectrum her eyes saw in, those were hard, but hard or not, by the end of the four-hour training session, she'd been able to control the Talus well enough that even Jakari couldn't complain.

"I'm fine," Hayami said. "I always get a little tense before a raid."

"This isn't a raid," Jakari said. "It's just a quick recon. We get in, we lay eyes on Nira. We get out. With any luck, we do it without a fight."

"Why not just take Nira out if we see her?" Hayami asked. "I'm not entirely sure I'm onboard with the murder thing, but if that is the plan, breaking in twice seems like a bigger risk."

"Nira's not going to be easy to kill," Jakari said. "I can do it, but killing Nira isn't our only objective, and if I kill Nira tonight, it will make our other objective harder."

"The research?" Hayami asked, a little embarrassed. She'd gotten so focused on the idea that they were going to try to assassinate the leaders of the Char that she'd forgotten why they were a danger to Earth in the first place.

"Exactly," Jakari said.

"Can I ask a question?"

"Always," Jakari said.

"The way you talked to Cikara...were the two of you close?"

"Define close?"

"You called them 'old friend,'" Hayami said.

"Ah," Jakari said. "We worked together during the rebellion. Honestly, I worked with all of them. Cikara, Jaya, Nira, and Saka. I liked working with Cikara best because they were more in control of themself than Jaya, and less creepy than Nira and Saka."

"Creepy?" Hayami asked.

"Nira doesn't really talk. She's capable of it. I've heard her speak a few times, but day-to-day, she's effectively mute. No one knows why, except maybe Jaya. Honestly, no one knows anything about Nira before the rebellion except that she's a Migrant."

"How do you know that?"

"The scar," Jakari said. "The fact that she has a fixed gender is also a pretty big clue, but the facial scar is the giveaway. A lot of Migrants carried things like that over. Tattoos, scars, their apparent age. I always figured the not speaking thing was something that got carried over too. That she was actually mute before the migration."

"And that creeps you out?"

"Yeah. I mean, not the fact that she's mute. That I could deal with, but there was something unnerving about her. When you looked in her eyes, it was like the light had already gone out. It was like looking into the eyes of a corpse. The silence just intensified the effect."

"And Saka?"

"Oh, Saka was just fucking broken. Literally. Their Phylactery was damaged by the Seichu. The closest thing I ever saw to an emotion from them was their loyalty to Jaya, and I was sure that was just a means to an end for them."

"You don't hate them, though, do you?" Hayami asked.

"No," Jakari said.

"Why not? Most people in your place would."

"Hating them would be hypocritical," Jakari said. "They're fighting for what they believe is best for the Gadan. I'm fighting for what I believe is best for the Gadan. We just...disagree on what that is."

"That wouldn't stop most people," Hayami said.

"I'm not most people," Jakari said.

"I've noticed."

"What do you mean?" Jakari asked.

"The way you talk to most people," Hayami said. "I heard you talking to Dubari before we left. The way you talked to them...most people aren't comfortable with that level of honesty."

"I don't see the point in lying."

"Yeah, you told Dubari the same thing. You talk to people like that, just completely honest, whether it hurts them or not, but then you turn around and try to get Dubari to reconcile with their family, or you go out of your way to watch over Mamachi after a traumatic experience."

Jakari turned towards her and stared for a moment before shaking her head. "You're doing it again."

"Doing what?" Hayami asked.

"Mistaking me for a good person," Jakari said. "I'm not."

"Are you sure?"

Jakari sighed. "You want me to be a good person because I'm on your side. In your mind, we're the heroes, and the heroes are supposed to be good, heroic people, but good, heroic people don't do the kind of things I do. They don't sneak into people's bedrooms and murder them in their sleep. They don't build a sniper nest and lay in wait to vaporize their target. They don't wire bombs to aircars. They don't blow up homes. They don't follow people down dark alleys and murder them.

"You see me talking and joking and laughing with you, Mamachi, and Skylar. You see me trying to help Prack and Dubari patch things up. You see me trying to protect human lives, and you think all of those things make me a good person, but they don't. Horrible people can be nice and kind when it suits them. Monsters can wear a pleasant face. They can love their wife and they can care about their friends, and they can still go out and blow up a hatchery or burn down a school. They can still torture someone's family in front of them to get information."

"War makes monsters of out of good people," Hayami said.

"No," Jakari said. "War gives monsters license to be themselves."

Hayami turned away from Jakari, trying to think of an answer for that, but the truck came to a stop and the comm crackled to life. "We're here," Mamachi said.

"Roger that," Jakari said.

Jakari touched a button on the side of her chair and it tilted back into a reclining position. Hayami did the same, then closed her eyes and issued the mental commands that brought her neural interface online. She took a couple of deep breaths and reached out, connecting to her Talus.

* * * *

There was a moment of disorientation and displacement as she opened her eyes and found herself strapped to a shelf. She reached over and hit the button to release her restraints and sat up, looking around the inside of the truck. She shuddered slightly, seeing herself laying in the recliner, still as death, but she pushed the feeling aside and hopped down off the shelf.

"It's hard to get used to at first," Jakari said, making Hayami jump slightly. She turned from where Jakari was laying in the recliner next to her, to where Jakari was standing beside the grav sled.

"Yeah," Hayami said. "This is weird." She looked down at her hands, which looked exactly like the hands she'd had her whole life, but which were made of TOP matter, and held in shape by a small computer embedded somewhere in her body, which was also made up entirely of TOP matter.

Jakari bent down and released the ratchet straps holding the grav sled in place.

"Get in," she said.

Hayami climbed into the rear seat of the grav sled. Jakari climbed in front of her, and Hayami wrapped her arms around Jakari's waist, holding on tightly as Jakari brought the sled online. The sled lifted off the floor of the truck's cargo area, and the rear door of the truck slid upwards, giving them a way out. Jakari guided the sled forward until they were clear of the truck, then turned and gave it a bit of throttle, sending them speeding through the dark towards their target.

Hayami shifted the spectrum her eyes picked up down into the infrared, and the area lit up like it was noon. It was mostly plants at first, but then the ruined buildings came into view. Some were nothing more than bare foundation, others were a few broken walls. Some were nearly intact. A whole town was abandoned when the coal mines under it had run dry. She spotted the building Jakari had selected as a probable access point to the ship below. A large brick building that was probably a coal storehouse once. The side was open, and a pair of steel doors had been dragged away from where they'd fallen, clearing the way in and out of the building. A sign of recent use.

They parked the sled a couple of buildings over, and when they had both climbed out, it reshaped itself into a rusted propane tank. Something which fit in perfectly with the rest of the surroundings. With their getaway vehicle secure, they quickly made their way over to the building in question and started looking around.

"What are we looking for?" Hayami asked in a hushed tone.

"Standard practice for the Char military is to mark hidden access points with a dim UV light," Jakari said. "Add UV to your current spectrum, then check the walls for eight glowing dots. You won't be able to see them from more than a couple of meters away."

Hayami nodded and switched her vision again, adding ultraviolet to the spectrum she could see. It took them about ten minutes before Jakari called her over, and sure enough, there were eight dim glowing dots arranged in a geometric pattern. Hayami couldn't quite place what the pattern was, but it didn't really matter.

"Keep an eye out," Jakari said. "This will go faster if I focus all my attention on it."

"I've got you covered," Hayami said.

Jakari placed her hand over the glowing dots and went still. Hayami switched her vision again, going back to straight infrared without the distraction of the ultraviolet, and dialed up the gain on her hearing, listening for anything out of the ordinary. She didn't hear anything other than a few crickets at first, but as the silence and the stillness lingered, she had to force herself to stay calm, and not jump at every shadow.

It took nearly ten minutes before anything changed, but just as suddenly as she'd gone still, Jakari started moving again. She took her hand away from the access point on the wall as a section of the ground began to open. She gave a small wave, indicating that Hayami should follow, then led them both over to where a platform with a raised control pillar had risen out of the opening in the ground. She stepped up onto it, and Hayami followed.

Once they were both on the platform, Jakari put her hand on the control pillar, and the platform sank down into the opening in the floor. Hayami watched as it closed above them and tried not to panic. The space they were in was small, and she had to shut her eyes to stop the feeling that the walls were closing in on them.

"It won't be long," Jakari said.

"I don't like this," she said. "How do you stand it?"

"It doesn't bother us," Jakari said. "We evolved from burrowing reptiles. We're comfortable underground. Most Migrants are more comfortable underground than above ground. Aashi and I couldn't afford anything cut out of actual bedrock, but we had a wonderful concrete den. We even had a real slab of granite on top of it for a basking stone."

"You mentioned a basking stone before, but I don't know what that is." Hayami said.

"It's just a large flat stone that's placed so it gets sunlight all day. It soaks up heat, so when you lie on it, you've got the sun on you and the warm rock under you. On the days we didn't have to work, we'd go up and lie in the sun at midday and just be together."

Hayami thought back to the morning she'd gone to wake Jakari up and found her under a heat lamp. It didn't take much to picture her curled up with another of her species, and maybe it was the Gadan resemblance to cats, but the picture was honestly adorable. So adorable, she barely noticed the platform coming to a halt.

A section of the wall opened, and Hayami looked out to see a massive hangar, filled with what had to be some kind of fighter craft. There were also larger ships that looked more like Jakari's transport, and an assortment of what looked like Earth vehicles, but were probably Taluses.

"Come on," Jakari said. She led them out of the elevator and across the hangar to a pair of double doors. Hayami watched as Jakari keyed in some sort of code, and the door opened. She followed Jakari through, into a corridor that was almost identical to the one on Napati's ship. Too tall, with a floor that had a rubbery give to it. There was one difference. Now that she could see in the infrared, the markings that had appeared to be black on Napati's ship were actually bright and easy to see.

"Your people naturally see in the infrared?"

"Our visible spectrum is about twice as wide as yours. We can see from about four hundred nanometers up to a micrometer."

"Good to know," Hayami said. "Do I want to ask how you got that security code?"

"Not now," Jakari said. "Ask me when we get back to base."

"Right."

Jakari led them deeper into the ship, following some unseen map. Occasionally, she would stop and place her hand on the wall and go silent for a few seconds, then wake up with a renewed sense of direction. Hayami was never sure what gave away the particular spots. There were no ultraviolet dots. No visible or infrared markings. Nothing that seemed to denote the places Jakari touched, and yet each time she picked a seemingly random spot, it turned out to be an access point. It was another question for when they were back at base.

They'd been moving through the ship for almost ten minutes before they saw anyone, but Hayami had to fight down the panic when they did. The first person they saw was a Gadan in their natural form, and she wondered if all the Gadan on the ship would be wearing their true forms, but a moment later, two people who looked human came around the corner, and the three of them started talking. The Gadan spoke in hisses and chitters and something close to a meow, while the humans spoke English with a Texan accent.

Jakari led them right by the three members of the Char crew with little more than a head nod in their direction and took another turn. Each turn Jakari took made Hayami that much more grateful for the Talus she was controlling. Without its built-in inertial tracking system, she would be hopelessly lost. As it was, she was sure she could find her way back to the platform they came in on, even if she wasn't sure she'd be able to operate it.

Jakari stopped them near an intersection in the corridor and turned to look at Hayami.

"Things are about to get tense," she said. "I need you to promise me that you will not shoot or kill anyone without my say so."

"I can do that," Hayami said.

"Good. Just, whatever happens, remember that we're only here through the Taluses. The Taluses are expendable. If this gets to be too much for you, just disconnect."

Hayami nodded.

"Good," Jakari said. "Follow me."

Jakari walked around the corner and Hayami followed. They went about ten meters down the corridor and came to a heavy door. Jakari reached out and punched a security code into the console next to the door. The door slid open, and both of them stepped through into a large office that had a single occupant.

"Hello, Cikara," Jakari said as the door slid shut behind them.

Chapter Eighteen

CIKARA STARTED TO SCRAMBLE out of their chair in a panic, but Jakari had expected that. She raised her arm, reconfiguring it into a launcher. The room filled with the sharp snap of the launcher and Cikara staggered back and screamed as they clutched their chest. They took their hand away to look at the wound, and Jakari smiled as Cikara saw the barbed dart sticking out of their chest.

Cikara looked up at her, fury written on their face. "You Form Locked me?" they asked.

"Yes," Jakari said as she pulled a signal jammer off her belt and activated it. She held up the jammer. "I wanted a private conversation, and I don't want you getting frisky."

"How did you even get in here?" Cikara asked.

"I've been bypassing Char security for nine thousand years. You don't have anything that can keep me out."

"Are you here to kill me?" Cikara asked.

"No," Jakari said. "If I wanted you dead, I wouldn't have Form Locked you, I would have just vaporized you. I told you, I'm here to confirm Nira's on site."

"Then why come here? Why Form Lock me?"

"Because it makes it look like I'm here to destroy your research," Jakari said. "Now, move away from the desk."

Cikara moved aside, and Jakari circled around behind the desk and sat down.

"Now, how do I access your files without setting off any tripwires?"

"You can't expect me to tell you that," Cikara said.

"Pretty sure she can," Hayami said.

Cikara looked over at her. "You're the human woman," he said. "What are you doing here?"

Hayami's hand reconfigured into a plasma cannon, and she pointed it at Cikara. "I'm here to make sure the twenty-three people you killed get justice."

Cikara stepped back.

"You forgot about them, didn't you?" Hayami asked, taking a step forward as the cannon began to glow a bright blue. "Well, I didn't, so I'd suggest you start talking, because if she doesn't need you anymore, then it's my turn."

Cikara looked over to Jakari. "We had a deal."

Jakari shrugged. "The deal was between you and the Suil. She's human."

"You won't let her kill me," Cikara said.

"Deal isn't final until I lay eyes on Nira," Jakari said. "And if I think for a second that you're going to try and pull anything shady, I will carry out my original orders. So, show me the Helot research. All of it."

Cikara looked over at Hayami again, then back at Jakari.

"Fine," Cikara said. "When you first log in, you'll see a small icon of an agacha. You have to tap it before you touch anything else, or you'll be locked out of the system and an alarm will sound."

Jakari reached over and placed her hand on the access point for the desk.

"Don't you need my user id and password?" Cikara asked.

"No," Jakari said. She connected to the system and quickly dropped down into the hardware level and began issuing commands to the system. It wasn't the fastest way to hack a computer, but it was absolutely the most reliable one, at least where TOP matter systems were concerned. The Char were actually pretty good about putting in hardware level security, but the problem with that was, any TOP matter system had two hardware layers. There was the hardware layer of the computer that was constructed out of the TOP matter, and then there was the TOP matter itself. The hardware layer of the computer was easy enough to secure, but the TOP matter layer wasn't, and most people never knew you could even directly address the TOP matter. Jakari only knew because she'd taken medic training with Rayak back during the rebellion, and it had taken her decades to realize the potential, but once she did, she took shameless advantage of it. She didn't so much hack the computer as she rebuilt it without any of the Char's security features in place, then she hacked the firmware from the hardware layer, then she hacked the operating system from the firmware layer.

By the time she was done, the computer cheerfully handed her a decrypted list of user IDs and passwords. Once she had that, she reset the system, erasing all evidence of her hack in the process, and then just logged in as Cikara. She made sure to tap on the agacha icon, then she downloaded a map of the entire ship. Once she had that, she pulled up all research related to the Helot program and downloaded everything, sending it through the Talus link back to her actual body in the truck, along with the map of the ship. Once that was done, she took a moment to look over the files and glanced up at Cikara.

"There's a file missing," Jakari said.

"Yes," Cikara said.

"What is it?"

"It's the final update for Shroud," Cikara said. "I've been holding off on uploading it because once I do, the system is finished."

"And Nira will kill you and take the weapon back to Jaya."

"Yes," Cikara said.

"Where is it?" Jakari asked.

"In my Phylactery."

"I need it," Jakari said.

"No," Cikara said. "You have everything else in front of you. You don't get that until Nira is dead."

Hayami took another step towards Cikara, but Jakari held up her hand. "That's reasonable," she said. "But once Nira is dead, I want that file." She looked over at Hayami. "You ready to move?" she asked.

"Yeah," Hayami said.

Jakari queried the computer to get Nira's current location. Once it told her Nira was in her quarters, Jakari downloaded a script into the desk's computer, then disconnected. "Let's go see Nira."

"What about me?" Cikara asked.

"The Form Lock will self-destruct in about two hours. I'll expect a comm call from you tomorrow at the same time to make arrangements."

"Why not just kill Nira tonight?" Cikara asked.

"Because I'm not ready," Jakari said. "Now, say goodnight."

"What?"

Jakari sent a command to the Form Lock, and a massive jolt of electricity shot through Cikara, dropping them to the floor and sending their Phylactery into lockdown mode.

"Did you kill them?" Hayami asked.

"Just knocked them out," Jakari said. "I left a script in the computer that will log back in and access the Helot data without deactivating the tripwire. When it does, and security arrives, it will look like we were after the Helot system and tried to torture the information out of Cikara."

Jakari headed for the door and Hayami fell in behind her. They slipped out into the hall and Jakari pulled up the map in her HUD, with the route to Nira's quarters highlighted.

"Why not just kill Nira tonight?" Hayami asked.

"I can't," Jakari said. "Cikara's good in a one-on-one fight. They had to be to survive in the gladiator pits. But there's a difference between good enough to survive, and good enough to become a legend. Jaya was the best gladiator to ever walk into the pits, and Nira was a close second. Saka was a bit more on Cikara's level than Jaya and Nira."

"But you said you could kill Nira," Hayami said.

"I can, but not while I'm remote piloting a Talus. I'm good, but I'm not that good. If I'm going to kill Nira, I either have to catch her completely unaware, or I have to fight her face-to-face."

"You can take her face-to-face?"

"Yes," Jakari said.

"You sound awfully sure of that," Hayami said.

"That's because I am," Jakari said. "Shift into preset two."

Jakari shifted her Talus from her human form to a randomly-generated Gadan form wearing a Char uniform. When she glanced back, Hayami had done the same.

"Is the translator working?" Jakari asked in Sabda instead of the English her throat and mouth could no longer pronounce.

"Yes," Hayami answered in the same language.

That was the last time they spoke until they reached the hall outside of Nira's quarters. Jakari shifted her vision deeper into the infrared and found the hotspot on the wall that indicated a hidden access point. She walked over and put her hand on the access point, then shifted her vision back to normal.

"Be ready," she said as she linked to the access point. She got a small nod of acknowledgement from Hayami and sent a command to the script she'd left on Cikara's computer, then pulled her hand away from the access point.

An alarm rang through the corridor, and Jakari counted to ten, then started walking towards Nira's door. She and Hayami were almost there when the door slid open and Nira stepped out into the corridor. Nira looked at Jakari and Hayami for a moment, then pointed at them, then herself. Jakari nodded, and when Nira started walking, she turned and followed her.

The three of them quickly retraced the route Jakari and Hayami had just taken, working their way back to Cikara's office. When they got there, Nira punched in a code to open the door and stepped inside. She immediately spotted Cikara on the floor and walked over, rolling them onto their back.

Jakari watched as Nira leaned down and examined the dart sticking out of Cikara's chest. Her hand reconfigured itself into a small, thin knife, and she carefully cut the dart out of Cikara's chest and held it up. Jakari watched as the wound on Cikara's chest healed itself, then glanced back at the dart in Nira's hand just in time to see it explode.

She took a step back, and Hayami did the same. Nira looked up with an expression of annoyance on her face.

"They'll head for the hangar," Jakari said. "To try and slip off the ship in the confusion. If we go now, we might be able to catch them."

Nira nodded and waved them away.

"Come on," Jakari said. She turned and headed for the door with Hayami in tow, pulling up the map of the ship and highlighting the fastest route back to the hangar. Once they were in the hall, they took it at a dead run, moving as fast as their Gadan forms would carry them, and far faster than they could ever have moved in their human forms. They got more than a few odd looks, since everyone else was headed in the other direction in response to the alarms, but they were Gadan in Char uniforms, so no one challenged them.

They reached the hangars, only to find them deserted. Jakari quickly led them over to the same platform they'd entered the ship on, and once they were both onboard, she activated it, sending them up towards the surface.

"Think we made it?" Hayami asked as they rode upwards.

"Maybe," Jakari said. "Won't know for sure until we're back at base."

Hayami nodded and didn't say anything else until they were back on the surface. Once they were, they both shifted back into their human forms and ran for the grav sled.

Jakari started reconfiguring the propane tank into the grav sled as they ran, and when they reached it, she waited while Hayami climbed in, then climbed in front of her. She relaxed as soon as she settled into the seat, the mental strain of running two separate Taluses fading as they connected. She relaxed even further when Hayami's arms slid around her waist. They weren't quite safe yet, but they were closer than she'd admit.

She gave the anti-grav engine a bit of juice and headed for the edge of town, keeping low and moving slow, trying to avoid detection as long as possible. Which turned out to be not that long. The sensor system pinged with the telltale warning of a building plasma charge nearby, and Jakari gunned the throttle and threw them into a series of evasive maneuvers, swerving and weaving and ducking behind obstacles where she could as the air filled with the bright blue glow of plasma.

"Shit!" Hayami screamed as a bolt sailed by close enough for them both to feel the heat. "I thought we'd made it."

"Told you we wouldn't know until we were back at base," Jakari said.

"I thought you were being paranoid."

"I was," Jakari said. "I was also right."

"Just shut up and drive!"

The grav sled's sensors lit up with hostile contacts, and Char grav sleds started boiling out of the buildings below them.

"*Fuck!*" Hayami said.

"We're not going to make it," Jakari said.

"You're sure?" Hayami asked.

"Too many of them, too few of us," Jakari said. "Lock your position and disconnect. You don't want to feel this."

"What about you?" Hayami asked.

"Just tell Mamachi to get moving," Jakari said. "I've done this before."

"Okay."

She felt Hayami go stiff behind her, the Talus no longer being controlled by its pilot. It made controlling the grav sled a little harder, since Hayami couldn't lean into the turns anymore, but that was fine. It wouldn't matter much longer anyway. She turned east and opened the throttle, making it look like she was trying to run for it while putting distance between her and the truck. She brought her weapons online as the enemy grav sleds tried to get into position behind her. She picked a couple of easy targets and fired, blowing sleds out of the sky. She might even have killed a pilot or two, though she doubted it.

She armed the grav sled's self-destruct system and swung it around in a tight turn, moving to rapid fire on all four forward-facing plasma cannons as she charged back towards the pursuing troops. They tried to scatter, tried to turn and run, but the distances were too short, and Jakari had been doing this a long time. She blew sled after sled out of the air as she rushed forward, the shock of the sudden, vicious attack keeping any of them from landing a shot even as she plunged into the middle of them. Then, as she reached the dead center of the enemy formation, she triggered the self-destruct.

* * * *

Hayami watched helplessly as Jakari jerked up and screamed as she fought against the harness holding her in her chair.

"Fuck!" Jakari yelled as she clawed at the harness.

"Easy," Hayami said.

"Fuck easy! Get me loose," Jakari snapped.

Hayami reached over and twisted the release on the harness, and Jakari scrambled off the chair and stumbled a few steps towards the rear of the truck before falling to her hands and knees. Hayami released her own harness and got to her feet as Jakari started retching violently. She took a couple of careful steps and dropped down next to Jakari, rubbing her back as the retching continued. Violent heave after violent heave rocked her, but she wasn't bringing up anything.

"Mamachi," she called out, not sure what to do.

"It's normal," Mamachi said over the comm. "It will last a few more minutes until her body realizes she's not actually dead."

"Told you that you didn't want to feel this," Jakari said between dry heaves.

"Doesn't sound like you want to feel it either," Hayami said.

"Not especially," Jakari said.

"Why didn't you disconnect?" Hayami asked.

"I wanted to make sure I got as many of them as possible," Jakari said. "The more I took down, the less chance they'd spot us before we were clear."

Jakari heaved again, and Hayami winced and rubbed her back a little harder, thankful that they were dry heaves and that she wouldn't have to spend the next ninety minutes in the back of a truck that smelled of vomit.

She didn't say anything else until Jakari's stomach calmed down, but when it was over, Jakari shifted so she was sitting with her back against the side of the truck and closed her eyes.

"How we doing, kid?" Jakari asked.

"No signs of pursuit," Mamachi said.

"Good," Jakari said. "That's good."

"Can I get you anything?" Hayami asked.

"Water," Jakari said. "Please."

Hayami got up and carefully made her way over to the ice chest they'd packed before leaving the base, pulled out three of bottles of water, and carried them over to Jakari. She sat down next to her and cracked open one of the bottles before handing it to her, then watched as Jakari downed the whole thing in one go. She opened a second bottle and handed it to Jakari, who nodded and took a sip before putting the cap back on.

"Try pressing it against the back of your neck," Hayami said.

"What?" Jakari asked.

"It's a human thing," Hayami said. "It helps with the nausea."

"Thanks," Jakari said. "The nausea's passed, but I'll remember that for next time."

Hayami nodded and opened the last bottle of water, then took a sip. "You do that a lot?"

Jakari shook her head. "No. Most of my missions are in and out. More like the first part of what we did tonight."

"What all did you get from Cikara's computer?" Hayami asked.

"The Helot tech. I got almost all of it. The Shroud design, the transfer algorithms for human consciousness, the Script code. I'm hoping that Rayak can use it to reverse engineer the Shroud and come up with a way to destroy it."

"You think that's possible?" Hayami asked.

"Yeah. We should be able to develop something like the Form Lock dart I used tonight. The Form Lock darts basically insert a Form Lock script into the target Vessel. If we can use a similar delivery method to inject a self-destruct script into the Shroud, we'd be able to free any Helots from Char control. It would make the whole system useless. It won't matter if we're able to take out Nira, Jaya, and Saka. Your people will be safe."

Hayami stared at Jakari, completely stunned.

"That's what tonight was about?" she asked. "You didn't give a damn about laying eyes on Nira. You were after the research."

"Oh, I wanted to see Nira," Jakari said. "I needed to make sure she was there."

"But you could have done that a dozen different ways," Hayami said.

"Yeah," Jakari said. "I could have, but this way, we have the Helot tech and can work out a hard counter, which will protect your people, and we ramp up the tension between Nira and Cikara, pushing Cikara more firmly into our camp."

"But won't it be harder to get back into the ship?" Hayami asked. "Now that they know we have their location, they're bound to dial up security."

"They'll probably move the ship," Jakari said.

"You say that like it's a good thing," Hayami said.

"It is," Jakari said. "Cikara will give us the location, so I'm not worried about losing the ship, but moving the ship disrupts their routines, puts them off balance, makes them vulnerable. And they'll need to find someplace they can hide quickly, so chances are, they won't be able to set down in a populated area. So if something happens to their ship, it won't wipe out a populated area."

"You thought a lot about this."

"Don't do that," Jakari said.

"What?"

"Start thinking I'm a good person," Jakari said. "I did this because I'm not going to walk into a situation where I know I won't walk out. Getting to a target is easy. I can get to anybody. Getting away after I've serviced the target is the trick. When a target is holed up somewhere where the security is too tight for you to get in and get out, the best way to handle it is to flush the target by making them think their security is compromised. They run for a new location, leaving themselves exposed, and you kill them before they get settled in somewhere secure. That's what I did tonight. I flushed the target. The rest is just gravy."

Hayami shook her head. "You are just completely fucking allergic to admitting you did a good thing, aren't you?" she asked. Then she leaned over and pressed a kiss to Jakari's forehead. "Thank you. Whatever your reason was, thank you."

"I...um..."

Hayami rolled her eyes. "Idiot," she said.

Chapter Nineteen

JAKARI STOOD AT THE back of the truck, watching in utter confusion as Hayami walked away. She'd spent most of the ride back to the base in a state of shock at what happened. Not on the mission, but after. She could still feel Hayami's lips pressed against her, and she didn't know what to do about it. She reached up, touching the spot, her eidetic memory replaying the moment in perfect detail, repeatedly.

"Jakari?" Mamachi said. The sound of her own name made her jump in shock because she hadn't heard Mamachi approach, which gave her another shock because no one had been able to sneak up on her since fairly early in the rebellion. She turned towards them, not sure what to say, or how to explain what had just happened.

"Are you okay?" Mamachi asked.

Jakari looked at them helplessly for a moment before turning and looking after Hayami. "She…"

"What is it?" Mamachi asked.

"She claimed me," Jakari said.

"*What*?" Mamachi asked.

Jakari turned back to Mamachi. "She claimed me."

Mamachi turned and looked in the direction Hayami had gone, then turned back to Jakari. "She couldn't have," Mamachi said. "She wouldn't even know how."

"She did!" Jakari said.

Mamachi shook their head. "No. She's human."

"I know."

Mamachi took a deep breath. "Okay, tell me exactly what happened."

"We were talking about the mission, and she asked me why I did things the way I did them. I explained that I wanted to retrieve the Helot research so we could develop a counter, and she got that look on her face that she gets sometimes."

"Which look?"

"Her eyes get soft, and she gets this sort of half-smile, and it always makes my stomach tie up in knots because I can tell that she's thinking that I'm some kind of hero. The one where I can look at her and tell that she's forgotten that I'm an assassin and not a soldier."

"You mean the one where she looks at you like you've just done something amazing?" Mamachi asked.

"Yes," Jakari said. "So, I told her not to do that. Not to think that I'm a good person. I told her I was flushing the target, and that everything else was just a bonus."

"And then what happened?"

"She leaned over and claimed me," Jakari said.

"How did she claim you?" Mamachi asked.

"She kissed me," Jakari said. "Right on the Cihna."

Mamachi reached up and covered their eyes with their right hand and bit their lower lip, and for a moment, Jakari was worried, but then she noticed their shoulders shaking and realized they were biting their lip to keep from laughing.

"You think this is funny."

"Yes," Mamachi said, as they burst out laughing.

"Fine!" Jakari said. She turned and started to walk away, but Mamachi reached out and caught her by the arm.

"I'm sorry," they said.

"It's not funny!"

Mamachi shook their head. "It kind of is," they said. "She didn't claim you."

"What? She did! She..." Jakari turned and looked after Hayami. "She kissed me, Machi. On the Cihna."

"Humans don't have a Cihna. They don't use scent marking at all." Mamachi reached up and rubbed the center of their forehead with the tips of two fingers. "It's just a bone plate. No scent glands. No nerve cluster. She didn't have any idea how...intimate of a gesture that would be for you."

She turned and looked in the direction Hayami had gone. "She didn't?"

"No," Mamachi said. "For humans, it is a gesture of affection, but it's a platonic one. Mothers and fathers often kiss their children in that spot. Friends as well. Romantic partners do use the gesture sometimes, but it doesn't carry the weight it does with us."

"Oh," Jakari said.

"Sorry to disappoint you," Mamachi said.

"I'm not disappointed," Jakari said. "I'm relieved."

Mamachi stared at her for a moment, then shrugged. "If you say so."

Jakari bit back the urge to ask what they meant by that, and instead headed towards the building and the waiting debrief, confusion swirling through her. She didn't want a wife. Especially not a human wife. She was better off alone, and Hayami was better off without her. She should be relieved. She was relieved. She was definitely relieved.

So why did she keep replaying the kiss over in her head?

* * * *

Hayami walked into the empty briefing room and took a seat. She really wanted to just go find her bed, curl up in a little ball, and sleep off the tension and adrenaline from earlier in the night, but she knew the debrief wouldn't wait. That didn't mean she had to like it.

The ride back to the base had been oddly stressful. Jakari hadn't said a word after Hayami had kissed her on the forehead, and she was left wondering if she'd broken some cultural taboo or something. Honestly, she wasn't sure what the hell she'd been thinking in the first place. She'd just wanted to let Jakari know that she was grateful. That she could see the good Jakari was doing, even if Jakari couldn't see it herself, but maybe that had been a mistake. Maybe she'd crossed some line she didn't know existed within Gadan culture. Or maybe Jakari was just so convinced that she was some irredeemable monster that any challenge to that self-image was bound to cause issues.

She wasn't sure which it was, but she did know that whatever was going on, she really hoped it didn't come between them. She liked Jakari. The more she got to know her, the more she liked her, and she thought Jakari could use a friend who hadn't been caught up in the war for centuries. Someone with an outside perspective.

She glanced up as Skylar took the seat beside her. "Hey," she said.

"How'd it go?" Skylar asked.

"Pretty good," Hayami said.

"You bring my Mamachi back in one piece?"

Hayami smiled. "Yeah," she said. "They're in good shape."

"Good," Skylar said. "I'd hate to have to rough you up."

Hayami laughed. "You really like them, don't you?"

Skylar's cheeks started to turn red, and she glanced towards the door before answering. "Yeah," she said. "Is that weird?"

Hayami shook her head. "I don't think so," she said. "It's pretty obvious they adore you."

"You think so?" Skylar asked. "I mean, sometimes I think so, but we've known each other for six years and we've never gotten any further than cuddling."

"Have you told them that you want to go further than cuddling?" Hayami asked.

Skylar sighed and shook her head. "I keep chickening out," she said. "I don't want to scare them off, you know? And, well, you've seen what Gadan look like in their natural form. Do you think they'd even find me attractive?"

"Do you find Mamachi's natural form attractive?"

"Oh, God, yes," Skylar said. "You haven't seen Mamachi's Gadan form, have you?"

"No," Hayami said. "I saw Jakari's and a few of the crew when we went down to the situation room that day, but that's it."

"Mamachi's beautiful," Skylar said. "All gold scales with black markings and muscles everywhere. It was a little weird at first, you know. I was never into any of that before I met them, but the longer I knew them and the more I saw them in their real form, the more I realized they were beautiful in any form."

"It probably doesn't hurt that their human form is a nice slice of beefcake," Hayami said.

"I didn't think you were the type to appreciate beefcake," Skylar said.

"Am I that obvious?" Hayami asked.

"Only when Jakari's ass is in your line of sight," Skylar said.

Hayami groaned and covered her face with both hands. "Oh, God."

Skylar laughed. "It's okay. You should see Mamachi in cheesecake mode."

"What?" Hayami asked, lifting her face out of her hands so she could see Skylar.

Skylar pulled out her phone and pulled up a picture of a gorgeous blond woman with light brown skin in a bright yellow bikini. It took a second for Hayami to realize that she was looking at a female version of Mamachi.

"Holy shit," Hayami said.

"Right?" Skylar said. "I spent the whole day afraid I was drooling."

"I didn't realize you were into cheesecake."

"I didn't either," Skylar said. "But having a gigantic crush on a genderfluid alien has made me realize I don't much care what kind of cake it is, as long as there's cake."

"Fair enough," Hayami said. "But I'm an old-fashioned girl. I'll stick to my cheesecake."

"Even if it has scales on it?" Skylar asked.

"What?"

Before Skylar could answer, the door opened and Mamachi walked in. They took a seat next to Skylar, and Hayami pretty much gave up any hope of getting an answer to what Skylar was hinting at. Though it didn't take much guessing, really. Especially after the comment about her staring at Jakari's ass. In her defense, it was a really nice ass, but then, everything about Jakari's human form was nice, and if Jakari were human, and not a coworker, she'd have been all over her.

The door opened again, and Jakari came into the briefing room and took the seat next to her. She smiled, but Jakari gave her an uncertain look that Hayami wasn't sure how to interpret, and before she could really consider it further, Napati, Rayak, Prack, Gomez, and Dubari all piled into the room.

* * * *

Jakari wasn't sure what to make of the look Hayami was giving her, which just compounded the confusion she already felt over the kiss. She tried to tell herself that Mamachi was right, that it was just a cultural misunderstanding. The problem was, it was such a specific gesture. She still remembered the night, after six months of asking Aashi to marry her, when Aashi had leaned in and kissed her like that.

Her thoughts were cut off by Napati, Gomez, Prack, Dubari, and Rayak filing into the room. She gave herself a small shake as they took their seats. It was time to focus on the mission and put everything else aside. Something she had a lot of practice at, thankfully.

"I know it's late, and the humans present need their rest, so we'll try to get through this as quickly as possible," Napati said. She looked at Jakari. "Tell us what happened."

"We approached the site of the Char ship without incident. As planned, Hayami and I used a pair of Class One Light Taluses in a doppelganger configuration, as well as a Class Two in a heavy grav sled configuration, to move from the transport to the entrance of the ship. We concealed the Class Two and proceeded inside the building I had identified as a likely point of entry. I was able to locate an access point, and hack through the Char security codes. We took a personnel lift into the base.

"Once inside, I was able to bypass ship's security far enough to get the computer to guide us to Cikara's office. I disabled Cikara using a Form Lock dart, broke into their account on the computer, and retrieved a map of the ship, Nira's location, and a portion of the Helot research which I hope will be enough to allow Rayak to develop a successful countermeasure.

"When we had everything I thought I could get from Cikara's system, I rendered them unconscious and proceeded to Nira's location while reconfiguring the Taluses into Char security personnel. I triggered a security alarm on Cikara's computer using a script I'd left running. Nira exited her quarters, and we were able to lay eyes on her and confirm that she is on planet per the intel we received.

"That's where we hit our first snag. Nira tasked us with accompanying her to Cikara's quarters. We went, and when she found Cikara, I suggested that their assailants were likely making for the hangar in an effort to escape. Nira gave us permission to pursue. We made it to the surface unchallenged, but once we brought the grav sled online, we were met with heavy resistance from in-place defenses and from enemy troops on grav sleds. I instructed Hayami to disconnect from her Talus, then flew all three Taluses into the middle of the pursuing enemies and set off the self-destruct system.

"Once the Taluses were destroyed, I woke up in the transport Mamachi was driving, and we returned here without any further signs of pursuit."

Napati turned to Mamachi. "Anything to add?"

"No," Mamachi said. "Everything was smooth on my end."

"Hayami?" Napati asked.

"No," Hayami said. "That covers the mission."

Napati turned back to Jakari. "So what's your next step?"

"Cikara is supposed to comm us tomorrow, to confirm that we're moving forward with the plan. I expect right now, they're in a mad scramble to move the ship—"

"What?" Gomez asked. "If they move the ship, how are we supposed to find them again?"

"Cikara wants us to kill Nira," Jakari said. "They will provide us with the new location."

"How can you be sure?" Gomez asked.

"Because Nira's paranoid. Even though I made it look like we attacked Cikara, she's got to be wondering why I didn't kill them, which is going to make Cikara even more desperate for our help. Moving the ship accomplishes two additional goals. First, it reduces the effectiveness of their security. As long as we strike quickly before they are fully dug in, we'll have a much better chance of getting in and out without casualties. Second, they are going to have to find a new place to hide quickly. That means that, most likely, they are going to put down someplace without people around, at least temporarily. That reduces the chances of collateral damage. No more risk of blowing one of your largest urban centers off the map if a stray plasma bolt cracks an anti-matter pod."

Gomez stared at her for a moment, then nodded. "I hadn't thought about that, but if you're right, that's definitely a good thing."

"We'll know tomorrow," Jakari said. "But if Cikara doesn't give us the new location, there are other ways to find them."

"Then I suppose there's not a lot for us to do between now and tomorrow," Napati said. "Are there any other questions or concerns before we adjourn?"

No one said anything, so Napati nodded. "We'll reconvene for the call from Cikara tomorrow. Until then, get some rest. I have a feeling once we get that call, things are going to move quickly."

Everyone started standing up to leave. Jakari moved around the table to find Rayak. "Have you got a minute?" she asked.

"No, but I have a feeling what you want is important enough for me to shelve everything else that needs doing."

"I want you to look over the Helot data," Jakari said. "You know more about the Phylactery system than anyone else alive. I need to know if anything is missing from the data I got."

"All right," Rayak said. "Let's go to my lab."

"Sure," Jakari said. "Let me just say goodnight to Hayami."

* * * *

Hayami watched as Jakari led Rayak over to them.

"Hey," Jakari said.

"Hey."

"I'm going to be in the lab with Rayak for a while," Jakari said. "We're going to start work on the Helot countermeasure. If you need me for anything..."

"I know where to find you," Hayami said. "Just follow the sound of grumpy here."

Jakari snorted while Rayak glared at her, but she just smiled back beatifically, daring Rayak to say a word. In the end, he just grumbled under his breath as Jakari led him away.

"I can't believe you got away with that," Mamachi said.

"What?" Hayami asked.

"Calling Rayak grumpy," Skylar said. "He's been known to throw a bone saw for less."

"That's why you call him grumpy *away* from the bone saws," Hayami said.

"You know, that's a good point," Skylar said.

"Come on," Mamachi said. "We'll walk you back to your quarters."

"Don't you have somewhere important to be?" Hayami asked as they headed for the barracks.

"Not really," Mamachi said. "My intel team is pretty self-sufficient."

"They'd have to be if you detached yourself from them for over a year," Hayami said. "I'm surprised you didn't get replaced."

"For a year?" Mamachi said.

Hayami thought about it for a moment and felt a little chagrined. "Right," she said. "Different time scales."

Mamachi tilted their head. "I suppose a year would be a long time for something like that among humans."

"Enough to get at least a temporary replacement into the role," Hayami said.

"I honestly wonder if I deserve the role," Mamachi said.

"Why?" Hayami asked. "From what I've heard, you're really good at it."

"Not good enough, apparently," Mamachi said. "Not when I miss something big happening in the back of the truck I'm driving."

Hayami looked at them and felt her stomach sinking. "Um, what do you mean?"

"I mean the part where you claimed Jakari as your future mate," Mamachi said.

Hayami stopped dead in her tracks. "I did what?" she asked at a volume that hurt her own ears.

"Claimed Jakari as your future mate," Mamachi said. "Honestly, I've never seen her that confused. One minute, she's fighting the Char, doing her thing. The next, the poor woman is sitting there wondering if she's finally gone round the bend."

"I...uh...what...I didn't..."

"Mamachi," Skylar said, "maybe you had better explain before her head explodes."

Mamachi shrugged. "She's the one going around kissing people on the Cihna," they said.

"What?" Hayami asked. She hadn't kissed anyone on the Cihna. She didn't even know what the fuck a Cihna was, but she knew she definitely hadn't kissed anyone there. She hadn't kissed anyone!

She froze, because that wasn't true. She'd kissed Jakari, but on the forehead. Not on the Cihna, whatever the hell that is.

"What's a Cihna?" Skylar asked.

"It's a marking gland," Mamachi said.

"A marking gland?" Hayami asked.

"Yeah," Mamachi said. "We use...well, we used to use scent marking. Not so much these days. After the Migration, all of our senses were improved, so it's not as important as it used to be, but we still have the glands. We use different glands for marking different things. The ones in our cheeks mark friends, family, children. The ones in our thighs mark territory." Hayami watched in horror as Mamachi reached up and tapped the center of their forehead. "The Cihna is reserved for marking our mates. Press the top of your head against your mate and rub, and a scent is released. Kissing someone there is a way of claiming them. An invitation for them to mark you."

"Oh, God," Hayami said.

"What?" Skylar asked, looking back and forth between Mamachi and Hayami. "What happened?"

"I kissed Jakari on the forehead," Hayami said.

Mamachi smiled and nodded. "Yes, you did," they said.

"Oh, God," Hayami said. "I...I asked her to marry me?"

Mamachi broke down laughing.

"Mamachi?" Skylar asked.

"I'm sorry," Mamachi said, gasping for air. "It's just, the look on her face."

"Jakari thinks I want to marry her?" Hayami asked.

Mamachi shook their head. "No," they said. "She did, for the entire ride back to base, but I explained it to her."

"You told her I didn't mean it?"

"Yeah," Mamachi said. "Should I not have?"

Hayami balled up her hand into a fist and punched Mamachi in the shoulder as hard as she could.

"You asshole!" she yelled. Then she hit them again. "You fucking asshole!"

"Hey!" Mamachi shouted, backing away and holding up their hands.

"You...argh!" Hayami turned and stormed away from Mamachi. She hadn't gotten more than a few steps when she heard Mamachi and Skylar both racing after her.

"Hey," Mamachi said, "wait up!"

Hayami spun around and pointed a finger at them. "You let me think Jakari thought we were engaged!" she snapped.

"Well, she did," Mamachi said. "For an hour and half!"

"So, what? You wanted to punish me for it?" Hayami asked.

"No!" Mamachi said.

"Hayami, just take it easy," Skylar said.

"I'm sorry," Mamachi said. "I was just teasing you. I didn't mean to upset you."

"Maybe you should go," Skylar said. "Just...let me take care of this."

"Okay," Mamachi said. "I really am sorry, though."

"No," Hayami said. "Wait."

Mamachi stopped. "What is it?"

"How bad did I screw up?" she asked.

"Not bad," Mamachi said. "She was just confused. She...the Cihna isn't just a marking gland. It's a...sensitive spot for us."

"So, I...violated her?"

"No," Mamachi said. "Once I explained, she was relieved. I think she was afraid she'd done something to give you the wrong idea."

"Fuck," Hayami said. "Just...fuck!"

She turned and started walking

"Hayami!" Skylar called.

"Just leave me alone," Hayami said.

She could feel Skylar and Mamachi's eyes on her, but she didn't look back.

Chapter Twenty

"THIS IS MORE THAN just a portion of the Helot research," Rayak said as Jakari set a hot cup of tea next to him.

"Yeah," Jakari said. "According to Cikara, there's only one file missing. The last design update. They've been withholding it because they think Nira will kill them as soon as they complete the tech."

"Not an unreasonable fear," Rayak said. "If Jaya thinks Cikara is compromised, they wouldn't hesitate to have Nira kill them."

Jakari took a sip of her own tea. "You know, I want to say I miss the days when we were all on the same side, but then I remember what those days were like."

"Easier," Rayak said. "You always knew who the enemy was."

"Did we?" Jakari asked. "How much easier would all of our lives be if we'd gotten rid of Arthan, Jaya, Saka, Nira, and Cikara when the rebellion ended?"

"I don't know," Rayak said. "It's easy to look back now, but then, they were the heroes who'd just won the war."

"And if we manage to kill Jaya, Nira, and Saka, what will that make us?" Jakari said. "Ten thousand years from now, are Mamachi and their friends going to be sitting around wishing they'd killed us when they had the chance?"

"No," Rayak said. "Because neither of us are stupid enough to go into politics."

Jakari laughed. "True enough," she said. "Besides, no one wants to call an assassin a hero."

"Doesn't mean you aren't one," Rayak said.

Jakari made a dismissive noise. "I'm not," she said. "A monster is about the nicest description for what I am."

"You are what you needed to be to survive," Rayak said. "I've told you before, blaming yourself for it is a stupid thing to do."

Jakari didn't say anything. It was an old argument between the two of them, and not one she really wanted to have again. Not when she had other things on her mind.

"Can you make a countermeasure with this?" Jakari asked.

"Most likely," Rayak said. "But I can't guarantee the effectiveness without that last file."

"I'll get it for you," Jakari said. "Just make sure you rig the darts to self-destruct once the countermeasure code is injected."

"Teach your grandmother to lay on a rock," Rayak snapped.

Jakari held up her hands. "Easy there," she said.

"Sorry," Rayak said. "Forgot who I was talking to for a second."

"It's okay," Jakari said. "How's Napati holding up?"

"Who knows," Rayak said. "Not well, I'd suspect, but you'd never know it."

"Plotting to murder the love of your life can't be easy, even if they've been trying to murder each other for nine thousand years."

"Sometimes I wonder if Jaya ever really loved her," Rayak said.

"I think they did," Jakari said. "I think that's why Jaya took it so hard when Napati sided with Arthan."

"Or maybe Jaya was just fucking insane to start with," Rayak said.

"I don't know," Jakari said. "Sometimes I think us Migrants are the ones who've gone insane. We were never meant to live this long."

"You got that right," Rayak said. "Sometimes, I think Bhaskor should have built a limiter into the Phylacteries. Everyone gets a century, and then the Phylactery just breaks down like a child's form limiter."

"Probably would have done all of us a favor if he had," Jakari said before taking another sip of tea.

"Well, what's done is done, and we have to live with it," Rayak said.

"Speaking of...what do you know about humans?" Jakari asked.

"More than I want to," Rayak said. "Why do you ask?"

"We're working with them," Jakari said. "We may be working with them for a while. I'd like to avoid any more misunderstandings."

"Any more?" Rayak asked. "I wasn't aware that there had been any."

"How would you know?" Jakari said. "You spend all day in your med bay."

"Good point," Rayak said. He picked up his tea and took a drink. "What do you want to know?"

"They seem very...affectionate."

"Ah," Rayak said. "You mean Skylar and Mamachi."

"I...um...how'd you guess?" Jakari sputtered.

"I have eyes," Rayak said. "Those two are so in love it's actually painful to watch. I honestly don't know what's holding them back."

"Maybe the fact that they're different species?" Jakari said.

Rayak waved his hand dismissively. "Hardly makes a difference when Mamachi can take any form they want."

"What about the fact that Mamachi will outlive her by tens, or even hundreds of thousands of years?"

"Or Mamachi might die in the raid on the Char ship a couple of days from now," Rayak said. "How long you might or might not live is no way to decide who you fall in love with."

"It's asking for pain," Jakari said.

"Maybe it's worth the pain," Rayak said. "Ask yourself, if you could go back and do it all over, knowing what you know now, would you still want to meet Aashi? Still want to fall in love with her, still marry her, still build a life with her?"

"Yes," Jakari said. "Of course."

"Even knowing how it would end?" Rayak asked.

"Yes."

"But what about the pain?" Rayak asked. "You've lived with that loss for ten thousand years, and you've never gotten over it. Not even a little bit. Was it really worth it?"

"Yes," Jakari said. "For her, anything."

"So, you see my point," Rayak said.

"Yeah," Jakari said.

"I've already talked to Napati about it," Rayak said. "Stationing Mamachi here for a few decades after we leave. A listening post, or a monitoring station. Whatever you want to call it. We can do without them for a few decades, and they get to be in love, have a life, be happy."

"You've given it a lot of thought," Jakari said.

"It's Mamachi," Rayak said. "I never quite figured out why everyone seems to want to adopt the little shit, but let's be real. Everyone thinks Mamachi is their kid."

Jakari laughed. "God, yes," she said. "You can't spend ten minutes around them without wanting to tuck them under a bask lamp and cheek mark them."

"You never had any kids, did you?" Rayak asked.

"No," Jakari said. "Aashi never wanted them. Not after what happened with her parents."

"Bad childhood?" Rayak asked.

"Really bad," Jakari said. "I was glad they didn't survive the bioweapon. I'm not sure what I would have done if they lived when she didn't."

Neither of them said anything for a while after that. They just sat and sipped their tea as Rayak looked over the Helot files, but eventually, curiosity got the best of Jakari.

"What about the other humans?" Jakari asked.

"What do you mean?" Rayak asked.

"Do they all get so attached?" Jakari asked.

"Not all of them," Rayak asked. "That pink haired girl, Kida..."

"The one that hangs around Prack?"

"More like follows him around like a puppy," Rayak said. "I think Prack's adopted her."

"But it's not romantic?"

"No," Rayak said. "She has a girlfriend. One of the guards. I've seen them together a few times."

"Any others?" Jakari asked.

"Why do you want to know?" Rayak asked.

"Just trying to understand them," Jakari said.

"I think Gomez has a thing for Napati," Rayak said.

"She does?" Jakari asked.

"Yes," Rayak said. "She hides it well, but every time she's around Napati, her pheromone levels go crazy."

"I didn't know you could detect their pheromones."

"Sure," Rayak said. "Give me a moment. I'll slug you the algorithm."

Jakari waited, and sure enough, a moment later, she got a wireless data transfer request from Rayak. She accepted, and the algorithm dropped into her download bin. She pulled it out and plugged it into her sensor package. There was a slight tingle as her olfactory nerves reconfigured themselves.

"Be careful, though," Rayak said.

"What?" Jakari asked.

"That human you work with. Hayami. Her pheromone levels spike a lot."

"They do?"

"Yeah," Rayak said. "Pretty much any time she's around a female human form. You, Gomez, Skylar, Kida. If I didn't know better, I'd think she was in some kind of mating heat."

"Do humans have those?" Jakari asked.

"Not really," Rayak said. "Or if they do, it's not in any of the medical literature I've reviewed. The females have a fertile period roughly once a lunar cycle, but the spike in sex drive is relatively small. It's not a full-on heat cycle. From what I understand of how humans work, I think Hayami is just young enough that she's actively seeking a mate. Gomez is older. Approaching the end of her fertile years. Kida has a mate, and Skylar is fixated on Mamachi, even if they haven't consummated the relationship."

"They don't scent mark, do they?" Jakari asked.

"They don't have the glands for it," Rayak asked. "Why?"

"Hayami did something that confused me," Jakari said. "It made more sense when Mamachi explained that humans don't have marking glands."

Rayak's eyes got a little big. "What did she do?" he asked.

"She kissed me," Jakari said. She reached up and tapped the center of her forehead. "Right here."

"Oh," Rayak said, fighting back a laugh. "God, no wonder you were confused."

"It's not funny," Jakari said.

"Yes, it is," Rayak said. "Of all the people she could have kissed, she picked you."

"What's that supposed to mean?" Jakari asked.

"What do you think it means?" Rayak asked. "Ten thousand years and you haven't even had so much as a tumble."

Jakari looked away from Rayak. "I never wanted one," she said. "I like being alone."

"Bullshit," Rayak said. "You think you deserve to be alone because you've got it in your head that you failed Aashi."

"I did," Jakari said.

"No, you didn't," Rayak said.

"You don't know what you're talking about," Jakari said.

"Yes, I do," Rayak said. "You sat there, and you watched the person you love most die, and you couldn't do a damned thing about it, but you were a gardener, Jakari. You took her to the hospital the second she got sick. You did everything you could."

"It wasn't enough," Jakari said.

"No, it wasn't," Rayak said. "I know, because it happened to me, too. You were a gardener, and you were helpless, but I was a doctor and it didn't matter. I was just as helpless as you were. I watched my wife, my daughter, my son-in-law, and my grandkids die that first day. All of them got the fast-acting variant. All of them except me. When the time for the Migration came, I considered refusing. I considered just going and joining the people I loved. You want to know why I didn't?"

"Why?" Jakari asked.

"Because they would have wanted me to live. They would have wanted me to go on, and have a good life, and be happy."

"But that's not what happened," Jakari said.

"No, it's not," Rayak said. "But the difference between you and me is, I haven't stopped trying. I haven't stopped hoping for something better. You just look for reasons you deserve to suffer."

"I don't have to look for reasons," Jakari said. "I can't forget them."

Rayak sighed. "You need to forgive yourself for what you did."

"I don't deserve to be forgiven."

"Yes, you do," Rayak said.

"I killed children," Jakari said.

"And they did a lot worse. The brothels. The gladiator pits. The slave markets."

"So that makes it okay?" Jakari asked.

"No. None of it was okay," Rayak said. "But you weren't the only one who killed children. We committed genocide. All of us are guilty of that. But we didn't have a choice. We didn't start the war. We didn't go looking for a fight. They attacked us. They dropped a bioweapon on us. They were killing us just as surely as we killed them. They were just doing it slower. We all fought back the only way we could, and when Napati gave you a better option than bombs and knives and terror, you took it. And when the war was over, you stopped. You went back to being a gardener. You tried to find peace.

"You didn't choose to become a monster. You chose to survive. You chose to fight back. And deep down, you know that. You don't feel guilty because of the things you had to do. You feel guilty because you survived when she didn't. That's what you can't forgive yourself for. Everything else is just an excuse."

Jakari stood up and took a deep breath. "That's bullshit," she said before she turned and walked out of the room.

* * * *

Cikara sat at their desk, rubbing the spot where the Form Lock dart had hit them. There was no pain, their body had healed the instant the dart had been removed, but there was the memory of being locked in a form and helpless.

Anger burned inside them. Anger at themselves for trusting Jakari and for needing Jakari. Anger at Jakari for the casual way she'd walked in like she had every right, for the way she'd overpowered them and then lorded her control over them. Anger at the realization that they had no one they could truly trust but themself.

They reached out and touched a button on the desk, opening a comm channel to Bayadani.

"Yes, General?" Bayadani asked.

"I need to see you in my office, right now," Cikara said.

"I'm on my way," they said.

Cikara cut the comm channel without another word and thought about the plan. Nothing had truly changed. Jakari was still their best chance of killing Nira. The difference was, they no longer believed they could trust Jakari not to kill them once Nira was out of the way. They needed insurance.

The door to the office opened, and Bayadani stepped inside. "You called?"

"I did," Cikara said. They pressed a button on their desk to lock the door behind Bayadani, then stood up and waved them to come closer.

Bayadani approached their desk. "What can I do for you?"

Cikara pulled out a device like the one that Jakari had used earlier and activated it, jamming any listening devices in the room. They stood up and approached the wall behind them, placing their hand on a specific spot and issuing a command through the hidden interface point. The wall opened.

"Come inside," Cikara said as they stepped through the opening. Bayadani followed.

Cikara took a seat in the hidden lab and gestured for Bayadani to sit down as well. Once Bayadani was seated, Cikara touched a control, sealing the room.

"I didn't know this was here," Bayadani said.

"No one does," Cikara said. "It's not on the schematics for the ship."

Bayadani nodded. "Clever."

"Thank you," Cikara said. "You have been the most loyal member of my staff since the day you were assigned. In the centuries you have served me, I have never had cause to complain about your performance. I want you to understand that."

"Thank you, General."

"You're welcome. But now, I have to ask a question I don't want to, but which circumstances have forced on me. Where do your loyalties lie?"

"General?"

"It's a simple question, Major."

"My loyalty is to the Char Oram."

"Of course. I never doubted that. The problem is that's no longer a clear loyalty."

"What do you mean?" Bayadani asked.

"Nira plans to kill me," Cikara said. "On Jaya's orders, I have no doubt."

"I see," Bayadani said. "And you want to know if I will side with Nira or you when the time comes."

"Not just that," Cikara said. "I know that you joined the Char because your sibling, Akasi, was killed in a Suil raid on the base where they were stationed."

"Yes, they were."

"I take it you understand that if Nira has orders from Jaya to kill me, then this will not end when Nira is dead. If I kill Nira, Saka will come with those same orders, and if I survive Saka, Jaya will come."

Bayadani, to their credit, took a moment to consider what Cikara was saying before giving a small nod. "Most likely, yes."

"Definitely, yes," Cikara said. "To be clear, I intend to be the one left standing at the end, but that brings with it other considerations. When I am the leader of the Char, I will do what is best for our people, and that may include making peace with the Suil."

"What?" Bayadani asked. "General, the Suil are the enemy!"

"No," Cikara said. "The Suil are Gadan, just like we are. The enemy is anyone who would hurt the Gadan. The Seichu were the enemy, and there may come a time when we have to fight some other aliens, but this civil war has gone on far too long. The Char and the Suil have killed more Gadan than the Seichu ever did. It's time for peace. To set aside arms and be one united people again."

"You're wrong!" Bayadani said. "The Suil are our enemies, and the only way there can be peace is if we crush them all."

Cikara nodded. "Very well," they said. "I have my answer."

Cikara reached over and touched a button on their desk and set their hand on the access point. "I want to thank you for your long service, Bayadani, and I want to assure you I hold no ill will towards you."

"General?" Bayadani asked, a moment before Cikara fired. Bayadani never saw the panel open behind them, or the dart launchers swing out. They never even felt the electrical discharge that forced them into Phylactery lockdown. They just hit the floor, unconscious.

Cikara picked them up and carried them over to the operating table. Once they set Bayadani down, they went over to the supply cabinet and retrieved one of the special Shrouds they had prepared for this eventuality. Bayadani would not lose all their memories like a normal Helot. Just the last few minutes. What would change was that they would be absolutely loyal to Cikara. Unable to question any order, willing to die in their defense, and more importantly, willing to kill for them.

* * * *

Hayami lay in bed, staring up at the ceiling. She'd pretty much given up on getting any sleep, and instead, was wondering how she could possibly have fucked up so bad. Oh, she knew there was no way she could have known that kissing a Gadan on the forehead was tantamount to a marriage proposal, but that wasn't the point. She shouldn't have kissed Jakari in the first place. Not on the forehead or anywhere else.

It was a stupid thing to do. Sure, she'd just wanted to say thank you for what Jakari had done, but that didn't require anything other than words. Except she'd gotten it in her head that Jakari would ignore the words because she was so determined to hate herself, but it wasn't her job to fix Jakari's emotional damage. The woman was a ten-thousand-year-old alien. She didn't need some cop from Texas playing amateur psychiatrist. Jakari could handle her own mental health.

Except she wasn't handling it. She was hurting and miserable and no one seemed to want to help her. Hayami had known the woman for a few days, and she could see how much pain she was in, how lonely she was. How could her friends not see it? Mamachi, at least, seemed to, but they didn't know what to do to help.

She rolled onto her side, thinking maybe staring at the wall would be more helpful than staring at the ceiling. It wasn't, which just pissed her off more than she already was. She growled in frustration and threw her pillow at the wall, which only pissed her off more, because it meant she either had to get out of bed and get her pillow, or sleep without it, which wasn't going to happen.

She grumbled when she got out of bed because the floor was freezing. She rushed over to get her pillow, then rushed back to the bed, which, of course meant she kicked the nightstand with her little toe. She stood there, staring down at her foot, waiting for the pain she knew was coming, cursing herself for following Jakari down that street and swearing that from now on, she would mind her own fucking business. A promise she knew was bullshit even as she made it. She was a cop. Minding other people's business was in the job description.

The pain finally hit, and she bit down on the scream she wanted to let loose and crawled into bed. She slapped the pillow a few times, then laid her head on it and pulled the covers up to her chin, wondering how the hell she, of all people, got stuck dealing with Jakari's mental health problems.

Just because she was a giant fucking lesbian didn't mean she knew a god-damned thing about women. In fact, her history with women pretty much proved that she was the worst person in the world to deal with a woman. Hell, she was pretty sure every lesbian in the metroplex had her name and a dire warning to avoid dating her at all costs. Not that she could really blame them. If she met herself, she would run in the other direction.

The question was, how do you apologize to someone for accidentally proposing marriage? Of all the ways she'd fucked up with women in the past, that was one she didn't have any experience with. Though given her record, she probably should have made plans for it. As big a fuck up as she was, she was bound to do it at some point.

At least Jakari wasn't disappointed. According to Mamachi, anyway. They'd said she was relieved. Which was another reason Hayami was pissed off. It was completely irrational, of course. She didn't want to marry Jakari. She wasn't even interested in Jakari. Jakari was a giant space cat lizard, and Hayami was a breast girl. Giant space cat lizards didn't have breasts, so she couldn't be interested in Jakari. It was still a little insulting, being told that someone was relieved you didn't want to marry them. What was so wrong with her that Jakari was actually relieved at the thought of not marrying her?

She rolled over and faced the other wall, since the one she was staring at hadn't been the least bit helpful. The new wall just stared back at her blankly, refusing to give any more help than the ceiling or the first wall, and she wondered for a moment where her gun was. Maybe the walls would be more helpful after she put a few bullets in them.

She huffed and rolled over, lying face down in the pillow, thinking maybe she could smother herself and not have to deal with any of this shit anymore.

Chapter Twenty-One

"MORNING, RAYAK," HAYAMI SAID as she stepped up next to him at the drink counter in the cafeteria. He turned and glared for a moment.

"Oh, it's you," he said, then went back to dumping a frankly frightening amount of sugar into his steaming cup of tea.

"Nice to see you too," she said.

"I didn't say it was nice to see you."

"No, but since that's what polite people would say, I just assumed the sentiment was implied, and that you didn't say it due to fatigue or a lack of proper caffeination."

"I've had plenty of sleep, and just because I'm wearing the form of a species of junkies doesn't mean I've developed an addiction to your stimulants," Rayak said.

"Now, see, that was rude," Hayami said.

"Yes. That was the point," he said as he started stirring his tea. "Rudeness usually makes you humans leave me alone."

"Well, I'm not your typical human," Hayami said.

"So I heard," Rayak said. "Proposing marriage in the middle of a mission does seem a little forward for your kind."

Hayami's cheeks suddenly felt like they were on fire and her eyelids felt like they were trying to climb her forehead. "You know about that?"

"Doesn't everyone?" he asked.

She closed her eyes and hoped like hell that her mistake hadn't spread that far. "I don't know," she said. She opened her eyes and looked at him again. "I didn't realize there's been a memo or whatever sent out to the whole base."

Rayak glared at her, but she could have sworn she saw one corner of his mouth twitch upwards. "What did you want?"

"I had a human question," she said.

"Obviously," he said. "Out with it."

"Mamachi said that he could go days on just a couple of donuts, but whenever I see most Gadan, they tend to have a drink in their hand. Water, coffee, tea. I was curious about why?"

"Walk with me," Rayak said.

Hayami picked up her tray and followed as Rayak started walking over to one of the tables.

"We don't require a lot of food," he said. "Most organics consume food as fuel. They run off chemical energy. We don't. Our bodies are built out of semi-biological nanotechnology." He reached a table that seemed to suit him and took a seat. Hayami did the same.

"Each individual particle of our body houses a power collection device. It works off the ambient energy in the environment. Since we don't require stored chemical energy to power us, food is mostly for replacing lost mass. We do shed material off our body in much the same way you shed cells, though at a considerably slower rate. What little food we do eat is converted into new TOP matter, or in some instances, into other specialized products, such as chemical fuel for certain types of weapons. That's why you'll sometimes see soldiers gorging themselves before a battle. They're loading their weapons."

"Right," Hayami said. "And the drinks?"

"Evaporation," Rayak said. "The particles exist as a particle-in-water emulsion, but as water is lost to the surrounding environment, the particles begin to lose their spacing. If we get too dehydrated, we start having serious problems. The first is losing the ability to shape shift, but it gets worse from there."

"How long can you go without water?" Hayami asked.

"We lose the ability to shape shift after about thirty-six hours. We start having serious functional issues by forty-eight hours. We'll shut down after about four days."

"Will you die?" Hayami asked.

"Eventually," Rayak said. "That can take months, or even years."

"Good to know," Hayami said.

"Yeah," Rayak said. "So, are you going to ask me what you really want to ask me, or are you going to keep wasting my time?"

"What makes you think that wasn't what I really wanted to ask you?"

"Because you're exhibiting anxiety markers, and you wouldn't be for such an innocuous question," Rayak said. He took a sip of his tea, and stared at her, waiting.

"Right," Hayami said. She picked up her egg sandwich and took a bite, chewing slowly as she tried to figure out how to phrase what she wanted to ask.

"You've known Jakari a long time, right?" she asked.

"I met her when Napati recruited her into the resistance fairly early in the rebellion, so ninety-eight hundred of your years, give or take."

"Right," Hayami said. "I'm just going to call that a long time and move on."

"Fine by me."

"And you clearly know about what happened on the mission last night," Hayami said.

"I've heard part of it," he said. "You kissed her on the Cihna."

Hayami sighed. "I swear I didn't even know what a Cihna was before Mamachi explained it after the debrief."

"Not surprising. We don't go around handing out a list of our intimate body parts to strangers."

Hayami closed her eyes and leaned forward. "Oh, God," she groaned. She waited, expecting Rayak to say something, but all she heard was him sipping his tea. Finally, she opened her eyes and looked up to see him watching her.

"How intimate?" she asked.

"I don't have much of a basis for comparison," he said. "I've reviewed the medical literature on human sexual interactions, but honestly, it leaves a lot to be desired when it comes to breaking down levels of intimacy."

"Right," Hayami said. "Of course it does."

"The other problem is, your people don't seem to have any sort of physical equivalent for marker glands, so it's hard to find a basis for comparison, but the Cihna isn't just a marker gland. It's part of the mating process. And by mating process, I don't mean the sort of casual copulation common among the young. I mean real mating. You don't mark someone with the Cihna unless you mean it. For a lot of our history, marking someone that way *was* marriage."

"And kissing someone there?" Hayami asked.

"It was a way of telling someone you wanted them to mark you. It was giving them permission to claim you as their wife or husband."

"Oh, God, I really fucked up, didn't I?"

"If it had been literally anyone else in the universe, I would say no. It's an understandable mistake."

"But it was Jakari," Hayami said.

"Have you heard the story of how she met Aashi?" Rayak asked.

"Yeah," Hayami said. "God, I messed up."

"Maybe," Rayak said. "Or maybe you did her a favor."

"What do you mean?" Hayami asked.

"I mean she's been wallowing in guilt and grief for millennia. Maybe a good sharp kiss in the Cihna was enough to finally snap her out of it."

"But it was a mistake," Hayami said. "I didn't know what it meant."

"So what?" Rayak asked. "Some of the best things in life start as mistakes, or accidents. How things start isn't nearly as important as what you do with them."

"You're not seriously suggesting I marry her, are you?"

Rayak shrugged. "Why not?"

"I barely know her," Hayami said. "We're not the same species. She's going to outlive me by tens of thousands of years."

"If you marry her, you'll have plenty of time to get to know her. She can be whatever species you want her to be. And how do you know she'll outlive you? She could be dead tomorrow."

"You're insane," Hayami said.

"No," Rayak said. "I just want to see one of the few people in this universe I genuinely care about stop hurting. Now, I don't know if it was the kiss that did it, or if it was already going on and the kiss just made her notice, but you have knocked her out of the hole she's been hiding in since her wife died. Maybe the two of you would work out, maybe you wouldn't, but you'll never know if you don't try. She could be the best thing to ever happen to you."

"Or I could hurt her so bad she crawls back into that hole and never comes out."

"I didn't figure you for a coward."

"I'm not," Hayami said. "I just know myself, and the long list of broken relationships I've left behind me is a pretty good sign that I'm not the person to save anyone's soul."

"So do better," Rayak said.

"Do better?" Hayami asked. "Just like that?"

"Just like that," he said. "You have a long list of broken relationships, that means you have a long list of things not to do. Don't do them. Do better."

"And if I just don't want to marry her? If she's not my type?"

"Then don't marry her," Rayak said. "I'm not saying you have to. I'm saying you could be good for her. You could make her life better. You could open yourself up to something that could be amazing, or you could walk away. It's your choice, but if you listened to her talk about Aashi at all, you have to know that she would love you fiercely, and she would love you forever."

Rayak stood up. "Now, if you're done bugging me, I have work to do."

Hayami gave him a dismissive wave. He turned and headed for the exit, and Hayami watched him go, wondering the whole time if all the Gadan had gone mad.

* * * *

Jakari sat in the conference room, waiting for the time to roll around when Cikara was supposed to contact them, but for once, the mission was the last thing on her mind. All she could think about was Hayami and the conversation she'd had with Rayak. He was right when he said she didn't like being alone, and when he said she thought she didn't deserve to be with someone.

It didn't really matter. It wasn't like there was anyone who wanted to be with her. Hayami had made a mistake. A cultural misunderstanding. She'd been crazy to think that anyone would actually claim her. She should have realized it was a mistake as soon as it happened.

She leaned back in her seat and closed her eyes, and the moment started playing itself out again in her mind. It wasn't a surprise. Every time she closed her eyes, she saw Hayami leaning in, felt her lips, felt…

Stupid. Stupid, stupid, stupid.

She closed her eyes, fighting back tears as another memory came to her. Staring at Aashi at the end of a date. Six months, they'd been together, and at the end of every date, every night they'd been together, she'd asked Aashi to marry her, but that night had been different. That night, she'd barely gotten the words out when Aashi leaned in and kissed her on the Cihna and whispered one word.

Yes.

She'd been so happy, so overjoyed, she'd thought her heart was going to explode. It had felt electric, like everything around her was brighter, louder, and more intense. Having Aashi in her life, knowing they were going to be together forever, had made everything better than it was before. It was a feeling that had never really gone away. Not until the bioweapon. Not until Aashi had died.

After that, all she'd felt for a long time was pain. Like she was nothing but a raw, open wound and someone was constantly pouring salt into it. She wasn't sure if the pain had gone away, or if she'd just gotten used to it, but after a while, she'd just been numb.

She wasn't sure what she'd felt when Hayami had kissed her. Shock. Confusion. But there had been something else. Something she didn't have a name for. Then Mamachi had told her it had all been a mistake, and the feeling had gone away, and not having it hurt.

It didn't make any sense. She didn't know Hayami. She didn't want Hayami. She didn't want anyone. She hadn't wanted anyone in a long time. Not since Aashi. So why did it hurt?

The sound of the door made her open her eyes, and she saw Mamachi walk in, looking like they'd just gone five rounds in the gladiator pits. Exhaustion hung off them like an ill-fitting suit. Jakari sat up and looked them over, wondering what had happened.

"Are you okay?" Jakari asked.

"I'm fine," Mamachi said.

"No, you're not," Jakari said.

Mamachi sat down and rubbed their eyes. "I had a fight with Skylar last night," they said.

"What happened?"

"I told Hayami what she'd done," Mamachi said.

"What? Why?"

"So she wouldn't make the same mistake again," Mamachi said.

Jakari fought down the urge to scream. It wasn't bad enough that it had happened, but now Hayami knew what had happened.

The door opened again and Skylar walked in, looking every bit as rough as Mamachi. She sat down next to them and looked over at them like an agacha that hadn't had its cheeks rubbed in hours. Jakari looked away, not able to deal with their problems when she had too many of her own, and the three of them sat in silence until other people started filing in just a few minutes before the scheduled comm conference. It was the same group as the last time. Napati, Rayak, Gomez, Prack, Dubari, and Dhom. Hayami was the last one to show up, but as she came in, she set a coffee in front of Jakari and gave her a weak smile. Jakari did her best to return it, though she wasn't sure how successful she was.

"Are we ready?" Napati asked.

"Yeah," Jakari said. "I've got everything set up same as last time."

"How long?" Prack asked.

"Should just be a couple of minutes," Jakari said.

Everyone sat in silence while they waited, but it was a tense, awkward silence. Jakari was trying to avoid looking at Hayami and Rayak, Mamachi was trying to avoid looking at Skylar and Hayami. Skylar was trying to avoid looking at Mamachi, and Jakari had no doubt everyone in the room could feel the tension.

When the time finally came, she put her hand on the access point, and a holo image of Cikara's human form appeared, looking almost exactly like it had the day before.

"Right on time," Jakari said.

"Were you expecting anything else?" Cikara asked.

"No," Jakari said. "I have the confirmation I need on my end. We're a go for phase one, if you're still onboard."

"After your stunt last night, I don't have much choice, do I?" Cikara asked.

"I told you what was going to happen," Jakari said.

"You didn't say anything about Form Locking me, or raiding my computer," Cikara said.

"No," Jakari said. "Because last night was about making sure I can trust you. And if I had told you what I had planned, you would have made sure I couldn't get to the Helot research."

"And what if I can't trust you?" Cikara asked.

"If you couldn't trust me, we wouldn't be having this conversation," Jakari said. "I could have killed you last night. I didn't. Just the same way I could have killed you in Freedom Plaza the last time we met. As long as you play straight with me, I'll abide by the terms of our deal. Your life, in exchange for Nira, Saka, Jaya, and the Helot tech."

"And what other surprises are you planning?" Cikara asked. "Are you going to lock me up in a Suil prison?"

"No," Jakari. "No more surprises. The deal is simple. You give us the current location of your ship, we come aboard, we kill Nira. In exchange, you give me the file we discussed. When Saka arrives, you contact us. We kill Saka. When Jaya arrives, you contact us. We kill Jaya. Once that's done, you sit down with the Suil leadership and hammer out a peace treaty while I go find a garden to tend, and everybody lives happily ever after."

"Good," Cikara said.

"I do have one request though," Jakari said.

"What is it?"

"How many of the human test subjects are still alive?" Jakari asked.

"All of them," Cikara said.

"We would like them returned," Jakari said.

"Why?" Cikara said.

"Because they're people," Jakari said. "Because they're of no use to you. Twenty-one soldiers, one way or the other, isn't going to turn the tide of the war, but these people had families, people who care about them. Lives that you've taken them away from."

"Fine," Cikara said. "Once Nira is dead, you can have the Helots, and the file we discussed."

"Good," Jakari said. "Where is your ship?"

"We're in the area the humans call Montana. I'm transmitting coordinates now."

"Received," Jakari said. "And Cikara..."

"Yes?"

"For what it's worth, I am sorry things had to go down the way they did last night."

"So am I," Cikara said. "I had hoped we could trust each other."

"If it was just my life, I would take the risk," Jakari said. "But there are billions of people on this planet, and what you're doing threatens every one of them. I had to be sure."

There was a long silence before the hologram nodded. "Understood," Cikara said. "Maybe someday, we won't be on opposite sides."

"Maybe," Jakari said.

"When will you strike?" Cikara asked.

"One moment," Jakari said. She muted the call and looked at Napati. "Tomorrow night?"

"That sounds good," Napati said.

Jakari reopened the comm line. "Tomorrow night," she said.

"Security will be tighter," Cikara said.

"How so?"

"We're cloaked and hovering a kilometer up," Cikara said. "You'll have to make an aerial approach."

"Understood. See you after," Jakari said.

"Until then."

Jakari cut the call and looked up at the rest of the group. "Okay," she said. "So, we go in tomorrow night."

"I think we can safely say humans are off the roster this time," Dubari said.

"Why?" Gomez asked.

"Unless you can fly without a machine, you won't be able to get aboard the ship," Dubari said.

"Dubari has a point," Jakari said. "We had a flying animal on our world called a pterocanis. They're generally a bit larger than we are, and they can reach altitudes of about five kilometers. It's a pretty standard form for most of us. We'll be able to fly aboard, but we won't be able to carry any humans with us."

"You're going in without Taluses?" Hayami asked.

"We'll go in with Class One Lights. Something like the power armor we gave you and the other humans," Jakari said. "Taluses aren't really all that great in boarding actions anyway. Once you get past the hangars, they're too damn big."

"Plus, if we need it, we can always steal TOP matter from the hangar to upsize what we take with us," Prack said.

"I don't like it," Hayami said.

"We *have* done this before," Dubari said. "We don't need babysitters."

"I know," Hayami snapped. "I still don't like it."

"Who do you want to take with you?" Napati asked.

"I'd prefer to go alone," Jakari said. "But I'm guessing you're going to say no to that."

"You're guessing correctly," Napati said.

Jakari sighed as she ran the possibilities in her head, and as much as she hated it, there really was only one way to build the team.

"Dubari, Prack, and Mamachi," she said.

Dubari looked over at Prack for just a moment, and she could see the tension in their face, but they couldn't say anything. Prack had been running covert ops since before Dubari was born.

"Just four of you?" Napati asked.

"Like I said, I'd rather go alone. In and out with Nira's head on a platter. But if I have to take a team, the smaller the better. Less chance of getting caught. And let's be real. Prack and I are the only ones who stand a chance in hell of taking Nira in a straight fight."

"You more than me," Prack said.

"I'm not gonna argue that," Jakari said. "Dubari and Mamachi are both good, but neither of them have the chops for Nira."

"Are you sure you do?" Napati asked.

"I've beaten her before," Jakari said. "It's not going to be easy, but I can take her."

"Maybe I should come along," Napati said. "Then you'd have three fighters who could match her."

"Frankly, that's a horrible idea," Jakari said. "In a straight up fight, yes. You can take any of the Triumvirate. I don't doubt that. But you haven't run a covert op since the rebellion, and nine thousand years is a hell of a lot of rust to knock off. You'd get us killed before we could get to Nira."

Napati didn't look happy with that answer, but one thing she had going for her over Arthan was a willingness to listen to her people. She nodded her assent.

"Are you sure you don't want anyone else?" Napati asked.

"I could go," Dhom said from the foot of the table.

Jakari looked over at them. "Aren't you a techie?"

"Yeah," Dhom said. "But I've been through special operations training. I've done plenty of covert ops."

"Simulated covert ops," Prack said. "No way, kid."

"But—"

"No," Jakari said. "Look, a mission like this isn't one you cut your teeth on. Ask Mamachi. Shit gets real way too fast out there."

"She's right," Mamachi said.

Jakari watched as the kid deflated. She couldn't bring herself to feel bad for them, though. Not when they wanted to go out and get themselves killed.

"So, it's settled," Jakari said. "The four of us will board the Char ship tomorrow night."

"Agreed," Napati said.

"Good," Jakari said. "Prack, Dubari, Mamachi, I want a word before you go."

"Dismissed," Napati said.

Everyone stood up and filed out, though Hayami and Skylar both took their time about it. Jakari waited until they were gone, then looked at Prack, Dubari, and Mamachi.

"I don't have to tell the three of you the level of shit we are walking into, do I?"

"No," all three of them said.

"Good. So, sort your shit," Jakari said. "I don't know if the two of you talked last night or not, but if you didn't, grab a room and yell and scream until it's done. I want your heads in the game tomorrow night, not up your own asses. Understood?"

"Yes," Prack and Dubari said.

"Then get out," Jakari said. She watched them leave, then turned to Mamachi. "Go find Skylar. Apologize, grovel, whatever it takes, but get it sorted. I need both of you rested and ready to go tomorrow."

"Okay," Mamachi said. "I take it you're going to sort your shit too?"

"Teach your grandmother to lay on a rock," Jakari snapped.

"Don't give me that bullshit," Mamachi said. "You're as out of it as the rest of us."

Jakari sighed. "Fine," she said. "I'll fix it."

"Good," Mamachi said. "Because if you die tomorrow, I will never forgive you."

* * * *

Hayami waited outside the conference room door with Skylar. She kept turning everything over in her mind. The conversation with Mamachi after the debriefing the night before. The conversation with Rayak that morning. Every conversation she'd had with Jakari since they met.

She honestly wasn't even sure why she was waiting for Jakari, but it felt like she needed to talk to her. To make sure they were okay. She wasn't sure what she was going to say, but she knew she had to say something. Jakari was going on a mission that she might not come back from. Four people against an entire Char dreadnought.

Of course, there had only been two of them last night, but that just proved her point. They hadn't made it out. Not even close. If they'd actually gone in instead of using the Taluses, they'd be dead now. Of course, if what Jakari said was true, she was more capable in person than she was through a remote-operated Talus, but that didn't stop Hayami from being afraid.

She wanted to go with Jakari, to be there to fight beside her. Her brain was throwing out wild ideas like hang gliders and wing suits. Things she would never be able to learn how to use before tomorrow night.

She looked up when the conference room door opened. Mamachi and Jakari stepped out, and Mamachi walked over to Skylar. She looked up at them, and neither of them seemed to need to say a word. Skylar took Mamachi's hand, and the two of them headed off in the direction of the officers' quarters.

Hayami looked at Jakari, who was looking at her like she might bolt at any second.

"Can we talk?" both of them asked at once. The words seemed to surprise Jakari as much as they surprised Hayami, and the two of them ended up standing there for a minute, just sort of staring awkwardly.

"Um...maybe somewhere private?" Hayami suggested.

"Right," Jakari said. "Come on. I know just the place."

She turned and headed towards the hangars. Hayami followed, having a pretty good idea of where they were headed. Sure enough, Jakari led the way to her ship. Hayami followed up inside, taking in the bright white walls and floors that were so different from the interior of the dreadnoughts she'd been aboard.

Instead of leading her to the cockpit, Jakari led her to a lounge with large, bowl-like furniture. She stopped just inside and pressed her hand over a silver disk on the wall, and one of the bowls reconfigured itself into a big, soft loveseat like the one she had in her living room. Jakari walked over and dropped down on one end and gestured for Hayami to take the other.

"Do you miss your usual form?" Hayami asked as she sat down.

"Sometimes," Jakari said. "Human bodies are so rigid. It's a wonder you're ever able to get comfortable."

"I never really thought of us as rigid," Hayami said. "Though I suppose it might seem that way given how flexible you seem to be in your natural form."

"I do miss being able to curl up properly," Jakari said.

"Would you be more comfortable in your natural form?"

"Probably, but I don't want to have a conversation through the translator, and my natural form isn't physically capable of speaking English."

Hayami nodded. "Right. Um...so, about last night."

"Mamachi explained it," Jakari said.

"Yeah, they said."

"Good," Jakari said. "I don't want you to worry that I'm going to try to hold you to it. Honestly, I wouldn't have held you to it if you knew what it meant."

"Why not?" Hayami asked.

"I'm not the kind of person anyone should be with."

"That's not true," Hayami said.

"Hayami—"

"No," Hayami said. "Look, Jakari, I'm a fucking mess. I go through relationships so fast my dad stopped bothering to learn my girlfriend's names because they don't last long enough to be worth the effort. I'm inconsiderate, inattentive, obsessed with my work, rude, heartless, and a complete bitch, and those are just the ones I've heard in the last year.

"You had a wife, someone you loved and who loved you back. Someone who mattered to you more than anything else in the world. You've been dedicated to her for ten thousand years. That's the kind of love humans dream of. The kind that lasts beyond death. The kind that lasts forever. I have trouble making a one-month anniversary. If either of us deserves someone better, it's you."

"No," Jakari said. "You don't know the things I've done."

"Maybe not," Hayami said, "but I have a pretty good idea. You made sure of that. You need to forgive yourself. You've done enough penance."

"I don't think that's possible," Jakari said.

"It is," Hayami said. "Look, I wasn't there. I don't know what the Seichu did to your world, to your people, but I know they murdered your wife right in front of you, and I'm guessing it wasn't an easy death. I've heard you talk about gladiator pits, slave pens, and brothels. We've had our own experiences with that sort of brutality here on Earth. Seeing it. Fighting it. It leaves a mark, but you are more than what they made you. You're the woman Aashi loved."

"She never saw," Jakari said. "She didn't know who I was."

"She did," Hayami said. "She knew who you were. She knew you were a kind, gentle woman who loved her. She knew you were a gardener who never wanted to hurt anyone. That woman is still there inside of you. She's a lot closer to the surface than you'd like to admit. I've seen her, almost every day since I met you."

Hayami reached out and took Jakari's hand. "That's why I kissed you last night. Not because you broke into the enemy ship, or because you disabled Cikara, or because you blew up a bunch of guards. I kissed you because you saved my life, because you saved the lives of dozens of people the day Ghuma and Birat came to the station, because you went after the Helot research and you scared them into moving the ship away from the city. I kissed you because you arranged for me to see my parents, and because you sat with Mamachi while they talked to Skylar about something hard for them to deal with. I kissed you because you're a good person. The fact that you regret the things you did, that you feel guilty about them, proves that you're not the monster you think you are.

"I didn't come here to apologize for what happened last night because you're a monster. I came here to apologize because I care about you, and because I'm afraid that I hurt you."

"You didn't."

"Will you just shut up?" Hayami said. "I'm trying to be nice here."

Jakari blinked, an expression of pure shock on her face for just a moment before she started laughing. It was a beautiful sound. Light and pure and free, and all the weight left Jakari's face, and for just a moment, Hayami could see the person she really was. Her heart slammed in her chest, and she leaned forward, cutting the laugh off with a kiss.

It was clumsy for a moment, like Jakari didn't quite know what to do, which sort of made sense since she'd never kissed someone in a human form before, but Hayami leaned into it, covering Jakari's lips with her own, letting her tongue slip out and caress skin that was even softer than it looked. Jakari's mouth opened, and Hayami took it as an invitation, deepening the kiss, letting her tongue slip into Jakari's mouth. She wasn't sure which of them moaned, but she moved closer, reaching up and resting her hand on Jakari's ribs.

"Jakari?"

Hayami and Jakari jerked away from each other, turning towards the lounge door. A moment later, Dubari stuck their head around the corner.

"There you are," Dubari said. "I got an alert that someone was on the ship, but you weren't answering your comm."

"Oh," Jakari said. "Sorry. We were talking."

"Ah," Dubari said. "Didn't mean to interrupt."

"It's okay," Hayami said as she stood up. "We were done."

"We were?" Jakari asked.

"Yeah," Hayami said. "I've got...things to do."

She rushed for the door before Jakari or Dubari could say anything else, practically shoving Dubari out of the way in her rush to escape. She followed the corridor back to the entrance ramp, and rushed down it, praying Jakari didn't follow and kicking herself every step of the way.

What the hell had she been thinking?

Chapter Twenty-Two

JAKARI STOOD AND STARED at the Fixture in front of her. The design was based on a human craft called a C-130J Super Hercules. It had been modified with Suil stealth and cloaking systems, which should let it go undetected and get close enough to the Char ship to deploy without raising an alarm. All of which was great, but didn't do anything to ease the dubious feeling she had looking at the craft.

"Humans really fly in these?" she asked.

"Yeah," Mamachi said. "I've ridden in one a few times."

Jakari turned to look at Mamachi. "And?"

"They're loud," they said. "The first couple of trips are rough, but once you get used to it, it just kind of rocks you to sleep."

Jakari turned back to the plane. "You're not filling me with a lot of confidence," she said.

"It's only a three-hour flight," Mamachi said.

"That fills me with even less confidence."

Mamachi laughed.

"Seriously," Jakari said, "how have you survived here for six years?"

"You're spoiled," Mamachi said.

"I'm used to civilization," Jakari said. "That thing doesn't even have counter grav engines."

"That thing also won't fall like a brick if the engines fail," Mamachi said. "There are tradeoffs."

Jakari sighed. "This would all be so much easier if I could just drop a few orbital lances through the target."

"I thought you preferred precision strikes to mass destruction."

"That was before I knew how we were heading to Montana," Jakari said.

Mamachi laughed again and shook their head. "You'll survive," they said.

Jakari looked over at them and couldn't help but smile. "I take it you got everything sorted out with Skylar?"

"Yeah," Mamachi said. "We talked most of the afternoon. We're good."

"That's good," Jakari said.

"What about you and Hayami?" Mamachi asked.

"We're good," Jakari said.

"Really?" Mamachi asked.

"Yeah," Jakari said. "Why do you ask?"

Mamachi pointed over their shoulder with their thumb. Jakari turned and saw Hayami standing at a distance, staring at them. She didn't look good. Jakari wasn't certain, but it looked like she hadn't slept.

"Go," Mamachi said. "I'll make sure everything gets loaded."

"Thanks," Jakari said. She turned around and headed towards where Hayami stood watching them.

"Hey," Hayami said.

"Hey," Jakari said.

"I...uh...I wanted to talk about yesterday."

"You ran away," Jakari said.

"I know," Hayami said. "I'm sorry. Like I said yesterday, I'm a fucking mess."

"So am I," Jakari said.

"No, you're not," Hayami said. "You're not. You're amazing. God, I've known that since I saw you dive out of that delivery van backwards, but I haven't been able to figure out how to tell you. At first, I was confused and scared, and then you didn't seem to want to hear it."

"I'm not—"

"No!" Hayami said. "Just let me talk, okay?"

"All right."

"You are amazing. I know you don't believe it, but you are, and I wanted you to believe that, but I just mixed up trying to tell you, and then when Mamachi told me what happened, I got all twisted up inside because I was afraid I hurt you, and I tried to talk to Rayak about it because I figured he's closer to your age than Mamachi, so he might have a better idea of how to fix things, but that just got me more confused, and when we started talking on the ship, I had all of this stuff running through my head about how I accidently proposed to you and how much you loved your wife and how long you'd been alone, and you started laughing, and I don't know if anyone has ever told you this, but you're really, really pretty when you laugh, and I was already thinking about how I kissed you in the truck the night before and honestly, I'm always a little stupid around beautiful women and I was worried about you going on a mission without me and that you might not come back and then I was kissing you and we got interrupted and I panicked and I'm sorry."

Hayami sucked in a deep breath when she stopped talking, and Jakari couldn't stop herself from smiling. She shouldn't have. She should have been focused on sorting out the mess between them, but there was just something ridiculously endearing about Hayami babbling away.

She reached out and took Hayami's hand, the same way Hayami had done the day before. "It's okay," Jakari said.

"It's not," Hayami said, looking down at their joined hands. "I keep messing up."

Jakari smiled. "I don't know," she said. "You're giving me plenty of reason to come back, even if it's just to see what you do next."

Hayami looked up at her, wide-eyed as her cheeks turned a dark shade of red. She reached up with her free hand and shoved Jakari's shoulder.

"You ass," she said, which only made Jakari smile wider.

"You know I'm not any better at this than you are," she said. "My big, winning strategy when it comes to dealing with women is to just ask them to marry me over and over again until they say yes just to shut me up."

"Well, if it works for you, you might as well stick with it," Hayami said.

Jakari stared at Hayami for a moment, a little surprised at what she'd just implied. She thought about it, turning everything over in her head. What Rayak had said. That her guilt was because she'd outlived Aashi. That she didn't deserve to be alone. A sentiment Hayami had repeated. The way Hayami had said she was amazing.

She wasn't sure she believed either of them. There were so many moments in her past she regretted, so many things she wanted to forget, but at the same time, she remembered what it had been like with Aashi. Being able to come home at the end of the day and just be with someone who loved her. The feel of a warm body against her, a soft touch when she needed it, a calming voice in the moments when it felt like everything was too much. She might not believe she deserved it, but given the chance, she wanted to have it again.

"If you insist," Jakari said. She took a step forward and reached up with her free hand to cup Hayami's cheek as she went up on her toes and pressed her lips to the center of Hayami's forehead. She heard Hayami let out a sharp gasp, which let her know Hayami understood the gesture for what it was. She pulled back and smiled.

"I'll see you after the mission," Jakari said. She lifted Hayami's hand up and rubbed her forehead against it before she let go, then she turned around and jogged back towards the plane that was taking them to Montana.

* * * *

Vrusti sat on top of the hangar at the Suil base, watching as the human craft lifted into the air carrying Jakari and a handful of other Suil soldiers north. They watched until the craft was out of sight, then leapt into the air, flying as quickly as the wings of their crow form would carry them until they were clear of the Suil base's detection range. Then they opened a comm line to Ghuma.

"They're on the way," Vrusti said.

"Acknowledged," Ghuma said. "Head for my location as quickly as you can."

* * * *

Cikara looked up at the comm signal they'd been expecting for most of the day. The signal was from Ghuma, only instead of coming in over the secure channel they usually used to keep things from Nira, it came in over one of the standard Char comm channels. Cikara hit the accept button, and a hologram of Ghuma appeared.

"General, I have news," Ghuma said.

"Go ahead," Cikara said.

"We've located the enemy base, and we've located the safehouse where the human's parents are being held."

"Excellent," Cikara said.

"I'm sending coordinates now on a subchannel," Ghuma said. "Orders?"

"Hold position," Cikara said. "I'll update you when we've decided on a course of action."

"Understood," Ghuma said.

Cikara cut the channel and went back to work, a smile on their face. It took all of five minutes before the door opened and Nira stepped inside. Cikara looked up and waved her in. Nira walked across the office and placed a pad on Cikara's desk. It showed two maps. One with the location of the Suil base, and one with the location of the safehouse.

"Yes," Cikara said. "I just received the news from Ghuma. I was planning on having Bayadani plan an attack tomorrow to grab off the human's parents, and then we could hit the base in a couple of days once we have our situation here settled."

Nira reached down and tapped the map impatiently.

"You want to attack now?"

Nira nodded.

"Which one?"

Nira spread her index and middle finger, pressing one to each map.

Cikara sighed. "I don't like attacking when we haven't secured our location."

Nira just stared.

"Fine," Cikara said. "But if anything goes wrong, it's on your head."

Nira picked up the tablet and headed for the door. Cikara reached over and hit the comm button.

"Bayadani, I need you to organize two strike teams," Cikara said.

* * * *

Hayami sat in the Combat Information Center in the Suil dreadnought, watching the status board. Kida, Prack's pink-haired human assistant, was there, along with Gomez, Skylar, and Napati. Unlike the day Ghuma and Birat had tried to grab her parents, they weren't watching live footage. Instead, they were staring at a map with an icon on it indicating the current location of the plane with Jakari's strike team.

Her nerves were frayed and her emotions were all over the place. Jakari was going into battle in just over an hour. Jakari had just asked Hayami to marry her. She was pretty sure she'd actually implied that Jakari should ask, which wasn't what she'd meant to do, but now that she thought about it, that was definitely what she'd done. All the Gadan were completely fucking crazy. Who the hell proposes to someone they have known for a week? Jakari, apparently, but then Hayami shouldn't be surprised, since she'd decided to marry her first wife before they'd ever spoken to each other.

The worst part was, she wasn't entirely sure she hated the idea. It was insane. It was completely fucking nuts. She was a disaster when it came to relationships. Jakari was a ten-thousand-year-old immortal alien cat-lizard woman. Hayami had once dumped a girl because they couldn't agree on what to watch on Netflix. She was pretty sure that she and Jakari were going to have bigger issues than that. Like what planet to live on. And Hayami was a breast girl, and Jakari didn't have breasts in her natural form. That had to be a strike against them, right?

"General, I have incoming comm traffic on comm frequency Charlie," someone said.

"Put it through," Napati said as she stood up and walked over to the control console. Napati hit a couple of commands on the console, and a blurred hologram appeared, and when it spoke, the voice was modulated so no one could have identified it.

"Is anyone there?" the modulated voice asked.

"This is Napati. I am not in a secure location and have you under an anonymity filter."

"Understood. Nira learned the location of your base. There is a strike force inbound. You have approximately seventy-five minutes before they arrive."

"Size?"

"Six hundred soldiers in Class Two and Class Three Taluses."

"The warning is appreciated. Is the situation on your end compromised?"

"No."

"Napati out."

* * * *

"Control to Dagger, do you read?"

"This is Dagger One. We read you loud and clear," Jakari said, a frown on her face. They were supposed to maintain radio silence for the whole trip. Napati calling them was definitely a bad sign.

"Dagger One, we have just received word from your source that the target has learned our location. A Char strike force is en route to us. Approximately six hundred strong."

Jakari turned towards the cockpit with every intention of ordering the pilots to reconfigure the plane into a proper Gadan ship and head back at maximum velocity. Every part of her was screaming to forget the mission and go back, to protect Hayami. Images of the hospital room where Aashi died danced in front of her head, only this time it was Hayami coughing up blood as her internal organs slowly liquified. This time it was Hayami she was holding as she cried and begged her not to leave.

She closed her eyes, taking deep breaths, counting backwards from ten, using calming techniques she hadn't needed in a long, long time to fight off a panic attack. She had to think, to focus. Breath in. Breath out. Breath in. Breath out.

Slowly, the panic abated, and she got control of herself back. Logic began to sink in. She had to complete the mission. There were plenty of

Suil troops at the base. Hayami would be in the situation room. She would be safe.

"Understood, Control. We will proceed with the mission. You just make sure we have a base to come back to."

"Roger that," Napati said. "We'll see you when you get home."

* * * *

Hayami stared up at the status board as the base went to full alert. Jakari wasn't coming back, and Hayami felt a sense of relief. If the Char troops were coming here, then they wouldn't be aboard the Char ship to fight Jakari, but that still left the problem of the six hundred heavily-armed enemy troops headed their way.

Before she could really even start processing it, she felt a tug on her arm, and she looked over to see Skylar looking at her.

"Come on," Skylar said.

Hayami stood up and followed her at very nearly a dead run. "Where are we going?" Hayami asked.

"The armory," Skylar said. "I figured we should hurry before Napati orders us to stay in the CIC."

"Good thinking," Hayami said. There was a part of her that knew she and Skylar absolutely should stay in the CIC where they were safe, but there was another part of her, and it was the part that was winning, that said there was no way in hell she was going to sit out a fight that could determine the fate of her planet.

They took an elevator up to the surface and ran for the armory. There were other humans there, and most of them were grabbing larger versions of the backpack Gomez had with her that day in the police station, along with large, heavy looking plasma rifles, and that was what Hayami expected her and Skylar to get, but as they reached the counter, Skylar spoke up.

"We need two Shims programmed with Skylar Pattern Seven, two Scripts programmed with Skylar Pattern Twelve, and two Scripts programmed with Mamachi pattern fourteen."

"Yes, ma'am," the armorer said. "Hands on access points so I can link the Shims."

She and Skylar put their hands on the indicated access points, and a moment later, the armorer handed them each three small cylinders. Then Skylar led them over to the TOP matter molds, where another armorer was waiting.

"Fill two molds with sixty-five kilos each, two molds with four hundred kilos each, and two molds with thirty kilos each," Skylar said. The armorer frowned but did as she was told.

"What are we doing?" Hayami asked.

Skylar looked at her with a smile. "You look like a girl who's seen some anime, am I right?"

"Yeah," Hayami said.

"Ever seen Bubblegum Crisis or Genesis Climber Mospeda?"

"Yes, and yes," Hayami said.

"Then you're going to like this," Skylar said.

* * * *

"We're approaching the drop zone," the pilot said over the radio. One of the other troops who'd come with them, and who was serving as the vehicle's load master, stood up, walked to the back of the plane, and opened the rear ramp.

Jakari and her team got up from their seats and pulled down the packs which were actually Class One light Taluses. They pulled them on and each of them began to reconfigure into their pterocanis forms. The flying creatures, native to Cruthanna, were built along similar lines to the dogs that the human security teams on the base used to help them patrol the perimeter. Large, muscular, sleek, with short fur, and unlike the dogs the humans kept, the pterocanis had absolutely massive wings. The best part was they were all but invisible to sensors in these forms.

"Now," the pilot called. Jakari didn't hesitate. She ran straight for the rear gate of the plane and jumped out into the sky. Her massive wings snapped open and filled with air as she started a slow turn westward towards the Char ship. She heard the faint rustle of wings around her, and a quick look confirmed Dubari, Prack, and Mamachi were with her. She started flapping her wings, heading towards the Char ship as fast as she could.

It took about ten minutes from the time they jumped until the time they spotted the Char ship. The cloak made it invisible, but one of the reasons the pterocanis was the go-to flying form for most Gadan was that they could sense magnetic fields. It was one of their base senses. So while the Char ship might have been invisible to the eye and to radar and most other forms of detection, it stood out like a raging bonfire to Jakari and her team. They sailed right through the cloaking field without hesitation and touched down on the top of the hull.

All four of them immediately shifted into their Gadan forms, and Jakari took a quick look around before heading towards the opening that led down to the hangar bays. The whole way, she did her best not to think about the fact that the Char would be hitting the Suil base at any moment.

* * * *

Skylar had been right that Hayami would like the gear she'd gotten them. They were both wearing Class One light Taluses configured as light power armor, but they also had large, heavy motorcycles which could switch over into a power armor mode that wrapped around and interfaced with the Taluses in their current configuration. On top of that, they both had massive plasma cannons to work with. Anyone who tangled with either of them would know they'd been in a fight.

Hayami was grateful for all of that, but the truth was, her mind was a thousand miles to the north, wondering and worrying about what Jakari was doing. At least until the alarms went off, announcing the first sensor sighting of the Char strike force.

Chapter Twenty-Three

A HUGE PART OF warp-capable starship design was dictated by two quirks in the laws of physics. The first was that warp drive rings had to be just that, rings. Perfect circles that surrounded the ship. The second was that the longer a ship was along the axis of travel, the more power it took to move the ship. That meant that the most efficient shape for a warp-capable star ship was a disk that flew through space with the flat of the disk pointed in the direction the ship was moving.

Those two principles meant that by and large, Gadan capital ship design had followed the same template since the first war with the Seichu, and Char dreadnoughts were no different. They were massive disks, ten kilometers in diameter, and a hundred and fifty meters thick. The top side of the ship had a circular depression in the middle some five kilometers in diameter, and fifteen meters deep. The bottom of the depression was covered with runways and landing areas, while the inner edge of the depression was lined with massive doors that opened to hangars that housed shuttles, transports, Taluses, and other tenders.

It was common practice on both sides to leave the hangars open when operating in atmosphere to allow various tenders to come and go at need. A fact that Jakari planned to take advantage of. She led her team to the edge of the depression where the hangars sat and circled around the perimeter quickly until they were directly above one of the gaps between open hangar doors. A quick look told her that most of the hangars were empty. Not really a surprise when the Char had sent their forces to attack the Suil base, but it did make things easier. The four of them slid down the curve of the hull to reach the bottom of the depression, then they headed to their right, making for the nearest hangar.

When they got there, the hangar was empty. Not a single craft in sight. It was a reminder Jakari didn't want of the danger Hayami was in, but there was nothing she could do about that except complete her mission. She waved for her team to follow and walked into the hangar like she owned it. One of the oldest rules on infiltration. Look like you belong there, and most of the time no one will bother you.

The four of them crossed to the back of the hangar, and Jakari found an access point that let her quickly orient herself in relation to Nira's quarters. That done, she quickly hacked the ship's computer and built root-level accounts for herself, Prack, Mamachi, and Dubari. Finally, she queried the system for Nira's location, then opened the door into the ship.

"You know where we're going?" Dubari asked.

"Of course," Jakari said. She transmitted Nira's location to the rest of the group. "We'll stick to the plan. All four of us go to take Nira down, then you and Prack will secure transport while Mamachi and I go find Cikara and pick up the prisoners."

Dubari nodded, and Jakari felt a bit of relief that there wouldn't be a fight over that. She'd worried that once they got to the ship, Dubari would insist on going with her to find Cikara, but she still didn't have any intention of letting Dubari within sight of Cikara.

"Let's go," she said, and headed deeper into the ship.

* * * *

Hayami had been in a couple of fire fights in her time on the force. She'd also been on more than her fair share of raids. She thought that it would prepare her for what was about to happen, but she was wrong. She didn't think anything could have prepared her for what she saw as the Char attack force came into range.

One second, the sky was dark, and the sounds of a quiet Texas evening filled the air. Crickets chirping, the occasional caw of crows, and the sound of the wind rolling down from the north. Then, like someone had flipped a switch, the ground split open and plasma cannons grew up like weeds as hundreds of fighters swarmed into the air. The sky filled with the bright, angry blue of superheated plasma, and the air rocked with the thunder of its passage.

The Suil base turned the very air into an inferno in an effort to defend itself, and the Char replied in kind, hurling down their own bolts of fire and death, burning enormous pits in the ground, melting away plasma cannons that were quickly replaced by new ones. The violence of the first few moments were unbelievable, and Hayami watched, entranced, as people on both sides began to die.

The spell was broken a few moments later when her suit sounded a tone in her ear. "Enemy will enter engagement range in thirty seconds."

Hayami hefted the massive plasma rifle she was carrying and pointed it to the sky, letting her HUD and her targeting sensors guide her.

"Enemy in range," her suit told her. Hayami waited, searching the sky carefully until her targeting reticle turned green. She squeezed the trigger and the plasma rifle kicked hard, but she barely noticed, too busy staring at the hole she'd blown in one of the enemy ships.

"Good shot," Skylar said. The words shook Hayami out of the trance she was in, and she started looking for another target.

* * * *

Moving through a dreadnought was an interesting experience at the best of times. The massive ships had crews of roughly five thousand people, which meant that the ship was practically deserted. Most people didn't realize just how big a ten-kilometer diameter circle was. Add to that the fact that most dreadnoughts had about fifteen decks, and it was pure luck running into anyone. The ships were built more as weapons platforms than as transports, which meant most of the space was taken up with guns and power collectors and other systems that fed its weapons. The people were almost an afterthought, only there to guide and control the enormous destructive potential.

Cikara's ship was no different. If anything, it was even emptier than most, because a huge chunk of the crew was gone. The ship still had four thousand four hundred people onboard, but it would be hard to tell that. Most were probably at some post or other, monitoring the progress of the battle to the south. Something that suited Jakari just fine. They were here for one person, and if they made it all the way to Nira's quarters without running into anymore, that would be just fine with her.

* * * *

As vicious as the opening phase of the battle was, it was over quickly. The Char formation didn't break out into dogfights and try to kill their enemies in the air. They must have known that would be suicide when the Suil fighters had ground support. Instead, they barreled through the anti-aircraft fire and the Suil fighters, absorbing losses like they didn't matter and heading straight for the ground.

Less than two minutes after Hayami had fired her first shot, the first Char Talus slammed down onto the tarmac. The thing was enormous, nearly ten meters tall, covered in armor, and carrying a massive shield. Plasma cannons swung towards it, but there were three more on the ground before they could finish targeting, and the four of them stood back-to-back, surrounding themselves with their shields and firing out at the cannons on the ground.

They opened fire as more and more of the enemy Taluses fell out of the air, clustering together for mutual defense as they started trying to burn down the defensive cannons.

Oddly enough, this was a situation that fit Hayami's talents. She dropped down to one knee and braced the rifle, picking a target carefully, and waiting until the right moment.

"Be ready to move," she said to Skylar as she lined up the shot.

"Got it," Skylar said.

Hayami waited a couple of seconds longer, then slowly squeezed the trigger. The flash of plasma and the buck of the gun were almost a surprise, but it was nothing compared to the ten-meter-tall Talus just liquifying after she blew a hole through it. She didn't have time to process what happened though.

She screamed, "Move," as the outer layer of her power armor shifted from exoskeleton to motorcycle mid-leap. She hit the ground already in motion and accelerated with Skylar right on her tail as the spot they had been in was lit up with dozens of plasma blasts. She opened the throttle as she began looking for her next sniper perch.

* * * *

Ghuma sat quietly in their Talus, currently configured as a blue Ferrari F8 Tributo, and watched the sky and the house where the human woman's parents were being kept. The strike team was running late, which annoyed them. Ghuma wanted this over while Nira was busy focusing on the attack on the base.

"I see them," Birat said over the comms. "Coming in from the north."

Ghuma looked and spotted them. There were five of them. Should be easy enough.

"Be ready," Ghuma said.

"I always am," Birat said in a tone that made Ghuma wish they could spend the evening doing all sorts of deliciously decadent things with Birat rather than doing Cikara's dirty work. Sadly, that would have to wait.

Five Char soldiers dropped out of the sky. Four of them were in Class Ones. Easy enough. The fifth was in a Class Three. A bit more of a challenge. Ghuma already knew Birat would take that one. This should be simple.

The human security forces responded to the attack, calling desperately for Suil assistance that would come far too late. Ghuma watched as the poor, doomed security guards died. They supposed they should have felt bad about that, since it was their report that sent those humans to their death, but Ghuma really only cared about keeping themself and Birat safe. Everyone else was expendable towards that end.

There. The humans were all dead.

"Now," Ghuma said. Their Talus reconfigured into a Class Two Light mech, while down the street, on the other side of the Char soldiers, Birat's reconfigured into a Class Two Heavy mech. The first two Char soldiers died without ever realizing Ghuma and Birat were there. That left only three of their shipmates for Ghuma and Birat to kill, and they set to the task with their usual efficiency.

* * * *

Jakari spotted the two guards outside of Nira's quarters as they turned the last corner leading to her door. The guards spotted them a second later, and from the way they tensed, it was clear they knew no one should be in that corridor at that time. Under other circumstances, Jakari would have admired their skill and dedication to their duty, but in the here and now, it just made her sad that she had to kill them.

They were just starting to turn towards her team, getting ready to issue a challenge when Jakari reconfigured her hands into plasma cannons. She didn't have to check that Dubari was already doing the same. They'd worked together enough that she knew they were.

"I've got far," she said as she raised her cannons. Four bursts of plasma shot across the distance, filling the corridor with a thunderous sound. The two blasts from Jakari's cannons vaporized the guard on the far side of the door while the two from Dubari's cannons did the same to the one on the near side of the door.

All four members of her team were in motion a moment later, running full out for the door. The element of surprise was gone, but with a little luck, they could still pin Nira in her quarters and contain the fight.

Luck, it seemed, was with them. They crossed the distance before the door opened. Dubari, Prack, and Jakari all took up position in front of the door, ready to attack the moment it opened as Mamachi laid a hand on the access point next to the door. They waited for what seemed like an eternity but which couldn't have been more than a second or two before the door opened to reveal Nira in her Gadan form, standing in the middle of an empty room, holding a sword in one hand and a shield in the other.

Mamachi lifted both of their hands, reconfiguring them into cannons and taking aim, and all four of them fired at once.

* * * *

The Suil fighters dropped out of the sky, reconfiguring into mechs as they fell. Like the Char mechs, each of them carried a shield that they used to cover themselves as they charged the Char formations, slamming into them and trying to break them up. It was a tactic that was met with mixed success. The Suil Taluses tended to be smaller than the Char ones, and Hayami could see why. They were going for fast and agile instead of the slow, ponderous bulk of the Char forces, but that meant they lacked the momentum to break the Char formations when they slammed into them.

Hayami didn't have a lot of time to worry about it. She and Skylar were still playing shoot and scoot. They'd fallen into a rhythm. Hayami would pick a target and go for the body shot. Skylar would piggyback off Hayami's targeting system and go for a headshot on the same Char Talus. Between the two of them, they were pretty much guaranteed a hard kill, because apparently, the Char all kept their Phylacteries either in their torso or their head. It made sense, but it also made killing them easier.

"Are we winning?" Skylar asked as they ran from their most recent sniper perch.

"I honestly can't tell," Hayami said. It was the truth. She wasn't sure if they were winning or not, but she didn't think they were. The Char formations had become hard points on the battlefield that the Suil forces were beating themselves against, and unless something changed quickly, she was afraid it was the Suil who were going to break.

Almost as if in answer to her prayers, the battlefield filled with the sound of metal on metal as several of the buildings folded open. Hayami and Skyler both stopped for a moment, watching as massive, lumbering machines marched out onto the field of battle. They had to be at least twenty meters tall, forty meters long, walking on four legs, and each one had a pair of massive cannons on their back, as well as pods hanging off the side with three smaller cannons built into each one.

At least two dozen of the behemoths lumbered forward, taking aim at the Char formations. The Char broke and started to run, but it was too late. The twin cannons bellowed, and Char soldiers died by the dozen.

"Okay," Hayami said. "Now we're winning!"

"Hell yeah!" Skylar said, just before the world exploded.

* * * *

Nira's quarters filled with burning plasma and vaporized TOP matter, but Nira herself dodged and danced around the incoming assault like a dancer floating across a stage. Jakari didn't want to believe anyone could be that good, but she wasn't really surprised. Nira was probably second only to Jaya when it came to fighters among the Char, which meant they were going to have to do this the hard way.

"Check fire," Jakari ordered, and almost as one the four of them stopped firing. When the smoke cleared, Nira ended up standing back in the same spot she'd been in when the doors opened. It was a deliberate taunt. Jakari knew it and was old enough that she wasn't bothered by it. She stepped forward into the room and Mamachi, Dubari, and Prack followed her. She shifted her hands, replacing one cannon with a sword, and the other with a shield.

"You three are on containment," Jakari said. "Nothing gets out of this room."

"Got it," Prack said.

Nira looked at her and Jakari could see the amusement on her face. An arrogant assurance that she'd already won the fight. Jakari just smiled at her, and shifted back to her natural form, and for just a moment, Nira froze, a look of shock and fear on her face.

Jakari leapt forward before Nira could recover, and Nira had to scramble to get her shield up between her body and Jakari's sword. It was a near thing, and it left Nira vulnerable, so Jakari drove her shield into Nira's chest and triggered an electrical discharge. Nira jerked back, a dark line burned into her chest and rage on her face. She spun her sword and rushed Jakari, and the fight was on.

Jakari hadn't spent nearly as much time in the gladiator pits as Nira, Cikara, Saka, or Jaya, but during the time she had spent there, she'd trained under all four of them, and by the time Napati had liberated them, Jakari had been very nearly the equal of any of them. Had it just ended there, the fight might still have gone in Nira's direction, but Jakari had spent the last nine thousand years as an assassin. She had not only trained constantly, but she'd seen more combat in that time than the four of them put together.

It was still a close thing. Nira was fast, cunning, and brutal, but Jakari knew from the first moment she had the fight. There was never a question in her mind. Sword met shield again and again, but the real battle was fought in their minds. Jakari watched Nira, waiting for the right moments. A block a little too far out, and Jakari would land a kick in Nira's gut. An attack that over committed, and Jakari would dodge and slam Nira with her shield. Every mistake, every taunting blow Jakari landed shook Nira's confidence.

It wasn't a one-sided fight. Nira landed her share of blows. A kick here, a pommel strike there, a shield block to the face. Every time, Jakari would just laugh at her and smile wider, covering every doubt, every moment of hesitation with bravado.

Jakari could see the end of the fight coming in Nira's eyes. She could see how close Nira was to losing control, and shifted her position just a hair, turning her shield side a bit towards Nira. Nira's eyes lit up when she instantly spotted the opening and moved in for a wrap shot, swinging her sword wide and twisting her wrist so she could hook the blade around Jakari's shield and catch her in the head with the back edge of the blade.

On an organic, it would have been a killing blow. On a Gadan, it should have at least stunned them, and since Nira and Jakari were both fighting with electrically charged blades, it might very well have sent Jakari into lockdown if it had landed. Instead, Jakari twisted back, her shield coming up and blocking the sword blow as she drove her own sword into the center of Nira's chest. She triggered her sword, releasing a massive discharge into Nira's body, and Nira froze as her Phylactery went into lockdown.

Jakari jerked her sword free as Nira fell forward. She stepped back, reconfiguring her hands into plasma cannons, and took aim. Four quick shots, and Nira was nothing more than expanding vapor, her Phylactery destroyed.

Jakari turned back to her team.

* * * *

Hayami was never sure where it came from. Just that one second their path was clear and the next there was a massive mech in front of them. It had to be at least thirty-five meters tall, and God only knew how much it weighed, but it was easily the biggest thing on the battlefield. Before either of them had time to react, it turned and fired at them. They both veered off, but Hayami heard Skylar scream over the comm as she caught the edge of the plasma blast. She looked back and saw Skylar go down, her motorcycle sliding away from her burnt and broken form before it exploded.

The colossus, Hayami couldn't think of anything else to call it, turned towards Skylar, and Hayami acted on pure instinct. She flipped the switch that activated the motorcycle's jump jets, and as soon as she was in the air, she triggered the transformation. The motorcycle twisted and formed, wrapping itself around her as she rose. Her hand found her rifle and she raised it, spewing fire and rage into the colossus, not caring where on the monstrosity her shots landed as long as she got its attention.

The colossus screamed and turned towards her, slapping at her again and again as she flew around it, her jump jets keeping her in the air and out of reach even as she fired again and again. She backed away, taking only a second to flag Skylar's position for a medivac as she lured the colossus away from her, trying to get it out in the open.

"Takahashi to all heavy units, I could use some help here," she called out into the general comm channel. She saw several of the behemoths turn in their direction and braced herself as they opened fire. The colossus staggered and let out a roar as it turned and fired at one of the behemoths, its massive gun blowing a hole clean through the smaller mech. The colossus turned towards the next behemoth, and Hayami realized the tide of battle had turned again.

* * * *

The trip to the hangar and the trip to Cikara's quarters took them in the same direction at first, so both pairs moved together down the first few corridors, heading for the point where their paths would separate. They didn't quite make it. They were two intersections back from the point where the path to the hangar would split off when the guards appeared, and they didn't seem to care that Jakari's team were in Char uniforms. They opened fire on sight.

Jakari and Prack, who were in front, both dropped prone and returned fire, vaporizing guards until the corridor in front of them was empty. She looked back to see where Dubari and Mamachi were, since neither of them had fired, and found Mamachi hunkered down over Dubari.

"What's wrong?" Jakari asked.

"I don't know," Mamachi said. "They took a hit, but they're not healing."

Jakari glanced over at Prack, who had a stricken look on his face. She knew Prack loved his child, even if Dubari could be an ass sometimes, but they didn't have time for anyone to fall apart.

"Mamachi, Prack, you take Dubari. Get to the hangar and find us a transport. I'll find Cikara and get what we came for."

Mamachi didn't argue. They just picked up Dubari and nodded.

"We'll be ready when you get there."

* * * *

The third behemoth went down and Hayami started to panic. They couldn't lose this fight. If they did, they lost the base, and whatever happened up north, they would be at a severe disadvantage when Saka and Jaya arrived. Something had to give, and Hayami was the only one close enough to do anything.

She swooped forward, letting her jump jets carry her, and grabbed hold of the colossus's head, using the motorcycle power armor's magnetic clamping system to lock on. Then she set its self-destruct system and punched out. The ejection system launched her into the air, and as she fell, she activated her Talus's jump jets and swooped down, scooping Skylar up off the ground and then running as far as her jump jets would carry her.

When the night sky lit up behind her, she didn't look back. She didn't want to see into the inferno the motorcycle armor's self-destruct had created, but the cheers that went up over the comm told the story. She'd killed it.

"Napati to Takahashi."

"Takahashi here," Hayami said.

"Good job," Napati said. "I'm sending you a guidance beacon. You've done your part. Follow the beacon back to the barn."

"Yes ma'am," Hayami said, not inclined to argue.

* * * *

Mamachi set Dubari down in one of the seats in the back of the transport, then followed Prack up to the cockpit. Getting to the hangar had been a fairly easy job and getting aboard the transport had been easier still. Mamachi wasn't sure how to feel about that. On the one hand, anything that made their mission easier was good. On the other hand, whoever was running security for the ship was sloppy, and that offended Mamachi's sensibilities.

"Flight controls are all on lockdown," Prack said. "The doors are open, but none of the ships can launch."

Mamachi sighed and dropped down into the co-pilot's seat. Apparently, the security wasn't as sloppy as it seemed. "Can you get past it?"

"Yeah," Prack said. "We've got root access to the system. When the time comes, I'll schedule a self-diagnostic then power cycle the fire control system to trigger it and authorize our launch. We should have a good five minutes to get clear of their range before they can shoot at us."

"What if they drop the weapons into manual?" Mamachi asked.

"Will only work if they have someone on the weapons mount," Prack said. "There's an active intruder alert, but no one has sounded battle stations."

"How much trouble do you think Jakari will have getting to Cikara?"

"I don't know, kid," Prack said. "But it's Jakari. She'll get the job done, trouble or not."

* * * *

Ghuma stared at the results of their and Birat's handiwork, who were currently sitting on the couch, looking at the both of them with fear in their eyes.

"You think this will work?" Birat asked over comms.

"I don't know," Ghuma said. "But the Suil are awfully soft on these humans. The fact that we killed our own people to protect the human woman's parents should definitely score us some points."

"I hope you're right," Birat said. "I hate all this cloak and dagger shit. I prefer a stand-up fight."

"That, my dear, is because you're twice the size of most Gadan. A fact that I appreciate for other reasons. But if Cikara is right, and Saka and Jaya have finally decided that they can do without Cikara's presence, then we need a fallback plan, because we're way too close to Cikara for Jaya to let us live."

"I know," Birat said. "Some days, I wish we'd never gotten involved with this war."

"Oh, I'll never say that," Ghuma said. "If I hadn't, I'd have never met you, and however this turns out, you're worth it."

Birat looked over at Ghuma, and Ghuma smiled. "I love you too," Birat said out loud.

* * * *

Jakari stopped in front of Cikara's door and hit the chime. No point in being rude this time around. The door slid open, and Jakari stepped inside. Cikara watched her until the door slid closed, and Jakari shifted from her Char disguise into her natural form.

"It's done," she said. "Nira's dead."

Cikara leaned back in their chair and let out a weary sigh. "Thank you," they said.

Jakari nodded. "I've come for the file and the humans."

"Right," Cikara said. They reached out and placed their hand on the access point for the desk. A few seconds passed, then they lifted their hand. "The file is in the computer."

Jakari walked over and placed her hand on the same access point, quickly accessing the system and pulling the file off Cikara's computer and leaving a small bit of insurance in the system at the hardware level. Once she was done, she lifted her hand off the access point.

She was just about to ask where the humans were when the door slid open.

* * * *

"Mamachi?" Prack called from the back compartment.

"Yes?" Mamachi asked.

"Where's Dubari?"

Mamachi frowned. They got up and walked into the back of the transport and saw the seat where they had left Dubari empty and felt their stomach sink. They reached for their comms.

* * * *

"Mamachi?" Jakari asked as they stepped into the room.

"Dubari woke up as we got to the hangar," Mamachi said. "I thought you could use the backup."

Jakari frowned. "I'd have rather you stayed where I sent you," she said, a little annoyed. It was odd for Mamachi not to follow orders, and for them to not follow orders in the field was nearly unheard of. "Is everything okay?"

"Yeah," Mamachi said.

Jakari nodded and turned back to Cikara. "Where are the—"

She was cut off when her comm tone sounded and Mamachi's voice filled her ears. "Jakari, Dubari's missing!"

There was no instant of confusion, no moment of hesitation. She just knew, and as she turned to the fake Mamachi, it was already too late.

Plasma sailed across the compartment, enveloping Cikara, vaporizing their head and torso. The limbs instantly reverted to the liquid form of uncontrolled TOP matter.

She stared down at the mess for just a moment, trying to fight down the nearly uncontrollable rage she felt. The mission had to come first. It had to.

"Dubari's with me," she said over comms. "We won't be able to retrieve the humans. Be ready to go as soon as we reach the hangar."

"Understood," Mamachi said.

She reached down and placed her hand on the access point and began digging through the data in Cikara's account. She pulled a full copy of both Cikara and Nira's user directories off the system, then initiated a purge command on both accounts, as well as on the shared research library for the Helot program, and finally sent self-destruct commands to all the Helot manufacturing hardware. Once that was done, she sent the stand down on the intruder alert, then disconnected from the computer.

"Let's go," she said, shifting back into her Char disguise.

"I'm sorry," Dubari said. "I had orders."

"I don't care," Jakari said. "We're over. You're not my partner anymore."

"Jakari..."

"Shut up," Jakari said. "Say one more word, and I don't care who your parents are. I'll kill you where you stand."

Dubari at least had the sense to realize she meant it. They didn't speak again until they got back to base.

Chapter Twenty-Four

JAKARI WAS CAREFUL NOT to make any sudden moves as she brought the transport in for a landing. She knew ground control had the ship tagged as friendly, but it was a Char ship, the base had just been attacked, and she didn't feel like dying because someone got twitchy. She set it down nice and slow, and then carefully powered down every system on the ship before getting out of the pilot's seat and heading back to the rear of the transport where Mamachi, Prack, and Dubari were waiting.

"Jakari," Dubari said. "I—"

"Shut up," Jakari snapped.

Dubari seemed to realize that in this case, discretion was definitely the better part of valor and shut their mouth. They stood up as Jakari activated the exit ramp and let Prack and Mamachi lead them down the ramp. Jakari followed, still fuming. Dubari had fucked things up so deeply she wasn't sure if there was any way to un-fuck them, but chances were, their shot at ending the war was gone.

She spotted the guards she'd asked for, standing beside Napati. Napati being there wasn't a good sign, but she figured that whatever new ration of shit was headed her way might as well come now, so she knew just how truly shitty her luck was.

"Take Dubari," she said to the guards. "Form Lock them and throw them in a holding cell. No one talks to them except me, Prack, or the General."

"Yes, Colonel," the guards said. Napati frowned but didn't say a word, even though she must be wondering what the hell was going on. She waited while the guards led Dubari away, then she turned to face Napati.

"Is there a problem, General?" Jakari asked.

"You and Mamachi should head for the medical bay aboard the ship," Napati said. "Now."

Jakari felt a chill run up her spine. She looked to Napati for some kind of reassurance, but there was nothing in her face, so she just nodded and started towards the nearest building with an elevator down into the ship. She made it two steps before she broke into a run, Mamachi right beside her.

* * * *

238

It had been a long time since Jakari had set foot in a real hospital. Gadan still kept medics around, but mostly they focused on dealing with damage to Phylacteries. Rare in a general sense, but common enough in a war. The Suil had plenty of organic allies, but Jakari had rarely had reason to deal with their sick or injured, so walking into the medical bay made her memories of the days after the bioweapon was released stand up and slap her in the face. Sitting with Aashi as she died. Carrying friends into the emergency room when they started showing symptoms. Triage centers that were too full to take any more patients. Homes turned into makeshift hospices.

Dozens of humans lay in various beds, almost all of them being treated for burns. Most of them seemed to be heavily sedated. Jakari could smell burnt flesh and blood and it made her want to gag and run away. She had never wanted to see this again.

She looked around desperately, trying to find Hayami, praying that Hayami wasn't one of the injured or the dying, but not holding out much hope. She froze for a moment when she spotted Hayami's parents down at the far end of the bay, afraid it meant the worst, that they had been brought here to see their daughter off to whatever came beyond, but then she felt an overwhelming sense of relief when she realized Hayami was sitting across from them. All she could see was Hayami's back, but it was enough to bring a sense of relief. She rushed down the length of the bay, Mamachi on her heels, and stopped by the bed Hayami was sitting next to.

All the relief she'd felt vanished as she realized who was in the bed. Skylar lay there, and Jakari had to look away.

* * * *

Mamachi followed Jakari from the elevator to the med bay, not knowing what to expect. The fact that Napati had sent them both here sent a chill up Mamachi's spine. There was only one reason Napati would send them, and all Mamachi could do was hope that however bad Skylar and Hayami were hurt, they would recover.

The med bay, once they entered, was horrible. The smell of burnt meat filled the air, and human and Gadan alike rushed from bed to bed, checking on patients, administering painkillers, applying wet bandages to the burns. Mamachi looked at Jakari, but she seemed lightyears away, and they wondered what memories she was lost in. Not good ones, Mamachi was sure.

Jakari started rushing down the length of the med bay, and Mamachi followed. They spotted Hayami sitting next to one of the beds, and the chill was replaced with ice cold dread. They looked down at the bed, and saw Skylar lying there, and it was like the wind had been knocked out of them.

The left half of Skylar's face was badly burned. Her left eye socket was empty, her left arm little more than a stump at the shoulder, and her left leg gone below the knee. She was on oxygen, and had several bags of IV fluids hung, including a bag of blood, but the worst part was, she was awake.

"Oh, thank God," Hayami said.

Mamachi looked at her.

"She refused to be sedated until you got here," Hayami said.

"She's right," Skylar said. "Can you guys give us a minute?"

"Sure," Hayami said. "Come on." She stood up, grabbed Jakari's hand, and headed somewhere. Mamachi didn't look away from Skylar to see where. They just felt relief that Hayami's parents followed.

Mamachi dropped down into the seat Hayami had been in. "What happened?" they asked.

"The Char had a Gestalt," Skylar said. "We fought it. I lost."

"You fought a Gestalt?" Mamachi asked, not sure they believed their ears.

"Fought might be an exaggeration," Skylar said. "If I drift off, wake me up. I'm on a lot of pain killers."

"You should be sleeping."

"I'll get plenty of sleep soon enough," Skylar said. "I just...there's something I wanted to say first."

"What is it?"

She lifted her good hand, and Mamachi took it, holding it gently.

"I love you," Skylar said. "God, I love you so much. And not just as a friend. I love you, and I wanted to spend my life with you."

"You do?" Mamachi asked.

"Yeah," Skylar said. "I suppose, in a way, I got my wish. I'm just sorry it was such a short life."

"What?" Mamachi asked. "No." They shook their head. "No, you're going to make it. You're going to be fine." They leaned in and pressed a kiss to Skylar's hand. "I love you too," they said. "And I don't care if the war is over or not. I'm staying with you. If you want me, I'll stay forever."

Skylar smiled up at them. "I'd like that," she said. "Do something for me?"

"Anything."

"Don't blame yourself," Skylar said. "I'm the one who decided to go out there and fight. I made the choice. It's not your fault."

"Hey, no, don't talk like that. You're going to be fine."

"I'm sorry, Machi," Skylar said. "I need to sleep now. Can you hit the call button?"

Mamachi pressed the call button, and a moment later, a nurse appeared.

"Are you ready?" the nurse asked.

"One second," Skylar said. She looked over at Mamachi. "I love you."

"I love you too," Mamachi said.

Skylar smiled, even though it obviously hurt. She turned back to the nurse. "I'm ready."

The nurse reached over and turned a knob on one of the IV bags, starting a drip.

"What is that?" Mamachi asked.

"Propofol. It will help her sleep," the nurse said.

"It's okay," Skylar said. "You're here. Everything is okay."

Mamachi looked down at Skylar, but her eyes were already closed. "Will she be okay?" they asked.

"I'll get the doctor," the nurse said. "He can explain."

* * * *

Hayami led Jakari out of the medical bay and down the hall to a waiting area. Her parents took a seat in one corner of the room while Hayami led Jakari over to another corner where they sat down.

"What happened?" Jakari asked.

"The Char had this big thing. Napati called it a Gestalt. It managed to blast Skylar and a couple of your really heavy mechs before I killed it."

"You killed a Gestalt?" Jakari asked.

"Skylar and I were in Taluses with add-on power armor. I borrowed your move from the night we met. I grabbed ahold of it, set the self-destruct on the power armor, and then punched out. I just wasn't fast enough to stop it from killing three of the heavies and blasting Skylar."

"The fact that you killed it at all is amazing," Jakari said. "How bad did Skylar get hit?"

"Bad," Hayami said. "You saw her, and that's just the surface damage. She fell from about six stories with damaged inertial dampers. She's busted up real bad. They don't think she's going to make it. She's got a bunch of internal bleeds that aren't clotting, even with medication, but if they open her up…"

Jakari closed her eyes and took a deep breath. "I need to talk to Rayak."

"Rayak? What can he do?"

"That will depend on what Skylar wants to do," Jakari said.

"Okay," Hayami said. "There's something else you need to know."

"What?"

"Nira sent a strike team after my parents."

Jakari looked over at them. "They look okay," she said.

"They are," Hayami said. "But only because of Ghuma and Birat."

"What?" Jakari asked.

"Cikara ordered them to protect my parents if any Char forces came for them."

Jakari closed her eyes. "Fuck," she said.

"What?" Hayami asked.

"Cikara really was playing it straight with us, and Dubari killed him."

"What?" Hayami shouted. "Why?"

"I don't know, exactly," Jakari said. "They said they were following orders. I'm guessing they went behind our backs and called Arthan. It's a mess, but right now, Skylar's a priority. Let's deal with that, and then we can see if we can salvage any of this."

"Okay," Hayami said.

* * * *

"Rayak?" Jakari called as they walked into the Gadan med bay.

"I wondered how long it would take you," Rayak called as he stood up from behind a piece of equipment.

"You know why we're here?" Jakari asked.

"I'm the chief medic," Rayak said. "Of course I know why you're here."

"Could the two of you enlighten me?" Hayami asked.

"We have the Helot tech," Jakari said. "Which includes details on how to transfer a human mind into a Phylactery."

"Okay?" Hayami asked, but a moment later, it clicked. "You can transfer Skylar's mind into a body like yours?"

"That's the idea," Rayak said. "My team is working on designing TOP matter prosthetics for the other injured humans, but all of them will live, with or without our help. Skylar is dying, and she deserves better. So does Mamachi."

"How soon can you be ready?"

"A few more hours," Rayak said. "The doctors tell me they can keep her stable for a day or so. I'm going to let her sleep until everything is ready. Then we'll wake her up. If she agrees, we'll transfer her mind into a Phylactery and get her into a Form-Locked Vessel."

"Good," Jakari said. "And Rayak? Thank you."

"I didn't do it for you," Rayak said.

"I know," Jakari said. "But thank you anyway." Jakari turned to Hayami.

"I need to go talk to Dubari," she said. "Do you want to wait here, or go with me?"

Hayami thought about it for a second, but there was never really any doubt. "I'm going with you."

* * * *

Jakari and Hayami walked up to the cell where Dubari was being held. Jakari pressed the control to move the blast door aside. The heavy door split and slid to the side, revealing a set of heavy bars. Dubari was sitting on the bed in the cell, staring out through the bars.

"Hey," they said.

"I'm not here for pleasantries," Jakari said. "I'm here to know why you did it."

"I had orders," Dubari said.

"When did you get the orders?" Jakari asked.

"When you decided to change the mission parameters, I contacted Arthan," Dubari said. "He ordered me to let you deal with Nira, then to kill Cikara and retrieve the Helot technology."

"Arthan wants the Helot tech?"

"Yes," Dubari said. "He thinks we can use it to win the war."

"How?" Jakari asked.

"I don't know," Dubari said. "He just told me to make sure to retrieve it."

"So you disobeyed a direct order from Napati by contacting Arthan, and you want to turn that abomination over to him to do God knows what," Jakari said.

"I was following orders," Dubari said. "Arthan is our leader. He's the reason the rebellion drove the Seichu off Cruthanna. He's the reason the Char haven't rolled over us."

"He's every bit as insane as Jaya is," Jakari said. "And it will be a cold day in hell before I give him the Helot tech."

"Jakari..."

"No," Jakari said. "I told you...you know what, forget it. You made your choice. Goodbye, Dubari."

Jakari closed the blast door, then turned to Hayami. "I need to go find Napati."

"I know," Hayami said. "Do you want me to come with you?"

"No," Jakari said. "Go back and spend some time with your parents. I'll find you when I'm free."

Hayami nodded. "Okay."

* * * *

Jakari found Napati in the combat information center. When she walked in, Napati looked at her and held up a finger, indicating that she'd be with Jakari in a minute. Jakari waited as patiently as she could as Napati finished talking to Dhom about something and tried not to think about how badly things were fucked up. She didn't want to break down until she was done with everything that needed doing, and she knew it was coming. She could feel her control fraying around the edges, and all she wanted was to find a hole to hide in.

Napati finished what she was doing and waved Dhom off, then walked over to Jakari. "Let's find a room," she said. Jakari nodded and followed as Napati led her down to the nearest briefing room. Both of them sat down, and Jakari could feel the exhaustion pouring off Napati.

"What happened out there?" Napati asked.

"Dubari," Jakari said. "They commed Arthan after we made our deal with Cikara, and Arthan ordered them to kill Cikara and retrieve the Helot tech."

"Cikara's dead?" Napati asked.

"Yes."

"And Arthan wants the Helot tech?" Napati said.

"Yes."

"Fuck," Napati said. "Do you have the Helot tech?"

"Yes," Jakari said.

"All of it?"

"All of it."

"Fuck," Napati said. "Who knows that?"

"You, me, Rayak, and Hayami know for sure. Dubari has probably figured it out. They know me well enough to know I don't half-ass anything."

"Fuck," Napati said.

"Yeah," Jakari said. "What the hell happened here?"

"Cikara was right. They dropped in battalion strength. We had to deploy behemoths, but they had a Gestalt with them. Hayami managed to kill the Gestalt, and once she took it down, we started kicking their ass. Eventually the Char broke and ran. We lost about sixty people and had a bunch of humans injured, but we killed about four hundred of them before the rest broke and ran."

"And Hayami's parents?"

"All the DHS agents protecting them are dead. Ghuma and Birat, of all people, saved them."

"How the fuck did that happen?" Jakari asked.

"I don't know," Napati said. "According to them, they had orders directly from Cikara to protect Hayami's parents at all costs. I'm guessing Cikara wanted to protect the alliance."

"Fuck," Jakari said. "This could have all been over. We really could have ended the war."

"I know," Napati said.

"We've got to do something about Arthan," Jakari said.

"I don't know what we can do," Napati said. "Arthan's still got popular support."

"So do you," Jakari said. "If you challenged him, demanded an election..."

"I'm a general, not a politician," Napati said.

"You're the only one that can challenge him," Jakari said. "Napati, the war is never going to end as long as Arthan's in office. He wants the Helot tech. You have to know what he's thinking. We can't let it happen."

"I know," Napati said. "I just don't know what to do."

"Think about it," Jakari said. "A public challenge. Let everyone know he sabotaged a chance to end the war."

Napati nodded. "I'll think about it."

Jakari stared at Napati for a moment, knowing exactly what her words meant. She'd think about it, and then do nothing. Jakari shook her head in frustration.

"What's Skylar's condition?" Napati asked.

"She's dying," Jakari said. "Rayak is setting up a Migration tank using the Helot research. When he's finished, he's going to wake her up and ask if she wants to Migrate."

Napati chewed her lower lip for a moment. "I'm not sure that's a good idea," Napati said.

"Why not?"

"If we help a human Migrate, Arthan's reaction could be bad."

"Ask me if I give a fuck." Jakari said.

"Jakari—"

"Do you want to tell Mamachi we're going to let Skylar die because Arthan might have a problem with it?"

Napati sighed. "No. No, I don't."

"It's the right thing to do," Jakari said. "You know it is."

Napati nodded her head. "Yeah. I do. For what it's worth, tell Rayak he has my approval."

"Like he gives a shit."

Napati laughed. "You have a point." She reached up and scrubbed her face with both hands. "What do you want to do with Dubari?"

"I don't care," Jakari said. "I'm done with them. I told them they're not my partner anymore, but technically, they disobeyed a direct order in time of war. That's a court martial offense. Not that Arthan will ever let them face charges."

"We could do it here. I have a full legal staff. Present it as a done deal."

"Arthan would just issue a pardon and reinstate them unless you actually shoot them."

"I couldn't do that to Prack," Napati said.

"Yeah," Jakari said. "I figured. It's a fucking mess."

"The whole thing is," Napati said. "I need to get back to the CIC. Let me know what happens with Skylar."

"I will," Jakari said. "But if I were you, I'd start looking for a replacement for Mamachi. I don't think they're leaving with us."

"Yeah," Napati said. "I think you're right."

Napati got up and headed for the door. Jakari waited until she was gone, then buried her face in her hands and tried to suppress the urge to scream.

Chapter Twenty-Five

JAKARI WATCHED AS THE human medics wheeled Skylar into the Gadan medical bay. Mamachi followed them, dancing around nervously. She could tell how much effort it was taking for them to not reach out and touch Skylar, so she walked over and slipped an arm around them.

"It will be okay," she said.

Mamachi looked at her for a moment, then turned back to Skylar. "I didn't want this for her."

"I know," Jakari said. "But it's not all bad. The two of you will have all the time you want now."

"You think so?" Mamachi said. "I know a lot of Migrants have trouble with it."

"We do," Jakari said. "But she won't ever have to see the things we did, and she won't have to deal with the losses we've dealt with. Plus, she'll have you. Look at Prack and Charvi. They're still together."

Mamachi smiled, and Jakari rubbed their shoulder. "It will be fine."

"I hope so," Mamachi said. "I love her."

"I know," Jakari said. "Anyone with eyes could see how much the two of you mean to each other."

Mamachi wrapped their arms around Jakari and hugged her tightly. "Thank you."

"For what?" Jakari asked as she hugged them back.

"For this," Mamachi said. "I know it wouldn't have been possible if you hadn't gotten the tech from Cikara."

Jakari rubbed her cheek against Mamachi's. "I'm just glad we could save her."

Mamachi let go and turned back to watch them load Skylar into the Migration tank.

Jakari gave Mamachi one last pat on the back and walked back over to where Hayami was standing. Hayami reached out and took Jakari's hand.

"Will she really be okay?" Hayami asked.

"As okay as any of us can be," Jakari said. "It's an adjustment, but she has a good reason to adjust."

"Yes, she does," Hayami said.

Jakari turned to look at Hayami. "We should find a place where we can talk," she said.

"Yeah," Hayami said. "I've been thinking the same thing."

Jakari gave Hayami's hand a small tug and led her towards the door of the medical bay, but before they got there, Jakari's comm beeped in her ear. She stopped and accepted the call.

"Go ahead," Jakari said.

"I need you in the conference room off the CIC now," Napati said.

"Why? What is it?" Jakari asked.

"I've got Cikara on the line."

"What?"

"Hurry."

* * * *

Jakari and Hayami reached the conference room at a dead run. When they stepped inside, Dhom, Prack, Gomez, and Napati were already there. Both of them stepped in and took their usual seats.

"What's going on?"

Napati tapped the comm control, and a hologram of Cikara appeared above the table.

"Hello, Jakari."

"Who are you?" she asked.

"I'm Cikara."

"How?" Jakari asked. "I saw...oh. A Talus doppelgänger."

"Yes," Cikara said. "After your little stunt the other night, I didn't trust you. A wise choice, it would seem."

"I'm sorry," Jakari said.

"I know," Cikara said. "It seems we were both betrayed. Where is Dubari, by the way?"

"In the brig," Jakari said.

"A good place for them."

Prack shifted in his seat and Jakari could see the anger in his face. She needed to shift the conversation.

"I should say thank you for protecting Hayami's parents."

Cikara waved dismissively. "A trifle," they said. "I was afraid Nira would make another play for them, and I couldn't have something so trivial destroy our alliance."

"Is there still an alliance?" Jakari asked.

"If you're still open to one," Cikara said. "Nira is dead, but that still leaves Saka and Jaya. Both bigger threats than Nira ever was."

"Agreed," Jakari said.

"Then we proceed as planned. I will inform Jaya that Nira is dead, and that I've encountered significant Suil resistance here on Earth. They'll send Saka to deal with it, and we arrange for Saka to meet a similar end to Nira."

"Agreed," Jakari said.

"I will also arrange for the delivery of the humans," Cikara said. "I keep my bargains."

"Thank you, Cikara," Jakari said.

"Given recent events, however, I do have one additional stipulation for our agreement."

Jakari braced herself, wondering if this is where everything fell apart.

"Dubari will remain in your brig for the remainder of our alliance. They will not be sent off world. They will stay in a cell, so I know where they are."

Jakari looked over at Napati, who gave a small nod. "Agreed. I have Napati's approval for that."

"Excellent," Cikara said. "Then our alliance is still intact. I will go ahead and make arrangements on my end to see to Saka's arrival and be in touch when it's time to make further arrangements."

"What do you want to do about Ghuma and Birat?" Jakari asked.

"Ah, thank you for reminding me," Cikara said. "Can you keep them? I'm afraid I can't bring them back here. After all, they killed five of my troops."

"I'll see what we can do," Jakari said.

"Good."

The line cut without any further comment from Cikara, and for a moment, the room was deathly silent. It was Jakari herself that broke the silence.

"We can still do this," she whispered, not quite believing it. She turned to Hayami. "We can still do this."

"Yeah," Hayami said.

Jakari reached out and pulled Hayami into her arms. "We can still do this!" she shouted.

* * * *

Cikara smiled as they cut the call with Jakari, taking a moment to savor their victory. Nira was gone, the Suil were still dancing to their tune, and now it was time to take the next step in clearing their pathway to control. Everything was falling into place. Even Dubari's little stunt played into Cikara's hands. It would push the wedge even deeper between Jakari and Arthan. Today was a very, very good day.

Cikara took just a moment to put on an appropriately grim face and entered the command to call Jaya. It would be late on Cruthanna, and the call would no doubt wake Jaya. So much the better for conveying a sense of urgency.

Sure enough, when Jaya appeared on screen, they were naked. Probably had just crawled off whatever poor person was warming their bed presently.

"What do you want, Cikara?"

"Nira is dead," Cikara said.

Jaya stood there for a moment, an uncomprehending look on their face, until finally they blinked and shook their head.

"Repeat that," Jaya ordered.

"Nira is dead," Cikara said.

"How?" Jaya asked, disbelief in their voice.

"Jakari killed her," Cikara said. "I don't know how, but she managed to get aboard the ship, kill Nira, and purge the research library."

"The Helot technology?" Jaya asked.

"We've lost months of research," Cikara said. "All the test subjects are gone as well. I can reconstruct a lot of it from data stored in my Phylactery, but delivery of the Helots will be delayed."

Rage spread across Jaya's face. "I'm sending Saka," Jaya said. "They'll deal with Jakari, and they'll help you complete the Helot system."

"Understood."

Jaya cut the line, and the grim look disappeared from Cikara's face, replaced by a smile. They got up and opened the door to their secret lab, smiling even wider at the sight that awaited them. The human woman's parents. They were unconscious, locked into machines that linked their minds to the Talus doppelgangers that Ghuma and Birat had left in their place. The machines boosted the range of the Shim connection far beyond the normal limit. As long as Cikara's dreadnought was anywhere on Earth, the doppelgangers would function perfectly, right up until the moment Cikara activated them.

Cikara walked over to the computer in the lab, opened the backup copy of the Helot research, and began working on a way to implant a Shroud from a distance. Something like the Form Lock dart that Jakari had used on them. Just a little bit of work, and Cikara would be able to control anyone they wanted. Including Dubari. Which meant the next time Dubari got close to Arthan, Cikara would have another very, very good day.

The Soulless God: The War of Souls Book 2

FOR THE FIRST TIME in millennia, Jakari has hope that the war between the Char Oram and the Suil Agam might actually end. With help from a traitor within the ranks of the Char, she managed to kill the head of Char Intelligence and bait a trap for Saka, one of the members of the ruling Triumvirate. If she can kill Saka, it might give her a shot at taking down Jaya, the leader of the Char, and ending the war once and for all. Normally, she'd be perfectly confident in her ability to get the job done, but thrown off balance by her partner's betrayal and the confusing feelings surrounding Hayami, the human detective she's working with, Jakari is beginning to wonder if she's up to the task.

Hayami Takahashi has a problem. Or more accurately, she has two problems. The first is the alien civil war that has spilled over into Earth and threatens the very existence of the human race. The second is that she's pretty sure she's engaged to an alien assassin she's only known a couple of weeks. She's not sure which one she finds scarier. What she does know is that Jakari is the best hope humanity, but given her own disastrous history with women, Hayami is terrified that she might end up breaking Jakari before the enemy has a chance.

With the fate of hundreds of worlds hanging in the balance, can Jakari and Hayami manage to get past their own problems and work together to deal with the threat Saka faces, or will they miss their only chance to end the war and save humanity?

Coming in August of 2023 from Desert Palm Press

About Molly J. Bragg

Molly Bragg is an autistic trans woman with a degree in Astrophysics and a love of storytelling. She loves science fiction, superheroes, and giant robots. Her hobbies include collecting Transformers, watching way too many crafting videos on YouTube, playing Dungeons & Dragons, and complaining bitterly about the way a certain comic book company treats her favorite superhero.

Connect with Molly

Email mollyjbragg@gmail.com
Website http://www.themollyjay.com
Facebook https://www.facebook.com/themollyjay
Twitter https://twitter.com/themollyjay
Tumbler https://www.tumblr.com/blog/themollyjay

Note to Readers:

Thank you for reading a book from Desert Palm Press. We appreciate you as a reader and want to ensure you enjoy the reading process. We would like you to consider posting a review on your preferred media sites and/or your blog or website.

For more information on upcoming releases, author interviews, contest, giveaways and more, please sign up for our newsletter and visit us as at Desert Palm Press: www.desertpalmpress.com and "Like" us on Facebook: Desert Palm Press.

Bright Blessings

www.ingramcontent.com/pod-product-compliance
Lightning Source LLC
Chambersburg PA
CBHW052027020726
47501CB00004B/1284